STOLEN KISSES

Slowly, very slowly, so as not to alarm her further, he lowered his dark head to hers, and gently pressed his lips over her own.

Heather appeared stunned when Adam was done, despite the fragility of the kiss. She opened her mouth to make some protest, but no sound would come; and he took advantage of her momentary confusion to kiss her again. This time strong arms held her firmly to his chest, and his lips were more ardent. As he kissed her, he felt a trembling begin in the slender body pressed close to his. "From that night, that brief moment when first I saw you, I have dreamed of holding you in my arms, of your sweet mouth beneath mine," he murmured huskily, his breath heated against her flaming cheek. "Each day since, I have cursed myself for letting you flee me, without so much as your name to find you by!"

Heather shook her head. "No, Captain, you must not entertain such thoughts—and you must never, ever kiss me again!" she cried. "You have gone far beyond the bounds of . . . of decency!"

"Decency be damned, my lovely Heather!" he breathed raggedly into the dark cloud of her fragrant hair. "I've found you at last. I won't let you go so easily a second time!"

CRIMSON ANGEL

PENELOPE NERI

ZEBRA BOOKS
KENSINGTON PUBLISHING CORP.

ZEBRA BOOKS

are published by

Kensington Publishing Corp.
475 Park Avenue South
New York, NY 10016

First printing: March 1986

Printed in the United States of America

For my parents, Rupert and Audrey Newson,

With all my love and thanks. I miss you, always.

Come, take my hand, my dear one,
And follow where I go.
We'll find a lasting treasure
Where the crimson angels grow. . . .

Part One

England and Scotland

Chapter One

"Off duty, are you then, Nurse Cameron?"

"Yes, at last, thank you, Mister Riggs! And what a long and tiring day it was too," Heather commented, her voice echoing in the hushed and empty corridors of St. Thomas' Hospital. Her tone was without resentment despite her words. "How is Mrs. Riggs today?" she inquired, stifling a yawn and flexing her aching back.

"As well as can be expected, I dare say," the porter said gloomily. "It's funny tho', she do seem awful big with this babe coming, not like the last two. Swells up she does, an' all—like balloons her feet are of a night! I must say, miss, it scares me, it does, t'see my Maggie looking that way." His long face with the lantern jaw seemed even longer as he sighed again, looking at her with his great, sad eyes like a mournful bloodhound.

Poor John, Heather thought, he must be at his wit's end with another child due within the month, four small mouths to feed already, and all on a hospital porter's meager wage. It was little wonder he appeared so glum! "I suppose an examination by a physician would be quite out of the question?" she asked, believing she already knew what his answer would be.

11

"Lawd, yes, miss! 'Sides, my Maggie don't hold with doctors, I'm sorry t'say, even could I find a way t' manage his fees, which I can't. Quacks and charlatans, she calls 'em! An' a pauper's bed would be quite out o' the question, quite! Our Maggie's proper proud, she is." He forced a smile as he saw the worried expression now upon Heather Cameron's face. "Now then, don't you worry none, miss. It'll work out!" he insisted with false brightness, tipping his cap. "You be off home fer a pleasant evenin'. I'll be seein' you in the mornin', miss. Careful how you go, now."

He held the door wide open to permit her merino skirts to pass unhampered through the narrow exit, and outside she saw Victor, her uncle's groom, about to come enter the hospital to escort her to the coach, his greatcoat lifting in the sharp wind.

"Evenin', Miss Heather." Victor greeted her, offering her his arm as he led her to the waiting coach. "It's a chilly night, isn't it?" he observed as he handed her inside, tucking a warm plaid carriage rug about her legs.

"A very chill night indeed," Heather agreed with a little shiver. "Do you think there'll be snow?"

The coachman sniffed the air, as if its very scent could hold the knowledge he sought. "No," he said at length, "No snow t'night—but we're in for a good thick fog, I'd wager, miss. Thick as pea soup!" His face, ruddy with cold, broke into a broad grin.

Heather murmured agreement as Victor slammed the coach door shut, sealing her inside the darkness that smelled of damp leather and a faint floral perfume, a lingering reminder of some past ball or soirée.

She braced herself against the slippery black leather as Victor started his horses and the vehicle jolted forward; then she leaned back, closing her eyes as weariness stole through her. Another long day, she thought;

yet a smile of satisfaction came to her lips in the shadowed coach. Yes, indeed, it *had* been long, and tiring, but infinitely satisfying! Had it been worth defying Uncle Jamie and Aunt Elise to get her own way? Yes! Besides, they had more or less resigned themselves to her nursing now, though that did not prevent them from commenting about her chosen vocation with sometimes annoying frequency, and always in a tone that intimated she had as good as thrown away her life—her chances for a good marriage and a wealthy husband—by following the dictates of her heart.

Had Miss Florence Nightingale faced such fierce opposition from her own family when she had decided to become a nurse, Heather wondered? That Florence's choice had been opposed by society in general was common knowledge, for in Florence's youth, nurses were considered little better than the unfortunates, the prostitutes that strolled the London streets by night! Happily, all that had changed over the past fifty years, thanks to Miss Nightingale's endeavors, and nursing had gained a measure of respectability, if not complete acceptance.

Opening her eyes, she recalled a sunny July afternoon last summer when she and three other student nurses who also attended the Florence Nightingale Nursing School for Gentlewomen, which was housed in the St. Thomas' Hospital, had been escorted by Matron to take afternoon tea with the founder at her home on South Street, to which she had temporarily retired on account of ill health. Though frail, Miss Nightingale had been gracious and kind, greeting the student nurses she knew with the affectionate nicknames she had bestowed upon them: the Pearl, the Dove, and others. To Heather's delight, upon her departure Miss Nightingale had given her a nickname too. *The Angel,* she had called her, a name by which Miss Nightingale had once been known. Heather could not have been more thrilled had she met Queen Victoria herself, so deeply had the heroic Miss Nightingale's good works impressed her. Oh, what she would have given to have labored alongside the Lady with the Lamp in the foul barracks of Scutari, tending the wounded and the fevered, the poor brave lads who had fallen under the Russian cannon for their country!

The coach, drawn by two sturdy matched bays, bowled briskly through the early-evening crush of the City, which was thronged with gentlemen dressed for the theater in silk capes, white scarves, top hats, and impeccably tailored suits, and ladies whose shimmering cloaks and evening gowns and long white gloves gave them a fairy-tale quality in the hissing light of the gas lamps. Clerks had quit their high stools and their offices, and had donned long knitted scarves over threadbare jackets for the brisk walk home. Barrow boys, or costermongers, trundled their carts of fresh fruits and vegetables back up to the East End. Match girls stowed away their wares and scampered through the dark mist to their pitiful cots. Yet courting couples braved the chill and damp of the night to stroll arm in arm along the shadowed Embankment where the Thames gleamed blackly, like pitch, and the chimes of Big Ben sounded, loud and clear, on the foggy air. As night settled swiftly over the sprawling, boisterous City of London, and her honest, hardworking and God-fearing citizens sought their fires, a hot supper, and a good night's rest, another London awoke. The dark alleys and narrow streets hummed and breathed with a different, sinister life as cutthroats and pickpockets, thieves, the gin-soaked, the unfortunates and their brutal, strutting masters—all the lowlife of the sprawling slums—stirred and began to go about their

14

dubious trades.

But Heather saw none of this as the coach made its way to the quietly elegant suburbs of Windsor Square, where Heather's Uncle Jamie and Aunt Elise had their elegant townhouse. Finally it turned through the tall gates of twisted wrought iron, and clattered up the driveway that curved through a sweeping expanse of lawn, dark with mist. The mellow stone walls and the high, pointed gables to the house seemed forbidding in the dusk, but their awesome aspect was softened by the amber lamplight that spilled through the open door-way and out onto the gravel drive in great golden puddles. As the coach rocked to a halt, Mrs. Reading came out to welcome her home.

"Why, there you are at last!" the housekeeper exclaimed. "Cook and myself had almost given you up for lost!" The tall, big-boned woman smiled as Victor assisted Heather down from the coach. She took her arm, bustling her inside the open front door of Cameron Hall, chattering all the while.

"Cook's had your tea brewed this past half-hour," Mrs. Reading confided with a little click of fond exasperation, "And no doubt it is well stewed by now! You will have to wait a few minutes for a fresh pot, I'm afraid."

Heather nodded as the little downstairs maid, Bridie, came to take her cloak and gloves and bonnet, damp now with the misty chill of the November evening. "I'm sure I shan't mind waiting at all, Mrs. Reading. Please, don't bother yourself on my account." Heather handed her bonnet to Bridie, and shook loose the cloud of flaming, reddish-brown hair that had escaped the severe knot into which it had been pinned. The damp tendrils curled about her face like a fiery halo, and Bridie gaped, awed as always by the vibrance of Miss Heather's beauty.

15

"Thank you, Bridie," Heather told the young girl with a smile.

"You're welcome, mum," the maid replied pertly, dropping a curtsy. With a flash of gray starched-cotton skirts, she turned quickly and whisked down the hall toward the kitchen, where the cloak would be sponged and dried, the bonnet brushed, before being returned to the armoire in Miss Heather's room.

"Come along. Into the parlor with you," Mrs. Reading insisted, taking Heather's arm and propelling her down the hall. "Indeed, with your training, Miss Heather, I'd have thought you'd know better than most the dangers of becoming chilled. There's a cozy fire in here," she added, swinging open the parlor door. "I'll tell Cook you're home and see to your tea while you warm yourself."

Heather turned in the doorway, "Is Aunt Elise not at home, then?"

"She is not. She has gone with your uncle to a musicale at the Ashleys, and is not expected back until quite late this evening. Miss Annabel is upstairs, though. I shall send Bridie to tell her you are home." With that, Mrs. Reading left her alone and went in search of Cook.

Heather crossed the parlor to the wide fireplace and glanced at the small white ormolu clock that ticked upon the mantel, feeling vaguely surprised. It was almost seven—little wonder she had received such a welcome home! They must, indeed, have thought her lost! She held out her hands to the fire, palms downward to warm them, and soon felt the heat send a rosy color to her cheeks. It reflected dancing golden flames in her deep violet eyes—eyes that a past admirer had likened to the velvety-deep violet of pansies in bloom, but in which her mother had fancied she saw the wild, purple heather of the highlands. Hence her name.

16

Those eyes, in combination with her gravely beautiful face, deep auburn, flaming hair, and exquisite figure and carriage, had turned more than one prospective suitor's head at the coming-out ball Aunt Elise had given in her honor two years before.

But, to Uncle Jamie's chagrin and Aunt Elise's despair, despite a considerable dowry in the form of an inheritance from her dear departed mother's side, to which Uncle Jamie had generously added out of his fondness for his niece, and despite her undeniable beauty, no proposals of marriage had been forthcoming throughout the entire season. Uncle Jamie had grumbled that the reason for this was, no doubt, the reputation Heather had gained—deservedly—for being somewhat independent and rebellious. These traits were not, Uncle Jamie had declared in his softly burred voice, what young men sought in a wife. No, not at all. Obedience and total dependency on a mate were what men prized in a woman. They wanted wives who could run their households, bear them numerous, healthy offspring to glorify their maleness, and entertain their business associates and peers. As hostesses wives were expected to exhibit the elegance, wit, and charm that befitted their husbands' positions in society and business. What a man definitely did *not* want, lovely though she might be, was a young woman whose education and personal studies might well have earned her the appellation of bluestocking, and who, furthermore, had a mind and a strong will of her own—and no reticence in expressing either!

So it was that Heather, to her Aunt Elise's dismay—and her own delight, had evaded the institution of marriage for the past two years. At the age of twenty she was considered past her prime and was expected to spend the rest of her days as a spinster, her energies directed to good works and charities.

17

Remembering, Heather smiled again as she sat, legs tucked beneath her, on the rug before the fire, her drab dark blue merino skirts billowing about her. A long-haired, smoke-colored cat uncurled itself from a pillowed wicker basket in the chimney nook to seek out her lap. As she petted it, the cat extended and retracted its needlelike claws. A starched white apron now lay in a crumpled heap at the young woman's side. No matter what her aunt and uncle might believe, she considered herself far from spinsterish! It was simply that, having decided what she wanted from life, she had reached for it with both hands, firmly grasping it and defying thereby conventional ideas of what was considered fitting for a young woman of her age and station. People—even dear, well-meaning people like her aunt and uncle—could simply not conceive of a girl working for her living, and enjoying every minute of it! Marriage, she had decided long ago, was an institution only to be considered when she had explored the other exciting possibilities life had to offer.

Nursing had been her dream since she was a little girl, busily bandaging and dosing her dolls in the schoolroom upstairs while her governess, Miss Sally, looked on with disapproval. Joining the C.M.S. and becoming a medical missionary to poor, disease-ridden heathens in far-flung lands had become her second goal, but at present it was too soon to broach her aunt and uncle with this. Indeed, they were still stunned by her first outrageous decision, poor dears! However, since she could not hope to be accepted by the Church Missionary Society without her nursing certificate, she was content to bide her time until she had acquired it.

"Then, Taffeta, we shall perforce tackle Aunt Elise and Uncle Jamie once more, h'm?" she murmured thoughtfully, scratching the cat beneath the chin, and feeling the vibration of its purr.

Mrs. Reading returned then, in her wake Bridie bearing a heavy silver tray weighted down with a silver teapot; a creamer and sugar bowl; a platter of thinly sliced, crustless bread, buttered and cut in perfect triangles; and a dish of strawberry preserves. On another plate were thick wedges of fruitcake studdied with enormous whole cherries and Cook's famous lemon-curd tarts. A pair of delicate bone-china teacups and saucers, decorated with deep pink tea roses, rested daintily beside the far-from-dainty repast.

"Oh, Mrs. Reading, you really shouldn't have gone to so much trouble!" Heather exclaimed as Bridie set the tray upon a low table drawn up to the fire. "A little cold meat and bread would have been more than enough."

"Nonsense!" Mrs. Reading declared firmly as Bridie exited. She shooed the cat from Heather's lap and seated herself in a wide, overstuffed chair that permitted her to be comfortable despite her bustle and the volume of her navy silk skirts. "You must fortify yourself after such a long day and in such nasty weather."

She proceeded to pour, and despite Heather's insistence that she was not very hungry, the steamy fragrance that rose from the elegant silver pot sent an unladylike growl of honest hunger reverberating through her.

The tea was delicious, an orange pekoe that invigorated and refreshed. Heather was sipping a second cupful and enthusiastically but decorously devouring a generous slab of Cook's fruitcake when the parlor door flew open and Annabel, Heather's cousin, tripped in.

Slender and petite, Annabel also possessed the famous Cameron hair, flaming, deep auburn tresses that seemed lit from within in some mysterious fashion.

However, whereas Heather's eyes were violet, the younger girl's were a clear, sparkling blue—clear as a loch reflecting a summer sky, Aunt Elise was wont to remark when waxing poetic as she often did.

Annabel could not be called beautiful, yet there was a forthright quality about her, an engaging honesty and good humor that more than one young man had found both intriguing and attractive. So attractive, indeed, that Annabel, not yet nineteen, had found herself spoken for by the end of her first season. She was to be married in the coming spring to one Anthony Winchester, second cousin to an earl, and one of *the* Winchesters so prominent in the woolen business. It was an acceptable match. Though it lacked brilliance, it was satisfying to Annabel and her parents were delighted for she had quickly developed a *tendresse* for her handsome fiancé.

Now Annabel skirted her way between the small tables strewn with fashionable bric-a-brac, and promptly sank to the rug beside Heather, ignoring Mrs. Reading's disapproving looks. She extended a graceful hand toward the plump cherry that winked like a great red ruby from the midst of the fruitcake resting upon Heather's plate. "May I, Coz?" she asked, smiling cajolingly.

Heather returned her smile. "You may—but only one, mind," she cautioned.

With the air of one stealing a priceless jewel, Annabel scooped up the cherry and popped it into her mouth. "Mmmm, heaven!" she declared.

Mrs. Reading sniffed. "There is ample fruitcake upon the tray, Miss Annabel, if you would care for some," she offered pointedly.

"No thank you, Ready darling, the one was quite sufficient. I'm afraid I made quite a glutton of myself at supper, and haven't an inch of room left for Cook's cake. It was just the cherry that I wanted." She and Heather exchanged merry glances, the look of two young women who have been conspirators in the past.

"Well, now that I see you are to have some companionship, I shall retire to my sitting room," Mrs. Reading announced. Her sensibilities quite offended by Annabel's unladylike behavior, she rose, and swept her skirts about her. Silk rustling noisily, she headed for the door with all the magnificence of a ship in full sail. "Good night, girls."

"Good night, Mrs. Reading. And thank you so much for waiting for me and keeping me company. It was very kind of you," Heather called after her.

At the door, Mrs. Reading turned, and her slightly frigid expression melted. "You are more than welcome, dear Heather."

Heather gave Annabel a surreptitious nudge in the ribs. Her cousin gasped, then added, "Good night, Ready darling. Do have a pleasant evening!" With a tight little nod, the housekeeper left the parlor.

Once she had gone, Annabel collapsed into giggles, her red ringlets bouncing over her shoulders.

"You're simply awful," Heather declared, smiling herself though she had tried to maintain a stern front. Within moments, her façade had crumbled entirely, and she, too, ended up laughing. "Why must you persist in calling her 'Ready darling'? You know how she hates it!"

"That is precisely why!" Annabel countered, looking in no way chagrined. "I do believe it is very beneficial for the stuffy people of this world to have their stuffing firmly pounded at regular intervals! Besides, I could never compete with Ready's 'darling Heather', so I shan't try. I say, Heather, might I have the last one?"

With a fond, exasperated smile, Heather handed Annabel the dainty china plate which contained the

21

last cherry. "You may. But don't blame me when your stays seem too tight and that tiny waist you're so inordinately proud of resembles dear Cook's in girth!"

"I won't," Annabel denied firmly, dismissing such a notion and devouring her second cherry. "I never seem to gain an inch, no matter how much I eat." She licked her sticky fingers and set the plate back upon the tray. "I say, Coz, did you read this morning's newspaper?"

"I scarcely had time for breakfast this morning, let alone reading! Why?"

"He struck again last night!" Annabel divulged, her expression bright with lurid fascination.

"The Whitechapel murderer?" Heather queried, paling.

Annabel nodded eagerly. "None other. Papa tried to hide the account in the *Times* from me, but I pried it away from Cook when she was done. You may be able to twist Ready around your little finger, but Cook is mine!"

"No doubt because you always do justice to her baking!"

Annabel shrugged. "Anyway, as I was saying, he struck again—another unfortunate, also in Whitechapel. She added darkly, "And apparently the police have received a letter from someone purporting to be the murderer, to all appearances signed in his victim's blood with the name 'Jack the Ripper.' Isn't it fascinating?"

Heather grimaced. "Fascinating—no." She shuddered slightly. "Ghoulish, yes! Honestly, Coz, your interest in this entire, awful business is quite disgusting, and more than a little disturbing."

"Oh, nonsense!" Annabel disclaimed airily. "Everything I do is, of a must, dainty and feminine—and utterly boring! Arranging the flowers. Paying calls with Mamma. At-homes. Teas. Why, there's nothing

22

with even the slightest, delicious taint of blood or scandal about it in my entire life! Is it any wonder I should be fascinated with 'Jack' and his doings?"

"Annabel!" Heather exclaimed, honestly shocked. "He *murdered* those poor, misguided creatures, murdered them horribly! Your attitude is quite unforgivable!"

"Isn't it?" Annabel agreed with a delighted smile. "Anthony, too, considers me quite shocking, but he says he would wager he will never find me boring as his wife, bless him! Come on, Heather darling, don't be stuffy! Don't you want to hear what else the *Times* had to say?" Without pausing for Heather's response, she quickly added, "It is thought he chooses only nights of heavy fog to do his evil deeds, and that because of the skill with which he . . . dispatches . . . his victims, he might perhaps be a surgeon. They speculate that he carries his knives in a physician's instrument bag concealed by a full dark cloak, and—"

"That is quite enough!" Heather exclaimed. Of a sudden, the cozy parlor, lit by the cheerful light of a single lamp and the flickering glow of the fire, seemed filled by the menacing presence of the Whitechapel murderer himself! The notion sent icy little chills dancing down her spine.

Annabel pouted sulkily. "I do declare, Coz, since you began this nursing business, you have become quite stuffy yourself—a younger Mrs. Reading, in the flesh!" Her pretty blue eyes sparkled mischievously. "Think on it, Coz, a surgeon! He might even be one of the physicians at St. Thomas' that you always speak so highly of. . . ." Heather's dark look silenced any further teasing on Annabel's part. She had gone too far this time, she sensed, and like a skilled strategist, she accordingly retreated. "Well, as you seem so upset about it, I will not speak of it again," she promised with

23

a contrite expression. "Did Ready tell you that Mamma and Papa have gone to a musicale at the Ashleys?" When Heather responded with a tight little nod, Annabel continued. "I do not know if you were aware of it, but Mamma confided to me that Edgar Ashley—the second son who was at Eton?—has eloped to the Continent with a governess! Isn't that just scandalous?"

"No!" Heather exclaimed. "Not the Edgar who was so priggish and righteous when we were children?"

"The same!" Annabel declared, inwardly pleased that she had so easily diverted the conversation to safer ground. "Imagine, Coz, Edgar, of all people, to do such a thing!"

They chattered on, the conversation turning from gossip to fashion, to the doings of the Royal Family presently wintering at Balmoral, and to Annabel's growing trousseau and her forthcoming marriage. By the time the two young women left the parlor and permitted the butler, Carmichael, to extinguish the lamp and bank the fire, the hour was late, and Heather's head was drooping like a lovely, weary flower upon her shoulders.

Later, tucked in her bed, her long hair braided and a warm flannel nightgown buttoned firmly up to her chin, she recalled Annabel's lurid remarks about the Whitechapel Murderer.

Just then the wind lifted, stirring the ancient elm below her window so that its leafless branches tapped upon the mullioned panes like insistent fingers as they threw dancing shadows on the floral-papered walls. Again came that shiver of fear. She pulled the covers up over her head and cowered beneath them until sleep claimed her. Fortunately, owing to her fatigue, she did not remain awake long.

Chapter Two

"I really must be leaving, Aunt Elise, Uncle Jamie, if you will excuse me," Heather murmured after a hurried breakfast the next day. She braced herself for the mild flurry her words occasioned each and every morning as she rose and pushed back her chair.

As she had expected, her aunt's delicately winged brows drew together in a ladylike frown of annoyance. Elise Cameron set down the post she held in her hand and pursed her lips. "So soon? Really, Heather, my dear, this nursing is becoming quite bothersome! It would be so pleasant to enjoy breakfast just this once as a family, all of us here together to start the day well." She smiled cajolingly. "Will you not consider staying at home this morning instead? Annabel and I have fittings at the dressmaker's at ten, but afterward we had planned to take a drive through Hyde Park and enjoy the brisk air. Later, perhaps, we will do a little shopping in Bond Street prior to luncheon. I'm sure you would find it a most pleasant day? . . ."

"I would truly love to join you," Heather murmured, coming to stand at her aunt side, "but I cannot. Do have a lovely day!" She kissed her aunt's cheek, catching as she did so the faint, pleasant fragrance of almond toilet water. Then she gave her uncle a dutiful peck upon the brow, and he absently returned it before she waved to Annabel and headed for the door.

"Heather!" her aunt called after her.

"Yes, Aunt Elise?"

"You will not forget this evening—the Rutherfords' supper and entertainment?"

"I will not," she promised. "Goodbye!"

Bridie was waiting with her heavy cloak in the paneled hallway.

"Oh, mum, you'll be late, you will!" she clucked. "Victor brought the coach around ages ago!"

"Matron will be furious!" Heather muttered under her breath, tying her bonnet strings and hastily snatching up her gloves and the portemanteau that contained a freshly starched lace cap and apron before flinging wide the door and hurrying out to the waiting coach.

Victor was waiting too, already seated upon his driver's perch, both reins and whip poised for a speedy departure. Whitton, his stableboy, handed her up into the coach, grinning at her cry of, "Lay on, if you please, Victor, or I shall be late!"

The coach rocked as the matched bays stepped out, the vehicle rolling rapidly around the curving driveway, out into the square and then on into a secluded thoroughfare lined with leafless trees that still wore a light veiling of early-morning mist upon their branches in the chill November air.

Heather gnawed at the tip of one of her kid gloves, willing Victor to urge the bays to an even faster pace as a vision of Miss Ratner, Matron, filled her mind. Matron was a veritable dragon of a woman, who took her position as guardian of the student nurses of St. Thomas' with alarming severity!

When establishing the school, Miss Nightingale had set down very strict rules governing the young women who would be permitted to attend it. They were to be young ladies of good moral character, who looked upon nursing as a lifelong vocation. While attending the school, they were to reside in a dormitory with other nurses, and to be closely chaperoned during all outside activities in which they participated. Only because Uncle Jamie and Aunt Elise were looked upon favorably by old friends of Miss Nightingale had Heather been permitted to remain at Cameron House while pursuing her studies, and even then Uncle Jamie had exerted his powers of persuasion to enable her to do so.

Matron had not been at all pleased that the Camerons had gone over her head and that an exception had been made to this rule in Heather's case, but she had been forced to accept what had been done. However, at times Heather believed that Matron went out of her way to be unpleasant and to make her life difficult. There had been nights when she had left St. Thomas close to tears, half-determined never to return. Only her sincere and deep commitment to nursing had given her the determination to return the next morning—that, and a reluctance to walk away from the patients who depended upon her and looked forward to her presence on the wards.

When the coach pulled up before the vestibule of St. Thomas' Hospital, Heather jumped down and ran inside before Victor could clamber down from his perch to assist her. Her cloak and merino skirts went flying as, holding down her bonnet, she sped across the cobbled street. Her cheeks were flushed, and one flaming curl had escaped its neat chignon to spill flamboyantly down over her shoulder as she all but fell inside the heavily paneled doors. She saw Mister Riggs standing at his post by the front desk and was about to greet him with a breathless good-morning when

27

something in his expression caused her to turn around.

Just inside the door stood Matron, her thin lips tightly pursed, her small, beady gray eyes cold and angry. She clasped her hands primly together beneath her bosom, and the white apron that she wore above her black wool, high-necked dress seemed to crackle with the pent-up irritation of its owner.

"Nurse Cameron," she said frostily, "You are precisely"—she paused and looked down at the gold fob watch, pinned to her formidable chest—"one and one-half minutes late."

Heather colored deeply. "Yes, Matron," she admitted, lowering her eyes. It would be useless to apologize or make some excuse. Matron would accept neither, she had learned from past experience.

Matron sniffed. "No doubt you had some other, more pleasant duty, that occupied your attention at home?" Before Heather could deny this, she continued, "However, it is only fair under your somewhat *special* circumstances here at St. Thomas that you should endeavor to adhere to the same regulations and rules of behavior as your less favored sister nurses. Tardiness is a flaw that I will not abide in my charges, Nurse Cameron! You will report to my office prior to going off duty this afternoon, at which time I shall inform you of what disciplinary measures I have decided to take. I shall expect you then. And please, endeavor to arrive *promptly*." With that, she turned a stiff back on Heather and stalked off down the corridor, her dark dress so long it created the impression she floated above the polished wooden floor, rather than walked upon it.

Heather's shoulders slumped. She turned slowly about and caught Mister Riggs's sympathetic expression. The porter came around his desk. "I tried t' tell her it ain't like you t' be late, miss, but she wouldn't

28

hear none of it," he said with a sympathetic shrug.

Forcing a smile, Heather held her head high. "Now, Mister Riggs, it was not your fault at all, it was mine. I was late, and I shall have to face the consequences. How is Mrs. Riggs today?"

"Not good, mum, not good at all. She were in bed as yet when I left this mornin', an' said as how she were feelin' too poorly t' get out of it. I tell you, Miss, I ain't never seen my Maggie lay abed of a mornin' 'ceptin' after she birthed our little 'uns. Not once."

"I'm sorry to hear it, very sorry indeed! But, if you will excuse me, I must be off." Heather hurried down the corridor, her high-buttoned boots tapping a staccato rhythm on the polished wood floors as she made her way to the student nurses' cloakroom. Once there, she hung up her bonnet, drew her white cap and apron from her portemanteau, and quickly put them on. A duty roster had been affixed to the wall, and Heather quickly scanned it. She was to make dressings, she noted with relief, before flying from the room.

Some student nurses were already busily cutting soft, old, white linen sheeting into strips for bandages, while others were rolling them into neat bundles. The faint smell of carbolic and camphor lingered in the room, which was barren save for a long table, several chairs, and a white enamel sink. A single high window let in a little light.

"There you are, Heather!" Charlotte exclaimed as she entered. "Matron is looking for you, and I fear she has blood in her eyes!"

"Had," Heather corrected ruefully. "Matron waylaid me upon my way in. I am to report to her office after duty this evening."

"No!" exclaimed Charlotte. "Oh, you poor darling—the dragon's cave itself!" The other nurses clucked sympathetically.

29

"What do you think she will do?" asked Roberta, a timid little creature with enormous dark eyes.

"Administer a flogging, at the very least!" Charlotte teased; then seeing the apprehensive look in Heather's eyes, she amended her dire statement. "Or more likely than not, assign you extra duty hours. A grand one for extra duties, our Matron is! She'll have you scrubbing the cutting-room floor from dawn to dusk for the next fortnight, I wouldn't wonder."

"If that's all she sets me to doing, then I shan't worry," Heather said firmly. She bit her lower lip. "You . . . you don't think she would dismiss me from the school, do you?"

"For being tardy just once in almost two years?" Charlotte asked. "Of course not, you silly goose!"

She cocked her fair head to one side and listened intently as a measured tread sounded in the corridor beyond the room. They all knew that step well and though it was not feared as much as the militant footsteps of Matron, it was respected.

"Sister's coming!" Charlotte hissed, and every head turned dutifully back to the work at hand.

Carefully rolling her third bandage, Heather wondered if all would turn out as well as Charlotte had insisted it would. Her violet eyes—great, dark pools—revealed her concern as she applied herself to the task at hand.

A fine, icy rain swirled about the hospital all that day, and the wards were chilly despite the roaring fires banked in every hearth. Through the windows, the city of London seemed wreathed in mist. Folks went about their business with their heads down against the weather, greatcoats and cloaks pulled warmly about them.

What a blessing not to be out in such foul weather, Heather thought as she finished helping one of the last patients on Victoria Ward, dear old Mister Ramsey, with his supper and bade him and the others a cheery, "Good evening!" They echoed her farewell and watched her slender, graceful shadow move down the whitewashed wall until she was gone.

She returned her tray of dishes to the kitchen and bade the cook and the scullery maids a good-night before turning her steps reluctantly to the nurses' cloakroom. The hour she had been dreading was at hand. Sister had dismissed her charges prior to their last duty of the day, which was seeing that the patients did justice to their suppers when able. All that remained was to don cloak and bonnet and make her way through the mazelike corridors to the small, austere room that was Matron's office—or as it was more commonly called, the Dragon's Lair!

Sister and the other nurses were already at the cloakroom, bundling themselves against the cold, damp weather in preparation for the walk to the nearby residence. A stone's throw from St. Thomas' Hospital, it provided living quarters for the student nurses. The young women formed an orderly line, in pairs, behind Sister, who called a crisp, "Good night, Cameron!" as she swept forth, the other young women filing demurely from the cloakroom in her wake. Charlotte, at the rear of the almost military column, hung back. She squeezed Heather's chilly hands and whispered a fierce, "Good luck!" before she hurried after the others.

Heather tied her bonnet ribbons, aware as she did so of the slight tremor to her fingers. "Silly goose!" she told herself firmly, but such self-encouragement did little to still the anxious flutters in the pit of her stomach as she stepped out into the long, now silent, corridor. She wished suddenly and fervently that she could be anywhere but here, facing any prospect but that which now awaited her.

"Nurse! Nurse Cameron!"

At the urgent tone of Mister Riggs's voice, she swung about to see him scuttling down the corridor toward her. Gone was his hangdog expression, in its place one of fear.

"What is it, Mister Riggs?" she inquired, dark brows arched.

"Maggie, miss, my Maggie! My eldest lad came alone across London t' tell me she's terrible sick, mum. He—he says he fears she's dyin'!" There was a whiteness about his lips and a trembling to his jaw that betrayed the rank terror inside him.

Heather's heart lurched with pity. "Mister Riggs, you *must* summon a physician now, do you not see? It does not matter if Maggie holds with them or nay. She is in dire need, and it is up to you to take the proper course if you would save her life and that of your unborn child!"

To her horror, his faded blue eyes filled with tears. "I know it, miss, d' ye think I haven't known it all along! But . . . but there's little coin for food, let alone physicians, don't ye see? Oh, please, miss, can't ye take a look at her? Wi' ye an' . . . an' the midwife, I'm certain you could do something for her. Please, Miss Heather?"

"Mister Riggs, there is very little I could do, even were I to come. Delivering a baby—and a difficult birth at that—would be quite beyond me, I know it!"

He reeled away from her in anguish, leaning up against the wall, great tears rolling down his cheeks and dripping from the end of his lantern jaw. "She's a goner then, my Maggie! A goner!"

Heather suddenly spied the small boy who had been clinging to the tails of his shabby frock coat. His grimy pinched face was streaked with tears, and even now he

32

was stuffing bony knuckles into his eyes to stem the hot flood that flowed forth. Despite the cold of the weather, the lad wore only a threadbare jacket, lovingly patched in mismatched cloth, and a knit muffler with several holes in it. His worn knickers were tucked into lumpy socks, and his fair hair appeared to have been hacked short by a demented barber. So thin, she thought absently, so very thin. . . .

"I will try to find a physician for her, Mister Riggs," she promised rashly. "Go home to your wife, and have no thought for the payment of his fee. I will see to it myself."

Riggs shook his head vehemently. "No, miss, no charity!" he insisted hoarsely.

"Not charity—a loan. No more, I promise you." He appeared about to protest further, but she silenced him with a stern, "Your children need their mother, Mister Riggs! We will discuss this when she is delivered and well once again. To what address shall I send the physician?"

"Number ten Dorset Street," Riggs supplied. "Oh, thank you, mum! An angel, you are, and no mistake!"

"Get along home, and hurry now!" Heather urged. She directed a long, intent look at Matron's closed door; then she turned about and went in search of a physician. She would be tardy, she realized grimly, but this was a matter of life and death. Surely even Matron would understand that when it was explained to her? Oh, Lord, Heather thought, I hope so!

Some thirty minutes later, she was forced to admit that not one physician had remained at the hospital. All had long since departed for the evening, heading to their homes and families, leaving the capable nurses who had already graduated from the Nightingale School in charge. What would the heroic Florence do when faced by such a dilemma? Heather wondered,

33

wringing her hands anxiously. The answer instantly came to her. She must do what she could for poor Maggie Riggs, however little that might be. Was that not her calling? With a sinking heart, she realized that in doing what she must, she would not only be tardy for her appointment with Matron, she would be forced to forego it entirely. *I shall worry about that when Mister Riggs's wife is seen to,* she told herself firmly as she sped out of the hospital entrance.

Her uncle's coach and Victor, the head groom and coachman, were nowhere to be seen, she noted with dismay. Oh, why did they have to be late tonight, of all nights! She started out into the street, shunning the shadows and instead scurrying from puddle to puddle under the feeble glow spilling from the gaslights. Ahead, the lamplighter was moving down the street with his little cart, still lighting some of the lamps. A chestnut seller tended his brazier on one corner, and the appetizing aroma of roasted chestnuts, as well as the buttery warm smell of toasted muffins from the muffin man farther down, were carried teasingly on the air, which was thick with the promise of fog. Heather looked to left and right, straining her eyes for the sight of a hackney cab, but there was none. An image of Mrs. Riggs lying in a pool of her own blood while her young son, in his pitifully threadbare clothing, wept tore at her heart. She clenched her fists. No! She could not permit that to happen, not when she might be able to do something to save the woman! There *must* be a cab somewhere. . . .

Three streets farther on, she came upon a hack drawn up before a public house. As she hurried toward it, the driver of the hack strolled out of the common room.

"Hey, gal! What the blue blazes are ye a-doing wiv my—Oh! Excuse me, mum!" he corrected himself, seeing that a young woman of some substance was inspecting his conveyance. "Were ye wanting a hack? There's no hackney finer than ol' Bloor's if ye are, an' no nag swifter than ol' Petey, though I say so meself!"

With frank dismay, Heather eyed the sagging horse in the traces, and her dismay was not alleviated when she turned her gaze upon its driver. But time was of the essence, if poor Maggie was to be helped. Good or nay, Bloor and his spavined nag would have to suffice. "Number ten, Dorset Street, driver, and whip up your horse. It's—it's a matter of life and death!" she cried.

The driver, reeking of ale and pork drippings and onions, thrust a mottled face into hers, and he grinned alarmingly. "Right ye are, mum. We'll have ye there right as ninepence afore ye can say Bloor's the best, an' no mistake!" He handed her inside and slammed the dilapidated door shut in her wake.

The coach lurched as he clambered heavily aboard, and Heather heard the loud crack of a whip and the protesting whinny of old Petey as the lash cut into his bony rump before the vehicle careened madly forward.

Chapter Three

Bloor, Heather learned to her chagrin, was emphatically *not* the best! He drove as if Lucifer himself handled the ribbons, and he lashed old Petey as if the poor beast were an obdurate Christian from whom he demanded a soul!

The hack jolted around countless corners, flinging Heather violently from one side to the other. It clattered over uneven cobbles, jarring her teeth and setting each nerve and muscle in her body a-jangle. It lurched. It rattled. And finally, after what seemed like an eternity, it shuddered and groaned to a halt. Tortured springs twanged. Leather creaked and groaned its protest of abuse. Then the snappings and poppings of overtaxed wood sounded loudly in the sudden silence.

She took a few breathless seconds to compose herself, then rose dizzily to her feet and flung open the door. Trembling somewhat, she felt her way down the step and into the street. The faint smell of cabbage struck her.

The fog had rolled in during the past half-hour, and Heather wondered what uncanny, or feral, instinct had guided Mister Bloor through it. The thick vapor wreathed about the hack like a poisonous yellow-brown breath from the gaping jaws of Hades. She could discern old Petey's bony rump, but nothing was visible beyond it. Damp, clammy air lay against her cheeks like a wet woolen muffler.

Bloor loomed up out of the fog then, his purplish face twisted into what passed for a grin. "Here we are, then, Dorset Street. Number ten's that way a step or two, miss." He rubbed his nose with a stubby finger that protruded from his knitted glove, and pointed into the fog.

Heather fumbled in her portemanteau for a coin, and handed it to him uncertainly. "I trust that will be sufficient for your trouble, cabbie?" she ventured, trying very hard to sound in control of the situation, though she had never hired a hackney cab before.

Bloor's eyes widened. He sucked in a gasp of sheer delight. The little chit had given him a whole bloody shilling, she had, for a bleedin' threepenny fare! "Oh, aye, it do be quite adequate, miss," Bloor said carefully, keeping the glee from his voice. "A good night to you, miss." Touching his cap, he leaped up onto his perch and gathered the reins in his meaty fists. In scant seconds, the coach had careened off into the fog, and Heather was alone.

She pulled her cloak about her and, stepping gingerly through the fog, traced the few steps Bloor had implied would lead her to number ten Dorset Street. But instead of a humble home, she found herself pressed up against a solid brick wall that, on closer inspection, appeared to continue on for several yards, with no gate or doorway that her frantic fingers could find!

A feeling of panic spread through her. Where had that horrible Bloor brought her? Not to Dorset Street, she was certain! She listened intently, hearing nothing but the slow dripping of water somewhere and the distant, mournful hoots of foghorns from ships on the Thames. The fog was growing thicker by the minute, closing in all around her! She pressed herself up against the wall and tried to regain her composure, but in truth she was very much afraid and quite lost. Hesitantly she set off, groping for her footing, her fingers grazing the wall for balance.

Her handhold suddenly ended. Off balance momentarily, she pitched forward into an open area. Scrambling to her feet, she saw the glow of a brazier several feet from her, dull red eyes leering at her through the heavy mist. About the brazier huddled several heavily bundled figures, foreshortened like dwarves as they squatted down on the cobbles to hug the warmth of the fire.

"Please," she began, her voice little louder than a whisper, "please, could you help me? I'm afraid I'm quite lost."

One of the "dwarves" uncoiled to stand and shuffled over to her.

"Lorst, are ye? Hee! Hee! Well, now ye're found, me pretty trull! Come over 'ere, along o' us fine fellows. We ain't seen a comely slut in many a day."

Gin fumes swirled from his chortling open mouth, and the foul stench of his body struck Heather full in the face like a fist. She had a brief glimpse of a visage that rivaled a water rat's for slyness before she let out a shrill squeak, hitched up her skirts, took to her heels, and fled. The raucous laughter of the vagrants gathered about the fire rang in her ears as she sped wildly through several more narrow streets lined with warehouses before she dared to slow her pace to a trot and, finally, a walk.

Suddenly a woman loomed out of the fog. She was upon her before Heather was aware that anyone was nearby, and she vanished just as quickly, flinging a

38

jeering comment over her shoulder. "Ye won't find no easy coin t'night, not in this bleedin' pea souper, luv! All them randy toffs are cozied up with their bloomin' wives!"

"Please, wait!" Heather cried, hurrying after the woman. The hissing light of the gas lamp at the corner revealed the woman's haggard, painted face, the garish plumes that spilled from the brim of her bonnet, the ragged fur trim that edged her shabby short cloak as she turned. An unfortunate, Heather realized, a lady of the evening. She swallowed. Annabel would love this, she thought grimly!

"Wot is it?" the woman demanded, fumes of gin emanating from her as she spoke. The look her faded blue eyes gave Heather was a calculating one. "Wot's up, dearie?"

"I'm looking for number ten, Dorset Street," Heather ventured, fumbling with the handles of her portemanteau. "The . . . the cabbie said I might find it hereabout?"

A great snort of laughter erupted from the woman. "He did, did he!" she exclaimed. "Ye wouldn't be after knowing this cabbie's name, would ye, ducks?" There was a brassy twinkle in her eyes now, even in the sputtering lamplight. "It wouldn't ha' been Bloor, would it?"

Heather blanched, her face assuming the color of wax. "Yes! That's him!"

The woman chuckled. "He played ye for a fool, luv, that sly old cock! Ye ain't in walkin' distance o' Dorset Street, specially on a bleedin' foggy night like this 'un! Dorset Street's clear across Whitechapel, it is. Beyond this 'ere wall is the Whitechapel slaughterhouse, and there ain't nothin' but pubs and boardinghouses and the like in the streets 'round these parts, as well your cabbie knew! I'd just bet Billy Bloor's downin' a foamin' pint in the Queen's Head, and laughin' his bloomin' head orf at the prank he's played ye!" The woman snorted again and sidled off, hips swinging exaggeratedly under her skirts. "G'night, ducks! Enjoy yer stroll!"

"Wait! Please, don't go! How shall I find another cab?" Heather implored, lifting her skirts and hurrying after her yet again.

The woman halted and shrugged. "Be buggered if I know!" she said coarsely. "Happen ye might try the Laughing Dog a street or two down, though folks in these parts don't have much call for hired hacks. Shank's pony—that's our bleedin' coach!" With that parting sally and a vague gesture to the left, the woman disappeared into the fog.

Heather started off in the direction the woman had indicated, s sick knot of dread in the pit of her stomach. Miles from here, if the coarse woman was to be believed, poor Maggie Riggs lay at death's door, while she wandered, lost, in the fog which, like some foul, slimy animal, insinuated itself through the heavy folds of her warm woolen cloak and wafted its foul damp breath against her cheek. Somehow, she had to find Dorset Street, she just had to! The lives of Maggie and her unborn babe depended on her doing so.

Heather halted at the next corner to get her bearings. With a sinking heart, she wondered if the woman, like that horrible Billy Bloor, had played her false, for she could discern no public house nearby—nor much of anything else, for that matter. Oh, surely there would be a constable on the beat in these parts. She craned her ears for his measured tread, and once she fancied she could make out the sound of footsteps nearby despite the steady drip-dripping of water. Yet despite the occasional disembodied voice that carried through the misty curtain all about her, she saw not another soul,

40

much less a police constable, and her panic grew.

It seemed that she had wandered blindly through the heavy mist for hours, her heart in her mouth, half-expecting *something* to leap out upon her at any moment. Finally, when she turned a corner, she could barely make out, across the narrow street, the feeble glow thrown off by a gas lamp, the gauzy veil of fog diffusing the light.

As she peered hopefully in that direction, she glimpsed a man standing in that hazy cloud of light. An amber glow limned his tall, broad frame and the swirling folds of his dark silk cape and top hat. Heather started eagerly through the fog toward him, intending to ask for directions. Then she saw that the woman she had happened on moments ago was clinging to his arm. Her painted face seemed frightened as it looked up into his, which was hidden by the dark shadow of his hat.

The hackles rose on the back of her neck, and a chill swept through her. Her feet suddenly seemed glued to the cobbles as she recalled, vividly, the evening before in the parlor at Cameron House, Annabel curled upon the rug beside her eating cherries and saying, *"concealed by a full dark cloak . . . he chooses only nights of heavy fog to do his evil deeds . . . he signs his name in his victim's blood as Jack the Ripper. . . ."*

Heather's hand flew to her mouth to muffle the shrill scream that built inside her as the man grasped the woman to him and fastened his fingers about her throat. A high-pitched giggle escaped the bawd. Her cry of, "Lawd 'a mercy, Bill, you are a one!" was cut off by a muffled groan as he struck her across the face.

Heather's attempt to silence her warning cry failed dismally. An involuntary shrill squeak, like that of a startled mouse, broke from her. Abruptly the man released the woman and swung about to see Heather standing only a few feet away.

"You, over there!" he growled. "Come 'ere, gal!"

Wide-eyed, Heather saw a pair of long arms, like black snakes, reach out to her. The motion galvanized her into action! "Never! Not on your life!" she cried, and she picked up her skirts, took to her heels, and ran—ran as fast and as hard as she could, giving no thought to the fog, nor caring that she had dropped her portemanteau in her flight.

Breath rasping from her open mouth, she sped like a crazed thing through the mazelike streets, the heavy panting and the loud footfalls of the man following her as she went. Twisting and turning, coming up against walls and lampposts, tripping and stumbling over her unwieldy skirts, she lurched off curbs and against boot-scrapes. In her terror, she sought desperately to escape him. Which way to run—which way to turn! Perhaps she would hurl herself into his arms if she chose the wrong direction. Dear God in Heaven, help me!

Several minutes passed before she dared to halt. Doubled over, holding her side where a vicious cramp knotted it, she listened with bated breath for the sound of that heavy breathing, for those ominous footfalls which had sounded like hammers of doom. There was nothing . . . not a sound except the steady drip-drip-drip of water . . . only the cold, wet fog pressing close about her like a shroud.

And then, she spied it—a golden rectangle of light that beckoned like a welcoming beacon from the open door of a public house across the street. The Laughing Dog! She had found it! Almost sobbing with relief, she flung herself forward off the curb, headed toward the light. She was only halfway across the street when the furious rumble of wheels and the deafening ring of hooves on cobbles sounded alarmingly close at hand. She looked up, wide-eyed, as she saw a coach and team thundering straight for her, careening out of the blanket of fog that walled her in!

She screamed and flung up her arms. In the scant seconds before thought became impossible, she glimpsed the driver upon his perch, a full black cloak flapping about him, his tall hat obscuring his features as he rode her down . . . and down . . . and down. . . . She felt that a tight band was squeezing her waist, had a fleeting sensation of flying through the air, and then everything went black, blacker than the bottom of a deep, dark pit.

How extraordinary! She felt as if she were swimming, swimming up out of a cocoon of blackness, yet there was no water, only a feeling of being quite weightless and drowsy. It was a marvelous feeling, so carefree, so relaxed. There was light beyond the darkness. Warmth. *Safety.* She sighed with relief and lay back.

All at once, she saw a tall, dark man before her, silhouetted against the light. He loomed over her, his tanned face but inches from her own. Tiny creases winged away from the outer corners of his eyes, and his jaw and cheeks, though cleanly shaven, bore a faint bluish shadow, while an engaging black curl spilled untidily across his brow. Prince Charming, in the flesh, she decided happily, and she favored him with a sleepy smile, which he returned, laughter suddenly twinkling in his curious gaze.

His breath fanned her cheek, warm and somehow as intimate as a caress. His unusual blue-violet eyes darkened sensually as his mouth came closer, closer to hers, and she watched it as if hypnotized. Who was he? What was she doing here, with him? And where was here? It didn't seem to matter. He was going to kiss her, but that didn't seem to matter either. *A dream,* a tiny voice whispered in her ear, *It's just a dream!* And, since none of this was real anyway, there was no need for her to be alarmed, none whatsoever. . . .

Her eyes closed as he finally covered her mouth with the flaming heat of his own, the startling contact of their lips so charged with sensation it seemed that a small jolt of electricity leaped from him to her. She gasped, her heart giving an enormous flutter, like a bird soaring into full flight; and she came close to swooning with excitement. Lord, his kisses made her feel devoid of strength or will, and so very, very strange . . . yet she could not bear it if he should stop!

Her slender arms eagerly twined about his neck, and her fingertips ruffled the errant commas of crisp hair that were molded to its nape. Mmm. Delicious! Quite *extraordinarily* delicious, she admitted silently, snuggling more closely against the broad, tweedy expanse of his chest. Strong arms tightened about her in response to her movements, and his provocative masculine scent filled her nostrils with a tantalizing combination of bayberry soap, fresh-laundered linen, and clean, male flesh. She moaned helplessly against his lips, willing him to continue. But as his tongue's tip probed boldly between the soft moistness of her lips to taste the honeyed velvet within, she wondered vaguely why it was only in her dreams that she was so reckless, so devil-may-care—never in her waking moments. . . .

"My dearest, only love!" she heard a husky, feminine voice whisper ardently, and with a start, she realized that voice had been her own! Though the tone was one she was quite certain she had never used before, the words themselves were only too familiar. They came from a scandalous novelette she and Annabel had sighed over. Her cousin had purloined the book from Bridie. Oh, if she could only stay asleep, and never, ever awaken!

Strong fingers moved over her face, tracing the line

of her cheek and chin, brow and nose as if to commit them to memory through the sense of touch. Dreamily she sighed and lay back, afloat on a golden sea of sensation—touch and scent and delight—as his lips moved over her face and then down to the pulsing hollow of her throat, trailing kisses in their wake. His fingers splayed across the slender ivory column of her neck, tenderly stroking. Their feathery pressure sent strange, shivery pulsings down her spine, but in some mysterious way, these sensations found their way to the very pit of her belly. The pressure of his fingers grew. Her dream lover's breathing became more heated and unsteady against her cheek. Somehow, it frightened her a little, that breathing. Oh, the golden sea was still there, lapping, lapping gently, but the euphoria was interspersed now with flashes of something not nearly so pleasant . . . something ugly and better not remembered. A glimpse of a tall, dark hat . . . a swirling cape . . . fog, fog everywhere . . . and strong, cruel hands curling about a vulnerable throat, squeezing, cutting off precious breath . . .

"Jack . . . oh, no! Dear God . . . Jack!"

The strong arms abruptly released her. Jolted awake by sheer fright, Heather sat bolt upright, her heart hammering. In that second she was completely at a loss as to where she was and whether she was awake or still asleep and in the throes of some terrifying nightmare.

Her dark red hair tumbled, loose, about her shoulders, a silky conflagration that fell in a rippling cape to her midback now that the pins and comb that had held it in place were lost. Her violet eyes were enormous, wild with fear. She looked frantically about her, then down at her person.

The tiny buttons that closed the front of her dress had been unfastened, and the froth of white lace that edged her bodice spilled provocatively through the

45

gap. Beneath it, the rounded swell of her ivory bosom could be glimpsed. In horror, she gasped as she realized that her stays—her *stays!*—had also been loosened! A moistened cloth lay upon her lap. It had fallen from her brow when she had come to and sat up.

She picked up the cloth and pressed its coolness against her flaming cheek, feeling suddenly weak at the import of her disheveled state. It was obvious that someone had seen fit to loosen her clothing . . . but who? And for what reason? Heat seeped into her cheeks as a vague recollection of heated kisses and a strikingly handsome man unaccountably filled her mind. She hurriedly cast aside this recollection, giving her head an irritated little shake.

A low, amused chuckle made her spin around as if jerked by a cord. Across the room she saw *him,* leaning rakishly against the heavy oak mantel, one arm dangling from it. The smile on his carelessly handsome face broadened as he saw her outraged expression and strode across the room to her side.

"Such a look of fury for the man who snatched you from the jaws of death, my lovely?" he inquired teasingly. "I would have thought a smile of thanks would be more in order!"

She gathered the front of her gown modestly about her and glared at him. "If it was indeed you who pulled me from the path of the coach, I'm most grateful to you, sir," she said coolly, her tone giving the lie to her words.

His smile deepened further to reveal the gleam of white teeth against a tanned complexion. He stood a moment in the light of the fire and of a single lamp. Then he clicked his heels together and made her a mocking bow. "You're more than welcome, Miss? . . ."

She chose to ignore his none-too-subtle ploy. Not telling him her name, she tossed her head angrily.

"Where is the woman who loosened my . . . my garments?" she demanded, the embarrassed flush in her cheeks staining them a deep crimson. "I would like to thank her for her ministrations, and to ask her to assist me in righting myself before I leave?"

"There was no woman," he answered, devilment dancing in his gentian blue eyes. He said no more, letting the brief statement stand for itself.

"No . . . no woman?" she echoed faintly. "You do not . . . you *cannot* mean . . . Oh!" The thought was so shocking she could not voice it, and as she saw him slowly nod, her hands flew to her breast in dismay. Her crimson face paled alarmingly, and for a second, she swayed dizzily. Immediately he reached out to steady her with long, tanned fingers, his expression no longer amused but concerned.

"You've undergone a considerable fright, Miss Anonymous. I would recommend that you relax for a moment or two longer before trying to stand." He pressed her gently back down onto whatever it was—a chaise, she fancied—that she was resting upon. "There, that's better. I'm certain that very soon your Jack will be along, and I'll then hand you safely over into his care, never fear."

"Jack?" she queried, turning white about the lips. She shook her head so violently that her flaming tresses stirred like a restless sea. "No! Dear God, not him!"

The man shrugged. "No one will force you to go with this Jack unless you wish to do so," he reassured her, alarmed by the utter terror he saw in her eyes at these words. He tugged at the wicked black mustache that gave a corsair's roguish flare to his handsome face, his concern evident. She was as pale as a ghost and was shivering uncontrollably. Not for an instant did the look of abject terror leave her face, but as his gaze lingered upon her, he was again struck by her vibrant

47

beauty. For the first time he knew what it was to be a moth and to be drawn, fascinated, into the dangerous radiance of the candle's bright flame.

Her hair was glory enough, each rippling wave rimmed with dark auburn fire, its coppery filaments glowing in the golden light. But added to that glorious, fiery tide was the magnificence of a complexion of peaches and cream, milk and roses—blemishless perfection that tempts caresses and beckons reckless kisses. Her eyes were a deep, true violet, luminous with the suggestion of tears sparkling in their depths. They were the velvet purple of pansies, crystaled with dew! The sum total of her innocent, glowing loveliness did rare and wondrous things to a man too-long absent from the fresh flowers of English womanhood; to a man grown disenchanted with the brown-eyed, dusky orchids of another clime's tropic flowers. . . .

He jerked his fanciful thoughts back to the moment at hand. The lovely young woman appeared quite pale and shocked as yet: a dangerous condition, he knew. "Some brandy will do the trick and bring the color back to your cheeks, I wager. Don't try to get up. I shall return shortly." With that, he turned on his heel in an almost military fashion and strode from the room, closing the door in his wake.

Despite his stern instructions, the very moment the door closed Heather sat up and swung her legs over the edge of the chaise.

The room was poorly furnished, the chaise on which she had lain lumpy and of inferior quality. The other sticks of furniture in it were of little account. The air bore a smoky quality that was mixed with the yeasty odor of ale and the sharper, almost medicinal, tang of strong spirits. She stood and gingerly made her way across the room, opened the door a crack, and peered out. The smell was stronger beyond, in the gloomy pas-

48

sageway. The sound of glasses chinked one against the other, and hearty voices raised in laughter, song, and banter confirmed her suspicions that the stranger, if he had indeed saved her as he'd said, had carried her into the Laughing Dog public house to which she had been headed.

She gnawed at her lower lip, anxiously wondering how best to escape both him, and the fresh predicament she found herself in. Oh, Lord, there was no telling what liberties he might have taken whilst she lay helpless and unconscious in his care! What if? . . . The very idea made her tremble all over. No, no, she would not even entertain *that* dreadful possibility! Surely she would know, somehow, if he had . . . if he'd . . . taken advantage of her? Wouldn't she? Or . . . would she? Despite her nurse's training, the intimate details of marital intercourse had never been discussed as part of the student curriculum, and she was suddenly furious at her ignorance about such matters.

But furious or not, there was no way to deny the disheveled state of her attire when she'd recovered from the swoon she had fallen into, nor the shameless, bold way he had admitted to having loosened her clothing and stays. And those kisses! He was an unprincipled beast—a cad of the first water, to take advantage of her helplessness! Tears brimmed in her eyes. If it ever came out that she had been alone and unconscious with a man, and a stranger at that, she would be ruined. She could never endure the shame of a scandal, for Uncle Jamie and Aunt Elise's sake more than her own. Thank God she had not given him her name! She would vanish, and somehow try to put this terrible night behind her! The chances of meeting that black-haired scoundrel in the circle in which she moved were virtually naught. . . .

Tiptoing rapidly, she made her way down the

passage, almost crying out in relief to spy a side door leading off it into the night. In a flash she was through it and out in the foggy street once again, her relief at having so easily fled the dark stranger was now mingled with dread that the Whitechapel Murderer might be out there, somewhere, waiting for her. She had seen him about his dreadful crimes, and he must perforce get rid of her—or risk the chance that she could identify him. He had attempted to do so once! He had no way of knowing that, thanks to the shadow cast by his hat, she had been unable to discern his features.

She scurried through the damp, chill murk and exited the alleyway at the front of the public house. Before it stood a hackney cab, the driver enjoying a pipe while he waited for a fare. He was not, she could determine by his blunt profile in the light from the open doorway, that awful Billy Bloor!

"Cabbie, is this hack for hire?" she cried.

"It is indeed, mum," the driver replied courteously, sweeping off his cap as he clambered to the ground. He made a bow. "Where might I be after driving you, mum?"

"To Cameron House—just off Windsor Square. Do you know the area?"

"Indeed I do, mum. But 'tis a fair drive, and will cost all of tuppence ha'penny," he advised her solemnly, tugging at his beard.

"No matter," Heather insisted hurriedly, her voice a trifle shrill in her desperation to be gone. "Only see me safely there, and I will consider the fare well spent."

The cabbie handed her carefully up into the coach, which though worn seemed well cared for and comfortable. Minutes later, the hackney pulled away from the curb at a discreet and comfortable trot. Heather leaned back against the seat and closed her eyes, saying a silent prayer for Maggie Riggs, whom she had temporarily forgotten in her upset, and another for herself. Oh, Lord, what a terrible, terrible night! Almost killed—and to all indications, her innocence taken, as well! She touched her lips, the vague, shamefully pleasant memory of a warm, masculine mouth—*his* mouth!—pressed ardently to hers stirring in her mind. Fantasy . . . or fact? How could she tell? Would she ever know the truth? Reaction set in then, and she cried softly against the hem of her cloak as the coach rumbled on.

As Heather was being swiftly carried far from the Laughing Dog public house, the tall, dark man was returning to the back room with a small snifter of excellent cognac cupped in his hand. The door was ajar, and as he stepped inside he saw at once that the lovely young woman was gone.

He set the brandy glass down upon a table and strode across to the chaise where she had lain, his attention caught by something that gleamed against the shabby chintz. Several bent hairpins were strewn there, as well as a small comb of mother-of-pearl that caught the golden glow of the flickering fire in its opalescent depths. He picked it up and turned it over in his hands, smiling ruefully. The disappointment that had filled him on finding her gone, like a pretty, exotic bird flown from its cage, was out of all proportion to the brief length of their acquaintance. Nevertheless, he felt a vague sensation of loss, an honest twinge of regret that he would never come to know her better. "A great pity," he murmured to himself, remembering her eager response to his stolen kisses. A wicked gleam ignited in the gentian blue of his eyes, and the black bars of his brows rose as he added in an amused tone, "A very great pity!"

Whistling softly, he drew his cloak and hat from the stand by the door and tucked them under his arm. Almost as an afterthought, he retrieved the comb he had set upon the mantel and looked at it once more. Cinderella had at least left her Prince Charming a glass slipper to find her by, he thought as he left the public house through the side door by which Heather had left scant minutes before.

"Awright, gov'na—where is she?" growled a voice as he stepped out into the alley.

He looked up, almost laughing aloud. An expensive top hat and a swirling silk opera cape did little at such close range, despite the meager lighting, to disguise the coarse and unlovely features of their owner, presently looming threateningly over him. A crooked nose, splayed malevolently across pitted, thickskinned cheeks, was a perfect partner to the fleshy, wide mouth below that boasted a sadistic curl. Eyes so pale gray as to appear quite colorless in the gloom gleamed greedily under a jutting Neanderthal forehead.

Nasty piece of work, Heather's rescuer thought, yet his disarming smile betrayed no inkling of his opinions.

"She?" he echoed mildly, black brows arched.

"Aye. The red-haired tart wot you brung in there," the man demanded querulously.

"What's it to you, friend?" Gentian eyes narrowed.

"Plenny," the lout growled thickly. "She were strollin' *my* gals' district—takin' the toffs right from under their bloody noses, she were! An' not s'much as a farthin' paid t'me fer the privilege, neither."

"And who might you be, my fine-feathered friend?"

The ugly fellow scowled, too great a dull-wit to know for certain if he was being insulted or commended. "Folks 'round these 'ere parts calls me Lord Bill."

"An' that ain't all they calls 'im, oftentimes, not by a long chalk!" added an indignant voice from the shadows.

For the first time, he realized that "Lord" Bill was not alone. He strained his eyes to plumb the inky alley in the direction of the voice, and saw a garishly painted bawd. Beplumed and beaded and decked out in shabby finery, she stood at Bill's elbow, laughing raucously.

"Shut yer bleedin' yap, Annie, an' sharpish," Bill growled, "lest I shut it fer ye wiv me knuckles, ye slut! Right, gov'na—where is she? I got a score t'settle wiv 'er!"

"The young lady has gone, my friend. Look inside for yourself if you don't believe me."

With a suspicious glance at him, Bill did indeed step inside.

Annie laughed. "A proper doubting Thomas our Billy is, make no mistake, luv! Wouldn't believe 'is own mother if she swore on a bloomin' stack o' Bibles! I told 'im straight out the gal weren't one o' us, but 'e wouldn't take Annie's word fer it, no sir. Seen she's a looker, 'e 'as, an' now 'e's minded t' find 'er and turn her out on the streets fer 'imself, the sod!"

The man's gentian eyes lit up. "You know her?"

"Gawd, no, ducks! She just came from nowhere, out o' the bloomin' fog. Said some cabbie had set 'er down there and left 'er. Scared witless she was an' all, t' find 'erself lost in these 'ere parts. Didn't talk like one of us workin' gals, neither. I had 'er placed fer a lady's maid, or summat." Her faded blue eyes grew calculating. "Bloody glad t' find she's gorn, I am tho', t' tell the truth. Enough o' us 'round here already, without one wiv *her* looks twitchin' her skirts and catchin' the blokes' eyes, Gawd yes!"

Lord Bill lumbered through the side door then. "She's gorn awright," he acknowledged sourly, "an' not a penny in me pocket fer it, neither. I've a mind t' show ye it don't pay to mess around wiv any but Lord Bill's lovelies in these parts, gov'na."

Bill hefted himself forward, meaty fists swinging up

53

to strike the man as he did so. But, neatly sidestepping with the virile grace of a fencer, the man easily avoided his fist and swung a smart punch himself, his knuckles connecting solidly against Bill's jaw with a ringing crack that sounded as if he'd struck a side of raw beef! Bill reeled backward, his elegant top hat tipping forward over his none-too-elegant face as he slammed against the public house wall, cracking the back of his skull in the process. The man stepped forward, lifted the hat with a murmured, "Excuse me, friend!" and dealt him a second punch square on his crooked nose. Cape billowing as he went, Bill slid down the wall without a sound other than a strangely childlike sigh.

"Gawd! I ain't seen no one so bloomin' 'andy wiv their dukes since Black Tommy McTavish beat Red Bob Mullens on Clapham Common three years ago. Blimey, luv, that were bloomin' poetry in motion, it were!" Annie exclaimed admiringly. "But 'e's like t' be right bullish when he comes to. Ye'd best scarper, mister!"

"Scarper, I will," the man promised, laughing. "But what of you?"

"Annie Garret'll manage, luv, don't ye fret none."

He nodded. "Then take this," he urged, drawing some coins from his pocket and giving them to her, "and lay low for a few days until he cools off."

"Why, bless ye, it'll come in right handy, luv!" Annie exclaimed. "Ain't much coin t' come by hereabouts of late, not after Bill's taken his cut, and wi' Jack about his dirty business," she added darkly.

"Jack?" he repeated. The lovely young woman had mentioned a Jack when she'd come to, and had seemed terrified of him.

"Aye, Jack the Ripper, they're callin' 'im now—the Whitechapel Murderer! Where've ye been that you ain't heard o' Jack? The papers ha' been full o' 'is evil doin's!"

"Abroad," he replied, deep in thought. Ha! It was little wonder the girl had been scared out of her wits, he realized belatedly. She'd thought the procurer, Lord Bill in his finery, was the Ripper himself—and he had unwittingly volunteered to see her safely into her Jack's care! Whoever she was, and wherever she was, he hoped she was safely away from these parts and off the streets.

He favored the bawd with a snappy salute. "Good night, Annie. Careful as you go," he flung over his shoulder, and whistling merrily on the damp, cold air, he made his way down the alley and out into the foggy streets of Whitechapel.

Chapter Four

Cameron House was ablaze with light when Heather, in the hired hackney, swept up to the front door. Servants bearing storm lanterns were scurrying about the driveway, and Victor was pacing anxiously back and forth alongside the coach with the matched bays, while Uncle Jamie barked orders to left and right. Aunt Elise stood in the doorway wringing her hands, still attired in the black-beaded gown she must have donned to wear to the Rutherfords for dinner.

As the cabbie handed Heather down from the coach, Mrs. Reading came hurrying from the house wearing a heavy cloak and bonnet. She drew up sharply upon seeing Heather, her handsome, if stern, face quickly adopting a furious expression.

"I was about to join the search for you! Where, may I ask, have you been, Miss Heather?" the housekeeper demanded.

"It is a long and involved story, Mrs. Reading," Heather began, hurriedly brushing away her tears. "We should go inside where you may hear it in comfort."

"We should, should we, miss!" Ready asked, her tone acidic. "Where, may I ask, were your thoughts for our comfort these past two hours? And furthermore, I ask again, where were you? Victor has been combing the streets for you! No one at St. Thomas' knew where you were. It was as if you had vanished from the face of this earth!"

"I—I didn't think," Heather stammered, realizing belatedly that all the lights, the uproar the house was in, were on her account. "The porter's wife was ill, and I wanted to help her if I—"

"Hmmph!" Uncle Jamie cut in, fastening his blue-gray eyes upon her with a severity she had never seen before. "It's this nursing business again, isn't it? Answer me, young lady!"

Heather's chin came up defiantly. "I suppose it is, Uncle," she admitted honestly. "But I made my decision to help others, and I will adhere to it. Mister Riggs's wife is very ill, and he had no money to pay a physician's fees. I hired a hackney to take me to their home in Whitechapel—"

"Whitechapel!" her Uncle exploded. "You went into that—that *stew,* and by night, unescorted?" He quivered all over now with rage. "Did you take leave of your senses, lassie? Och, 'tis lucky you were no' set upon—or worse!" As usual when he was agitated, Jamie Cameron's highland burr became decidedly pronounced. He jabbed a rigid finger toward the house. "Go t' your room! We'll talk more o' this in the mornin', aye, that we will!"

"No." The single word trembled on the crackling silence.

"No?" her uncle thundered, his expression incredulous.

For emphasis, she shook her head, her jaw hardening defiantly now, her former tears forgotten.

"No, Uncle Jamie! As I tried to tell you, there's a very sick woman in Whitechapel—a woman who might well die in childbirth if I cannot get there to help her! She

57

has several small children and a husband who need her desperately, and they have no money for a physician's fees. I've—I've tried to be an obedient niece to you, Uncle, but in this matter I regret I *must* defy you. I mean to have Victor drive me back into Whitechapel immediately. I would rather have your permission to do so, sir, but I regret that with or without it, I shall go. Every minute counts, Uncle Jamie!" Her voice was husky, filled with desperate pleading yet with a steely edge of determination to it. The plea was in her eyes too.

Jamie Cameron's shoulders slumped. "John Riggs's wife, you say?" John's brother had been a groom for the Cameron's some years back. The porter at St. Thomas' was a fine, hardworking man, to all accounts. Nodding at his niece, he sighed heavily in resignation. "Then go to your room, lassie. I'll take Victor myself and we'll go after a doctor for the woman, never fear." He waggled his finger at her again, a ferocious scowl on his ruddy face. "But don't take it into your daft wee head that this changes anything, Heather Cameron!" he bellowed. "I'll still be seeing you in my study in the mornin', lass. Aye, and don't ye forget it! *Victor!*" He strode rapidly away toward the stables.

Heather felt tears prickle anew in her eyes, tears of relief mingled with gratitude. For all her uncle's displeasure with her, he would keep his promise, she knew. He was not a man to renege on his word. "Thank you. Oh, thank you, Uncle!" she managed. Then she picked up her skirts and held her head high as she went into the house.

Mrs. Reading stood stiffly by the door. As Heather made to pass her she implored, "Will you please see that the cabbie is paid, Mrs. Reading? I have no change, and he has done nothing wrong!"

In answer, the housekeeper gave a tight little nod,

and Heather brushed past her and ran up the curving staircase to her room where, her brave façade crumpling, she flung herself across the bed and wept again, half in relief that she had returned safely after her frightening adventures and that all that was possible would be done for Maggie Riggs, and half at the realization of the predicament she was in.

Her tears were all cried out when a sharp rap sounded upon her door some time later. She sat up in bed, her long hair braided, white flannel nightgown primly buttoned to her chin. Only a telltale flush to her cheeks betrayed the burst of weeping she had given way to. Only the lavender shadows beneath her eyes gave any inkling of the shocking new discovery she had made whilst bathing—several faint blue bruises about her upper arms and upon her thighs. Further proof, to her way of thinking, that her worst fears were true!

"Yes? Who is it?" she asked, tired and wishing she could fall asleep.

"It's Mrs. Reading. May I come in?"

"Enter," Heather bade her, drawing a deep, shaky breath.

The housekeeper did so. With an unusual lack of formality she perched upon the edge of Heather's bed.

"Heather, my dear," she began after some slight hesitation, "your aunt asked me to come and speak with you about your escapades tonight. She is dreadfully upset herself, and has retired to her bed." She frowned, drawing circles on the counterpane with a restless finger. "I wonder if you fully realize the seriousness of what you have done tonight? You must know that your aunt and uncle were dreadfully concerned when Victor returned alone and said he could not find you! We—all of us—we feared you had been abducted, or had met with foul play of some kind. When people are concerned, their relief is often replaced by anger. The anger does not lessen the love they feel. Rather, it is in proportion to their fear. Do I make myself plain?"

The controlled expression upon Heather's face softened a little. "Oh, yes, Mrs. Reading, I know that—I know that Aunt Elise and Uncle Jamie have only my well-being at heart, as do you." She reached out and squeezed the housekeeper's large hand. "But," she added gently, "I cannot live my life as the fragile, useless female they would have me be—I just can't! Since I began studying at the Nightingale School, I have learned the joy of having a purpose in my life. Tonight, I had hoped to use what little knowledge I have acquired to help someone in dire need—to *really* help someone, Mrs. Reading." Her violet eyes were earnest, her expression grave and deeply sincere. "Admittedly, the way I chose to go about it was wrong. I should have left word, so that your minds would have been at rest, but I'm afraid I acted first and weighed the consequences afterward. I was stupidly thoughtless! Forgive me?"

Mrs. Reading patted her cheek. "You know that goes without saying, dear girl. But I fear you will have far more difficulty persuading your uncle to forgive you so readily. He instructed me to sternly remind you that he will await you in his study after breakfast in the morning."

Their eyes met, and both women acknowledged in that silent exchange that Jamie Cameron's interview with his niece was likely to be a most difficult one.

"You are so like your father, Heather," Mrs. Reading observed. "He was ever one to act and weigh the consequences of his actions after. But he was a good man, a man to be admired, for all his impetuousness." A faint smile hovered about the housekeeper's lips.

60

"And also a man who continually flouted convention! Do you remember him at all?"

Heather regretfully shook her head. "I sometimes have a vague recollection of a woman, a very beautiful woman with a sweet voice who used to sing me to sleep. I've always presumed that she must have been my Mamma. But of Papa, I have no memories whatsoever."

Mrs. Reading nodded. "It is surprising that you should even recall your dear mother. You could have been only two years old when she passed away." Her eyes took on a faraway look. "Her last words to me were to take you home, to England, to your Uncle Jamie. She knew he would raise you with all the love he would lavish upon his own children. And he has, child. He and your Aunt Elise have loved you dearly from the very first day I brought you to them, despite your father and Jamie having quarreled so bitterly about your Papa's determination to spend his days as a medical missionary in Africa. He was a brilliant man, your father, and I suppose being the eldest brother, Jamie believed Alex should heed his counsel, and go into the family woolen business, instead of 'wasting' his life doctoring heathen savages!" She sighed heavily. "I don't expect you would consider his life wasted, though, would you, Heather?"

"My father did what he felt he had to do, Mrs. Reading. I cannot help but admire him—or any man— for following his heart. Mamma must have loved him very much to have sacrificed everything for him, to have married him despite her family's protests, and to have spent the remainder of her life working alongside him?"

Mrs. Reading nodded. "She did. Oh, what a pair they made—he so very handsome, she so very beautiful! Were it not for your hair, which is the Cameron

61

auburn from your father's side, you are the very image of Isobel!" Her gray eyes twinkled. "But it is your father's obstinacy you have inherited, not the biddable nature of your dear, fragile Mamma, God rest her soul!"

Heather smiled. "You still miss her a great deal, do you not?"

The housekeeper acknowledged by her faraway, pensive expression that she did. "We were dear friends until the end. More like sisters than mistress and companion. She would have done anything for me, and I for her. I even left my position without giving notice to go with her and your father! Were it not for your aunt's generosity and understanding, it would have been nigh impossible for me to find another place when I returned to England. As it was, they were kind enough to offer me employ as their housekeeper, and I was most grateful to accept. I believe your aunt realized that I had grown fond of you, and would wish to be where I might watch you grow to womanhood. They are a wonderful couple, Heather. You have been most fortunate."

Soberly, Heather nodded. "Yes, Mrs. Reading. I—I would not hurt them for the world!" Nor bring them shame, she added silently, a deep ache beginning in her heart.

Mrs. Reading stood and bent to place a kiss upon Heather's brow. "Of course not, my dear. In the morning, you must tell your uncle that. He loves you. He will not be overly stern with you, I am certain. Good night, child. A good night's sleep will better prepare you for the morning's storm—and I am willing to hazard that it will be a severe one."

"Is there any news of Mrs. Riggs yet?" Heather called after her.

"None so far, I'm afraid. But your uncle told me that

he had found an excellent physician for her—a Doctor Stewart, who has his offices on Harley Street. She is in the best possible hands, my dear."

"Yes. Doctor Stewart is excellent." Heather acknowledged, immeasurably calmed by the knowledge that Maggie had the care she so desperately needed. "Please thank Uncle Jamie for me, Mrs. Reading."

"I will. Good night!"

Heather murmured her reply as the housekeeper left the room.

If you but knew the entire story, dear Mrs. Reading! she thought grimly when she was again alone, I hazard that you would swoon, at the very least!

Lord, if she closed her eyes, she could still recall with horrifying clarity, the rolling white eyes of the horses; the flecks of foam that sprayed from their mouths; the shadowed countenance and flowing cloak of the man who leaned forward over the horses' rumps and lashed them to greater speed as they rode her down! Hot on the heels of that nightmarish memory, the remembrance of a delicious stolen kiss and the roguish grin of the man she had wakened to find herself quite alone with filled her mind . . . for although she tried very hard, she could not help thinking about him! On reflection, his attire and voice had been markedly out of place in such an area as Whitechapel, she mused. Ah, yes, but those carelessly handsome, dark good looks would not have been *nearly* so unlikely in one of the lurid romantic novelettes she and her cousin secretly wept and sighed over, a wicked, unbidden voice hinted in her ear, or upon the stage in one of the new music halls—or even in a fairytale! It was quite unfair that any man so unprincipled as he had been should be so extraordinarily handsome.

She frowned as she snuggled under the bedcovers. She felt completely the same—a little tired, perhaps, from her escapade, a little frightened still, but certainly not different as she had imagined she would feel after having been the victim of a man's passion! Would she ever know what had really happened? Would her future husband be able to tell if she were virgin or not upon their wedding night? Or would she carry her shameful suspicions to the grave, a spinster, never knowing the truth? Aunt Elise and Uncle Jamie and Mrs. Reading would doubtless suffer apopleptic fits were they to learn she had lain, unconscious, in a man's care, without benefit of a chaperon of any kind! Were her uncle to learn of it, he might go so far as to seek the man out and demand at gunpoint that he marry her and thus save her from ruin. Imagine, she might be forced to marry someone she did not even know or want to know. Whatever other admissions they might be able to pry from her, she would never reveal the dark stranger's part in her night's escapades, she vowed with a shudder.

Her nerves, like tautly coiled springs, tensed as the door opened a crack. A waft of pretty perfume drifted into the room ahead of her cousin Annabel.

"Are you asleep, Coz?" Annabel hissed loudly into the shadows.

"If I had been, I would not be so now," Heather retorted. "Turn up the lamp, if you will?"

With a rustle of silk skirts, Annabel obediently did so before twirling about to face her cousin. Her blue eyes danced with excitement, and there was a high color to her cheeks. In the glittering gown of deep blue, decorated with tiny shimmering blue beads from the ruched hem to the daring décolletage, and with long white gloves encasing her lower arms, she was quite beautiful. "Well! It appears you have been creating a scandal, Heather, dear!" Annabel declared, grinning wickedly. "How marvelous of you! I had thought my evening at the Rutherfords would quite enthrall you, but now I fear it pales in comparison to your exploits. Quickly, tell me all!"

With a rueful smile, Heather told Annabel about John Riggs's wife and the horrible cabbie, Billy Bloor, and about the rest of her frightening experience in the foggy streets of Whitechapel. She carefully omitted any reference to the man who had pulled her from the path of the racing coach, casually saying, "Luckily, someone happened along, and pulled me aside in the very nick of time. And here I am, safe and sound and none the worse for my adventures." She forced a smile.

"You actually *saw* the Ripper at his work?" Annabel whispered hoarsely. "Oh, my! Oh, my Lord! But—you must tell Papa!" she exclaimed. "Do you not see, Heather? What you saw might lead to his arrest!"

"No, Coz, I didn't see his face, remember? I could tell Scotland Yard nothing that they do not already know. Please, do not tell Uncle Jamie a word of this! It would only further convince him that I should give up nursing, and I could not bear that he should force me to do so. I intend to tell him only that the cabbie tricked me, and that I lost my way in the fog, nothing more. Give me your word that you'll say nothing!"

Though blatantly disappointed, Annabel nodded and solemnly crossed her heart with a white-gloved fingertip. "I promise—not a word." However, she looked at Heather with new interest, her opinion of her cousin obviously elevated by her cousin's brushes with death and with the Whitechapel Murderer, and by her seemingly resigned and calm attitude to it all. "But what if he comes after you, Coz?" she asked. "Why, your very life might be in danger!"

Heather shrugged. "I'll have to be careful, that's all. Besides, how could he ever find me in a city such as London, teeming with hundreds of thousands of people?" she argued rationally.

Annabel nodded. "Yes, I suppose you're right." She leaned forward a little . "Would you like to hear about the Rutherfords' dinner and ball now? I regret that it was not nearly so exciting as what happened to you, but all the same it proved quite entertaining."

"Go on, do, you little goose! Of course I want to hear everything!" Heather insisted. Annabel promptly sat down upon the bed.

"Well, when you did not return with Victor, Mamma insisted that Anthony and I should go ahead to the Rutherfords in his coach—and offer our apologies for Mamma and Papa, with the hope that they would be able to join the gathering later, once they had found you.

"After dinner, we all retired to the music room, and Lydia Halsey gave one of her loathsome pianoforte recitals, accompanied by her sister, who, I confess, gave me a violent earache with her screeching!" She giggled. "After the gentlemen had finished their brandy and cigars, and the women had torn everyone to shreds with their gossip, Lady Rutherford invited us all to dance, and the evening became very jolly, for I was not once lacking for a partner!

"Anthony was properly jealous as befits a fiancé. When he whirled me into a waltz, the music had not yet ended when a tall, dark man tapped him on the shoulder and cut in in the most bold fashion! Poor Anthony! He was quite furious, as you can imagine. The young man whisked me across the floor into the shadows, and behind a curtain he tilted my face to his. 'So, Cinderella, we meet again!' he whispered. Well, as you can imagine, I was quite at a loss for words, for I could not recall ever having met him before, and he was quite handsome enough that I doubt I should have forgotten him if I had! When I looked into his face, he was

66

startled, and seemed taken aback. He apologized profusely, and explained that he had mistaken me for someone else. I suppose I should have been quite put out about it, but he was so very *galante* that I instantly forgave him."

"And did you ever learn this man's identity?" Heather inquired, smiling.

"I did. He is Captain Adam Markham, of the Berkeley Square Markhams." She said the latter with such an air of triumph that Heather wrinkled her brows in puzzlement.

"And what if he is?" Heather pressed.

Annabel sighed exasperatedly. "Don't you remember, Coz? He's the second brother—the so-called black sheep of the family?"

"I'm afraid the intricacies of society gossip escape me," Heather remarked wryly. "In what way is this Captain Markham a black sheep?"

Annabel sighed a second time. "Colonel Markham left the family estates to the eldest son, Hunter Markham. Some years before his death, he bought a commission for the second son, Adam. The third son—Rory, I believe his name is—joined the church. Adam served with the dragoons in India—and quite courageously, too, from what I was able to discover—but there was some sort of scandal which was hushed up, and soon after, he resigned his commission. Apparently this made old Colonel Markham so furious, he struck Adam from his will! Captain Markham fancies himself an explorer now, and spends much of his time in the jungles of Darkest Africa, which explains why we have heard so little about him before. An explorer! Isn't that exciting?"

"Very," Heather admitted. "But hardly a secure means of acquiring a livelihood."

"Oh, pooh!" Annabel was disgusted at her cousin's

practicality. "Nothing practical is ever romantic or exciting!"

"Not even the woolen trade?" Heather asked innocently, eying her cousin whose fiancé was a part of that trade, as was her uncle.

"Anthony is the exception," Annabel contradicted firmly. "He is wildly romantic and exciting, wool trade or not!"

Heather laughed. "I agree. Anthony is very sweet and quite handsome himself—daring, too, if he would risk his sanity by making you his wife!"

Annabel stuck out a small, pointed pink tongue and grimaced horribly in her cousin's direction. "If you will tease so, I shall be off to bed," she declared, feigning a wounded tone. "Good night, Coz." She leaned down and kissed her cousin fondly, and Heather, suddenly overcome with tenderness for her dear cousin however well they might both tease to hide those affectionate feelings, hugged Annabel fiercely, wishing she could confide her secret.

"Good night to you, too, Coz. Sweet dreams!"

"They will be," Annabel vowed, "for I shall dream of my Anthony *and* that handsome rogue, Captain Markham!"

And I, Heather thought fervently after Annabel had waltzed through the door, pray that I do not dream at all!

Nevertheless, when sleep claimed her that night it was not dreamless as she had so desperately hoped. A tall, cloaked figure pursued her relentlessly through the corridors of her mind, his boots pounding the cobbles, his mocking laughter echoing over and over until she covered her ears and screamed for him to stop.

But every time he finally captured her and held her

fiercely in his arms, she found herself gazing up into another's face—a face lit wickedly by eyes of gentian blue, almost as violet as were her own but set off by a tanned, weathered face and glossy black, curling hair. In her dreams, he reached for the buttons of her gown and unfastened them one by one. She felt the touch of his warm, virile hand upon the curve of her quivering breast, his warm breath fanning her flushed cheek, the firm pressure of his heated lips as they covered her own; then she woke up, her face wet with tears, to find herself quite alone—and burning with shame.

Chapter Five

Uncle Jamie did not appear at breakfast the next morning, and after a subdued meal, during which Aunt Elise had sighed countless times and had given her numerous doleful glances, Heather excused herself and made her way from the breakfast room and down the hall. She knocked upon the paneled door to her uncle's study and, receiving no answer, let herself inside.

She had expected to find him lost in his work, his sandy head bent over some ledger, deaf to her knock upon the door. To her surprise, the study was quite empty, a cozy haven of leather chairs, paneled walls, and bookshelves crammed with classical works in Latin and Greek and English. There was a teak gun case against one wall and beneath a window that overlooked the square stood a colorful papier-mâché globe that spun in a stand. When she and Annabel had been younger, they had loved to come in here just to spin it, she recalled. They had delighted in jabbing their pink little fingers indiscriminately against its surface and declaring that where it stopped, there they would live when they were "growned-ups." Annabel, crafty minx that she was, had unerringly managed to land her finger directly upon Paris each time, whilst Heather, less obvious but equally conniving, had opted for Africa! She spun the globe once more, for old times' sake, before turning away, restless in her anxious state and wishing Uncle Jamie would hurry up and get what promised to be an unpleasant dressing-down over with.

She had completed her toilette with great care that morning. A mauve morning gown of wool, with a darker violet fitted jacket fastened down the front with intricate froggings served to keep out the cold of the vast house, and also to create the sober and responsible impression she had been striving for. If the interview were begun within the quarter hour, there was a chance she would have time to change into the dark merino gown that was her uniform, and still be on time at St. Thomas'. . . .

The door opened then, and Uncle Jamie stalked in. Heather looked up expectantly, surprised by the resigned expression upon his face for she had anticipated a look of controlled annoyance. He came around the desk and pulled a heavily carved chair up to it for her, gesturing to indicate that she should be seated before seating himself opposite her. Wringing her hands in her lap, she waited for him to begin, and after clearing his throat innumerable times, he did so.

"Heather," he said hesitantly, "it has been almost eighteen years since your Mamma died, and Mrs. Reading brought you here to us. At that time, we had no little ones, and it seemed that in takin' away my poor brother and his bride, God in his goodness had seen fit to give ye t' us in their place." His voice thickened with emotion. "Believe me, Heather, my dear, you could not have been more loved had Elise borne you and had I fathered you myself. I—I want you to know that we think of you not as a niece, but as a daughter, a beloved sister for Annabel."

A lump swelled in Heather's throat. Oh, this was far,

71

far crueller, than any scolding could ever be! "And—and I love you both, dear Uncle Jamie!" she whispered huskily.

"Good, good. I'm very glad to hear it," her uncle acknowledged. He coughed. "Also, like many fathers and daughters, we have not always seen eye to eye on certain matters—your nursing, in particular. I know you are well aware that your aunt and I had hoped you would make a brilliant marriage, have a husband and children and a fine household of your own. But since ye seemed so earnest about your . . . your calling, we realized that, like your father, you had chosen t' follow a different path. Consequently, we agreed that you should be permitted to try the Florence Nightingale School, and if you'll recall I took it upon myself to use my connections to allow you to continue to live with us at home while doing so?"

Heather nodded. "Yes. You and Aunt Elise have done so much for me, and I shall always be grateful, for I understand that you did what you could despite your disapproval." She paused. "But I fail to see in what way this is connected with what occurred yesterday evening, Uncle Jamie?"

Her uncle reached for the sheet of paper that he had lain upon his desk top, and handed it to her wordlessly.

She was frowning as she took it from him, but as she read the brief letter written upon it in a crabbed dark hand, her face grew first white, then red with anger; her hand shook upon the vellum, crumpling the corner. "What!" she cried. "But—but this is so unfair! How can Matron dismiss me from the school? I was late only the one time, just that once, Uncle, I give you my word!"

He nodded. "I know that, Heather. But Miss Ratner—Matron—expressly states that you were instructed to report to her office after duty yesterday, and that you never put in an appearance at all. That, dear child, is the reason for your dismissal." He sighed. "Please believe that whatever my feelings about your nursing, and however angered I might have been by your running off unattended last night, I would never have wished such a punishment on you, never. I . . . I know how much it meant to you." He looked suddenly older than his forty-odd years, and deeply troubled.

"But, there must be something we can do!" Heather cried, jumping to her feet and pacing agitatedly across the Turkey carpet, before flinging about to face him. "I know! I shall appeal to Miss Nightingale! She has taken a liking to me, Uncle, I know that she has. She even gave me a pet name when I went to take tea with her last summer—she called me her Angel! And she gives such names only to her favorite students. Oh, please, dear Uncle Jamie, will you not take me to South Street to speak with her? I'm certain she would give me another—"

"I have just returned from South Street, Heather," Jamie said heavily. "I went there immediately upon receipt of this letter, which arrived by a message-boy early this morning. That is why I was not here when you arrived, as I promised to be." He came around his desk and crossed the room to his niece, taking her by the shoulders and holding her at arm's length. "Your Miss Nightingale was a great woman in her youth. A heroine. The good she did to reform the conditions in military hospitals and in the hospitals here at home in England cannot be measured. She saved countless lives by the sheer dint of an iron will and by her refusal to admit defeat or accept the denial of anyone who stood in the way of her goal, however exalted their position. Such a woman can follow her purpose only by exerting the most stringent discipline upon herself; by sternly foregoing the little everyday pleasures that we indulge ourselves in. And what she expects of herself, she also

73

expects of others.

"I explained to Miss Nightingale your reasons for not keeping the appointment with Matron. I told her everything about John Riggs's wife, and that your intent was to go to Whitechapel to help her, but it is my sad duty to tell you that Miss Nightingale was moved not a whit by it. 'No excuse!' she said. 'Nurse Cameron should have informed Matron of her intent. She did not. Nor did she obey Miss Ratner's explicit instructions to report to her office. I have no choice but to agree with Matron's decision, however harsh it may appear.' So you see, my poor, wee child, you ha'e no options left to you."

For a second, she swayed, and he feared she was about to swoon. But then her shoulders squared and her chin came up. She looked him full in the eyes. "I see," she said in a small voice. "Then I have no recourse. Thank you for doing what you did, Uncle. I am very grateful for your efforts on my behalf, and especially so since it went against your own wishes to make them. Now, if you will permit me, I should like to go to my room. To be quiet and alone, so that I can think."

Inwardly cursing that damned, termagant Florence Nightingale, the dragonlike Matron Ratner, and the nursing profession in general, Jamie Cameron nodded. He drew Heather gently against his chest and kissed the crown of her head, wondering how far she would get before she crumpled, lost the brave façade she was maintaining now. Her slender body trembled ever so faintly in his embrace, and his heart went out to her. She was so like Alex, his younger brother, had been. So determined, so fine, so very hard to understand! "Run along, my dear," he said huskily, wishing he could find some words to comfort her better in her anguish. Silently, she left, drifting to the door as if she walked in her sleep.

Despite what she had told her uncle, Heather did not go immediately to her room. She went instead up the winding staircase to the second floor, then up another to the third and to the day nursery that she and Annabel had shared as children. It was now used only when guests with boisterous offspring stayed at Cameron House, which was rarely.

The ink-stained desks were covered with dust sheets, as were the dappled rocking horse with the mane and tail of frayed blond rope, and the enormous Gothic dollhouse in the corner. Beneath the window sat a heavy trunk, and Heather ran to it, knowing even as she flung up the lid what she would find within. Numerous dolls stared back up at her, their exquisitely painted bisque or porcelain faces still pretty in the wan November sunlight that streamed through the narrow windows. She took several out and sat them upon the window sill, bravely smiling through the mist of tears that had gathered before her eyes, for she had no trouble in recalling which of the dolls were hers, and which Annabel's. Heather's dolls all wore plasters and bandages upon their limbs and heads, and after all these years they still smelled faintly of camphor and liniment! Poor babies, she thought, I never did make you all well again. She rested her head upon her hands on the dusty window sill, and cried out her disappointment and her anger.

It was in the day nursery that Annabel found her some time later, curled upon the window seat with a large porcelain doll cradled in her arms, staring unseeing through the murky panes at the bleak, misty lawns of Cameron House.

"May I come in, Heather?" Annabel asked, unusually

subdued. She had learned what had transpired in her father's study, and she had known how deeply upset her cousin must be at the fragmenting of her most cherished dream. Seeing Heather nod, she went and stood behind her. "Father is quite shattered, you know, Coz," she said softly. "Despite their doubts, I do believe he and Mamma were quite proud of your determination, in a funny sort of way. How are you? Does it hurt very much?"

"Yes!" Heather whispered, blinking rapidly. "But—but there is nothing that can be done to mend things, and so I am angry quite as much as I am upset."

"At Papa?"

"No, not at Uncle Jamie, bless him, nor at Matron or Miss Nightingale, come to that. At myself, Annabel! I should have thought before I reacted so rashly. If I had but taken the time to inform Matron of my intent, and to apologize because our interview would be postponed, she would have had no basis to dismiss me! I worked so hard to enter the school, remember? I begged and pleaded and became quite contrary with Uncle and Aunt Elise. And in one rash action, I threw it all away!"

"What will you do now?"

Heather shrugged. "As you do, I suppose. Take the air with Aunt Elise. Arrange the flowers. Apply myself to my needlework"—her voice broke—"and die of utter boredom!" A long silence followed.

"Then you will have to do so at Moorsedge," Annabel divulged at length.

"What?"

"Yes. Mamma and Papa were discussing it. They are very much afraid you might succumb to a depression if you remain here in the city. They have decided to close Cameron House for the winter, and to whisk us both off to Scotland—isn't that grand? It's been—what?—

76

two years since we wintered there, and I do so love Papa's family home and the heaths and the snow, and Cook Shelagh's delicious scones! I know how terrible everything seems now, but do try to look a little excited, you poor dear, for Mamma's sake. I know she's hoping her idea will completely win you over. "And," she added with a happy little smile that she quickly smothered, feeling guilty, "Anthony is to be invited to stay with us, and they are planning to have shoots and routs and hunt suppers to fill the days. It won't be dull at all. Most of society retires to Scotland for the winter, anyway, so we'll have loads more fun there than if we were to stay in town! Mamma intends to invite plenty of young men to our social occasions. I do believe they are nurturing the fond hope that, with your nursing days ended, you will perhaps look more favorably upon the subject of marriage."

Heather decided to offer no comment regarding this, and instead asked, "When are we to leave?"

"If everything can be packed in time, on Thursday morning. Most of the servants will come with us, with just enough of them left behind to keep the house in order until we return in the spring." She headed for the door. "I'll leave you to recover now, Coz. I do so hope I haven't intruded? Oh, and by the way, Ready sent Victor to St. Thomas to enquire after Mister Riggs's wife. She knew you would be concerned. Mrs. Riggs had a trying time of it, but is doing well. They have a new baby daughter, a tiny little darling, to all accounts. John Riggs was most distressed to hear what had become of you on his account, and he sends his deepest apologies. Their daughter, Ready said to be *sure* to tell you, is to be named Heather, after you. Isn't that sweet? Mamma has had Cook pack a basket full of treats for the older children and some nourishing foods for Maggie Riggs, and Witton is to deliver it this afternoon." She paused. "I know it won't make any difference to the way you feel right now, but . . . I want to say how very much I admire you, Coz. If not for your perseverance, Maggie and the baby might both have died."

After Annabel had gone, Heather returned the bandaged dolls to their trunk, and left the nursery herself, closing the door firmly in her wake. Her nursing, like her childhood, was all in the past now. The purpose that had given her life so much meaning was gone. All that remained for her now was her duty, her duty to Uncle Jamie and Aunt Elise. She must try not to disappoint them again, since they had been so dear and good to her.

She went downstairs to face their sympathetic expressions with a brave smile, a smile that hid brilliantly the emptiness in her heart.

Chapter Six

So efficiently did Aunt Elise and Mrs. Reading engineer the remove to Moorsedge, that Heather had little time to grow despondent over her disappointment. They had not been installed in the rambling gray stone house situated on the edge of the wild, snowy Scottish heaths for even forty-eight hours when invitations were sent out for suppers, hunt breakfasts, and routs.

Aunt Elise, determined to occupy her cherished niece's mind with pleasant thoughts, engaged her assistance in writing the invitations and in helping with the preparations. Maids flew hither and thither, dusting and sweeping, polishing, beating rugs and draperies, or airing bed linens before roaring fires. The chimney sweep was summoned to sweep the numerous chimneys. A trap was sent into the nearby village and returned laden with various foodstuffs, and several similar trips were made before Aunt Elise declared the pantry and shelves stocked to her satisfaction. Hams hung from the ceiling in the cellar, as did grouse and pheasant and quail. Preserved fruits gleamed within glass jars from the depths of the cupboards. Cheeses and fresh butter, cream and eggs sat under muslin cloths in the stone-flagged pantry that was deliciously cool in summer, but frigid in this month of November. Annabel remarked delightedly that it was as if "dear Mamma were laying in stores for a siege!" and Heather echoed her sentiments.

Acceptances to their invitations were returned promptly by those members of London society who, following the custom of the Royal Family, passed the winter season in Scotland. They were eager for diversion in any form, and Elise Cameron and her husband, Jamie, had a reputation for being excellent hosts and for laying on sumptuous repasts and innovative entertainments for their guests.

"Oh, my word!" Elise exclaimed as they sat at the breakfast table, opening the last of the post that had arrived a few hours earlier. "Lord Douglas Dennison has accepted our invitation to supper tomorrow evening!"

"Of course, Mamma," Annabel said patiently, "Everyone knows that Elise Cameron's suppers are the high points of any winter season! He'd be a cad to refuse!" She fondly kissed her mother's brow.

"But you see, Annabel, my dear, I did not expect Lord Dennison to accept! He is the governor of some outlandish place in Africa, and is rarely to be found in England, or at his estate here! I merely issued him and his mother an invitation out of courtesy, you see, as is proper, and he has accepted!" She turned to Heather, who was making a list of those who had accepted their invitations in readiness for the careful lettering of place cards that would follow. "Heather, my pet, you simply must meet Lord Dennison! He is outrageously handsome, as well as titled and extremely wealthy!" Elise confided with relish, her eyes sparkling, her expression hopeful.

"I am quite certain that I shall meet him if he is to

come to Moorsedge tomorrow night, dear Aunt Elise," Heather teased. "I say, Annabel, the black sheep Markham fellow that you met at the Rutherfords is to be at the supper also. Apparently he is visiting with Reverend Rory Markham at the manse in Kirkenmuir, and the reverend has asked that the invitation should be extended to include him."

"Then of course, it shall be," Aunt Elise agreed. "According to Mrs. McGregor in the village, everyone is quite impressed with Reverend Markham. He was sent here to take over the parish almost two years ago, after Reverend Kinney passed away, and has done wonders, to all accounts. It is not the reverend's fault that he had the misfortune to be born brother to a young man of Adam Markham's somewhat dubious reputation."

"Adam Markham? Oh, how delicious!" Annabel squealed with delight. "He truly is a most handsome rascal, Heather, believe me! Imagine, a lord *and* a rascal—in the same room! I warrant I shall swoon with excitement!" She leaned languidly against the window frame and passed a limp hand across her brow in imitation of a swoon.

"Not to mention a certain fiancé?" Heather reminded her, smiling.

"Oh, and of *course,* my Anthony! I had not forgotten my sweet darling for an instant!" Annabel hastily amended. "He is to arrive on the noon train today. Shall I go alone," she wondered aloud, eyes sparkling mischievously, "or will you take the trap with me to the station to meet him?"

"Naturally, I will," Heather agreed, "since I am certain Aunt Elise will not permit you to meet him alone. Will you, Aunt Elise?" She winked over her aunt's bowed head at Annabel, who returned the wink with a broader one of her own.

Elise looked up, brows crinkling. "Mmmm? Unchaperoned? No, no, certainly not!" she agreed, peering over the reading spectacles that were perched dangerously on the very tip of her nose. "Heather, you will accompany Annabel, of course. Run along now. We shall continue this after luncheon."

Less than an hour later, Heather and Annabel, warmly cloaked and wearing fur hoods, their cold, gloved hands tucked into fox-fur muffs, were being briskly bowled along a rutted country road to the nearest village of Kirkenmuir. A winter wonderland of white heath and silvered firs stretched for miles all about them. Moorsedge, with its gables and turrets and gray, weathered stone, rose from that pristine whiteness like an ancient keep at their backs. Far away and to the east, atop a craggy tor, rose the ruins of a castle, an ever-vigilant guardian of the little glen below. Beyond that lay the misty purple-blue of the Grampians, sleeping giants bearded with snow.

"Oh, do hurry, Heather!" Annabel cried, almost losing her seat on the trap in her excitement. "Look! The train was early for once! I can see the smoke from the engine from here! Dear Tony will believe I have forgotten his arrival!"

Sure enough, great gouts of steam were rising in the frosty air above the little platform which comprised the entire Kirkenmuir train station. "Don't worry, Coz," Heather said reassuringly, "I am quite certain your Anthony will still be there. After all—where else could he go?"

Kirkenmuir was the only village hereabouts, the next station being that to the north, at Balmoral, where the Queen was in residence at her castle on the River Dee. Nonetheless, Heather flicked the whip lightly across the broad rump of the pony, and the animal stepped up its gait, bowling them smartly past the few cottages and

82

shops, the church, the public house, and the school-room that made up the village before coming to a bouncing halt before the platform. Annabel scarcely waited for the vehicle to stop before she clambered down and sped across the station to where her fiancé waited, his baggage at his feet. Heather carefully devoted her entire attention to the pony, turning a blind eye to the pair's shamelessly ecstatic reunion as she did so.

"Well, I'll be damned!" exclaimed a deep voice behind her. "I never thought to find my Cinderella in this outlandish spot!"

The voice was one that had become horribly familiar in her dreams—rather, her nightmares—and her stomach turned over. She turned slowly about, coming face to face with the dark-haired stranger from the Laughing Dog public house. Her cheeks grew hot, then cold, then heated again as she dared a glance at his face. Yes, it *was* him! There was no mistaking that urchin's smile, those dancing, dark blue eyes alive with roguish merriment, that deep tan offset by a wicked black mustache! Gulping, she forced herself to remain outwardly calm, while inwardly her emotions seethed. "Forgive me, sir?" she queried, her brows delicately arched in an expression of ladylike dismay. "I do not believe we have been introduced."

His delighted grin wavered and she stared blankly at him. "Not introduced? No, damn it all, I suppose we weren't, come to think of it!" he admitted; then he winked. "But don't expect me to believe you have forgotten me, my lovely, not when I recall the dramatic circumstances of our first meeting?"

Heather allowed a slight frown to knot her smooth brow, and she pursed her lips as if considering his statement. "On the contrary, sir, I have no recollection of ever having met you before, none whatsoever! Perhaps

83

you have confused me with someone else?" she suggested, smiling patronizingly as if at his error.

A dark scowl wreathed his handsome features. "Come now, Miss Whoever-you-are, I am not mistaken—unless you have a twin! You are she, the vision I snatched from the jaws of death, not two weeks past in Whitechapel!"

A tinkling laugh escaped her, silvery on the frosty air. "There, you see, you are mistaken, sir! I can assure you that I would *never* venture into that area, not on any account! Now, if you will excuse me? . . ." She inclined her head and started to sweep past him, toward where Annabel and her Anthony still stood, clinging ardently together.

With a curt nod, he stepped back to allow her to pass him, his gentian eyes turbulent, his expression one of anger and frustration as the slender, gracefully cloaked figure moved on toward the pair upon the platform. The wind blew a sudden flurry of snowflakes into his face, and as she turned to glance back over her shoulder at him, he glimpsed a stray curl of flaming hair that had escaped her hood to toss wildly in the current of air. His jaw hardened.

"Heather!" Tony Winchester exclaimed, his handsome face beaming. "Lord! If you aren't more beautiful than ever!" He grinned. "Perhaps I shall jilt this minx here, and run away with you to Gretna Green!"

Well accustomed to dear Anthony's teasing, Heather laughed merrily, turning her cheek for his kiss of greeting.

Annabel glowered in mock ferocity. "Try it, my dearest Anthony, and you will sorely regret it! 'A woman spurned!' . . ." she hinted in an ominous tone, and Anthony smiled and hugged her fondly. The expression in his eyes confirmed more eloquently than words that he would do no such thing!

In brotherly fashion, Tony offered one arm to each of the young women, and after nodding at a porter to follow them with his bags, they made their way to the trap. With a start, Heather realized that that awful man was still standing there.

"Why, Captain Markham!" Annabel exclaimed, hurrying toward him, and Heather's heart sank. "We had heard you were here at Kirkenmuir already. Can it be you have only just arrived?" There was a pair of suitcases at his feet.

Taken aback, Adam Markham nodded. "Why, yes, Miss Cameron. Mister Winchester and I had the pleasure of sharing the same compartment up from Glasgow."

"Ah! Then your brother must have accepted my mother's invitation to supper tomorrow in advance of your arrival," Annabel realized aloud.

Captain Markham nodded. "I daresay," he agreed, smiling now. "But Rory is deucedly practical, for a man of his calling. It's more likely that he saw a means to get rid of his older brother for an evening so that he might pore over his beloved classics without interruption, and he took it!"

"Oh, Captain Markham, for shame!" Annabel said, laughing. "I'm certain he thought nothing of the sort." Belatedly, she remembered Heather, still clinging to Anthony's other arm. "Oh, forgive me, Coz! You have not been introduced, and here I am, chattering on! Captain Adam Markham, my cousin, Miss Heather Cameron." She turned to Heather. "Heather, perhaps you will recall I mentioned I had the pleasure of meeting Captain Markham at the Rutherfords a week or so ago?"

"I—I do seem to recall something of the sort, yes," Heather confessed, recalling only too well that particular night.

Adam caught Annabel's tone and grimaced ruefully. "Ah! Then I am certain Miss Annabel must also have told you that I mistook her for . . . someone else on that occasion, and that I behaved quite unforgivably?" He grinned. "It is apparently becoming a habit with me—mistaking people's identities?" He paused, black eyebrows quirked, but Heather raised her eyes to his unflinchingly.

"Perhaps that is but confirmation that you are in need of the tranquillity and relaxation to be found here in the solitude of Kirkenmuir, Captain?" she suggested coolly.

"Perhaps," he agreed, his mocking gentian eyes boring into hers in a way that made her heart go into gyrations. "I am honored to make your acquaintance, Miss Cameron," he declared with a half-bow.

She offered her hand to him, knowing if she refused Annabel would want to know why she had done so. "And I yours, Captain Markham. I trust you will have a pleasant winter in Scotland?"

"I was in some doubt before, I must confess," the captain said candidly. "But now"—he lightly kissed her hand after the French custom—"I am quite convinced that my stay will be . . . delightful!"

She drew her hand away from his warm one as if burned, and then inclined her pretty head politely. "Thank you, Captain. And now, if you will forgive us, we must be on our way home. I do believe there is further snow on the way, judging by the sky."

"Yes," Tony Winchester agreed. He handed Annabel up into the trap, then assisted Heather into the rear seat, before taking up the reins himself. "I say, Markham, are you being met by anyone?"

The captain shrugged. "Supposedly, yes. But it is not unlikely that Rory might have forgotten. Once he starts writing his sermons, Armageddon could come, and he'd not notice it!"

"Is the rectory far off the road to Moorsedge?" Anthony asked his fiancée.

"Not at all, Tony," Annabel insisted. "We'd be delighted to take you, Captain, it's no trouble at all. Climb on up."

Without further ado, Adam Markham swung his bags into the trap, and climbed agilely into the seat beside Heather, who scowled and drew her skirts aside, giving him wide berth. She turned her head rigidly away from his.

The trap set off at a brisk pace, turning at the King James' Arms onto the road across the heaths, which was little more than a deeply rutted track even at the height of summer, when it was bordered by wild purple heather and fragrant yellow gorse instead of snow.

Oh, Lord! Heather thought, staring dismally at the wintry heaths and the distant mountains. Why did he, of all people, have to come here! Inside her muff, her fingers twined anxiously together, and she gnawed worriedly at her lower lip. Could she continue to maintain her pretense of never having met him before? Could she convince him that he had met someone else who merely bore a resemblance to her? With a sinking heart, she acknowledged that was unlikely. He was so bold, so certain of himself—and quite without any sense of propriety whatsoever!

She was jolted as the trap took a curve in the road a little too wide, and she almost toppled from her seat. At once, Captain Markham's strong arm came out to steady her, sliding smoothly about her shoulders and remaining there long after any danger had passed. She could feel the firm masculine pressure of his fingertips against her upper arm through her cape. Why, it seemed his fingers were afire. . . .

"Sorry, everyone!" Anthony apologized over his

87

shoulder. "It's been awhile since I've driven a trap. I'm a little rusty, I'm afraid!"

"Think nothing of it, Winchester," the captain declared. "We're quite comfortable back here—are we not, Miss Cameron?"

"Quite, thank you, Captain," Heather said icily. "You may release me now."

"On the contrary, Miss Cameron," Adam countered smoothly, "I do believe it would be far safer if I were to keep my arm exactly where it is, in the event of another jolt like that one. We would not wish to see your lovely self thrown to the ground beneath the wheels of the trap, would we, now?"

She turned to look at him; high, angry color blooming in her cheeks at the feigned expression of concern and innocence he wore, despite his slightly mocking tone. Her violet eyes flashed. "There is little fear of that, sir, I can assure you," she gritted hotly. "I have never been prone to accidents, and I do not intend to become so in the near future."

"Never, Miss Cameron?" he asked, gentian eyes roving her lovely, furious, flushed face with the fleeting warmth of an intimate caress.

He edged a little closer, and his thigh, encased in tweed trousers, brushed intimately against her own. A pulse drummed in her temple, blood pounded in her ears. "Never!" she insisted weakly as the trap bowled on, the racing beat of the pony's hooves as rapid as the galloping beat of her heart.

Heather dressed in an apple green silk gown the following evening for the formal supper her aunt had planned. The neckline was daringly low, the straps mere gossamer ribbons of silk sewn with tiny, green glass beads. The style showed off to advantage her flawless ivory shoulders and arms and the curves of her high, full breasts, but it made no concession to the snow that drifted down about Moorsedge and sent a chill throughout the old house. Her dark flame hair, swept dramatically away from her lovely face, had been dressed by her aunt's French maid, Nanette, in loose, heavy coils which were threaded through with the long strand of tiny, perfect emeralds left to her by her paternal grandmother, Alexandra Cameron.

"Bien, Mademoiselle Heather! You are ready—and very beautiful, yes?" Nanette declared, loosening tiny tendrils of hair from the shining, smooth coiffure and curling them about Heather's brow with a dampened finger to make enchanting sweetheart's curls to frame her face.

"Do you really think so?" Heather wondered aloud, eying herself doubtfully in the cheval-glass mirror. "Perhaps another gown? . . ."

Nanette laughed. *"Non, mademoiselle,* that one, it is perfect! Here, *chérie,* your fan, and your shawl. I will wait up to help you undress, *oui?"*

Heather nodded as she clipped on the small emerald pendant earrings that matched the necklace. "Yes. Thank you, Nanette."

She hesitated at the head of the staircase, then drew a deep breath before starting gracefully down it, one gloved hand lifting the skirts of her gown from the polished wooden floor, the other gliding gracefully down the carved balustrade. She was extraordinarily nervous, and she knew the reason why. Adam Markham would be at Moorsedge tonight. There would be no escaping him or his pointed comments that only she would understand—or the searching glances from those mocking, devilish, deep blue eyes that made her feel peculiarly bare and vulnerable. Just thinking about him caused the strangest little catch in her throat, and it gave her heart a peculiar little twist. She bit her lip. She *must* stick to her guns, deny ever having met him before yesterday—until the bitter end if need be! Duty was her lot in life now. She must not bring shame upon her aunt and uncle, not on any account.

"Why, there you are, my dear girl!" Elise Cameron exclaimed, coming to greet Heather as she reached the foot of the stairs, and leaning forward to press a motherly kiss to her brow. "My word, you look enchanting! Doesn't she look bonny, Annabel?"

Annabel, quite lovely herself in a gown of pale pink satin, a dramatic but effective foil for her flaming locks, nodded agreement. "Indeed yes! After this evening, I wager Moorsedge will be flooded with gifts and calling cards and invitations for Miss Heather Cameron from her countless suitors!"

"Oh, shush," Heather begged. "I am certain I do not want gifts or calling cards or anything of the like! Or suitors, come to that!"

"You may not, but my dear Mamma does!" Annabel confided as her mother drifted away to see to her guests. "She is quite expecting this round of entertainments she has planned to result in a husband for you, Coz."

"I know," Heather acknowledged gloomily. "I feel much like a horse must feel at a horse fair—everyone appraising me and wondering if I am sound in both wind and limb!" She sighed. "It's really quite barbaric."

"Don't complain, Coz," Annabel advised. "After all, Mamma and Papa have at least given us the opportunity to choose our future husbands, unlike most poor girls who have the choice made for them, like it or not. I say, that must be Reverend Rory Markham over there by the door! He's rather attractive too, don't you think—though not nearly so dashing as brother Adam!"

Heather looked in the direction her cousin discreetly indicated and saw that a serious, dark-haired young man had just entered. He was even now handing his hat, coat and gloves to Carmichael, the butler, who stood in attendance at the door.

"The Reverend Rory Markham, and Captain Adam Markham!" the butler announced.

Heather then saw that Adam had entered first and was standing off to the left of his brother, concealed by an antlered stag's head that jutted from the wall. She wanted to bolt, but there was no time to do so as Rory and Adam came toward them, both impeccably attired in evening wear.

"Reverend Markham, I'm Annabel Cameron, and this is my cousin, Miss Heather Cameron. Welcome to Moorsedge! We are delighted that you could join us," Annabel greeted him prettily. "And good evening to you, Captain Markham! Won't you go on through into the salon, and avail yourself of some refreshment before supper?"

"I would be delighted," Rory Markham accepted warmly, smiling. "Adam?"

"In a moment, Rory, old chap. First, I must pay my respects to Miss Heather. Musn't I, Heather?" he added in a lower voice, looking down at her. His dark eyes glowed as he viewed the stunning picture she made, and warm color seeped into Heather's suddenly pale cheeks as his inspection of her lengthened. He drew her hand into his and kissed it. "A very good evening to you, my lovely Miss Cameron."

She snatched her hand away and forced a smile. "And to you, my dear Captain Markham," she rejoined, her voice heavy with sarcasm. "Please, won't you go on into the salon? As my cousin said, drinks are being served. I'm sure after your cold drive across the heath, a hot toddy would be very welcome? Uncle Jamie has some excellent whiskey. Or perhaps brandy would be more to your liking? If not there's also rum punch and—"

"You're babbling, Heather," Adam remarked, his teeth flashing white beneath his black mustache as he grinned. "A certain sign of nervousness, I've been told." His gentian eyes twinkled with wicked brilliance as he noted the tremor that swept through her at his words.

"Nonsense!" she declared firmly. "What on earth should make me nervous?"

"You. Me. The Laughing Dog public house."

"The Laughing Dog?" She shook her head. "You are speaking in riddles yet again, sir. I have never heard of the place before. Where is it?" she demanded.

"You know quite well that it is in Whitechapel, my dear," Adam retorted softly. "As were you that night!"

"I must insist, sir, that I was nowhere of the sort!" she flared, her voice somewhat shrill. "If you persist in this ridiculous notion that we have met before and continue to plague me with your misguided beliefs, I will have no recourse but to ask my uncle to see that you leave Moorsedge without delay!" The color in her cheeks was brilliant now, and her eyes were very bright. The thrust of her breasts against the green silk of her gown was emphasized by the erratic quality of her breathing. Her pendant earrings swung violently.

"Damn, but you're magnificent when you're angry, my sweet!" he declared, and snapped her a mocking salute before nodding to Annabel and his brother and weaving his way between the throng of guests to the refreshment tables. Her knees felt ready to buckle with relief once he had gone, and Annabel, at last relinquishing Rory Markham to the gathering, looked at her oddly. "What is it, Coz? You seem upset?" Annabel, usually so deceptively featherbrained and guileless, could also be amazingly shrewd at times, not unlike her mother. "Did Adam say something to annoy you?"

Heather forced a smile. "Nothing that should not be expected from a man who's obviously an incorrigible flirt." She forced the words from between clenched teeth.

"He tried to flirt with you?" Annabel whispered breathlessly. "Oh, Heather, I would turn quite green with jealousy were it not for my dearest Tony! Don't you like him? Don't you think he's handsome—not even the teeniest little bit dashing? As Heather vigorously shook her head she declared, "Oh, nonsense, I don't believe you!"

Heather was saved from further interrogation by the arrival of more guests who were entering Moorsedge with snowflakes clinging to their capes or coats, their cheeks ruddy with cold. The eminently suitable and eligible Lord Douglas Dennison was among them, and Heather noted that he seemed quite as charming and attractive as her aunt had claimed.

After greetings had been offered, Heather and Annabel circulated through the gathering to ensure that none of the guests felt left out or bored, or were in want of drinks or canapés. Shortly after, Carmichael announced that supper was served, and all of the guests found their partners and trooped into the long, paneled dining room where the buffet had been spread. To her immense relief, Heather found herself escorted by the Reverend McGraw, while Adam seemed quite comfortable with the large, handsome matron on his arm. Heather had never before seen the woman who was attired in black silk, but she proved to be Aunt Elise's Mrs. McGregor from the village, Squire McGregor's wife.

The evening passed quickly from then on, supper being followed by brandy and cigars for the men in the billiard room, while the women retired to relax and freshen up, then sip demitasses of coffee. The ladies and gentlemen came together later for charades, which Heather declined to play, pleading a slight headache. She sat in an overstuffed chair in one corner, exquisitely aware that Adam, lounging comfortably in a chair far across the crowded room, was watching her every move. When she glanced his way, he winked wickedly or doffed her a smart salute, smiling his mocking smile, and each time she crimsoned at his boldness. Oh, but he was insufferable! A cad! she fumed silently. Why could he not be a gentleman and let well enough alone? Had he not done enough already to ensure that she would be quite ruined if the truth ever came out? No one would believe her pleas of innocence, not with such a rogue as he involved . . . if she was indeed still innocent!

The game of charades was declared over shortly after, Annabel's team having scored a rousing victory over her mother's team. With much laughter and friendly argument over the outcome, the guests spilled noisily into the long hall for dancing. Annabel hooked her arm through Heather's and led her after them.

"You're just like Taffeta when there's a mouse at large in Cameron House," Annabel remarked shrewdly. "What on earth is it that has you so on edge, Coz?"

Heather shrugged, inwardly alarmed that Annabel had read her uneasy mood so easily. "Do I seem on edge?" She forced a smile. "I don't feel so. It's a lovely party, isn't it?"

Annabel nodded. "Indeed it is. Mamma is in her element as hostess. I declare the local gentry are quite dazzled by her!"

The two young women laughed as a flushed Elise Cameron, on the arm of a towering, bearded laird took to the floor again and was soon whirling to the rousing music of a lively Scottish reel. She wore a length of the Cameron plaid draped over one shoulder and across her breast. Pinned by a glittering thistle brooch at the waist, it gave a decidedly highland flair to her elegant dark gown. Her slippered feet were as nimble as a young girl's in the intricate steps of the reel. Jamie Cameron stood to one side, the proud smile upon his face occasioned by the admiring glances his wife was drawing. Heather and Annabel smiled and made their way to the refreshment tables for a warming mug of mulled rum punch. Despite crackling fires in the vast fireplaces, Moorsedge was colder than a tomb in winter months.

Heather sipped her punch and took advantage of Annabel's momentary distraction with the Reverend McGraw of the High Kirk of Scotland, to cast her eyes over the guests. Her relief was great when she saw that neither Adam Markham or his brother Rory were among the dancers. They must have adjourned to the smoky billiards' room with several of the other men. A respite at last, she thought weakly, sipping her drink.

"May I fetch you some more punch?"

She stared at the etched crystal mug in her hand in vague astonishment, about to protest that it was still full when she saw that it was now quite empty! When had she drained it? she wondered in dismay. She looked up, and saw Lord Dennison smiling down at her. It was he who had spoken, she realized belatedly.

He plucked the glass from her stiff fingers and ladled more punch into it. "There," he murmured, returning it to her.

She flashed him a grateful smile. "Thank you, Lord Dennison."

"Please, I insist that you call me Douglas. And, if you will permit me, I shall call you Heather."

"Of course," she agreed. Warming to his pleasant

95

manner, she sipped her punch, eyeing him covertly as he watched the dancing.

As Annabel had said the morning before, he was a striking man. He wore his fair hair a little longer than was strictly fashionable. It curled over his collar in back and fell forward across his brow in an engaging cowlick. His thickly lashed blue eyes were startling against his golden bronze complexion, and his nose and lips were finely chiseled, almost delicately so. On a woman, such features would have been considered quite beautiful, but it was his tall build and lean, hard physique that kept his handsome face from appearing overly feminine. His impeccably tailored coat and trousers, accented by a satin brocade vest, showed to advantage the broad sweep of his shoulders and narrow hips. She was vaguely surprised that such a charming and handsome man—one possessing a title and considerable wealth, to boot—had never married.

"If you have not yet promised it to some other lucky fellow, I would consider it an honor if you would permit me the next dance," Douglas stated.

"The honor would be mine," Heather responded graciously, and setting aside her punch glass, she allowed him to escort her to the floor for the next dance, which happened to be a waltz. Drifting in his arms, she felt quite relaxed as he conversed wittily, and she was flattered by his admiring glances which had none of the wolfish quality of those of the other young men visiting Moorsedge. Their looks both confused and annoyed her. *Like Adam's,* she thought distantly.

". . . most unusual for a woman possessed of such stunning beauty as yours, my dear Heather."

She had not heard the start of his compliment, but she smiled and thanked him anyway. Fortunately, he seemed not to have noticed her distraction.

"Will you be riding to the hounds tomorrow?"

"No, I'm afraid not. Fox hunting has never been something I enjoyed."

"What a pity! I would have found it far more pleasurable with such a fetching huntress as yourself amongst the field," he said ruefully, sky-blue eyes twinkling.

"You are far too kind!" she declared with a small, deprecatory laugh.

"At the risk of sounding trite and boring you with compliments that I am certain you have heard countless times, I must insist that it is not kindness that prompts me, but your own exquisite loveliness, Miss Cameron."

His words sent a warm blush rising up her throat. "Enough, Douglas!" she begged. "My head will become quite swollen with false pride if you do not cease this flattery!"

"Very well," he said with a smile, as he turned her expertly in time to the music, "I shall admire you mutely, if adoringly—but only if you will consent to allow me to escort you in to the hunt supper tomorrow evening?"

"A bargain I agree to very willingly, Lord Douglas," she promised. Following these words, she favored him with a coquettish laugh and lowered her long lashes as she looked up into his face. Both gestures seemed more what Annabel might have done in her place, she thought immediately after making them, and she was at a loss as to what could have come over her tonight. It must be the effect of the rum punch, she decided.

The music ended and Douglas Dennison swept her from the floor and returned her to her cousin's side. With a formal bow and a dazzling smile, he thanked her and excused himself. Annabel grinned, her blue eyes narrowing as she watched the tall, distinguished man weave his way between the dancers, now in the throes of a rollicking polka, and head in the direction of the billiard room.

"Well!" she exclaimed, turning to Heather. "I do believe our little blue stocking has made yet another conquest!"

"Oh, hush!" Heather scolded. "I danced with him. That's all." There was a becoming flush to her face, a luminosity about her lovely eyes, that belied her words.

"And you expect me to believe it was the slow, dreamy waltz that put such a high color in your cheeks? It had nothing to do with certain compliments a handsome, *rich,* titled man just might have been showering upon you?"

"Nothing at all. It's—it's warm in here, that is all," Heather denied firmly, and laughed.

Annabel was wrong. It was not Douglas Dennison's handsome face that filled her dreams that night. It was the roguish Captain Markham's! It was not Douglas who whispered her name, and waltzed with her held dangerously close in his strong arms, but Adam. *Adam!*

Chapter Seven

The baying of foxhounds, the nervous whinnying of numerous horses, and the clatter of their iron-shod hooves upon the cobbles below her window woke Heather the next morning before Nanette, the ladies' maid that she, Annabel, and her aunt shared, came to do so. She shivered as she fastened a warm dressing gown about her, and then she hurried to the window, scratching a hole in the frost-feathering on the panes to peer below.

The Master of the Hunt, Squire Alistair McGregor, sat his massive chestnut hunter in the center of the cobbled stableyard, resplendent in his "pink" coat—a vivid scarlet despite its name—spotless white jodhpurs, black boots, and black top hat. He was in the act of partaking in the traditional stirrup cup of sherry, as were several other red-coated riders. Meanwhile, the Whipper-In was attempting to control his pack of forty or so foxhounds, who were snapping at each others' heels in their excitement. Lord Dennison, Heather saw, was among the dozen or more riders. He was deep in conversation with her Uncle Jamie, also mounted. Douglas looked very dashing in his black coat and fawn breeches, a sky-blue silk ascot in the collar of his coat, she noted absently.

A sharp rap sounded upon her door but before she had sufficient time to answer it, Annabel, already dressed, burst into the room.

"You won't *believe* who's downstairs, giving Aunt Elise a lecture on raising tropical orchids under glass in Scotland, of all things!" she cried.

"Oh, Lord, no. Not Adam Markham?" Heather wailed, sinking onto her bed, a horrible grimace on her face. Like the proverbial bad penny he had shown up again!

"The same!" Annabel confirmed. "Mamma appears to have taken an enormous liking to him, Coz, despite his reputation. Twice since he arrived I have heard her call him 'you dear boy' in that voice she uses when she's particularly pleased with us. And once, she even patted his cheek! Imagine that!"

"Does he appear to be planning to leave soon?" Heather asked hopefully.

"Not for ages, I don't believe. He's sitting in Papa's chair, his legs comfortably stretched out and a glass of sherry from the Hunt Meet in one hand, and he's talking about orchids. He's convinced Mamma that she could raise them here, and she's enthralled by the idea and talking about hiring a master gardener from Glasgow or Edinburgh to see to the erection of the greenhouse. He's even promised to bring Ready a parrot when he returns from Africa the next time. A parrot!"

"Oh, damn it all!" Heather exploded crossly, and Annabel's eyebrows arched upward in shock. "Then I shall go back to bed!" Heather tossed back and rumpled blankets, dived beneath them, and pulled them up over her head.

With a smile, Annabel marched across the room and flipped the counterpane away. "It's too late to hide, Coz! Mamma sent me up here to instruct you to come down to the breakfast room and help entertain Captain Markham. She said that since you had not planned to ride to the hounds, it was the least you could do."

"Oh, bother! Confound him!" Heather gritted out irritably, stalking across the room.

The hounds below her window struck up a ferocious baying then, and her scowl dispersed, to be replaced by a broad smile. She pursed her pretty lips thoughtfully. "Do you know, Coz, I've had a sudden change of heart! I do believe I shall join the hunt after all!" She grinned wickedly. "And since I will now be unable to help Aunt Elise with her guest, you must offer her my deepest regrets! Quickly, Annabel, help me, and I will be indebted to you forever!"

A half-hour later, she hurried to the stables and breathlessly bade Victor saddle her horse, one of several loaned to the Camerons by the McGregors of Kirkenmuir. In the dark blue velvet riding skirt and jacket and the elegant top hat—about its brim rested a filmy white scarf, the ends of which trailed down her back—and with her hair a flaming coil draped charmingly over one shoulder, Heather made a striking picture against the snow.

She thanked Victor, touched her crop to the bay's rump and trotted him after the other riders, who were presently following the Hunt Master, the Whipper-In and his hounds across the sweeping heaths toward a distant spinney. The pack raced ahead, noses lifted to the wind in the hope of sniffing a good scent, tails waving like standards of fawn or brindle or black.

The bay was fresh and eager for a gallop. Taking a firm grip on the reins, Heather made certain that she was secure in the sidesaddle before urging him into a brisk canter in an attempt to catch up with the other riders. The hunt made a picturesque sight, scarlet coats and glossy horses contrasting dramatically with the

101

pristine white of the heaths and the purple of the Grampian mountains beyond.

The foxhounds, longeared little white beasts patterned with black or fawn, circled eagerly about, baying continually now as their excitement grew. They swarmed into the spinney, noses to the ground. Minutes later came the thrilling winding of the hunting horn to signal that they had found a scent, and the pack was away!

Heather reined in her horse at the rear of the group of riders to watch as a flash of russet color broke cover and streaked down the glen from the wooded area, the baying of the hounds rising to frenzy pitch as they blasted from between the trees in pursuit of the fox, the riders leaping snowy hillocks and bare hedges to follow them.

Heather crossed her fingers. "Run!" she muttered treacherously. "Don't let them catch you!"

She made little effort to keep her horse abreast of the others as, with excited whoops, they followed the hounds. As she had told Lord Douglas the evening before, she did not much care for the "sport" of fox hunting. Instead, she trotted the bay leisurely after them, enjoying the bracing air, the beauty of a countryside mantled in virginal white, and the sparkling webbing of frost and snow feathers that veiled the trees. It was a beautiful, crisp morning—far too beautiful for dying, she thought with a shudder; and she offered another prayer for the safety of the hunt's quarry.

She had ridden over three miles and had just entered a second spinney when the crack of a branch behind her made her turn swiftly about in the saddle. To her horror, she saw Adam Markham standing in the copse, a sack dangling from one of his hands, a sack in which something wriggled furiously. Beyond, tethered to a tree, was a handsome gray stallion.

102

"So! If it's not one vixen, it's another!" Adam declared ruefully.

"What on earth are you doing here?" she demanded, looking down at him from her horse's back, her dismay evident. "I thought that you were—"

"Safely back at Moorsedge with your Aunt Elise? How could I bear to stay there, knowing you were gone!" he remarked teasingly. "I rode the back way, around the loch, hoping to run into you. And I did!" He grinned wickedly, deep blue eyes dancing at her furious expression. "My prayers have been answered, my wild, highland Heather! We are quite alone. At last."

Furious, she realized that he was right, and her heart began to throb madly. "Nonsense!" she denied. "The— the rest of the field will be along soon."

He shook his head. "I doubt it. They're all riding around in circles at this moment, wondering where their fox has gone!" He raised the sack in his fist. *"Voilà!* Ze fox! A little aniseed spice, 'borrowed' from your aunt's kitchen—your Cook, Shelagh, is such an old darling, by the way. Bless her!—and sprinkled on the snow by yours truly, will lead the hunt a merry chase, I shouldn't wonder."

"You didn't!" she exclaimed, half in horror, half in reluctant admiration.

"I did indeed," he insisted. "Barbaric sport . . . it serves them right to go chasing after shadows all day! This poor little lady was exhausted. She hadn't even the strength remaining to run from me when I spied her beneath the oak over there. I threw my coat over her and bundled her into this sack."

"Which you just *happened* to have with you?"

"Correct! The ungrateful little vixen gave me a nasty nip for my trouble, though," he added. "That's the trouble with vixens—no sense of gratitude at all."

103

There was a devilish twinkle in his eyes.

She ignored his none-too-subtle reminder and instead gasped as he raised his other hand, which was badly bruised and bleeding from several deep puncture wounds.

"You must have that washed and bandaged at once!" Heather cried, forgetting her dislike of him in her concern. "Why, foxes carry hydrophobia and all manner of diseases in their bites!"

He shrugged. "I've survived Africa and her wild life these past five years, my sweet. I doubt one pretty little English vixen will be my downfall." His gentian eyes sparkled as he cocked his head to one side and considered her thoughtfully, lips pursed. "Then again . . ."

"You should not jest about such an injury," she scolded, dismounting. She drew the white silk scarf from her hat brim and went toward him. "Give me your hand!" she commanded sternly.

"Take it, pretty vixen. And my heart too, if you will have it!" he teased, extending his injured hand nonetheless.

With a ferocious scowl, she grabbed his hand and bandaged it with dexterous fingers, as briskly and efficiently as Florence Nightingale herself could have wished. "There! That will stop the bleeding, but you must see that it is well washed with both soap and hot water, and disinfectant applied. If not, there could well be some infection."

"Yes, Nurse Cameron," he promised solemnly.

Flushing hotly at his teasing tone, she gave him a cool, dismissive nod and started to remount her horse, but as she did so, she saw him totter a little and close his eyes, as if he were close to fainting. Quickly, she turned back to him, steadying him by the upper arms.

"What is it?" she asked, breathless.

He turned his head. "I do believe my injury is worse

104

than I thought," he said softly. "I find myself in need of some support." Obligingly, she offered him her arm, which he took, suddenly spinning her about and pressing her back against a convenient tree trunk. His dark head dipped and he would have kissed her had she not belatedly guessed his intent and quickly ducked under his outstretched arm.

"You—you—*Oh!* Words to describe your behavior quite fail me!" she cried, her cheeks a rosy pink that had little to do with the crisp winter air.

"How about dangerous? Or bold? Or even . . . de-lightful?" he suggested wickedly.

"I was thinking more on the lines of incorrigible, or disgraceful!" she snapped with an angry little toss of her head. "Good day, Captain!" She stormed off across the snow toward her horse, petticoats rustling noisily beneath her velvet skirts.

"Won't you ride with me? We'll set this little lady free a safe distance from here," he called after her, gesturing to the sack in his fist and its wriggling, yelping bundle. "After all, you didn't appear to be overly keen on the hunt yourself, the way you were hanging back." He strode casually toward her. "Come on, Heather, stop being so prim and stuffy! You're a very, very beautiful young woman, and I adore you! Be daring— be reckless for once in your sweet life. Take a chance. Come with me!"

"Certainly not!" she refused quickly. It was such recklessness that had got her into difficulty the last time!

"As you wish," he agreed with an exaggerated sigh. "Oh, and by the way, if you happen upon Lord Douglas, offer him Adam Markham's sincere regrets that the fox got away, will you?"

"Lord Dennison? If I see him I shall, yes," she promised reluctantly.

"Oh, you'll see him," Adam insisted, an unfathomable expression in his eys. "After the way the two of you were dancing together last night, I daresay you'll be seeing a great deal of him. He enjoys pursuing helpless little creatures—like vixens."

"Lord Dennison behaved perfectly toward me last night. He is a gentleman in every sense of the word—which is more than could be said for you!"

"There are a great many things that *could* be said about Douglas Dennison," Adam remarked grimly. "But that he is a gentleman 'in every sense of the word' is not one of them. May I assist you to mount?"

"If you would be so kind," she gritted.

"It would be my pleasure. We will meet again, Miss Cameron . . . and discuss that night we met in Whitechapel at leisure."

"Since I have never been to Whitechapel, as I have told you several times before, Captain, that will be quite out of the question!" Heather insisted.

"Will it, indeed?" he challenged. "We'll see about that!" His laughter followed her as she rode away.

The strain of running into Adam Markham had been too much, Heather decided wearily as she sat at her dressing table that night, combing out her waist-length dark-flame hair after Nanette had assisted her in undressing. Her nerves felt quite shattered! From here on, she decided, she would shun any gatherings to which Adam Markham—confound him—had been invited. She would spend her mornings quietly at Moorsedge. Her afternoons she would pass in riding one of the excellent mounts Squire McGregor had offered Uncle Jamie for the use of his guests and the members of his household. And in the evenings, she would curl up by the fireside and read poetry, embroider, write in her journal, sketch—do anything that would avoid the risk of running into Adam

Markham again! And if, by some horrid chance, she ran into him anyway, she would continue to pretend she did not know what he was talking about! Aunt Elise would be bitterly disappointed that she did not attend the functions that had been arranged with her in mind, but that just couldn't be helped. Sooner or later, surely Adam must leave his brother's house, and when he did she would be able to breathe freely again!

A brisk, chill wind was blowing as she rode from the Moorsedge stables some two weeks later on what had become her customary afternoon ride across the heaths. Again, the horse she rode was the handsome, bay gelding, spirited and glossy coated. Once away from the grounds of Moorsedge he responded to the pressure of her knees and stretched out in a beautiful, invigorating canter that sent her long flame hair streaming behind her as she rode.

Free, at last! she thought rebelliously. Oh, but it was growing harder and harder each day to escape Aunt Elise and the plans she had made for this dinner or that rout or musicale, or whatever! That she had caused her Aunt great displeasure she knew only too well, but it could not be avoided. It seemed that at every turn she ran into that awful Adam Markham, and the infuriating man never missed a chance to remind her of the night she had been lost in Whitechapel and had lain unconscious in his arms! Once, she had come perilously close to letting slip that the woman had indeed been she, and that near calamity had made her feel weak, yet even more determined to avoid him like the veritable plague.

I shall not think of him, she told herself. It was far too pretty a day for thoughts of that unprincipled rogue, for all that it was the first week of December.

The sky was a clear, untrammeled blue. Frost sparkled on the bare bushes like diamonds, and the fir trees were feathered with snow. The gelding's hooves threw up powdery drifts in their wake as Heather and her steed sped across the vast whiteness toward the glistening, iced mirror of Loch Cameron.

So involved was she with the beauty of the day and in controlling the massive gelding that she did not at first see a rider galloping swiftly toward her from the direction of Kirkenmuir. The dark gray stallion was quite close when she first spotted it and as she recognized its rider, a curse that would have done credit to a trooper escaped her gritted teeth.

"Come on, Treacle," she muttered to her horse, her violet eyes now lit by angry sparks, "Get up there, old fellow!" The horse responded eagerly, stretching out its black-maned neck and lengthening its stride, haunches working furiously, bay legs barely striking the snowy heaths as his rider leaned forward in the saddle and urged him into a thundering gallop.

With a whoop, the rider of the gray stallion urged it after the bay, and the chase was on!

Treacle fairly flew across the heath, a mere stream of color that contrasted sharply with the snow. Heather, the reins grimly wound around her fists, urged him to go even faster, calling to him and drumming her heels into his sides. The gray was gaining on them, she saw, daring a glance over her shoulder!

"Faster, Treacle, faster, my lad!" she cried, her words wrested away by the wind. Pins and ribbon dropped from her hair as she rode, and a dark-flame tide escaped her hat and tumbled down in a rich cascade over the bay's neck, mingling with the furled dark mane of her horse. Riotous color filled her cheeks, hectic against the dark violet of her angry eyes. "He will not catch us!" she muttered furiously. "He must not!"

She risked another backward glance and then gave a little groan of dismay. Drat him! He was gaining on them, leaning forward over his gray's neck and standing up in the stirrups like . . . like a jockey, as if he had been born in a saddle, that rogue, that—that cad! A flutter that could only have been fear started in her belly and sent a throbbing, excited heat into her groin. For a second, she felt light-headed and, close to swooning, almost lost the bay's reins during her disorientation.

A thicket of firs lay ahead, and beyond, the silvery frozen loch. On either side rose treacherous rocky outcroppings coated with ice—far too treacherous for a horse, she realized belatedly. She must bring Treacle around or risk becoming trapped or falling. She pulled hard on the reins, then caught a flash of dark color to her right, and saw that Adam Markham had guessed her intent. He meant to cut her off! Furiously she lashed Treacle's broad rump with her crop in a frantic bid to outdistance him—but it was too late! She reined in the bay, rocks at her back, fir trees on either side, hopelessly trapped.

He, too, reined in his horse, and sat there, quietly watching her as the horses' breaths steamed in the cold air. He was hatless, she saw now, clothed in a short coat of dark Scottish tweed and fawn jodhpurs and black boots. The rolled collar of a knitted sweater showed through the turned-up collar of his coat, the same shade of blue-violet as his gentian eyes.

"At last, we meet again, Cinderella! And I have here, in my pocket, the 'glass slipper' that you left behind in Whitechapel that night . . . if you would have it returned?" There was the unmistakable ring of challenge in his voice. He leaned forward over his horse's neck and patted it affectionately while he awaited her answer. The gray stallion snorted and tossed its head, breath pouring from its nostrils in smoky plumes that, in the cold air, mingled with its rider's breath.

"Slipper? I left no slipper that night!" Heather replied, at once realizing the folly of that denial. She muttered an unladylike curse under her breath and tossed back the riot of fiery hair that spilled from beneath her hard hat in a gesture of irritation.

Adam Markham grinned in triumph. He urged his horse across the snowy moor and under the whispering firs, toward her. His curling black hair made a striking contrast to his tanned face. His cheeks were ruddy with cold and with vigor, his dark gentian eyes alive and dancing with wicked merriment. "So, you do admit that it was you? You do remember that night, Heather Cameron? Then you must also recall that it was I who saved you from certain injury, if not death itself! You'd almost convinced me that I was mistaken after all. I've been feeling damned put out that you could so easily forget my face if it was indeed you that I rescued, for in the past, certain young ladies have assured me that I am not too unpleasant to look upon." His grin widened.

She snorted at his breezy lack of modesty. "I won't stay here and listen to your teasing," Heather snapped, gathering her reins in her fists. "I thanked you quite properly that night. As far as I'm concerned, that's an end to the matter. Good day." She would have wheeled her horse about and ridden past him, but he reached from his saddle and grasped her mount by the reins, close to the bit, effectively halting it.

"You didn't seem nearly so eager to leave when you lay unconscious in my arms that time," he said with heavy sarcasm. "Rather, you sighed languidly and rested your lovely head cozily upon my shoulder, with no regard for propriety whatsoever. It took great forbearance on my part to relinquish you to the chaise, believe me!" His gentian eyes sparkled wickedly.

"You unprincipled beast!" she stormed, crimson seeping into her cheeks and an angry fire igniting in her violet eyes. "Sir, you are *no* gentleman, not when you remind me of a moment of weakness—a weakness over which I had no control, if you recall!" Her breasts heaved with outrage. Her slender shoulders shook.

He shrugged. "Nevertheless, I warrant your uncle would not see it that way were I to tell him of it. Unless, of course, you have already told him?" The black bars of his eyebrows arched innocently.

"You wouldn't!" she cried, half-outraged, half-imploring.

"You said yourself that I am no gentleman, Miss Cameron. Anything is possible with an 'unprincipled beast'—I believe that was your expression?—such as myself!"

"You make yourself quite plain, Captain Markham—"

"Adam," he cut in.

"Very well, *Adam,*" she snapped. "Simply name the price for your silence, and I will see to it that you are paid. But do not set your sights too high, sir, for I am of limited means until my majority next year."

"Price?" He threw back his head and laughed heartily, the deep, rich sound rolling off his lips. "You're delightful, Miss Cameron—quite as delightful as you look!" he declared when his laughter was done. His eyes appraised her appreciatively, darkening in frank pleasure at the vivid picture she made in the fitted forest green, velvet riding jacket and divided skirt, her vibrant coloring accented by the froth of white lace spilling from the collar, a tiny gold-encased cameo pinned in its snowy depths. Her riding hat was perched jauntily atop her loose, tumbling auburn curls, which were quite without pins or combs to hold them in place.

Her tresses, furled in the crisp, invigorating wind that swept across the heathlands, framed her lovely face in their fiery web. "I regret that I implied I wished a payment of money for my silence, Heather. Rather, I had something of little account to demand of you."

Relief filled her, for it would have been deucedly hard to pay him off without arousing her Aunt Elise's curiosity. But then her relief rapidly changed to suspicion. "What is this something of 'little account'?" she demanded.

A smile tugged at his lips. "A ride with me across the heath, to the ruined castle up ahead. In return, I will give this back to you." He drew from his pocket a mother-of-pearl comb that she recognized all too well. "Your slipper, Cinderella! Is my price too high?"

Heather was tempted to say that it was. But if she did so, what would his reaction be? "Very well," she agreed at length. "I will ride with you. You are certain there is nothing more . . . no further price upon your silence?"

"None at all, Heather Cameron," he promised solemnly, returning the comb pointedly to his pocket.

With a tight little nod, she touched her heels to the hunter's massive sides and trotted on, leaving Adam to urge his horse after her. With a chuckle, he did so.

"Tell me, how was it you came to be in Whitechapel alone that night?" he asked her curiously when he had brought his mount alongside her own.

In short, brittle sentences, she told him, wishing there were some way to wriggle out of the promise she had made.

"Nursing?" He looked at her with new eyes. "Your father wouldn't have been Alexander Cameron, would he?"

"Why, yes. You have heard of him?"

"In Africa, yes, a great deal. To all accounts, he was a man to be admired."

112

"I was born in Africa. My mother's companion brought me back to England to be raised by my Uncle Jamie, Papa's brother, when Mamma passed away from a tropical fever."

"I see. How old were you then?"

"Only two years of age—far too young to remember my parents or that continent, I'm afraid." He nodded, seeming genuinely interested in the story of her young life, and a little of her tenseness and irritation eased.

"It would appear you and your father both shared an interest in medicine?" he observed.

"Yes. I would rather have become a doctor than have trained for nursing, but my aunt and uncle would not hear of it. Are you aware that there are but two female doctors in the entire medical profession? It is a monopoly men have held for far too long! However, I was satisfied to obtain their reluctant permission to enter the Florence Nightingale School and I would have received my nursing certificate next year were it not for . . . well, circumstances."

The finality of her tone warned him not to delve further into what was obviously a distressing matter to her. They both fell silent, the stillness of the vast white emptiness being broken only by the occasional blowing of their horses and by the soft crunching of hooves in the powdery snow. The sky above was baby blue, and there were few clouds save those that milled like woolly gray sheep upon the distant looming mountain peaks. Up ahead, the ruined castle walls etched a dark, ragged tear in the sky beyond.

"This castle belonged to the Camerons, you know," Heather remarked. "It fell into ruin over two centuries ago, and no laird since then has bothered—or had the funds—to restore it. I should like to do that, I think, if it were possible someday."

Despite the gallop, their horses were still fresh and

113

found the climb up to the castle upon the tor no challenge. Soon Adam and Heather were walking their mounts between the snow-covered mounds of fallen stone, looking about them with keen interest. "Here!" Adam called. "This must have been where the horses were stabled." He pointed to a portion of a wall in which black iron rings were still set.

"It was," she confirmed. "The armory was over there," she pointed, "and the Great Hall lay beyond. Most of the walls are still intact there."

Adam dismounted and looped his horse's reins through an iron ring. He strode across to her horse and looked up at her, smiling his disarming smile. "Will you walk with me into the hall, my lady Heather?" he teased, bowing low and doffing an imaginary cap.

What urged her to accept, she did not know, but she found herself suddenly answering him in kind with a merry "I will, my lord!" and thanking him as he lifted her down to the ground beside him.

They walked through the crumbled walls and into the ancient hall, Adam taking her elbow from time to time to assist her. The vast stone walls towered above them on all sides, yet the sky showed through far above for the upper stories and towers and battlements had long since fallen to the onslaught of harsh highland winters and the ravages of time. Heather picked her way between the snow and the rubble to lean through an arched window which commanded a view of the glen below and of the white-mantled heaths all about.

"Look! You can see the chimneys of Moorsedge if you look there, beyond the loch and to the east a little." She pointed, and Adam obediently looked where bidden. "Annabel and I used to come up here when we were children and play at being great Cameron ladies of bygone days. We fancied when the wind blew, we could catch the skirl of bagpipes upon the air, and we

114

scared ourselves witless for fear some ghostly piper, kilted in the Cameron plaid, would appear!"

Laughing, she turned to look up into his face, alarmed to find him standing so close behind her that, for a second, she was pressed against the rough tweed of his coat. The scent of clean male flesh was, for an instant, full in her nostrils, coupled with a heady, exciting warmth that caught her breath in her throat. That strange quivering in her loins returned anew. Quickly, she drew away, suddenly afraid of something dangerous she read in his dark eyes, something that the woman in her recognized—and responded to.

He sensed that at any second she would dart away from him. To ward off such a move, he planted one hand on either side of the window arch, blocking her escape. His gentian gaze had all the intimacy of a caress as he looked down into her startled face. Slowly, very slowly, so as not to alarm her further, he lowered his dark head to hers, and gently pressed his lips over her own.

She appeared stunned when he was done, despite the fragility of the kiss. She opened her mouth to make some protest, but no sound would come, and he took advantage of her momentary confusion to kiss her again. This time his strong arms held her firmly to his chest, and his lips were more ardent. As he kissed her, he felt a trembling begin in her slender body, pressed so close to his.

"From that night, that brief moment when first I saw you, I have dreamed of holding you in my arms, of your sweet mouth beneath mine," he murmured huskily, his heated breath against her flaming cheek. "Each day since, I have cursed myself for letting you flee me, without so much as your name to find you by!"

Heather shook her head. "No, Captain you must not entertain such thoughts—and you must never, ever,

115

kiss me again!" she cried. "You have gone far beyond the bounds of . . . of decency!"

"Decency be damned, my lovely Heather!" he breathed raggedly into the dark cloud of her fragrant hair. "I've found you at last. I won't let you go so easily a second time!"

"Please . . . I must go back to Moorsedge!" she pleaded, still stunned to the core by the startling magic his kisses had worked upon her. Her heart was turning handsprings in her breast, and her lips tingled as if they had been stroked by lightning. "Aunt Elise will have the grooms out looking for me if I do not return soon."

His eyes were the turbulent blue of a stormy sky, violent as a tempest at sea. An angry scowl darkened his tanned face still further, deepening the faint blue shadows along his jawline. "No!" he said sharply, his voice cutting like a whip through the silence of the ruins. "It has taken me far too long to chance upon you alone. I will not permit you to leave me yet . . . unless I have some reassurance that I shall see you again. Alone."

"No, Captain, please, do not ask it of me, for I can give you no such assurance! You have already gone too far," she insisted, suddenly darting forward and past him. "What of my reputation? . . ."

His hand snaked out and coiled tightly about her wrist. "Damn your reputation! I will see you again. I must!" He looked down into her lovely, frightened face. "Did you feel nothing when I kissed you? Was there no answering spark in you to the fire that leaped through me?"

Without responding, she tried to pull free of his hold upon her, but he demanded roughly, "Was there, Heather?"

"Yes!" she admitted, filled with shame, "Yes! Now, please, let me go!"

"Shall I see you again?" Will you come here, at the same time tomorrow?"

Miserably, she nodded.

"Your word?" he demanded.

She said nothing, simply staring at him, her wide violet eyes filled with silent pleading. He muttered a curse and shook her. "Give me your word!" he insisted again.

"I . . . I will be here," she agreed in a small voice.

Satisfied, he reluctantly nodded and released her. Velvet skirts and dark flame hair streaming behind her, she flew back the way they had come, between the crumbling ruins to where the horses were tied. Unaided, she managed to clamber up onto the sidesaddle by means of a convenient fallen slab of stone, and she cantered the hunter from the castle ruins at reckless speed.

She rode down the hill and quickly away, back across the snowy heathlands to Moorsedge, without giving Adam Markham a single backward glance. She did not trust herself to do so. . . .

Later that night as Heather lay wakeful in bed in her room at the front of Moorsedge Hall, watching the play of shadows cast by the bedroom fire upon the ceiling, Adam's handsome face remained imprinted on her mind. His deep, sensual voice still rang in her ears: *"I will see you again! I must!"*

She tossed and turned restlessly, hearing the village clock in the distance chime first one, then two, and still feeling far from sleepy. Finally, in desperation she rose and wrapped herself in a warm dressing robe, lit the oil lamp at her bedside, and drew a slim volume of Swinburne's poetry from her bureau drawer, before settling down to read. Yet the pages blurred and ran together. The words separated into single letters that danced and tumbled across the pages like tiny black elves, refusing to make sense, and in the end she set the book aside and stared dreamily into the fire.

Gently she touched a fingertip to her lips. Strange, but she fancied they felt slightly swollen, as if his kisses had left their mark. She could almost taste the firm pressure of his mouth over hers, feel the graze of his fingertips against her spine, the steely embrace of his strong arms holding her so very tightly!

She had decided she would not keep her rendezvous with him the following day—but could she resist the temptation to do so? I must go, she told herself firmly. I have no choice, none whatsoever. If not, he might make good his threat to tell Uncle of that night in Whitechapel, and my reputation would be ruined!

But that was not the real reason she would meet Adam in the castle ruins. It was not the *real* reason she would fret and pace and worry over her toilette, her attire, her hair, for the greater part of late morning and early afternoon of the next day. That was not the real reason at all. And she knew it!

Chapter Eight

"You came!" he breathed, his expression one of amazed delight.

"You left me no choice in the matter, as I recall!" Heather retorted, but there was no sting to her tone. Rather, there was a breathless excitement in it that she was at a loss to control. Her lashes swept down as her heart began to hammer wildly. Lord, the way he looked at her! It was shamelessly bold! And he was so very handsome—every bit as handsome as she remembered him from the afternoon before. Those hungry, deep blue eyes did funny things to her breathing. . . . Stop it, Heather, stop it, foolish girl! Such thoughts are wicked beyond belief! Where has your practicality flown? Oh, shush, she told her conscience recklessly. He is so exciting, so dangerously, wonderfully masculine! She raised her dark lashes again and smiled up at him.

Two strides, and he was holding her by the fingertips, raising her to stand beside the cold slab of stone on which she had perched to wait for him.

"Heather!" he groaned as he buried his face in the fragrant wealth of her hair. "Can it be only yesterday I first kissed you?" He held her tightly in his arms, arching her pliant body against his lean length as he covered her mouth with his, crushing her breasts to the hard broadness of his chest with the ardor of his embraces.

Her limbs turned the consistency of porridge as he parted her lips and his tonguetip delved hotly between them, exploring the velvet sweetness of her innocent mouth, their kiss more intimate than she would ever have believed it possible for a kiss to be. The tender throbbing in her loins quickened at his sensual kisses, a fierce heat that she was powerless to control and did not understand building in her most secret parts. The effect of his kiss sizzled from her mouth to her fingertips, her breasts, her belly—everywhere—spreading heat and liquid fire! She laced her fingers in his crisp dark curls, relishing their vibrant, springy softness, and the roughness of his face when her fingers drifted down over his cheek as he kissed her. "Adam! Oh, my lord, Adam, don't!" she moaned against the rough tweed of his coat when his lips left hers to rain kisses upon her hair and her neck above the froth of lace that spilled from her jacket. "This is wickedness—madness—you must not!"

"If it's madness, then you are quite mad too, my angel!" he breathed. "And if it's wickedness . . . then let us both be damned, for I would sooner sell my soul than let you go! What I'm feeling . . . you feel it too, I know it!" he breathed raggedly, his voice strangely husky, his gentian eyes aflame. "I never dreamed I could feel this way for any woman—not until you, my dearest Heather!"

Even had she wanted to respond to his impassioned words, she could not, for the fiery hunger of his mouth possessed hers again and again, tearing forth a savage response that matched his own from some untamed, wanton well buried deep within her. *I want . . . I must . . . I need! . . . Oh, Adam, Adam, my darling, please!* . . . she cried silently, desperately, arching the lovely, bare column of her throat so that he might brand it with masterful lips. What it was her whole being clamored for, demanded, pleaded for, she did not know. But she sensed instinctively that Adam did, that Adam would understand. Her fingers dug into the tweed of his jacket. Her lips were the color of summer strawberries, wild and ripe from the firm pressure of his kisses, when he released her at length.

"I want you—you know that?" he declared huskily. "Damn me for it, but I want you, my innocent angel!"

A sudden light-headedness brought her close to swooning. "I . . . I know!" she managed brokenly, her voice a whisper. She stumbled and fell against him, her legs giving way. Suddenly she was lifted, swept into his arms, and he was striding between the castle ruins to their horses. He bore her up, onto his gray stallion's back, still held fiercely in his arms. Then, leading the bay gelding behind them, he rode swiftly away from the ruins.

"Where? . . ." she murmured.

"The manse," he answered. "There'll be no one there but the two of us, my darling. Rory has gone to see his bishop in Glasgow. We'll be quite alone."

Alone—alone with him! The thought, the knowledge of what being alone with Adam implied, filled her with trembling excitement. She clung to him while his horse carried them swiftly across the heaths toward the outskirts of Kirkenmuir, wondering if she were not, as he had so heatedly said, quite mad, for surely no sane, well-brought-up young woman would be behaving so shamelessly! Snowflakes drifted down about them as they rode, but she was nestled warmly in his embrace, mindless of the cold, mindless of anything but the heat of his lips, the smoldering dark fire of his eyes, the feel of his arms cradling her firmly against his broad chest.

Soon they were at the manse, a quaint residence of weathered stone bowered by gloomy pines and silver birches veiled with snow. The horses sheltered in the stable, he lifted her again and carried her inside, to a hallway that gleamed with polish and the fine grain of old wood, and on, up a staircase to a chamber where a fire crackled cozily in a wide hearth, and touched everything with topaz. Their shadows trembled upon the walls as he took her in his arms and kissed her long and lingeringly.

"You won't regret this, my angel!" he murmured, stroking her cheek. "I'll bring no shame upon you, only love and delight, I swear it!"

"Then you didn't . . . didn't take advantage of me that night in Whitechapel?" she asked haltingly.

His soft laughter rippled against her hair. "Other than a single, delightful kiss, my sweet, no! Did you think I was such a rogue that I would take advantage of your helpless state?"

"Yes," she candidly confessed. "You seemed quite capable of having done so!" He laughed, and color filled her cheeks. "But what of my clothing? It was unfastened!"

"Only to permit you to breathe more freely and to recover from your swoon, my silly little love, nothing more," he reassured her.

In the firelight, he undressed her pin by pin, button by button, hook by hook, until she stood quivering and bare before him, clothed only in the glory of her hair. Her garments made a frothy puddle of lace and satin and velvet at her feet. I am melting, she thought dazedly, shivering with delight at his delicate touch, melting away under the heat of his caresses and the erotic sensation of knowing his dark eyes were lovingly appraising her body. Should she cover herself? Should she feel shamed to stand so exposed before him? Did other women behave so? Would he think her wanton if he knew, knew that she loved the smoldering heat of his gaze upon her full, womanly breasts, her hips . . . the mystery between her thighs that was hidden from his eyes by only a soft fleece of fiery curls?

"My God! You're more lovely than any man deserves!" he breathed huskily, his voice catching at the sight of her. Her creamy flesh was patterned with flickering firelight and with shadow, her dark-flame hair glinting with fiery copper threads as it stirred about her shoulders. Her high, full breasts and the curves of her hips caused the bittersweet ache in his loins to become an unbearable pressure. "Come to me, my lovely angel!" he commanded, holding out his arms. His husky tone brooked no refusal. His gentian eyes were aflame with desire. "Come here, and let me claim you as my own for all time!"

She went to him, and he drew her hands between his own, kissing them tenderly before he placed them over the buttonings to his shirt. With a small, unsteady breath, she unfastened the buttons one by one, drawing aside the garment to bare his chest. It was as smooth and hard as carved oak, as deeply tanned as teakwood, and it was lightly forested with springy black curls that disappeared beneath his wide belt buckle in a tapering line. She tugged his shirt free, baring arms that rippled with muscle. They were wiry, strong, but capable of such gentle embraces. Her fingers paused, trembling, at his belt. "I . . . I cannot!" she whispered. "You must help me, Adam."

He nodded and unfastened his belt, drawing off boots and jodhpurs to stand magnificently, proudly naked before her. His lean, hard thighs and flanks fulfilled the promise of his shoulders and chest; taut, well muscled and tanned to a burnished dark gold by a hot, relentless sun far fiercer than that which shone

123

upon English shores. His manhood reared from its curling dark bed with an arrogant power that made shivers of apprehension mingle with her innocent desire.

He gathered her into his arms and lowered her to the bearskin rug beside the fire, dropping to his knees before stretching out alongside her. Tenderly, he spilled the dark-flame river of her hair through his fingers, his manhood surging at her beauty, at the contrast of her hair's vibrant color against the silken pallor of her ivory flesh—flesh with the texture of creamy white rose petals, flesh that exuded a subtle perfume that tantalized and delighted even as it enflamed his senses. He dipped his dark head to her breasts, nuzzling the delicate pink buds that surmounted them, drawing each one deeply into the flaming heat of his mouth until they swelled, unfurled, became achingly swollen and deliciously taut against his moist tongue. She tensed under his caresses, and he could hear the sudden racing of her heart as he made love to her, alternating the sweet plunderings of his mouth with the gentle strokings of his hands and fingertips until she arched upward to meet them.

He kissed her lovingly, his hand drifting down across her rib cage and on over the velvet plateau of her belly to nestle against the tangle of flaming curls that shielded the treasure within. Trembling, she stiffened, refusing him entry. He knew then that she was afraid— of him and of their passion. He stroked the silken columns of her thighs, gliding higher and higher until, with a small, defeated cry, she parted them to permit his hand to caress between. He tousled the soft curls, gently, so gently, from time to time, allowing his fingertip to graze the trembling bud within, but each time returning his caresses to the silken triangle that concealed it until she cried aloud with her need. Only then did he part those shielding petals and penetrate with his touch the chaste flower within. He half rose and watched her face as he enflamed her with rhythmic caresses, each one surging tenderly, deeper and deeper, into her silken sheath until her eyes darkened and, in the light of the fire, were filled with reckless pleading. The golden flames were reflected in their violet depths, symbols of the fiery passion he torched within her.

God, how skillfully, wondrously, he built the fire that raged through her, vanquishing her maidenly doubts and fears, and replacing them with helpless longing! His kisses were more arousing than she had ever dreamed mere kisses could be! Her breasts, tingling from his kisses and caresses, felt full, their vulnerable crests now aching little points of pleasure, while in her belly was a tense knot, and between her thighs. The earlier throbbing, tickling sensation had become a fierce, sweet ache that demanded more—far, far more—than his caresses, the touch of his hands alone.

He sat up, his shoulders burnished by fire, his ebony hair glossy with blue lights, and gently grasped her thighs, lifting and parting them as he knelt between them. Their gazes met, held; and she was lost, melting under his gentian gaze, drowning in deep violet-blue that was like a midnight sea flecked with moon gold. "The choice is yours, my love—to stop, or to go on?" His voice low and unsteady with desire, his hard form sliding up the length of her quivering body as he leaned forward to cup her face in his hands.

"No. No, don't stop . . . don't!" she heard herself whisper, and it was a stranger's voice that had spoken, a voice husky with passion and filled with tender yearning.

She gasped as she felt the hard, probing heat of his manhood against her vulnerable core, and eyes closed, she tensed for the awful, rending agony that must surely follow. Perspiration dampened her brow as he clasped her firmly to his chest, for she knew by the smoldering desire in his eyes there would be no turning back, not now—not ever again! He gazed deeply into her eyes. "I love you, my angel! Never forget it," he whispered, and thrust tenderly within her, staunching her moan of pain with his kisses, then holding very still to permit her to recover, to relax, to give her body time to expand and accommodate his entry.

"And I love you, my dearest Adam," she whispered, her vow from the heart. The rending pain was soon over, and was replaced by an exquisite pressure and fullness. Oh, how wonderful it felt to hold him deep within her, to feel his arms enfold her, his kisses on her eyelids, her lips, her breasts!

And then, he began, flexing his muscled hips and flanks to fill her and recede, fill and recede, moving slowly, deeply, until she feared she must surely burst with delight. Her fingernails carved tiny crescents in his tanned, muscled back as he made slow, unhurried love to her. She sighed blissfully as he quickened his pace, arching her body now in some instinctive rhythm it seemed she had always known matching his movements as he loved her with ever greater ardor. The rough, dark curls upon his broad chest rubbed sensuously against her sensitive breasts as he thrust tenderly into her, inciting shivers of delight that exploded through her like tiny charges of lightning. "Oh, oh, Adam, I cannot bear it—I cannot!" she cried aloud. She arched suddenly like a bow beneath him, remaining quite still, quite motionless, as rapture claimed her.

For seconds that seemed an eternity, multicolored lights dazzled her eyes. Fireworks exploded in her vision, bright chrysanthemums of gold and rose and flame. Sensation washed through her until it seemed she must surely drown in its hot flood, incoming tides of heat building to a towering tidal wave of delight that crashed over her. The wave filled her with dizzying pleasure that ebbed but gradually, finally cradling her gently downward to reality. Belatedly, she realized that Adam lay beside her now. Beads of sweat, topaz-colored in the firelight, gleamed upon his chest and brow. His breathing was quick and ragged, yet the expression in his eyes was infinitely tender as he drew her against his chest and kissed her sweetly, full upon the lips.

"I knew it, my angel," he murmured. "I knew it would be that way between us! I used to scoff at poets and romantics, believing there was no such thing as love at first sight. But when I first saw you, my lovely Heather, I knew that they were right, and I was wrong! I was a moth, drawn to your beauty as if it were a bright flame—not caring if I singed my reckless wings in its heat!"

She laughed delightedly, her expression becoming intent as she caressed his handsome face, tracing the black bars of his eyebrows down to the arrogant nose with the endearing little bump at the bridge, then outlining the stubborn thrust of his chin. From there she moved upward again, a smile curving her lips as she drew the wicked line of his mustache that tickled deliciously when they kissed. "A moth . . . *you,* Adam? Oh, no! I imagine you as a far more handsome animal. A panther, perhaps. Sleek, dark, and powerful, and yes, quite dangerous! Or a fierce tiger, padding silently through the jungle. But a moth—no!"

He grinned down at her. "You're a tease, my love. A delectable creature, but a tease nonetheless. How is it such a treasure could have escaped marriage this long?"

"By having the reputation of possessing a strong will and a mind of my own, either one of which is enough to keep any prospective suitor away!" Heather confided with a rueful smile.

"Then those men are all fools!" Adam said huskily. "They'd never buy a horse without spirit, or a hunting hound with no backbone; and yet they'd look for blind obedience and submission in their mates! I'll have no such spineless creature for my bride!"

She held her breath, wondering if he meant to propose to her, but he rose from the bed and padded barefoot across the room to collect his fallen clothes and put them on. His boots followed. He blew her a kiss and left the room with the promise that he would return very soon.

Heather slipped from the bed. Winding the rumpled sheet about her, she perched upon a tapestry stool set by the hearth. Her chin resting on her palm, she gazed into the dancing golden flames, feeling drowsy and starry eyed. Lord, she had never dreamed anything could be so wonderful as the way Adam had made her feel! Imagine, she had once thought him a rogue, had hated him for what she believed he had done to her at the Laughing Dog public house that night!

Filled with restless energy, a combination of nervousness in the wake of their lovemaking, and excitement over the new discoveries she had made that afternoon, she stood and wandered about the room, touching this, straightening that. Adam's knitted jersey lay where it had fallen earlier in the heat of the moment, and she picked it up and folded it, intending to lay it tidily across a chairback. But on impulse, she buried her face in its fuzzy warmth and inhaled his warm, masculine scent, her eyes growing misty and tender, before setting it aside.

Several books, all well thumbed, lay upon the nightstand. James Bateman's *A Second Century of Orchidaceous Plants,* Bartle Grant's *The Orchids of Burma,* and several others, both in French and English. She wrinkled her nose in distaste. Definitely not her own taste in reading materials! Surely they were not her teasing, devil-may-care Adam's either?

She looked up a little guiltily as the door opened and he came in, bearing a pitcher of steaming water, fresh linens, and soap. He set them down upon the dresser and cleared his throat self-consciously. "I thought you'd want to? . . ."

"Oh, yes! Thank you, Adam," she murmured, blushing, astonished by his consideration.

He nodded. "I'll find us something to eat meanwhile, if Shona hasn't locked the pantry."

"Shona?"

"My brother's housekeeper. She's a wonderful old dear, but I'm afraid she doesn't trust me not to raid the larder!" He grinned boyishly, and Heather laughed. "Do you like orchids?" he asked, noticing the book in her hand.

"Yes. Yes, I suppose I do. They're very exotic, aren't they, and lovely to look at? I've enjoyed the hothouses at Kew Gardens countless times," she acknowledged, then wrinkled her nose in distaste. "But I'm afraid I'd find *reading* about them very dull—all those long Latin names to remember—don't you?"

"On the contrary. I find it fascinating."

"But this one's in French!"

"What of it?"

"You must read French very fluently?"

"Naturellement, ma belle! My mother was French, didn't I tell you?" She shook her head. "Her family were émigrés. They fled across the Channel and settled in Cornwall after the Revolution. Dazzling creature, my mother, very parisienne. Dark and lovely, vivacious, intelligent—she completely bowled over my poor stick-in-the-mud father, who was the stuffy

129

military type, what! But then, *la belle* Eugénie Rivière dazzled everyone. I inherited my good looks, winning ways, and coloring from her side of the family, *tu comprends,* and my fascination with orchids. She loved them. Orchids have become something of a hobby of mine, too." He winked and grinned. "Ranking second only to making love to incredibly beautiful redheads!" He saw a becoming blush stain her cheeks, and chuckled. "I'll see to the food, *chérie,*" he promised as he left the room a second time.

She had bathed and dressed and was sitting in a chair by the window when he returned with the food he had promised. On a tray were cold pheasant, sliced chicken breast, buttered scones, glasses, and a bottle of white wine.

"Come, we'll sit by the fire and have our little picnic here on the rug," he declared, dropping promptly to the bearskin and beckoning her to sit beside him as he uncorked the bottle with a loud pop. "Nothing very fancy, I'm afraid. I'm more at home cooking over a campfire out in the bush than in a kitchen, to be honest!"

They ate in companionable silence, the only sounds the snapping and crackling of the fresh logs he added to the fire and their own laughter when he teasingly fed Heather the most tender morsels of the food. It was an afternoon she would treasure always in her heart, she vowed dreamily as she gazed across at Adam's handsome face. The firelight alternately cast his virile, strong features in light or shadow, so that at times his eyes seemed those of a devil in a dark angel's face, while at others he had the eyes of an angel in a roguish devil's face. Which is he? Heather wondered, stretching like a contented kitten. Angel or devil? Replete in every way, she leaned back and sighed blissfully. Leaning against his broad chest, his strong arms lovingly enfolding her, they watched the fire together in silent intimacy.

"I wish I could keep you here always, my sweet, but I can't," Adam murmured regretfully much later. "Tea-time is past. I must see you safely back to Moorsedge, before they call out those grooms you threatened me with just yesterday!"

Yesterday! Heather thought as Adam pulled on his shirt and jersey. Was it just yesterday he had kissed her, held her for the very first time? It seemed a lifetime ago. Lord, everything had happened so quickly!

The dazed but happy feeling lingered long after he had kissed her farewell, having promised that they would meet again the next afternoon. He left her a half-mile's ride from Moorsedge, and as she rode across the heath toward the rambling old house, she wondered if anyone would be able to tell what had occurred, for she felt quite different inside in a way that went far beyond the slight tenderness between her thighs. She was glowing, alive, more tinglingly aware of herself and everything around her than she had ever been before. The snow seemed brighter, more crystalline, where it lay in sparkling drifts upon the heaths. The afternoon sky, fading to amethyst now, was lovelier than it had seemed before. The crisp air was like a chilled, tangy wine of which she could not drink her fill.

Douglas Dennison was riding away from Moors-edge as she rode up. He swept off his hat and wished her a good-afternoon, smiling down at her from the back of his massive black hunter.

"And a good afternoon to you too, Douglas," Heather replied.

"I came to Moorsedge to invite you to take tea at Heathlands tomorrow afternoon. My mother would be honored if you could come?"

"Tea? Tomorrow? I . . . I do believe I have a prior engagement, I'm afraid, Douglas. But please express my gratitude to Lady Dennison for her kind invitation, and tell her that I would be delighted to take tea with her another afternoon when it is convenient for her to have me."

Douglas Dennison nodded, his sky-blue eyes flickering over her appreciatively, as if admiring a beautiful statue or a priceless work of art. "You look very lovely this afternoon, Heather—your hair tousled by the wind and your cheeks so bright and flushed."

"Do I?" She shrugged, embarrassed by his compliments and the husky tone in which they were delivered. "Why, thank you. I . . . I've been riding. The cold weather is most invigorating."

"So it would appear," Douglas agreed, his blue eyes narrowed as he gazed intently at her.

She flushed under his gaze. "Well, if you'll excuse me, I must be getting home. I'm so sorry that your journey was wasted."

He nodded and tipped his hat again. "Nonsense, my dear. Seeing you was quite reward enough."

Muttering her thanks, Heather rode quickly away from him, through the curling wrought-iron gate of Moorsedge.

For a few seconds, he sat and watched her; then he turned his horse and rode back the way she had come. The powdery new snow had been churned up by her horse's hooves; her path easily followed. Some half-mile's distance from Moorsedge, he found a second set of hoofprints alongside the first. So, the lovely Miss Cameron had not been riding alone! He had a suspicion of just where those two sets of hoofprints would lead him.

Aunt Elise and Annabel were in the blue drawing room taking tea when Heather went inside. Her cousin

132

looked up expectantly from the buttered scones she was devouring crumb by crumb.

"Why, there you are! You just missed Lord Dennison, Heather! He came to invite you to take tea tomorrow at Heathlands."

Heather nodded. "I know. We passed on the road."

"And?"

"And what?" Heather replied innocently.

"Did you accept his invitation, silly?" Annabel pressed. Aunt Elise looked up hopefully, awaiting her answer.

Heather shook her head. "No, I did not. I . . . I made the excuse that I had a prior engagement."

"You didn't? Oh, Heather, how could you!" Annabel exclaimed. "What an opportunity you have missed!"

"That is a matter of opinion, Coz!" Heather declared pertly.

Annabel shrugged. "Oh, well, to each her own," she said airily. "I expect you'll be wanting your tea. Fruitcake or scones?"

"Oh, nothing for me, thank you," Heather refused. "I'm not very hungry, to be honest." Not after the delightful little 'picnic' she and Adam had shared on the bearskin rug before the fire, she added silently! Heat reddening her cheeks, she hurriedly fled, using the excuse that she had to change from her riding clothes.

In the sanctuary of her room, which was decorated in forest green and cream shades, she looked at the little ormolu clock atop the mantle with dismay. Almost four! Twenty-two endless hours must pass before she would meet Adam, her wonderful, wonderful Adam, again at the castle ruins—an eternity! However would she survive? . . .

"Rory will be back from visiting his bishop tomorrow morning," Adam murmured, lazily leaning upon one elbow and watching the play of the firelight on Heather's lovely face. "We'll have to find some other place for our trysts then, little love."

"I know. But don't let's think about that now, please, Adam? I don't want to waste these precious moments we have together." She reached out and traced his handsome profile with her fingertip. When she reached his mouth, he tenderly trapped her finger and pretended to bite. Then he turned his ravenous attentions to her slender arms, nibbling up their length to burrow his dark head against her throat, which she bared to him gladly, twining her fingers through his crisp, black curls and giggling helplessly as he growled and endeavored to devour her anew. "I wish these afternoons could never end." She sighed as he took her in his arms. "The hours between are endless!"

He chuckled softly, brushing a wandering flame curl from her cheek and thinking anew how very lovely, how wonderfully passionate, she was, so unlike most respectable women who, unless of dubious character and morals, never admitted to finding pleasure in the arms of any man, not even those of their husbands. They merely yielded submissively. Yet Heather made no secret of the pleasure he had awakened in her, or the joy she experienced during his lovemaking; and his own pleasure was heightened because of it. She came to him gladly, gave herself freely with an innocent seductiveness that fired his blood as surely as a torch touched off a hayrick. He parted her lips beneath his, touching the tip of her tongue with the tip of his own. Breaths commingling, reveling in the sensual taste, scent, and feel of each other, they kissed long and deeply.

As they kissed, his hand enfolded her breast and a shiver of delight rippled through her as the nipple rose, tingling, against his palm. Desire pooled hotly in the

134

very pit of her belly, and she grew breathless at the thought that soon, very soon, they would be joined once more, moving in ageless rhythms, locked in each other's arms, inseparable body and soul in that exquisite moment of soaring rapture that would follow.

He broke their kiss and leaned back, then began a trail of kisses that he vowed, husky-voiced, would encompass every lovely, silken inch of her body. Quivering, burning, she lay very still, moaning softly with her need, gasping as he drew first one delicate bud deep into his heated mouth and savored its sweetness, then the other. His tongue tip danced in circles about the sensitive areolas until she writhed in delicious torment and implored him to stop. But he would not! Along the silky inner columns of her thighs, he kissed and caressed her until she grew breathless, lost in feverish yearning. And then, wonderfully, his lips moved higher—maddening, tormenting lips that were at the same time deliciously gentle and inflaming. Soon after, she was moaning in abandon and feeling the crescendo of rapture begin. It lifted her on soaring wings, bearing her to some place that was bathed in golden light and filled with explosions of dazzling colors that throbbed and pulsed like stars in a sky gone mad. She lay quite still, and let the madness envelop her.

When she opened her eyes, Adam was smiling down at her, his own gentian eyes smoldering with desire. He moved easily upon her, parting her trembling thighs with his knees as he entered her, showering kisses over her face and shoulders as he thrust into her welcoming heat. She twined her legs about his hard hips, locked loving arms about his waist, and whispered again and again how much she loved him, wanted him, needed him. Her endearments were wings that sent his passion soaring. Swiftly, deeply, he loved her, until restraint became an impossibility, further denial an exquisite torture. With a groan of delight that was muffled by the silken curtain of her fragrant hair, he was done.

Within a few seconds he had recovered himself, and he then cupped her face in his hands, his eyes earnest, his expression grave. "I love you, angel," he breathed huskily. "I love you more than life itself. You're my heart, my soul."

"Until I met you here in Scotland, I thought my life would never have meaning or purpose again," she confessed, stroking his black curls and tenderly wiping away the perspiration that glistened upon his brow. "Now all that's changed . . . because of you."

They lay quietly together, embracing, exchanging tender little kisses and drowsy words in the afterglow of their lovemaking. The shadows lengthened on the walls. The logs upon the hearth burned down, finally casting off only an orange glow that bathed the room in ruddy light and winked off brass lamps and glassware. Exhausted, they slept.

Adam wakened first and swung from the bed, running his hands through disheveled black hair as he groped for the small clock upon the nightstand. He groaned when he saw that it was well past five. The hour of Heather's customary return to Moorsedge had passed. Shona, his brother's housekeeper, would return shortly from her afternoon off. Damn! There would be the devil to pay if he didn't return Heather too her uncle's house, and swiftly. He scowled as he dressed, cursing the conditions that forced them to keep their love a secret for the time being. He had no fondness for skulking around like a thief in the night, stealing away with his beloved for a few stolen hours of delight, being unable to shout to the four corners of the world that she was his! But for now, he acknowledged bitterly, they had little choice. He had far too few prospects, and far too much pride, to ask her to marry a pauper!

As he went to wake her he paused for a second, looking down at her as she slept. Love and tenderness overwhelmed him. The curves of her cheeks were flushed in contrast to the white linen of the pillow, and one lovely bare arm, upflung, framed the riot of dark-flame hair that tumbled about her satin shoulders. Her lips were slightly parted and moist, the crescents of her lashes made sooty smudges on her cheeks. The swell of her breasts rose and fell evenly against the sheet he had drawn over her with the dying of the fire. "Soon, my angel! Soon we can sleep the night away in each other's arms as man and wife, I promise you!" he murmured with fervor. Hating himself for having to wake her at all, he woke her with kisses.

There was alarm in her eyes as she hurriedly washed and dressed. For teatime had come and gone, and she had never returned from her ride at such a late hour! Please God, let them not have noticed the time! she prayed fervently, pulling gloves, grown suddenly unwieldy, onto trembling hands.

"Ready?" Adam asked.

"Ready!" she confirmed with a nod.

He hesitated. "Heather, my love, I wish with all my heart it didn't have to be this way! Soon, I—"

"I understand, Adam." She silenced him gently. "I must be gone from here. Will you ride with me?"

"All the way," he answered, silencing her protests with a glance. "If your uncle is angry, then I'll bear the brunt of his anger, not you."

She shook her head. "No. You'll leave me at the usual place, and I'll ride the remainder of the way alone. If you accompany me, they'll suspect something is amiss. I'll . . . I'll tell them that I rode too far, and forgot the time."

137

"No! No more lies, sweet."

"It's for the best. Now, let's be on our way," Heather, practical as always, insisted.

They cantered their horses from the stables of the manse, but once they were outside the wrought-iron gate, Adam reined in his mount. "Did you see that?"

"See what?" Heather cried, reining her horse in beside his.

"Someone was here, I'm certain of it. Look. The tracks of the horse lead straight through the gate and on up the drive. I'm certain I caught a glimpse of a rider as we came through the gate. Could your uncle have someone following you to ensure your safety?"

"No! Uncle Jamie trusts me. He would never do anything of the sort without telling me." *Yes. He trusts me,* she thought silently, *and I have betrayed his trust.* The feeling of guilt that welled up inside her was not one she welcomed. It tarnished the glow of their long, idyllic afternoon, of all the afternoons they had shared these past weeks, and so she hurriedly cast it aside. "Perhaps it was a visitor for your brother?"

"Would a visitor have left the manse without knocking?" Adam countered thoughtfully as they rode swiftly on.

"Perhaps he knocked, but we never heard him?" Heather suggested softly, a smile drawing up the corners of her mouth. She eyed him archly.

Adam nodded, grinning now at her mischievous expression, his suspicions allayed. "Perhaps," he admitted, and urged his mount into a gallop, Heather's bay following.

At the usual spot where they parted, he leaned from his horse and kissed her farewell. Flame curls furling in the wind, she rode swiftly on to Moorsedge, and when she looked back over her shoulder, he was still sitting where she had left him, watching her. He cut a

138

strikingly handsome figure upon his gray horse, his dark silhouette etched against the snowy heath. He raised his hand in salute, and she waved in return, the tears that smarted in her eyes turning chill on her cheeks in the bitter wind.

Stolen moments. Secret trysts. Cherished hours torn from long, empty days—hours when she felt truly alive again for the first time since her dismissal from St. Thomas, tingling and vibrant—were no longer enough. She wanted so much more for them! To share all life had to offer. To drink at the well of experience, be it bitter or sweet, from a communal cup. And at night, to climb the stairs with him, arm in arm, and then lie in his embrace until dawn pinked the sky, with no need to leave in secrecy and shame like a thief in the night. To care for him, and he for her, be they well or ill, rich or poor, for all their days. To carry his babes in her belly and to bring them forth in travail softened by love and pride. Would that day ever come for them? Would Adam, one day soon, ask her to marry him? And if he did so, would Uncle Jamie accept his suit despite Adam's reputation as a penniless black sheep and a scoundrel? A lump welled in her throat and refused to be swallowed. *He must!* She loved Adam so!

Chapter Nine

"Christmas Eve! I can't believe how the past weeks have flown!" Heather said.

Annabel grinned. "Time has a way of flying, Coz, when you're in love."

"Is it so obvious?"

"Only as plain as the nose on your face!" Annabel teased. "Pass me the red and green garlands, will you?"

Heather smiled self-consciously and handed her the paper garlands. Annabel balanced precariously on the chair she was using as a ladder to attach them to the picture railing in deep swags. "There! That looks lovely!"

Her cousin was right, Heather reflected. It did look lovely. Moorsedge wore her Christmas finery like a grand old pagan queen bedecked in boughs of holly and evergreen, sprigs of mistletoe, and the inevitable garlands. The house smelled festively of pine and plum pudding, mince pies and sausage rolls, sherry and port. In the corner of the drawing room towered a young fir that Victor had felled only two days before. It was decorated with tinsel, tiny candles in miniature silver-plate candlesticks, shimmering crimson satin balls, and matching plump satin bows, as well as dainty colored-glass birds with real feathers in their tails. Mysterious little packages, gaily wrapped and beribboned, poked tantalizingly from between the furry green branches. On the topmost, spirelike central branch shone a glittering silver star that Heather and Annabel had made themselves the last Christmas they had spent at Moorsedge, two years before.

"There! What do you think?" Annabel demanded, clambering down from the chair and surveying the room with a critical eye, her fists on her hips.

A cozy fire crackled in the wide fireplace, and dozens of tiny candles flickered golden light like countless fireflies. The satin balls gleamed. The holly and the ivy wreaths added splashes of color to the faded floral and beige Aubusson carpet, and enlivened the brocade papered walls, their red and green colors repeated in the garlands.

"It looks just perfect," Heather murmured in approval.

"Oh you!" Annabel exclaimed, "I doubt if you'd notice a crooked holly wreath if it jumped down and bit you today! Is Adam coming this evening?"

"Yes," Heather confessed with a smile.

"Then I daresay you'll be utterly useless for the remainder of the day." Annabel sighed. Her feigned sternness softened. "Truly, I'm so very happy for you, Heather! After that business with your nursing, I despaired of ever seeing you smile again. We have Adam to thank for that glow about you, and I intend to do so tonight." She hugged her cousin warmly, thinking Heather had never looked more beautiful, more radiant, than she had these past three weeks. "Mamma and Papa are expecting him to ask for your hand any day now, do you know that? Has Adam mentioned when he intends to do so?"

The luminous smile Heather wore wavered fractionally. "No, no, he hasn't, not yet. Perhaps he intends to wait until the New Year?"

Annabel nodded. "I expect so. A new year, and the beginning of a new life for the two of you. It is fitting." She smiled brightly. "But whether he asks Papa for your hand tonight or a week from now, the most important thing is he loves you and wants to marry you. The rest is just a matter of formalities," she declared breezily. "It took my dear Tony an eternity to pluck up the courage to ask Papa for my hand. Men are all the same. For all their bravado, they are mortal cowards when it comes to broaching the subject of marriage! No doubt your Adam will get around to it in his own good time. When does he plan to return to Africa?"

"In February," Heather replied, her mind not really on the subject of Adam's return to Africa at all. No. She had another worry, beside which all else paled. . . .

"Ah! Then we can expect a very brief engagement and a romantic winter wedding!" Annabel decided while returning unused decorations to the large wicker hamper that had been brought down from the attic. "Lord Douglas' nose will be sorely put out of joint when the announcement is made, I'd wager. Why, anyone can see he admires you and holds you in great affection! Adam had best hurry, or Douglas will pop the question first!" Annabel teased. Then her smile quickly became a puzzled frown. "You know, he and your Adam seem quite distant and cold toward each other—even hostile. I've noticed it several times when they've both been here at Moorsedge. That's rather strange, don't you think, considering they both live most of the time in Africa? One would think their common love of the continent would dispose them to being friends, rather than enemies. What do you suppose can be the reason for it? Jealousy?"

Heather shrugged. "I asked Adam once, but he seemed reluctant to discuss it. I gathered it is a dislike of long standing, though. Perhaps something happened when they were in India, in the army. Douglas was Adam's commanding officer there, you know."

"No, I didn't. Here, Coz, would you ask Carmichael to see this returned to the attic?"

Annabel handed Heather the wicker hamper and she took it and went in search of the butler. Her errand completed, she paused to pet Taffeta. The cat had been brought with them to Moorsedge, and she now had a new litter of kittens in her basket by the kitchen fireplace. As Heather stroked their silky fur, she thought about what Annabel had said. "He has never mentioned marriage, not once, Taffeta," she murmured, rubbing her cheek against the mother cat's silver-gray coat. The cat purred loudly. "Love, yes. Desire, yes. But marriage—never." Her expression was grave as she left the kitchen, her mood so pensive that she collided full tilt with the housekeeper, Mrs. Reading, in the hallway.

"Forgive me!" she exclaimed.

"Of course, my dear. Here! These were delivered for you a few minutes ago. Aren't they lovely?" Mrs. Reading handed her an enormous bouquet.

"Red roses . . . this far north, and in December? Where on earth can he have found them?" she cried, quickly removing the tiny envelope that was tucked amongst the long-stemmed red roses the housekeeper had handed her. The heady perfume of the flowers filled the hallway as she opened the note, her fingers trembling with excitement, her misgivings of moments before forgotten in her pleasure. Red roses carried the message of abiding love and admiration, did they not? Oh, how foolish she had been to doubt Adam! But her delighted expression fled as she read the few words

143

written on the enclosed card in flowing copper-plate script:

Even the rare beauty of red roses in the midst of winter cannot match the rare and wondrous beauty of she to whom I send them.

> Your affectionate admirer,
> Douglas

"From Captain Markham, of course?" Mrs. Reading asked, smiling fondly.

Heather, crushed with disappointment, shook her head. Her expression was bleak. "No. They're from Lord Dennison."

"Ah, I see. Well, I do believe you will have a choice to make before long!" the housekeeper ventured.

"No, Mrs. Reading. I find Lord Dennison very pleasant and charming, but—"

"But it's Adam that you love," Mrs. Reading finished for her. "To be honest, I'm not at all surprised to hear it, my dear. You look as I remember dear Isobel, your mother, did when she fell in love with your father. She had that same glow about her." She took the bouquet from Heather. "I'll put these in water for you, shall I?"

"Yes, thank you. If you'll excuse me, I think I'll lie down for a while before luncheon."

"You are not unwell?"

"No, of course not! A slight queasiness, nothing more. It's probably just all the excitement of the past week, what with Christmas Day tomorrow."

"Oh, my! I do hope it's not the winter grippe! It would be so unpleasant if it were and you missed all the festivities, my dear." The housekeeper's square-boned face showed concern.

"I'm sure it's not, Mrs. Reading. A short nap, and I

shall be fine," Heather reassured her; then she excused herself and escaped to her room.

She hurriedly penned a polite note to Lord Dennison, thanking him for the lovely bouquet, after which she pulled the bellrope to summon Bridie, instructing the maid to see that the note was delivered to Douglas' residence. When Bridie had scurried off, Heather removed her morning gown and slipped a wrapper over her undergarments before sinking wearily to the bed. Several nights spent in wakefulness had taken their toll, she realized with a heavy sigh. Furthermore, the bright façade she had maintained these past seven days had drained her still more.

"Oh, Adam, she thought, staring up at the ceiling, I love you so much! Do you feel that way about me? she wondered. True, he had said he loved her countless times, but not once had he mentioned marriage. Not once during those snowy afternoons at the manse when she had nestled in his arms, drowsy from his passionate loving, had he asked her to be his wife! She gnawed her bottom lip, tears pricking her eyes. And now it appeared very likely that their lovemaking had had far-reaching results. Oh, dear Lord, what could she do? she wondered silently, a shudder coursing through her. She was almost certain that she was carrying Adam's child!

Her monthly inconvenience was a week late—she had always been so regular before—and from time to time this week she had felt light-headed and queasy, as she did now. What else *could* it be? She rolled over, buried her face in the counterpane and wept. First, she must tell Adam, of course. Oh, Lord, what would his reaction be? Would he be furious? Or would he say that he had been waiting for the right moment to ask her to marry him, that this would just set their wedding day forward by a few weeks? She hoped so. Oh, God, she hoped so!

Unbidden, Adam's dear, handsome face filled her mind, his gentian eyes dark with desire. She recalled her fanciful imaginings that first afternoon when they had become lovers, that they were the eyes of a devil . . . or an angel. Which was he, deep inside? There were times when she felt she didn't really know him at all, despite the intimacy they had shared. Oh, what a rash, lovesick little fool she had been to let him sweep her caution and propriety aside and to make such passionate love to her! But she had been caught up in the dangerous spell he wove, irrevocably and recklessly charmed by him, by his kisses and caresses and embrace. Her senses had reeled and her heart, like wild horses, had thundered out of control, leaving her heedless of anything but her love for him. Certainly she had given no thought to what the consequences of their lovemaking could be. Tonight—*tonight*—she *must* tell him. . . .

"I'll always remember you as you are this evening, my love," Adam whispered against her cheek as they waltzed that evening. Her gown of pristine white satin, sashed in Christmas evergreen, billowed about them as they danced, her dark-flame hair spilling a riot of long, fiery curls over her creamy bared shoulders.

She gazed up into his handsome face, her breath catching in her throat. His hand upon her waist was firm and warm, the other, holding her own, equally so. His clean, masculine scent filled her nostrils. The very nearness of him played havoc with her resolution, and her heart gave a frightened little flutter. If she lost him in the telling . . . She forced her thoughts away from such ideas, and tried to concentrate on the music, music that washed about them like a golden sea, carrying them hither and thither on its glorious tide. His sensual deep blue eyes never left her face, not once, and she knew by his expression that even now, even here upon the crowded floor of the ballroom, he wanted her! The thought sent a little quiver spiraling through her, and she missed her footing. At once his strong arms righted her. His expression was concerned as he set her upright.

"Enough dancing," he whispered, taking her by the elbow and steering her between the whirling, laughing couples. "Tonight, I want you to myself, my sweet."

He guided her down the hallway to the cloakroom, where he wrapped her fur cape about her bare shoulders and then donned his own overcoat. "Come on!" he urged in a whisper. Silently, she nodded agreement and tucked her small hand in his large one.

Elise Cameron saw them leave the dance-floor and started after them. But she had taken only a step or two when she resolutely turned away, back to her guests. Her dear Heather's face had been so radiant, so filled with love, and Adam's expression had been equally tender. Heather's aunt was certain that any day now a nervous Captain Markham would arrive at Moorsedge, hat and heart in hand, to urgently request a private meeting with her husband in order to ask for Heather's hand. What harm could come from letting the sweethearts have a precious moment or two alone together? It could only be a matter of days before an engagement announcement would be forthcoming, judging by their expressions. And she remembered only too well the magic of being in love, she thought fondly as she gazed across the room to where her Jamie's sandy head showed above the heads of the other guests. . . .

Elise was not the only one who observed the lovers' departure. From across the room, Douglas Dennison watched them slip away, a calculating smile playing about his lips as he sipped his whiskey.

Adam led Heather to the cobbled stableyard of Moorsedge Hall, where numerous coaches waited. Off to one side stood a sleigh, a sturdy dapple-gray horse in the traces. With a deep chuckle at her surprised and delighted expression, he swept her off her feet and deposited her inside, tucking plaid carriage rugs about her legs before nodding to Victor and jumping in beside her. He took the reins himself and clicked to the horse, breath rising in plumes from his mouth in the crisp, cold air. In seconds they were off, gliding swiftly across the snow.

The silvery jingling of the harness' bells, the wet swish-swishing of the sleigh's polished runners and the dull thudding of the horse's hooves on the powdery whiteness were the only sounds. Adam slipped one arm snugly about her shoulders and drew Heather close, brushing a kiss to her cheek as the sleigh sped on, almost flying over the frosted snowy heath that was sparkling in the moon's silvery brilliance. Only the fili-gree patterns of leafless trees marred their pristine winter wonderland. Moonlight gleamed upon the creamy wings of an owl as it glided over the glen, and the distant loch glistened like diamonds, flashing hidden blue and silver fires.

On a slight incline above the loch, he reined in the horse, turned to her, and took her in his arms. He held her so fiercely, kissed her so ardently, she grew weak beneath his sweetly savage lips. Helpless to deny him her mouth, her kisses, her embraces, she laced her fingers in his thick black curls and returned his heated kiss, thrilling to the hard strength of his chest against her breasts as she arched against him, the feel of his warm hands—his long, tanned fingers—cupping her face. His lips tasted of brandy, and were as warm and intoxicating as wine. When at length he drew away, they were both breathless, trembling with leashed desire, almost speechless with emotion. He burrowed one hand beneath her dark-flame hair, brushing aside the soft curls and the luxurious collar of her fur cape to stroke her throat.

"You're so beautiful by moonlight, my lovely Heather," he murmured tenderly, taking her cold little hand in his and kissing her fingertips. Reluctantly, he released her and delved into the pocket of his coat, withdrawing a small box-shaped parcel wrapped in gold foil and festooned with quantities of scarlet ribbons. He pressed it into her hand. "I wanted us to be alone, so that I might give you this. Merry Christmas, my love."

She turned enormous violet eyes up to him, her lashes sooty smudges in the silver and gray moonlight. "A gift? Oh, but I left yours at the house . . . upon the tree!"

"Never mind. You may give it to me later. Go ahead. Open it!"

With shaking fingers and much laughter, she managed to unfasten the ribbons and she began carefully removing the foil.

"Good Lord, woman, that's no way to open a gift!" he teased. "Tear off the paper! Savor the moment!"

Laughing still more, she did as bidden, then tugged free the ribbon that held the box of black velvet within and lifted the lid. She had wondered if perhaps there was a ring inside, but had realized the box was far too big. Something larger lay inside, something carefully wrapped in tissue paper. She unfolded it. In her palm lay a tiny unicorn of crystal that sparkled like diamonds in the moonlight. It was complete and perfect in every detail, right down to the little magical twisted horn and each dainty hoof. The mane and tail were spun threads of glass, almost as fine as real hair.

"It's wonderful!" she exclaimed, eyes shining, pleasure sending warm color to fill her cheeks.

"I'm glad you like it. For a moment, I was afraid that you wouldn't."

"How could I not like anything so precious and beautiful?" She leaned across and kissed him gently on the cheek. "Thank you, thank you, dear Adam! I will treasure it always!"

His grin was like that of a schoolboy, who was enormously pleased with himself, as he lowered his dark head to kiss her again. "I found it in Edinburgh last week," he continued after their kiss. "I was searching for a pair of glass slippers to give my Cinderella, and found this instead! Somehow, it reminded me of you—a creature so beautiful, so magical, you seem to have stepped straight from my wildest fantasies. Sometimes I wonder if I'll wake up one morning, and find I've dreamed you!"

She nodded, feeling tears choking her throat. How could she bear to break the magic of this moment, with the moon spilling silver across the starlit snowy heaths, and Adam's arms around her, his deep voice whispering the silly, wonderful words that do not seem silly to those in love? . . . But she had to!

"Please, don't say such things, Adam," she implored him, pressing her finger across his lips to silence him. "I don't deserve them. I'm no mythical creature—I'm just a woman. Very real. Very imperfect. And vulnerable, too—oh, so vulnerable! Just say that you love me, nothing more, that you'll always love me. That . . . that one day very soon, we can be married. That we'll spend the rest of our lives together!" Her violet eyes held the

150

glimmer of unshed tears in their depths as she looked up at him, her palm cradling his cheek.

He stiffened under her touch and drew away from her. In that single flinching, the magic was gone, shattered into a million splinters that pierced her heart.

"I'm afraid marriage is quite out of the question, Heather, for the time being," he said curtly. "Damn it, I have nothing to offer you, nothing at all. And I will not make you a poor man's wife. I want to give you everything you've ever dreamed of—and more!"

"But there's nothing I want but you, Adam, nothing at all!" she whispered urgently. "We'd have each other. We'd manage somehow, I know we would. Besides, my mamma left me some money, to be used as a dowry. There's enough to tide us over for a while, until you are able to find a position somewhere. I wouldn't mind making do, as long as I had you. Money isn't everything."

"Damn it, Heather, it's easy to say that when your uncle has always seen to it that you've lacked for nothing!" he flung back at her, scowling darkly. "If I went to him and asked for your hand, he'd demand to know what prospects I have, as is his right. And I would have to tell him none, none whatsoever. And what do you think his answer would be to my suit then?" He paused, his expression bitter. "He'd laugh in my face!"

"But you must ma—"

"I will, my love. But not yet. Very soon, things will be different, I promise you. Then I'll be the proudest, happiest man in the world to take you for my wife! Just last year I heard rumors of a treasure hoard that has been lost in the African jungles for over two hundred years!" His gentian eyes glittered with feverish excitement. "I intend to find that treasure!"

"You see, it's said that in the 1700s, a great Dahomey king named Agaja ascended to the throne of his people. He was a wise king, with an uncanny knack for drawing people to him. Under his rule, women were considered equals with men, and also fought in times of war. The women of his royal army were much like the legendary Amazons. Legend has it that the king deeply loved one of his Amazonian warriors, a tall, svelte beauty with flashing dark eyes. During a fierce battle with the enemy Oyos, this lovely creature was killed, and Agaja was inconsolable.

"Now, the Fon people of Dahomey, of whom Agaja was king, believe that their rulers are descended from a fierce and valiant warrior king, who was the son of a mystical union between a human princess and a leopard. Because of this union, the kings of Dahomey are believed to possess supernatural powers. So it was with Agaja. When Agaja wept for his lost beloved, the tears that fell were miraculously transformed. And do you know what they became, according to the legend? Diamonds, my angel! Crystal, glittering diamonds! There are reputed to be thousands of them! During the wars, the neighboring Oyo people stole the Tears of Agaja away, intending to keep them for themselves. But from that moment, bad luck followed the Oyo. Their power dwindled. Their vast empire collapsed. Superstitious people, they concluded that this was because the treasures they had stolen from the Fon king were cursed. Old King Oyo sent several of his most trusted men to the southeast, with instructions to hide the treasure deep in the bowels of the Congo, where it was to remain hidden for all time.

"That's why I returned to England originally, Heather. There's a man named Robert Elwood who lives somewhere in Norfolk. Years ago he accompanied

152

the explorer, Doctor Livingstone, on many of his expeditions into the African interior. It is said that he found the fabled Tears of Agaja while lost in the jungle, after he became separated from the main expedition. By the time friendly natives found him and returned him to civilization, he was half-dead from fever and hunger. His hair had turned white overnight. He could no longer remember the way to the Tears, but babbled on of the great riches he had seen. To my knowledge, he is the only white man still living who has been there. I have a friend in London, a lawyer who is attempting to contact this man for me. It was this man I had business with in Whitechapel that night we first met. I'm certain if I could just talk with this man I could persuade him to tell me about the time he was lost and, from what he tells me, be able to find the Tears of Agaja and other treasures. Few men know Africa better than I. We'll be rich beyond imagining, my darling!"

She gaped at him in disbelief. "Tears of diamonds? Leopard kings? Be sensible, Adam! If this lost treasure trove truly existed, if it *could* be found, that would have been done long ago. You can't be the only man who has tried. You're wasting your time—chasing shadows, building castles in the air, whatever you wish to call it! I'm here, Adam, and I'm *real*. I love you! We can have a good life, a wonderful life together. Forget these foolish dreams, I beg you!"

"Forget my dreams?" He set his jaw grimly and shook his head. "No, my sensible little girl, I can't. I would as soon cut off my hand! A man without dreams is already half-dead, by my reckoning. If you love me, as you say that you do, you won't ask that of me. You'll trust me. And be patient."

"But, Adam . . . I'm carrying your child!" she cried in a strangled tone, the words torn from her in

153

her anguish.

Even in the moonlight, she saw that he paled.

"Good God!" he muttered under his breath. "Are you certain?"

She nodded. "Yes. There . . . there is every indication that I'm with child," she whispered, misery in her heart.

"Damn!" He turned abruptly away from her. For several, endless moments he said nothing. "I suppose this changes things somewhat," he said heavily. "We must be married, of course. And soon."

"Yes. I suppose we must. For the child's sake." She reached out and took him by the arm, tugging him gently to face her. "Adam, please believe that I wouldn't intentionally have trapped you into marriage this way, not for the world. You must believe that!"

"Trapped me?" The anger faded from his face. He took her by the shoulders and shook her slightly. "Good God! You silly little idiot! Is that what you thought I'd think? When I wanted you so badly that I took advantage of your innocence, my darling? I'm to blame, if anyone. You haven't trapped me—and it's not you at whom I'm angry. I'm angry at myself. I wanted everything to be right when I made you my bride, and now . . . ! Don't cry, sweet! I can't stand to see you cry!" He wiped away the hot tears that rolled down her cheeks with the ball of his thumb, smiling down at her. "Feminine tears are my one weakness, my Achilles' heel, if you like. Yours are thorns in my heart!" He held her tenderly. "How long have you suspected?"

"About a week."

"Lord, what you must have gone through, my poor darling!" he said with feeling. "Don't cry anymore. I'll speak to your uncle first thing tomorrow. I doubt he'll be happy to hear that you are to become the wife of a man who has nothing but prospects of 'fabled treasure,' but I'm certain he can be persuaded to agree to our marriage . . . by telling him of your condition should it become necessary. Dry your eyes, sweet. It's not such a tragedy after all. We have our love, and each other. And in a few months, we'll have our child. It'll work out, I swear it! I'll make this up to you somehow. But for now, it's Christmas Eve—a time to be happy."

She nodded. smiling bravely through the watery mist that filled her eyes. "Yes, you're right, Adam. I'll try. But now, you should take me back to Moorsedge, if you will, before we're missed." She grimaced. "My reputation will be in serious doubt soon enough, without adding tonight's indiscretion to it."

"I will, very soon, I promise. But first, a kiss from the future Mrs. Adam Markham for her future, very loving husband."

Laughing, her fears for the moment stilled, Heather tilted her head obligingly and offered him her lips.

Carolers from Kirkenmuir were entertaining the assembly in the hall when Adam and Heather, faces flushed from the frosty night air, slipped in amongst their numbers. Relieved, Heather saw with a glance at the grandfather's clock in the hallway that they had been gone less than an hour, though it had seemed far longer.

"Well? How was the moonlight?" Annabel whispered, her arm linked through her Tony's, who was brandishing a sprig of mistletoe.

Heather's already rosy color deepened. "You noticed?"

"I did—but I believe I was the only one. I told Mamma you had gone to the kitchen for more refreshments when she asked where you were. She believed me."

Heather nodded. "Thank you, Coz." She smiled. "The moonlight was heavenly!" From across the circle, Adam caught her eye, winked reassuringly, and blew her a kiss.

Unnoticed by the lovers, Douglas Dennison witnessed the tender exchange, and his lips tightened in displeasure.

Chapter Ten

Christmas morning dawned crisp and cold, the suggestion of further snow in the air. Heather awoke feeling jittery and flushed, conditions she blamed on Adam's forthcoming meeting with her uncle. Nervous, she took longer than usual to wash, dress, and arrange her hair despite Nanette's patient assistance. Finally she went downstairs, her feet leaden.

After Christmas greetings were exchanged, a breakfast of porridge and grilled bacon, ham, kidneys, and poached eggs was served. That eaten, the Camerons donned warm coats, bonnets, scarves, and muffs; and Victor brought the coach around to carry them to St. James's, the little church in nearby Kirkenmuir, for the Christmas morning carol service. Each stained glass window was alive with the merry glow of candles, and holly berries twinkled from the numerous wreaths that adorned the window sills. Yet Heather could not concentrate on the festive sermon Reverend Rory Markham had prepared, nor on the joyous carols the congregation sang with such gusto. Watching Rory Markham in the pulpit, she could think only of his brother Adam; handsome Adam, dashing Adam, who, if all went well, would soon be her husband. "Oh, God,

157

please make Uncle Jamie say yes!" she prayed fervently, pressing her palms to her still-flat belly beneath her fur-lined coat.

Adam Markham sat down to the enormous breakfast Rory's housekeeper, Shona, had cooked for him, and dug in with an appetite that would have done justice to a starving man.

"Och, 'tis a bonnie appetite ye have, sir," Shona exclaimed in delight as drop scones and scrambled eggs, grilled kidneys, and kippers disappeared in short order. "I wish the reverend were the same, och, aye, I do. A terrible finicky appetite your brother has, an' no mistake. Can I get ye a spot more o' the tea, sir, or will ye ha'e another kipper?"

"No, thank you, Shona. I swear I would explode if I ate another bite!" Adam declared. "Did Rory leave for the church yet?"

"Aye, he did, not ten minutes ago."

Adam nodded, dabbed at his lips with a linen napkin and pushed back his chair. "That was a grand breakfast, Shona. Why don't you take the morning off and go into Kirkenmuir and visit your sister and her family? They'll be happy to see you on Christmas Day."

"Och, but Wednesday was my day off, Captain, d'ye recall?"

"Well, you've earned another," Adam insisted. "That slave driver brother of mine needs a good talking to, not thinking that you'd want to spend some time with your family over Christmas. Go on, Shona, be off with you." He grinned. "If you don't, I'll be thinking you've grown sweet on me, and can't bear to leave!" He winked.

"Och, sir, 'tis a rascal ye are, an' no mistake. Sweet on you, indeed!" Shona scolded, giggling. "Very well, sir, I'll see to the pots and then I'll be off for a wee while. I'll be sure to return in time t' put the turkey in the oven, so you and the reverend need not fash yerselves for your Christmas dinner. There's steak pie in an ashit in the pantry, if ye're feeling peckish later. And . . . thank you, Captain Markham, sir!"

"My pleasure, Shona."

Adam left the dining room and strolled down the hallway to his brother's study in search of the whiskey he knew Rory kept inside a cabinet there. He'd need a drink before facing Heather's Uncle Jamie, he thought ruefully. Because of the rumors that had flown about when he'd resigned his commission, and later when his father had cut him off without a penny in his will because of that scandal, his desirability as a husband had been sorely reduced. Jamie Cameron would likely as not be none too happy about his niece's choice. Adam's suitability as a husband hadn't bothered him overmuch until now, until Heather. . . .

The post from the previous day still lay on a silver tray upon his brother's badly scarred desk. There were several letters for Rory, among them an accounting from the vintner's in the village. Adam whistled under his breath at the amount, and shook his head, grinning. "You take after Father, little brother," he muttered under his breath as he sifted through the others. There were none for him. He picked up the well-thumbed copy of the *Iliad* that lay beside the post, poured himself a drink, and carried the book to a chair by the fireside, intending to pass the time until the Camerons returned to Moorsedge from church in reading. He opened the leather-bound book, shaking his head as an unopened letter—obviously used as a bookmark by Rory—slipped from between the pages and onto his lap.

But his smile turned to a thunderous scowl, and he

159

cursed under his breath when he saw that the letter was addressed to him and that it bore a London postmark dated the week previous! He hurriedly slit the envelope open with the letter opener he had brought Rory, as a joke, from Africa—a voluptuous and alarmingly large-breasted fertility goddess carved from ebony wood. Groaning in dismay, he quickly scanned the contents. The letter was, as he had expected, from the lawyer he had hired, telling him that a meeting had been arranged between himself and Robert Elwood, the man who was reputed to have once seen the Tears of Agaja.

"Damn you, Rory!" he muttered grimly as he took his pocket watch from his waistcoat and saw the time. "Your preoccupation with your classics may have cost me dearly!" The meeting was scheduled to take place in London that same evening. He had lost an entire week in which he could have made the journey south to the City, thanks to Rory's absentmindedness, and it was doubtful if, this being Christmas Day, any trains were running! If he were to make it to London in time, he had to leave now.

He raced up the stairs three at a time, and flung his clothes haphazardly into a bag. Then he returned to the study and hurriedly scribbled a brief note to Heather, explaining his reasons for being unable to come to Moorsedge as planned. He ended the message with a promise to return in a few days. Adding a declaration of his love, he tucked the folded letter into an envelope and thence into his pocket.

The Camerons would still be at church, he realized as he whipped the gray horse into a gallop. Hopefully, Victor would be waiting outside with the carriage and he would be able to give the groom the letter to deliver to Heather. The horse careened into the churchyard, churning fresh snow under its hooves, vapor streaming from its nostrils. Several coaches and grooms waited outside beneath the ancient yew trees, but the Camerons' coach was not among them. He cursed again.

"Were you looking fer someone, sir?"

Adam flung about in the saddle to see a coachman lounging against a fine black coach, smoking.

"Victor, the Cameron's coachman—where can I find him?" he demanded curtly.

The scrawny little coachman grinned. "Ah, he went t' wet his whistle at the King James' Arms, I'll wager!"

"Do you know if the trains are running today, man?"

"There's just the one, sir, besides this mornin's milk train, on account o' the season. She leaves at ten. If ye were t' step on it, you could make it."

Five minutes to ten. I'll have to step on it, all right, Adam thought grimly! He whipped the envelope from his pocket. "Do you know the Camerons of Moors-edge?"

"Of them, aye, sir, that I do."

"Will you see that Miss Heather Cameron gets this letter directly after the service? There's a florin in it for your trouble?"

"No trouble, sir, no trouble at all," the coachman declared, touching his cap. He took the letter and the coin from the young captain, and he wished him luck as Adam dug his heels into the gray's sides and rode from the churchyard.

When Douglas Dennison exited the church following the service shortly after, his coachman was waiting for him.

"What's up, Glover?" he demanded suspiciously. The coachman displayed a crafty grin that, over the years, Douglas Dennison had come to know well.

"This sir. I thought you might be interested. It's from your old friend, Captain Markham, for Miss Heather Cameron. Seems he had to leave Kirkenmuir in some-

161

thin' of a hurry, sir," Harry Glover confided slyly.

"Did he, now?" Douglas replied with a frown, taking the letter that the coachman waved tantalizingly before his nose. He drew away from the church door and stood beneath a snow-laden yew while he tore open the envelope and read the contents.

"He's found Elwood," he snapped angrily when he was done. "They're to meet tonight, at the Victoria Hotel in London. He's not to keep that appointment, Glover, do you understand me? He's not to arrive there—nor is he to return here in the near future."

"You want 'im dead?"

Dennison laughed. "No, my friend. As appealing as that prospect sounds, it would be far too easy. No, I have other plans for Captain Markham. I intend to make him squirm, as he once made me squirm! Just see that he's delayed in returning here. Considerably delayed."

"Gotcha, gov'na," Glover acknowledged with a wink. "I might be able t' make the train, if I were t' leave now?"

Dennison nodded. He drew a sheaf of pound notes from his pocket, peeled off several and handed them to Glover. "Go to it, man!" Harry Glover shuffled rapidly off toward the train station. Dennison took the envelope and its contents and tore them into tiny pieces before tossing them to the wind. "Just like confetti!" he murmured as they showered to the ground. He chuckled softly.

He was still standing outside when Heather and the Cameron family exited the church minutes later.

"Merry Christmas, Miss Cameron," he greeted her. She smiled, but there was a distant quality to her that Dennison noted and inwardly relished. The pensive expression only added to her vibrant beauty. He thought again how perfect she was for what he

162

intended—so glowingly beautiful. Her passionate nature was hinted at by her exquisitely feminine, rounded figure, her seductively long-lashed violet eyes, and yes, those lips that seemed always to have just been kissed, they were so rosy and full!

"And to you, Douglas. I wanted to thank you in person last night for the lovely bouquet of roses, but Moorsedge was so crowded. It was most kind of you to send them!"

"Not at all!" he denied, knowing quite well she had not given the matter a thought, not with her moonlight tryst with Markham in mind. "As I said in the card, their beauty quite pales beside your own, my dear." He smiled a disarming smile, his blue eyes twinkling, his blond hair attractively disheveled by the brisk wind. "Ladies, I see Jamie is in conversation. May I escort you out of the wind and to your coach?"

"You may, Lord Dennison," Elise Cameron accepted his offer graciously, extending her arm and watching her niece's pale face. As she had expected, Heather seemed not in the least animated by his offer. Inwardly, she sighed. It appeared things were as she had thought last night at the ball. The Markham fellow had made a far deeper impression on dear Heather than had Lord Dennison, despite his questionable financial status and his dubious prospects. She dearly hoped Adam had some independent means unknown to them, so that if he should ask for Heather's hand, Jamie would be able to approve the match. After they had retured last night, she had hinted to Jamie of what was in the wind, but her husband had been very doubtful regarding Adam Markham's suitability as a husband for Heather. She pursed her lips. Adam is such a dear boy, despite his reputation as a rascal, she thought as Lord Dennison led them to their conveyance. She could well understand a young woman's attraction to Adam and his dark good looks, but looks faded . . . it was security she wanted for Heather, and happiness. Poverty, however genteel it might be, provided neither.

· Victor had returned from the public house with the coach, and Lord Dennison handed the women inside, accepting Elise's invitation to visit Moorsedge very soon.

"My mother has asked me to again extend her invitation to you and your aunt to take tea with her, Miss Cameron," he told Heather. "May I tell her that you will?"

Elise nudged her niece in the ribs and Heather gasped. "But of course, Douglas," she agreed reluctantly. "I would love to."

"Would next week be convenient? Say, Thursday at three?"

"Why . . . yes, I suppose so." By Thursday, the whole world would know that she and Adam were betrothed!

"Marvelous! I shall send my coach to fetch both you and your aunt. Have a wonderful Christmas, Mrs. Cameron, Heather."

All during the drive back to Moorsedge and later when she had changed her clothes and joined her family and Tony Winchester in the drawing room, Heather wondered when Adam would make his appearance to speak with her uncle. She jumped nervously at each knock upon the door, and she experienced no pleasure when the family gathered beneath the Christmas tree to unwrap their gifts, nor in the carols they sang, so jittery was she. When the others complained of the chill, she rubbed her moist palms on her skirts and hoped they would not notice the high flush to her cheeks. Lord, her stomach felt as if butterflies were practicing crash landings inside it and there was a tightness in her chest that threatened her breathing! Where was he? He had promised to come to speak with her uncle in the morning. Where could he be?

Luncheon came and went, and then the afternoon marched by on leaden feet, each pace measured by the loud and suddenly irritatingly regular tick of the mantel clock. When daylight faded, the maids hurried to draw the velvet draperies against the night. The aroma of roasting turkey, of chestnut stuffing, chicken and steak pies, plum duff, and treacle pudding wafted through the wings of Moorsedge from the kitchens, and everyone talked expectantly of the upcoming feast. But Heather felt no anticipation. The smell of the food made her feel queasy, and later, as they sat at a festive table adorned with silver platters and snowy linen cloths, bunches of crimson holly berries, and tall, wavering crimson candles, she might have been at a wake rather than a Christmas supper, for the delicious food tasted like sawdust on her tongue. The feverishness she'd experienced earlier that day returned, and it made the candleflames dance crazily before her. Uncle Jamie's and Aunt Elise's faces became enormous. Their features seemed grotesquely distorted, and their voices sounded far away. Blood pounding in her ears, she rose shakily and begged to be excused, but she managed only two faltering steps before dizziness and heat overwhelmed her. She tottered, then righted herself to find Uncle Jamie's arms firmly about her, offering their support. Aunt Elise hurried to her side and placed a cool hand upon her brow.

"Why, upon my word, Jamie, she is burning up! Quickly, carry her upstairs to her room! The poor child is quite ill!"

Mrs. Reading and her aunt undressed her and tucked her into bed, hot bricks at her feet, extra blankets added to her coverings. Hot toddies of whiskey with lemon were pressed upon her, the bedroom fire was fueled with fresh logs. Cocooned now, and more than a little drunk from the whiskey as well as groggy from the fever, she fell into a restless sleep.

In her fevered dreams, she searched for Adam, calling his name. Sometimes he came to her, his gentian eyes dark with desire. He held her in his strong arms and kissed her, his mouth like flame upon her bare body, burning until it seemed his kisses must consume her, that she would curl up and disintegrate like ashes in the wind. Then just as suddenly, he was gone, and there was only darkness, inky and absolute. She was alone—so alone . . . so very, very alone.

The rhythmic clackety-clack of the train was like a noisy lullaby after so many hours on the rails Adam thought, jerking his head up and stifling a yawn. Booted feet propped up comfortably upon the velvet-upholstered seat opposite him, he gazed out of the window at the countryside.

He couldn't see much at all now, really, for it was well after four, and darkness fell early in winter. Purple night cloaked the little villages and towns the train clattered through, its presence against the ghostly white of endless wintry fields betrayed only by tiny points of lamplight piercing the gloom like fireflies. Usually, he enjoyed trains enormously: the shiny, magnificent appearance of a gleaming engine; the smoky, exciting way they smelled and shot great fountains of hissing steam into the air, the heady feeling of break-neck speed as they clattered rapidly and noisily over the rails, their progress punctuated by the occasional triumphant blast of a whistle. But the appointment with Robert Elwood made him eager to be done with traveling, to be in London and en route to the Victoria

Hotel. He was eager to take the first step toward their future—his and Heather's.

A knock came at the compartment door, and Adam looked up to see a ticket collector in a navy blue uniform standing in the corridor, swaying slightly with the movement of the train.

"Ticket, sir?"

"Right here," Adam responded with a grin. Fishing in his waistcoat pocket as the collector stepped into the compartment, he handed the man his ticket for punching. "Where are we?"

"About ten minutes outside of the city, sir. You'll hear the whistle as we enter Charing Cross station."

"Thanks." The collector tipped his hat and left, and Adam heard him moving away down the corridor calling, "Tickets, if you please! Tickets, ladies and gentlemen!" as he went.

Impatient now that the end of his journey was so close at hand, Adam swung his bag down from the net baggage rack above his head. As he did so, he heard two strident whistles and he knew they must be approaching Charing Cross station. Good! He had a little less than forty-five minutes to find a cab and reach the hotel. Despite everything, it looked as though he was going to make it in time! Shouldering into his greatcoat, he picked up his bag and made his way out of the compartment, moving sideways down the narrow corridor toward the door.

"Excuse me, sir?"

Adam turned to see the ticket collector behind him. "Yes?"

"Would you be Captain Adam Markham, sir?"

"I am." Black eyebrows came together in a frown.

"Then I have a message for you, sir. There's a gentleman back there, in the baggage compartment, who says he has some information for you. He instructed me to

167

tell you that if you were interested in a certain item that has been lost for several years, you were to meet him back there before the train puts into the station." The collector shrugged. "Sorry to be so vague, sir, but that's all he said."

Still frowning, Adam nodded and slipped the man a tip. "No problem." He turned and made his way back down the corridor to the rear of the train where the baggage compartment was. *What the Devil is this all about?* he wondered as he went. *Who knew that he had boarded this train, and how? Could the "certain item" which had been "lost for several years" be the Tears of Agaja? And if so, who was his mysterious informant?*

He turned the handle to the baggage compartment and swung open the door. Mountains of cases and trunks, milk churns, wicker hampers, and chicken coops, complete with clucking contents, cluttered the long car. He stepped inside and looked around. No one.

"If you have something to say to me, come out and say it to my face, whoever you are!" he challenged, a dark scowl wreathing his face. He sensed a quick movement at his back and spun about—just a fraction of a second too late! Something hard and cold thudded heavily across the back of his head, filling his vision with stars.

"*Christ!*" he groaned, then folded to the floor without another sound.

He came to aware of a vicious ache at the back of his skull. Then he sensed pins and needles in his hands and feet and a nasty crick in his back. Groaning and cursing under his breath, he tried to stretch, but found he could not. He was inside something dusty and prickly, and there was no room to stretch.

168

He remembered the ticket collector's mysterious message and his entry into the baggage compartment, the ringing blow to the back of his head. *You bloody, gullible fool!* he upbraided himself disgustedly. Damned if he hadn't played right into their hands—whoever "they" might be—walking into their little trap like a lamb to the bloody slaughter!

By squirming uncomfortably about, he managed to touch the sides of his prison, which appeared to be a large, rectangular wicker hamper. Shouldn't be too difficult to break out of this, he decided, encouraged. After all, how strong could a wicker hamper be? Clenching his jaw, he strained against the sides with his palms and feet, sweat pouring from his brow and his head throbbing agonizingly. But the basketwork refused to give. After several fruitless moments, he gave up temporarily and concentrated instead on getting his bearings while he regained his strength for a second attempt.

Somehow, he sensed that he was no longer aboard a train. The rhythm of the movement was different, rocking rather than shuddering from side to side. He strained his ears for a sound of some kind that might give him a clue to his whereabouts. Faint, disembodied shouts reached him, and once, he thought he caught a scream, like that of a gull. A boat, perhaps? It was possible. Since he had no way of knowing how long he had been dead to the world, whoever had struck him might well have bundled him into a conveniently empty hamper, removed it from the train, and had it loaded onto a boat.

Rested somewhat, he determined to escape again, this time using different tactics. He flung himself to left, then right, rocking the heavy hamper from side to side in the hope that it would topple over and the catch would break loose on impact. He rocked, harder and harder, almost whooping in triumph as the hamper tottered momentarily, then rolled heavily over with his weight, slamming him hard against the ground, or whatever was beneath it, upside down. Damn it all! he thought, silently fuming and cursing whoever had woven the basket to form such a perfect, inviolable cage. The bloody catch was still fastened, still intact. Obviously, this called for more subtle methods! Temporarily resigned to his fate, he began to tug laboriously at the wicker strands, one by one, breaking them free. If brute force had failed, then maybe nibbling himself a hole to crawl through might succeed? *Like a blasted mouse,* he thought, disgusted, as he broke off yet another short strand.

He guessed that almost two hours had passed before he had a hole big enough to crawl through. It was too dark to see his watch. Instinctively, he reached for it. It was gone, as were his leather wallet, several pound notes, and all of his personal papers and effects! What he said next would have sent old ladies into purple convulsions. He was still consigning the thiefs to various unpleasant demises when he heard voices, loud foreign voices, very close at hand, speaking in French, his mother's tongue. He understood every word perfectly, and he stiffened, though he made no sound. If they were the ones who'd cracked him across the skull, then let them think he was still out cold.

Scraping noises and thumps and bumps and clatters followed, and he realized that there must be many cases and crates all about him. Judging by the sounds, whoever was nearby was shifting them about. After several minutes, he felt the wicker hamper he was in move as someone tried to lift it.

"Mon dieu! Jacques, mon ami! Give me a hand! I think there's a body in this one!" A burst of loud, deep laughter followed.

"A body? Unless it is that of a woman and very much alive, I am not interested, François. Lift it yourself!"

"I'm telling you I can't!"

A muffled curse then. Heavy footsteps. More hands fumbling, heaving at the hamper. Someone panting heavily nearby, and groans as the other man also tried to lift it.

"Merde! For once, you're right," the man, obviously Jacques, agreed grudgingly. "Ah! No wonder! See what it says here, François? Bibles. Your sins and mine must weigh heavily upon us if we cannot even lift one little hamper full of holy books, *oui?"*

"Speak for yourself," François growled. "Come on. The *capitaine* said to look lively, yes? You take that side. I'll take this one."

Adam felt himself lifted and raised up, then he heard the clank of metal as a hook was attached to a rope looped around the hamper. Brilliant light assaulted his eyes as the hamper was lifted. He looked down, through the hole he'd made, and saw water beyond, then the deck of a small ferryboat directly beneath. He squirmed about until he hung by his arms through the hole, and he dropped to the deck, aware of two amazed white faces gaping up at him. He landed upright, bending at the knees to take the impact of the fall and immediately bouncing back up onto the balls of his feet.

"What the devil's going on here?" he demanded, gentian eyes crackling with anger, fists planted arrogantly on his hips. "Who are you? Where are we—and what the devil was I doing in there!" He gestured toward the empty hamper, swinging violently to and fro above him in midair from a loading hoist.

"They," said a voice behind him, "are two members of the crew of this vessel, *La Mouette.* We are presently just off Calais, and about to unload our cargo. As to

171

what you were doing in there, *m'sieu,* I expect that you'd know the answer to that far better than we, yes? After all, we presumed the hamper contained only Bibles, not a stowaway."

Adam flung around and glared at the man, a short, stubby fellow with a pugnacious stance and expression. He appeared no more in the mood for playing games than was Adam.

"A stowaway?" Adam laughed scornfully. "I've no time to waste on your little jokes, *m'sieu.* If you'd be good enough to fetch him, I'd like to speak with your captain. Now."

The man laughed unpleasantly. "You would? Then speak away, *m'sieu.* You see, *I* am ze *capitaine!* You have approximately ten minutes before we dock to entertain me with *your* amusing little story for when we arrive I will summon the gendarmes!"

Heather awoke to see snow swirling down like feathers beyond her bedroom window; heard the sound of lowered voices from across the room. She struggled to sit up, aware now of a dull aching in her temples, a sharp pain in her lungs that made breathing difficult. She was alarmed at how dearly this effort cost her, for she was trembling and clammy with perspiration when she finally made it up onto her elbows.

"She's awake!" she heard Annabel exclaim. "The fever has broken!"

"My dear child!" Aunt Elise's voice. "Thank God!"

Aunt Elise, Annabel and Mrs. Reading hurried to her bedside and stood there, smiling foolishly as they looked down at her. There were tears in their eyes.

"You've been very ill with lung fever, Heather," her aunt explained gently. "We were afraid we would lose you! Child, why didn't you tell me you were feeling

172

unwell on Christmas Day? That ride to the church in a drafty old coach, and then standing about in the wind and the cold afterward—why, it is a blessing—a miracle, you have recovered at all!"

"How long have I been ill?"

"A week," Annabel disclosed. "Drifting in and out of a fever most of the time. Oh, Coz, we were so frightened! How are you feeling?"

"Strange . . . and very tired. My chest pains me."

"That's to be expected. The doctor said he had seen few cases of pneumonia as severe as yours. Your recovery will take time."

"Has . . . has Adam been here? Does he know that I've been ill?"

Elise Cameron turned away from her. "Why, just look at these lovely flowers upon the bureau! Aren't they delightful? Douglas Dennison sent them," her aunt commented hurriedly as if she had not heard Heather's question. "He has been to Moorsedge every day to inquire after you. The poor man has been terribly worried."

"But what about Adam? Has he been here too?"

Her voice had grown shrill, and the housekeeper and Aunt Elise exchanged anxious glances. "Now, Heather, it could be dangerous for you to become so excited. Try to remain calm and quiet, there's a good gir—"

"No! I demand that you tell me about Adam this instant, Aunt Elise! There's something you aren't telling me, I know it! What is it? Has something terrible happened to Adam?"

"Mamma, Ready darling, please, go on and rest." Annabel urged the two older women gently. "You've sat with Heather so many nights, you must be utterly exhausted. I'll sit with her now. I'll—I'll talk to her." Their eyes met, and silent glances of understanding were exchanged.

173

"Very well," Elise agreed with a heavy sigh. "Come along, Mrs. Reading. I do believe we have earned a good, hot cup of tea." She turned to Annabel. "I'll have Shelagh prepare some beef soup and a custard for Heather. She needs some nourishment."

Annabel hugged her mother and kissed her brow fondly. "That sounds perfect."

After they were gone and she and Annabel were alone, Heather turned her head to watch Annabel as she crossed the room to her bedside. "Why are you all avoiding my eyes?" she demanded, her thin little face anxious, her violet eyes dark and enormous. "What is it that you won't tell me?"

"Adam has gone, Heather." Annabel spoke the words bluntly. There was no way to soften them and so she made no attempt to do so.

At her words a cold clutch of fear gripped Heather's belly. "Gone?" she echoed. "What do you mean, gone?"

Annabel sighed heavily and perched on the bed beside her cousin, drawing her hands between her own. "When you were ill and at the height of the fever," she began, "you called for Adam continually, repeated over and over how much you loved him. The doctor suggested that you might be calmer if Adam were here. He felt that you would sense his presence and be comforted by it, and so recover more rapidly. Mamma and Papa were beside themselves with worry. Papa went to the manse to ask Adam to come, but Rory told him that Adam had left Kirkenmuir, where and for what reason he had no idea. He told Papa that when he returned to the manse after the service on Christmas Day, he learned that Adam had given the housekeeper a few hours off. In her absence, he had packed his bags and left. Rory found his gray horse later at the train station. Not a word has been received from him since."

174

"No!" Heather cried, her face paling alarmingly. "He would never do such a thing—he wouldn't leave without telling me, I know it! He loves me! He . . . he promised to come on Christmas Day to ask Uncle Jamie for my hand!"

But despite her impassioned words, dread coiled snakelike in the pit of her belly. *He had gone.* The words were repeated over and over in her mind like a litany, a horrible, unbearable litany. The very day after she had told him she was carrying his child, he had left without word to anyone, not even a farewell for her or for his own brother! Oh, Lord, she felt that her heart was broken clean in two, the ache was so exquisitely painful! Tears burned behind her eyes, scalding torrents that threatened to burst forth like a ruptured dam. She turned her head away, and the tiny crystal unicorn he had given her greeted her eyes. On the mantel, it was aglitter with amber light from the fire. *Oh, how could you, Adam? I loved you so! Adam, what of me—what of our child?*

She wouldn't cry. She would not! If he had truly deserted her, he was not worthy of her tears. And if he still intended to return, well, then there was no occasion for them! Could he have just been using her? Every word he'd spoken, every promise he'd made, were they only lies? *No!* She had believed his vows of love. But why? Because he had been so sincere . . . or because she'd desperately wanted to believe them? Because she loved Adam, and Adam's loving her in return made their passionate interludes less shameful?

Love! Perhaps he had never loved her, she thought bitterly? Perhaps to him she had been only a toy, to be played with and cast aside when she ceased to please or when a more serious consequence—such as the threat of a forced marriage—dulled his pleasure? No. She would never believe that of him, not unless she heard it from his own lips. Her love and trust were not so fragile that they foundered on the rocks of uncertainty. What was a week, after all? Nothing!

To Annabel she insisted obstinately: "He'll come back. It's been only a week. Who knows what may have happened? I . . . I'm certain there must be a very good reason for his leaving. Soon he'll come back and explain it all to us. I know it!"

"Of course he will, Coz," Annabel soothed her, frightened by the wild light in her cousin's eyes and by the two spots of hectic color that had flared anew in her cheeks. "Of course."

Chapter Eleven

He paced back and forth in the narrow cell like a caged wild cat. Ten paces forward. Ten back. Six paces to the barred, square window. Six paces back to the rough wooden bunk. Hardly enough blasted room to swing a cat, he thought, scowling and running irritable hands through his disheveled black hair.

Ten days he'd been here, and there was no indication that he'd be released in the near future. Ten days had limped by since he'd rashly knocked out the captain of *La Mouette* and dived overboard. All hell had broken loose after that, he recalled!

The two merchant seamen had leaped overboard after him, but he'd realized immediately, with a wild surge of elation, that he was a far more powerful swimmer than they. Only minutes later he'd heaved himself up onto the stone-walled jetty of the Calais harbor, streaming water, and he had taken to his heels.

Unfortunately, the enraged crewmen's cries had alerted several people on the wharf, and fishing nets and lading papers had been hastily cast aside while they'd joined the pursuit of the stowaway! Seconds after, he had heard the strident nasal blasts of several police whistles, and he'd ducked down a narrow alley just in time to evade the caped and capped gendarmes that the livid Captain Rouget, still groggy from a ringing uppercut to the jaw, had hastily summoned. A merry chase had ensued, and, Adam remembered ruefully, he'd given those little bastards a run for their money before their sheer numbers had proved his undoing and they'd cornered him. A brick wall at his back, over ten feet high, had blocked his escape.

"That's it, then!" he'd declared in French, throwing up his arms in surrender. "You've got me, *monsieurs!* I'll come peacefully." He'd grinned.

But a peaceful surrender was the last thing on the provincial gendarmes' minds. Action of any sort was rare here, in sleepy coastal Calais, and these men were hungry for excitement. That this arrogant Englishman had evaded them, made fools of officers of the law for close to two hours, had tried their mettle. It was unforgivable! One of them whipped a baton from his belt and came menacingly at Adam, smartly slapping the billy club against his palm.

"I regret, *m'sieu,* that I do not understand you," the gendarme had murmured slyly, raising his baton over his head. Adam had ducked, whirling to one side to evade the blow, as the constable had lunged at him.

"'Don't understand' my eye!" he'd gritted out, drawing back his fist and slamming it into the gendarme's hard belly with such force the jolt all but broke his wrist and knuckles. "Did you understand that, eh, you bastard?" he'd panted.

The winded gendarme had collapsed to the cobbles with an explosive "Oof!" and on glancing up, Adam had seen his fellow officers advance en masse, their expressions ugly, their batons raised. At that moment he'd known that as far as he was concerned, the fight was as good as over.

I gave them a good run for their money before they

178

laid me out, he thought with great satisfaction, as he went to gaze broodingly out of the barred window that looked onto the depressing mud flats of Calais beyond. He'd come to here, freezing cold in this miserable little cell, the stench of urine and old sweat in his nostrils, feeling as if he'd tangled with a gorilla. His splitting headache made the last one seem trivial. Livid bruises had mottled his face; they were only now beginning to fade. A cut had opened on his brow and lip and it had stung like blazes. He'd tasted salty blood in his mouth as he'd staggered to the crude bucket in one corner to spit. Thank God, his teeth were still intact, though his body felt as if someone had tried to tear his arms and legs off at the sockets and rearrange the pieces.

He'd gone at once to the grilled door and bellowed that he demanded to see the sergeant of gendarmes. After half an hour of bellowing, the sliding aperture in the door had been pushed aside and a narrow, foxlike face had peered in.

"What is it you wish, *m'sieu?*"

"I demand to see the sergeant, constable, and to be told why I'm being held here?" The best form of defence was attack.

"Why?" A scornful laugh. "I would have thought the answer to your question was obvious, *m'sieu!* The captain of *La Mouette* has lodged charges against you for stowing away on his vessel, *non?* And there is the other little matter of your resisting arrest, of striking an officer of the law in the performance of his duties, *n'est-ce pas?*" A foxy smile. "You are in very serious trouble, I'm afraid, *m'sieu.* Very serious."

"I demand to see a lawyer!"

"You have money, *m'sieu?*"

"You know damned well I don't!" Anger had crackled in his gentian eyes.

"Then I would suggest, *m'sieu,* that you are in no

179

position to demand anything!"

The opening had slid shut with a resounding thud.

And that, for several days, had been that, Adam recalled. Seething, he'd had no recourse but to return to the foul little bunk with the stained and stinking tick mattress, and to think. And, God, how he'd thought! Of Heather, most of the time. Poor angel! What must she have imagined, when he'd not returned to Scotland after three or four days as he'd promised in the letter and when she'd had no word from him? She must think he'd become ill, or been injured somehow. She must be half out of her mind with worry—as he would have been, were their situations reversed.

He closed his eyes, a clear picture of her lovely face and body filling his mind—the woman he loved who carried inside her his child. *Their* child. Strange, he'd never seen himself as a father before! Heather's announcement had rocked him back on his heels more than he cared to admit. He knew his expression when she told him must have been an incredulous one, but the news had been so damned unexpected! Belatedly, he'd seen the strain in her shadowed eyes and had realized, with a wave of guilt, the hell she must have gone through, wondering those past days if she was with child or no, worrying about what his reaction would be when she confessed her secret. *And you, you unfeeling bastard, reacted badly,* he declared to himself.

He imagined her pale little face, tense with worry, her violet eyes shadowed by weeping and brimming with tears, her expectant response to every knock upon the door. God, what he'd give to be able to hold her, comfort her, tell her he was—

A piercing shriek ruptured the silence, and Adam got up and went over to the window. A young lad, perhaps twelve years old, stood with raised fists before the lum-

180

bering Constable Lapin, whose uniform was splattered with mud and slush.

"Go on then, you big ox, hit me if you dare!" the boy challenged, his eyes blazing defiance.

"I'll do more than hit you, you little weasel," Lapin panted, "I'll kill you! I warned you what would happen if you threw mud at me again, didn't I?"

"So what!"

"So this is 'what,'" Lapin threatened, lunging for the boy.

"Lay a finger on me, and I'll tell my uncle!" the youngster taunted, and Lapin halted as if stopped by a bullet.

"Oui, you would, wouldn't you?" he growled, apprehension in his eyes.

"But of course. What else is having an uncle who's inspector of gendarmes good for, eh, Lapin! See this bruise here—and this one, right here? I'll tell him you made those! He'll have you rounding up waterfront whores for the rest of your life!"

"A boy your age shouldn't talk that way," Lapin muttered.

"A boy my age shouldn't do a lot of things that I do," the lad retorted cockily. "Now, how about it, Lapin? Ten francs, and I'll tell Uncle nothing!"

"But . . . I never laid a hand on you!"

"You and I know that, but who do you think Uncle Raoul will believe?"

Lapin hesitated. "You dirty little—"

"I'm waiting, Lapin."

With a curse, the constable dug into his pocket for the coin and flipped it to the boy, who caught it expertly. "A wise decision," the urchin commented. Then he ran off screaming, "Uncle! Uncle! Help me! Lapin is hitting me! Ow! Ow!"

Adam shook his head. The young rogue had played

the blundering Lapin for the fool he was!

He grasped the bars and shook them, more for something to do than in a real attempt to break free. Besides, he'd tried them several times before that first week, and they hadn't given by so much as a fraction of an inch. He stared out, past the mud flats to the gray-green swells of the English Channel beyond.

"I'll make all the worry and waiting up to you, my sweet," he promised a startled gull fervently. "Just as soon as I get out of this blasted cell!"

"Well, Heather, here you are at last! Mother and I had despaired of your ever coming to Heathlands Hall, you know."

"I'm sorry. My illness . . ." She shrugged expressively. "I've needed these days to recuperate, Douglas."

"Of course. Forgive me, Heather. I didn't mean to sound accusing. Only to impress upon you how very eagerly your visit has been awaited. Mother was delighted that you were finally able to come. She and your aunt appear to be getting along quite splendidly, do they not?" He glanced back over his shoulder, through the glass windows of the conservatory to the salon where the two women were conversing beside a low table spread with the remnants of the delightful high tea Lady Dennison had served.

"Yes, they do," Heather agreed without enthusiasm, casting about her for a topic to change the conversation. "These plants are wonderful, Douglas. The effect in here is quite tropical, despite the wintry weather outside. What are they?"

"Varieties of palms and ferns that I brought back from Africa for Mother. Gardening is her passion! Do you like them?"

"Oh, yes, very much. They're so lush and enormous—so very different to British plants." *Like orchids,* she thought with a pang, remembering Adam's passion for the rare plants.

"At my residence in Nairobi, the gardens run riot with such as these after the rainy season—some as tall as houses, others low and spreading. And the flowers! Crimson, white, yellow and mauve—gigantic blossoms! They are exotic beyond belief! I do believe you would like it there, Heather."

"Perhaps," she admitted, feeling apprehension well up inside her as she realized the direction in which he had deftly steered the conversation. His very smoothness flustered her. "Thank you for showing them to me, but I do believe we should return to the salon now, Douglas. My aunt would not approve of my spending so much time alone with you." She managed a little laugh. "She is quite old-fashioned in regard to such matters."

"Nonsense!" he declared, smiling and flicking the blond cowlick that fell across his brow from his eyes. "They can see us from where they are sitting, so we can hardly be considered unchaperoned! Besides, I'm certain if your aunt had no objection to your riding across the heaths unaccompanied every afternoon, she can have no objection to you being here with me, where you are in plain view." Fair eyebrows rose inquiringly, and then he added as if it was an afterthought, "Oh, but you were not *completely* unaccompanied, were you?"

Her head jerked up in alarm. "What do you mean?" she demanded.

"You and Adam Markham used to ride together, did you not?"

"You . . . must be mistaken, Douglas," she insisted.

"No, I think not," Douglas contradicted, taking her elbow and drawing her behind a tall, fronded potted palm where they could not be seen from the salon. "I saw you together on more than one occasion—once leaving the manse, I do believe, and another time, exiting the ruins of the castle above the loch. You didn't seem overly concerned about a chaperon then." He smiled knowingly.

Two spots of hectic color filled her pale cheeks. "Oh!" she whispered, suddenly recalling Adam's suspicions one afternoon that they had been followed. He'd been correct.

He chuckled. "Don't be alarmed, my dear. I'm a man of the world, after all. I know how a handsome rogue such as Markham can turn an innocent young girl's head! And I confess, I wasn't too surprised to learn he had left Kirkenmuir rather suddenly, knowing him all these years as I have. Love 'em and leave 'em, that's his style, my dear girl! No doubt he heard the deafening clamor of wedding bells in his ears, felt the marriage knot starting to tighten about his throat, and he determined to leave before the situation got even stickier, mmm?" He drew one of her dark-flame curls between his fingers and rubbed it. Then his handsome features grew stern. "Damned fool! I would never have left you so cavalierly, my dear Heather!" A light kindled in the sky-blue eyes. "Never!" he repeated softly, drawing her cold little hand to his lips.

"Douglas, I must ask you not to—"

"Hush, now, you mustn't cause a scene. It would upset Mother and your aunt terribly, and all for nothing." He smiled. "You see, I love you, Heather! I'm sure you must have realized that by now? I came to Moorsedge each and every day when you were at the height of your illness to inquire after your progress. I— I was beside myself with worry, my darling girl! Won't you permit me just one little kiss in return for my concern?"

Before she had time to protest, he lowered his fair

head and pressed his lips to hers in a chaste kiss that left her quite unmoved. "There! No more than a brotherly token of affection. That wasn't so terrible, now, was it?"

"No," she agreed reluctantly.

"I'm certain your Adam's kisses were not nearly so respectful, were they?" he added knowingly. "But then, the man is quite without scruples. Did you know that he served under me out in India before he resigned his commission?"

"I had heard that he did, yes."

"Let me tell you, it was fortunate for him that his father had some influence with the War Office, else he would have been given a dishonorable discharge at the very least! As it was, old Colonel Charles Markham was able to pull strings here and there and hush things up, and Adam was permitted to resign without a scandal. He told you about what happened, of course?" His blue eyes were piercing as he put the question.

"No, he did not. And—and I don't think I wish to hear it now," she protested.

"Oh, but you should!" Douglas disagreed smoothly. "I believe the anguish you are suffering now on account of Markham's . . . departure . . . would be far easier to bear were you to understand what a scoundrel the man truly is, and how fortunate you are to have escaped his seducer's wiles before it was too late." His voice was like honey dripping into her burning ears, wheedling, convincing. With no prodding or comment from Heather, he continued quickly. "We were engaged in besieging a city, you see. Others thought we should retreat, yet I believed we had an excellent chance of securing it. As it happened, I was proven to be correct. After several weeks of siege, we took the city. The inhabitants were rounded up and brought to the main square, men to one side, women and children on the

185

other. Markham and his men had charge of the women and children. I gave strict orders that the prisoners were to be well treated, fed and watered. They were pitiful creatures, enemy or no! The siege had left most of them starved, you see, incapable of resistance or escape.

"I awoke a night or so later to learn that your Captain Markham and his men had gone beserk! They had violently raped and brutally abused the women in their care, then had gunned them down like cattle—the innocent little children with them, some no more than infants still nursing at their mothers' breasts! He claimed later that they had attempted to escape, and that he'd had no choice. A pack of lies, of course."

"No! I won't believe that of Adam!" she cried, shaking her head vehemently, horror in her violet eyes.

Douglas shrugged. "That is to be expected, my dear. He can be a charmer with the ladies when he puts his mind to it, as well you know, my poor girl! But that doesn't alter the fact that he is like a rosy apple that conceals the rotten core at its center! I pressed charges against him for his actions, and started proceedings for a formal court-martial. But Colonel Markham's influence squashed all of that, and Markham was simply asked to leave the service. Adam has never forgiven me for my part in forcing him to resign his commission, which resignation resulted in his father cutting him out of his will. After I retired from Her Majesty's Service, I accepted the position of Governor of Nairobi. Shortly after, Markham came out to Africa, to explore, so he said. I have no such delusions, however. He's but awaiting the moment when he can get even with me! His bitterness is like a disease, Heather, riddling him with its poison. He never misses a chance to provoke me, never. If he thought he could get away with it, he'd kill me without batting an eye. But he hasn't dared, to date! I have friends in high places too."

"Why are you telling me all of this?" she demanded, shaken to the core but not convinced by his tale.

"Why?" He smiled and tenderly stroked her cheek. "I think you know why, Heather. I want you to understand me, to know all there is to know about my life and the part Markham has played in it. I want no secrets between us. You see, my dearest, I want you to be my wife. Will you marry me, Heather?"

She snatched her hand from his as if burned, her thoughts in turmoil. "Marriage? But . . . this is all so unexpected, Douglas!"

"Not so very unexpected, surely?" he contradicted. "Can you honestly say you didn't know, or at least suspect, the very great affection and admiration I have for you?"

"Yes," she admitted reluctantly, "I'd suspected something of the sort, but—"

"But you were hoping that Adam would return and ask your uncle for your hand?"

"No, I . . . yes," she confessed lamely.

"He won't, you know. It's been two weeks since he left Kirkenmuir! Have you had any word from him in that time—a telegram, perhaps, or a letter?" He knew quite well that she had not, but had he not known, her crestfallen expression would have betrayed the truth. "Ah, I suspected as much! He has a return passage booked on the *Cassiopeia,* which is scheduled to leave Southampton for Africa on the twelfth of February—a little over two weeks from now. I know. I have passage booked aboard her too. He'll be on that ship, my lovely Heather. I'd wager all I possess on it!"

He took her hands and drew her to him, his handsome face eager as he gazed down into her shining, tear-filled eyes. "Forget Markham! He's not worthy of your tears. I want you, darling! I adore you! Become my wife—let me spend the rest of my life cherishing you, loving you. I would never shame or desert you. I offer you my heart and all that I have, Heather, if you'll only say you'll be mine?"

Her pulse pounded in her ears. Alarm flared in her violet eyes. "I cannot possibly decide such an important matter so quickly, Douglas. I must have time to consider your . . . proposal," she hedged.

He nodded. "You shall have it," he agreed. "But, if you honor me by accepting, we must be married very soon. You see, I leave for Africa on the twelfth of next month. If you consent to become my wife, I'll go ahead and make certain all is in order for your arrival before you join me. There is another vessel leaving for Africa in March. It is my dearest wish that my bride, my lovely Lady Heather, will be upon her!" He clasped her to him his blue eyes hungry as they roved her exquisite, pale face. "We could have a wonderful life together, Heather! There's a hospital under my jurisdiction in Nairobi that is badly in need of a skilled hand to reorganize it. With your nursing experience, you could provide that skill. We could do great things there, worthwhile things such as your father and mother did together in Africa. You would be returning to your birthplace to offer something very valuable to its people: knowledge."

A hospital! It was as if Douglas could read her heart, could see the pain that relinquishing her nursing had left, buried deep inside her. He was offering her a chance to rebuild her dreams, a little voice whispered in her ear. A hot flush swept over her. It was Adam she loved, not him! What were dreams without the man she loved to share them? No, it was Adam she wanted, wanted desperately still, with every fiber of her being! Marriage to Douglas could never be anything more

188

than a travesty, at best.

"Well?" he demanded, very much the ardent, impatient suitor.

"As I said, I cannot answer you immediately, Douglas," she said softly. "But I promise I will do so very soon. And I . . . I am deeply honored by your proposal."

He nodded. "Good. Then I shall pray each day that your answer will be the one I long to hear!"

And I will pray each day for my Adam to come back to me, she vowed silently, though to Douglas she only smiled and politely inclined her head.

Chapter Twelve

But her prayers were not answered, not that day or on those following.

The bright flame of love and trust, the torch she had carried in her heart for Adam, began, if not to dim, then at least to flicker when her spirits were at their lowest ebb. And in those dark, bitterly cold January days, her spirits were often low.

Her doubts and fears, for Adam and for herself and for their unborn child, ran frantically round and round in her mind like a mouse upon a treadmill. What should she do? Where and to whom could she turn?

There was no recourse for a young woman such as Heather, except perhaps the shelters manned by the Salvation Army, whose militant Christian volunteers, in uniform, defied public censure to offer aid to unfortunates and fallen women. *Fallen women.* I am now one of them, Heather thought bitterly, a bona-fide scarlet woman. What would scandal-hungry Annabel have thought had she known her dear but "stuffy" elder cousin could legitimately have been branded upon the forehead with a scarlet letter! The thought, however, was one which Heather did not find in the least amusing.

Worry had robbed her of both appetite and sleep these past weeks. Days of little nourishment and less rest, coming so soon after her illness, had left her noticeably thinner. Her violet eyes were shadowed with lavender. Her complexion had the pallor and translucent quality of fine porcelain. The bloom of vibrant beauty she had worn when Adam was still at Kirkenmuir was dulled, and though heartbreakingly lovely still, she was now a melancholy beauty. Aunt Elise and Annabel looked at her with loving concern as they watched her moving listlessly about Moorsedge. Countless times she would glance up to find them exchanging worried glances over her head, their eyes quickly shifting away when they saw that she had noticed them. For their sakes, she tried to act cheerfully, to smile when she felt like crying, to laugh when it seemed to do so might shatter the brittle veneer of strength she affected. The strain told. She longed to lose herself in grief, to wallow in the luxury of blessed tears, and to give way to the pain inside her, without thought for anyone's hurt but her own. One afternoon, unable any longer to stand Aunt Elise's studiedly light conversation or Annabel's carefully bright chatter, she excused herself and escaped to her room, hoping to find a haven in privacy.

But her room offered no haven this afternoon. Instead, it felt like a cage, stifling her with its warmth and its narrow confines. She felt a sudden yearning to be outdoors, in wide, open spaces. She wanted to feel a heady rush of cold air tingling and prickling her skin, to feel a bracing wind streaming through her hair while her horse thundered beneath her, galloping across the snowy heaths at breakneck speed.

Acting on impulse, she hurried to her wardrobe and flung open the door, selecting a warm green-and-black plaid skirt, a white blouse, and a long, knitted cardigan

191

that belted at the waist. She quickly changed, cramming a bright emerald tam-o'-shanter atop the dark auburn curls that hung free about her face and shoulders, and then winding a heavily fringed green plaid scarf about her throat. Pulling on her boots, she almost ran from the room and down the stairs. Haste was necessary, as was stealth. She knew without a shadow of a doubt that Aunt Elise would forbid her to go riding so soon after her illness, and she had no intention of being apprehended!

She slipped down the long, paneled hall and was about to cross the kitchen and go out through the rear door when the unmistakable sound of weeping brought her up short. It sounded as if it were coming from the coal cellar, of all places! Stepping gingerly to avoid Taffeta's fluffy, squirming kittens, now all quite mobile and able to clamber out of their basket by the fire, she crossed the flagstoned floor and flung open the cellar door. The weeping abruptly stopped. A pale face peered up at her through the sooty gloom.

"Bridie! Why, what on earth's wrong? Whatever are you doing in there?"

Loud sniffles. "Oh, mum, I'm every so sorry, aye, that I am! I didn't mean t' make so much noise. I—I were just after gettin' some coal for the drawin'-room fire, that's all, mum." She lowered her red, swollen eyes, obviously embarrassed to meet Heather's shrewd glance.

"Simply fetching coal doesn't cause such weeping, Bridie," Heather insisted. "What is it, dear? You can tell me, you know, whatever it is. I promise I won't say a word to anyone, unless you want me to?"

Her kind, caring tone proved the little scullery maid's undoing. Bridie emitted a great howl and flung her white apron up to cover her soot-streaked face.

"Oh, Miss Heather, mum, 'tis Victor an' me, aye,

it is!"

Heather nudged the distraught girl out into the kitchen, closing the cellar door in their wake. Patiently, she tugged the filled coal scuttle from the girl's clamped fingers and pressed her down into a chair.

"Now, Bridie, tell me what's worrying you, do," she urged, filling a kettle and setting it on the top of the black range to heat. "I'll make us both a nice, hot cup of tea while you talk. Now, what is all this about Victor?"

"No, no, I can't tell ye, mum, I just can't! 'Tis . . . 'tis too wicked t' tell, what with me being a good Catholic girl, an' all!"

"Bridie," Heather said sternly, "tell me, and have done with it!"

"W-well, mum," Bridie began, interspersing each word with soggy hiccups and rubbing her swollen eyes with grimy knuckles dark with coal dust, "Victor an' me, we've bin steppin' out together—courtin'—for about a year now, an', well, I do like him awful bad, mum. So, when he—when we—back in London—and now— Oh, mum, I think I'm after havin' Victor's babe!" Fresh wails ensued now that the truth was finally out.

Heather blinked. "You're having Victor's child?" she echoed stupidly. That Bridie's troubles should parallel her own astonished her.

"Aye," Bridie confessed in an enormous sob.

"And he won't marry you?"

"Well, I haven't told him yet, mum," the girl whispered, blowing her nose on her apron.

"Why not?"

Bridie shrugged. "I was frightened to. Why, he's head groom, to be sure, an' me nothin' but a scullery maid!"

"You were good enough for him to be courting for a whole year, Bridie," Heather pointed out. "Who's to say he won't jump at the chance to marry a pretty, hard-working girl like you? You must tell Victor, Bridie, and right away. At least give him the chance to have his say. He's a good man. I'm certain he won't let you down once he knows."

"Do ye really think so, mum?" Bridie asked hopefully, her eyes dry now.

"I do," Heather confirmed. "Tell him, and be sure to let me know what he says."

"But . . . but . . ."

"There's more?"

"Aye," Bridie confessed unhappily. "Bridget—her what is chambermaid over at the McGregors' place?—I told her I thought I was in the family way, an' she says the only thing t' do is t' get rid o' the babe." She fished in her apron pocket, drawing out a much-handled scrap of paper, which she handed to Heather. On it a name and an address were scribbled in a childish scrawl. "'Tis a woman who lives in Kirkenmuir," Bridie explained. "She's bin known t' help girls in trouble, she has," she added darkly.

"Help? You mean to help them lose their babies?" Heather flung herself about from the stove, where she had set the big blue teapot while the tea brewed, alarm in her eyes.

"Aye."

"Bridie, promise me you won't do anything so foolish—that you won't go to this woman. Please?" Heather implored the girl earnestly, grasping Bridie by the shoulders and squeezing so hard the maid winced. She'd seen at St. Thomas' what these old women, often well-meaning but ignorant, could do to "help" poor, frightened girls like Bridie more times than she cared to count. Butchers! "If Victor proves difficult, then come and tell me, but don't go to this Aggie creature, whatever you do. Promise me?"

"I promise," Bridie said quickly. "I—I don't think I could ha' done it anyway, mum," she confessed. "A babe's a babe, is it not, wanted or otherwise?"

Relieved, Heather nodded and poured them both hot tea, handing a sturdy mug of the steaming brew to Bridie. They sipped in silence, and Heather wondered, as she glanced at the little maid's dry-eyed but still tear-streaked face, what Bridie would say if she knew Miss Heather was in such a predicament as her own. But there was no Victor for Miss Heather to turn to. . . .

"I'll be off now, mum," Bridie said shyly when her cup was drained. "Thank ye ever so for hearin' me out an' tellin' me what t'do. Ye've been ever such a help, ye have, Miss Heather. I'm goin' to talk to Victor right away!"

"I'll go with you to the stables. After he's saddled my horse for me, you will have him all to yourself."

"Should you be ridin', mum, so soon after being sick, an' all? Ye still look a wee bit peaked t'me?"

"The fresh air will do me good," Heather declared. "Come on. Let's get it over with."

Shortly after, Heather was cantering Treacle out through the wrought-iron gates of Moorsedge. Looking back over her shoulder, she saw Victor slip his burly arm about Bridie's waist, and arm in arm, heads bent in earnest conversation, the couple made their way toward Victor's cozy quarters above the stables. Relief filled her. Bridie had found a happy ending, by the looks of it. Would she ever find hers?

She was riding up the hill toward the castle ruins before she realized the directions in which she had unconsciously turned the bay. She reined in her mount and sat there, still and quiet, staring at the crumbling gray stone walls etched darkly against the pale, wintry skies and the lavender mountains beyond, but seeing nothing.

". . . ride with me across the heath, ruined castle up ahead. . . ."

Adam's words sounded so clearly in her mind that for an eerie instant she fancied if she but turned she would see him there, astride his gray stallion, his black hair whipped by the wind, his tanned cheeks ruddy with health and vigor, his gentian eyes sparkling as he threw back his head and laughed merrily at her surprise to find him there. But no . . . Only the beautiful sweep of snow-covered heathlands lined the little glen. Beyond was the silvery gray glint of the loch. The mournful scream of a hawk high above broke into her daydreams. She flicked her head to clear it, then rode on up to the castle.

She and Annabel had often fancied the ruins were haunted, but today, as she stepped between the fallen gray stones to the arched window and gazed through it to the wintry landscape below, there was but one ghost here. The wind, searching through the broken towers and crumbling halls, bore his name to her on chill breath:

Adam . . .

Leaning back against the archway, where he had once crushed her ardently into his arms and kissed her, she gave way to her grief, letting the controlled façade she had maintained at such cost melt in a hot flood of tears that poured forth like a dam unleashed. Here she didn't have to pretend, didn't have to hide her wounds under a cloak of pride.

She sank to her knees and pressed her burning cheek against the icy stone, crouching there and sobbing as if her heart was broken, as indeed it was. She remembered the sweet, fiery weight of Adam's body as it covered hers, imagined the feather-light caress of his tanned fingers upon the curves of her aching breasts— the wild rapture that had swept her away. She remembered his loving, and her pain became a living thing, a tormenting monster that ripped and shredded and gouged yet still was not done with her.

"I have dreamed of holding you in my arms . . . of your sweet mouth beneath mine. . . ."

"I will see you again! I must! . . ."

Memories bombarded her. She hugged herself tightly and wept because Adam's arms were not holding her, because his lips did not warm her cheeks, only her own scalding tears. "Wherever you are, Adam, know that I love you," she whispered sadly. "Know that I believe in you. Dear God, hurry back to me, my darling! Tell me your love was no lie!"

How long she remained curled up there she never knew. The afternoon light faded, becoming amethyst. It was pricked by tiny points of light as the villagers of Kirkenmuir lit their lamps for the evening. Snow began to fall, drifting down about her like feathers, clinging to her hair and lashes. It was time to go back, she decided, before Aunt Elise set up a hue and cry for her.

She burrowed in the pocket of her cardigan for a handkerchief to dry her eyes, but she found none. Instead, the scrap of paper that Bridie had handed her fell out and fluttered to the ground. She picked it up and stared at the words scrawled there, and for a second, the temptation was great.

For a second.

No! The denial sounded in her head, as loud and as piercing as the scream of the hawk had been earlier. She could never take the life of the precious child she and Adam had created, from their passion if not from their love, whatever the cost. As she walked wearily back through the ruins to where her horse was tethered, she counted on her fingers, realizing with a sinking heart that she was entering her second month. Soon, it would be too late to hide the truth. She must decide what to do, and quickly.

Time was running out—and hope.

Each night for the next week, Heather paced for countless hours in her room at Moorsedge, still wondering desperately what to do. Should she run away? Take what little jewelry she possessed and sell it to give herself and her child a start somewhere else? Should she tell her aunt and uncle, and watch their trust and their pride in her wither and die? No! She could bear anything but that!

Marry Douglas, whispered a small, insistent voice inside her. *Marry him, and give your child a name. Save your family and yourself from shame and scandal!*

But she felt no love for Douglas, none whatsoever! Indeed, she fancied she could never trust herself to love again, not as she had once loved Adam—as she still loved Adam, despite everything.

This past week however, that love had become tainted with bitterness and disillusionment. She had begun to believe that it might be as Douglas had so cruelly pointed out at Heathlands Hall: Adam had only used her, toying with her affections and lying to her to bring her to his bed. Damn his very soul! She should hate him with every ounce of her being, she knew. She should. She tried to . . . but she could not.

Was there to be no escaping the hold Adam had upon her heart? Each night, each long and *empty* night, she dreamed of him, of his handsome face poised above her own, of his kisses searing her body like a brand, of the passionate tenderness of his arms which curled about her while he whispered promises of love. At such times, her body tensed and sang like a plucked string. But when she awoke, it was only the down-filled pillow she clutched so desperately to her breast. Not Adam. Dear God, never Adam! . . .

She whirled about in response to a soft rapping upon her door. Lord, it was close to midnight! Who else could be up and about at this ungodly hour?

"Who is it?" she asked, her ear pressed to the door.

"Ellen Reading, my dear. I noticed the light under your door. May I come in?"

"Of course," Heather replied, and opened the door to let the housekeeper in.

Mrs. Reading stood in the doorway, her gray hair wrapped in curling irons bound with rags, her large, square-boned body clad in a sensible dark blue dressing gown that was trimmed flamboyantly with ostrich plumes about the neck and hem, an incongruity that faintly surprised Heather, who had never suspected Mrs. Reading capable of the least frivolity in either dress or manner.

"I have endeavored, and most strenuously so, to mind my own business, Heather dear," Mrs. Reading began. She stood uncomfortably in the center of the room. "But anyone who knows you cannot help but realize that you are dreadfully unhappy. One could speculate that this is entirely due to young Captain Markham's departure . . . or one might wonder if perhaps there is something else, something more, that is troubling you?" She strode across the room and took Heather by the shoulders, turning her firmly to face her. "Forgive me if I am overstepping the bounds of my position and our friendship, but is something else wrong? Believe me, my dear child, there is nothing you cannot tell me, your Ready. I will keep any confidence you should choose to share. On your dear mother's grave, I swear it!"

"There's nothing wrong, Mrs. Reading, other than my upset over Adam leaving," Heather lied. "Please, go back to bed, and don't worry on my account. I'll be fine." She forced a smile.

"Do not presume that I'm a fool, Heather," Mrs. Reading said sternly, her lips pursed. "I have watched you grow from an infant. Twenty years, Heather! My dear, I fancy I can read your expressions almost as well as I can read my own thoughts. You're lying to me, aren't you?"

"No! Of course not!" Heather protested.

Mrs. Reading clasped Heather's face firmly in her hands. "Look into my eyes, child, and tell me that again," she insisted stubbornly.

Heather broke away, a shudder running through her. "I can't!" she whispered. "Please, go away!"

"Then there *is* something more? Oh, I knew it! My dear, trust me. I want to help you!" Mrs. Reading cried in an anguished voice.

"Very well," Heather whispered, her defenses falling because of her desperate need to confide in someone. "I'll tell you."

She turned away from the housekeeper and stared steadfastly into the fire. "I'm carrying Captain Markham's child, Ready." Across the room, the housekeeper gasped. "And last week Lord Dennison asked me to marry him. I'm so confused. I feel nothing for Douglas, nothing at all, but—"

"But you wonder if you should marry him to give your child a name," Mrs. Reading finished for her.

"Yes!" Heather confessed. "It would be wrong of me, terribly wrong, I know, and there's no telling how Douglas would react once he learned the truth, but—"

"How would he learn it?"

"Why, the child would be born too early for him to have fathered it, do you not see?"

"Some babes are born early, that's all Douglas would ever need to know. He can't be certain the child

200

is not his, not once you are wed and the marriage has been . . . consummated."

Heather drew a deep breath. "No, it would never work."

"It has worked before, who knows how often! These are hard times for men and women who love deeply and passionately and fully, as you loved your Adam," Mrs. Reading said wistfully. "I would be willing to speculate that more babes than you would imagine are born eight months after their parents' wedding day and are passed off as prematurely born. Douglas loves you, does he not? He'll believe what he wants to believe. Marry him, Heather, and solve all your problems! I cannot stand to see you grow gaunt and haggard with worry and despair."

"We are to go to Africa if I accept his proposal, Ready," Heather said thoughtfully. "He plans to leave on the twelfth of next month, to go ahead and prepare everything for my arrival. I would follow him at the end of the month, as his wife."

"Then marry him! You have everything to gain, my dear, as well as a solution to your immediate problems. He is an attractive man, with position and wealth, and he loves you. You could do far worse than accept his proposal."

"But what of Adam? What if he should come back, what if there is some . . . some perfectly acceptable reason for his departure?"

"You're grasping at straws, my dear girl," Mrs. Reading said gently. "Adam has been gone an entire month. He could certainly have sent a letter or a telegram by now—if he wanted to. Surely you realize that?"

Miserable, Heather nodded. Her slender shoulders slumped. "Yes. Yes, you're right. A part of me knows it quite well. It's just that—that another part of me refuses to admit I can have been so terribly wrong about him!"

"That is the burden a trusting and loyal heart places upon one, my dear. Accept that your trust in him was misplaced, and look forward, never back. Forget Adam. Build yourself a new life out of the ruins of the old, a better life!"

Heather's jaw came up. Determination swept through her. Mrs. Reading was right, of course she was! Tears solved nothing. She must take a firm hold on the reins of her life, and steer it in the direction she wished to go. She could do far worse than marry Douglas. He loved her, did he not? And there was the hospital. She was needed there. He had said so. There would again be a purpose in her life. Three purposes, in effect, she amended. Her child, her husband, and the hospital. It all sounded so perfect, the pieces coming neatly together like parts of a wooden jigsaw. Her shoulders slumped. Her determination dwindled. Yes, *too* perfect, considering there was a missing piece: her heart.

She drew a deep breath. "You're right, Ready. I've been over it a thousand times or more myself. Marrying Douglas would solve everything. And who knows, perhaps in time I would grow to love him as he loves me. But . . . I can't marry him!"

"Can't?"

"Can't, or won't, whichever you prefer," Heather said heavily. "It wouldn't be fair to Douglas, or to me or my child, not when I feel the way I do about Adam. Oh, Ready, what's wrong with me? I should hate him. But even knowing how he took . . . took advantage of me, used me, I still love him so!"

Ellen gave a helpless shrug. She went across the room and took Heather in her arms, stroking her hair as she hugged her fiercely, tears misting her own gray eyes now. "I know, my dear girl, I know. Dry your eyes.

202

We'll think of something else, you'll see. Hush, now, hush, my sweet, dear child."

In the distance, the clock in the tower of St. James's church, in nearby Kirkenmuir, struck midnight, ushering in the twenty-fifth day of January. Adam had been gone a month.

Chapter Thirteen

"Psst! . . . Yes, you!"

The lad turned around, eyebrows cocked inquiringly. *"Moi, m'sieu?"*

"Yes. Come here, will you?"

"But why, *m'sieu?"* The innocently blank expression grew crafty. "You are a prisoner, and *très dangereux,* are you not?"

I am indeed. And getting more dangerous by the minute, you little rogue! Adam thought, muffling a heated curse. "Nonsense," he said calmly, no sign of his irritation showing. "I'm no more dangerous than you! Come over here, by the window."

The boy edged warily closer, suspicion bright in his dark eyes.

"That's better," Adam coaxed, smiling as he looked down at the lad through the bars but feeling like a damned ape in a zoological garden. "How would you like to earn some money?"

"How much money?"

"Fifty francs, if you do what I tell you."

"Only fifty?" the lad jeered. "You waste my time, *m'sieu! Au 'voir!"*

"Wait! A hundred, then?"

"That depends on what it is you want me to do? I want no trouble with *les gendarmes.* My uncle, he is Inspector Raoul Poirier, yes?" The boy spat, wiping his mouth on the threadbare sleeve of his jacket.

"You'll have no trouble, I swear it. Not if you do as I ask. Just send a telegram for me, and the fifty francs is yours."

"The boy scowled. "You said a hundred!"

"All right, blast you, a hundred!" Adam hastily amended, thinking he had not underestimated the lad. "Will you do it?"

"Very well. Where is the message?"

"Here." He handed a piece of rumpled paper through the window to the boy.

"Bien. And the money?"

Adam winced inwardly. This was where it got difficult! "No money until after you deliver it. Do you think I'm a fool?" he said gruffly.

The boy snorted. "And do you think I am, *m'sieu?"* He crossed his hands over his chest. "No money, no telegram. You pay me half now, and half when the job is done."

Adam sighed. Poirier's relatives were as crooked as he. But, he reflected, he was counting on that. "And where would I get money, locked in here?"

The boy grinned slyly, and Adam was fleetingly reminded of the shrunken heads he'd once seen impaled on sharpened poles out in Africa. "That's your problem, *oui?"* He turned to leave, dragging his shabbily shod feet across the mud flats as he went.

"Go on with you then, damn you!" Adam roared. "I had you figured for a likely lad, eager to make a few extra francs here and there, but it's easy to see you don't have the guts for it. Your loss, my young friend. Your loss!" He turned away from the window, sat down on his bunk, and waited.

After a few moments, which to Adam seemed like hours, a reedy voice chirruped indignantly from below the window, "I have courage, *m'sieu!* If you were only out here, instead of in there where I cannot get at you, I would show you just how much courage I have!"

"Talk is cheap, *petit garçon,*" Adam retorted mockingly. "You'll have to do better than that if you want to prove yourself to me." He strolled back to the window. "Perhaps take a chance?"

"Explain yourself."

"As you said, I have no money to pay you . . . or to send the telegram. But the man to whom I wish to send it has a great deal of money. Get it to him, and I'll see that you get the hundred francs I promised you, plus the money for the telegram, and more."

"Much more?"

"Much! Say, five hundred francs for your trouble?"

The boy gulped. His eyes widened. "It must be a very important message, *m'sieu!*"

Adam nodded. "It is. Five hundred francs worth. Now, isn't that enough to take a chance for?"

"*Oui!*" The lad gasped the word out. "Give me the message."

Adam did so, and the boy raced off.

Lying on his bunk, staring up at the damp ceiling, Adam wondered if his bid for freedom would work. Lord, he hoped so! Over the past few days, all other hope for speedy release from this blasted holding cell had diminished. In answer to his demands that he be formally charged with whatever crimes he'd been accused of, he had received only double-talk.

"Who's paying you off, Poirier?" he'd demanded finally. "Who is it that has you in his pockets, eh?" He'd lunged forward, bent on taking Inspector Poirier by the throat and dragging the truth from him by force, but two of Poirier's men had pulled him off before he

206

could do any damage.

The inspector had only smiled and shaken his head, his crafty black eyes sliding uncomfortably away from Adam's unwavering glare. "There are no payoffs here, *m'sieu!* My department is clean. Now, your violent temper has got you into serious trouble once already, *non?*" he'd said mildly. "Take my advice and remain calm, *m'sieu,* or it will be the worse for you. The wheels of justice move slowly here in France. Be patient, and your case will be reviewed in good time. Constable Lapin, take the prisoner back to his cell!"

But Adam was convinced he was right. He'd seen Captain Rouget of the ferryboat *La Mouette* in the inspector's office on several occasions, had even seen money change hands. Whoever had him bundled into the hamper had paid off the captain, he was sure. And Rouget, in his turn, was lining the pockets of the inspector, but for whom and for what reason, he had not the faintest idea. Frustration roiled through him. Damn! It infuriated him to have to pace back and forth here day after day, trapped, knowing that back in Scotland, Heather must think something terrible had happened to him. Thank God she was the sweet, loyal woman she was! She'd fret, but she'd be there, waiting for him. That knowledge helped to keep his flagging spirits up, and it gave him the determination necessary to set his plan into action.

"Soon, my sweet. Soon, all going well," he murmured.

He tormented himself as he lay on the bunk in the freezing cell, imagining her lovely body, warm and rosy with desire, pressed ardently to his. The warm, woman-fragrance of her flesh, the faint floral scent of her tumbling red hair, came full and sweet, to his nostrils. The sensation of creamy flesh trembling beneath his fingertips as he loved her was palpable. God! The memory of her filled him with love and throbbing desire! He groaned aloud at the thought of the anxiety she must be enduring now, but he knew for the time being he was powerless to end her misery.

"Come through for me, lad," he muttered to the dripping ceiling, "or I'll wring your greedy little neck!"

Had he but known it, the lad was doing just that!

"Uncle!"

"Go away." Julian's uncle, Inspector Raoul Poirier of the Calais Police Department, did not so much as glance up at his nephew. Silently, he cursed the hand of fate that had left his sister-in-law a widow and had made him the guardian of both her and her brat. He continued his paperwork.

"But, Uncle, I—"

"Julian, I told you to go away! Can't you see I have work to do? *Allez! Vite!*" An ink-stained hand jabbed irritably in Julian's direction, and the boy yearned to crane his head forward and sink his teeth into those stubby fingers!

He pouted, his lower lip jutting out several inches beyond the upper one. "Very well, Uncle," he said quietly. "I will not show you the telegram the prisoner gave me to send." He turned abruptly and started to speed toward the door.

It took a few seconds for the boy's words to sink in. When they did, Poirier's head jerked up as if yanked by a leash. "What? What did you say? Julian! Come back here, at once!"

"Oui, Uncle Raoul?" The boy turned, his expression guileless and bland, dark eyes shining through his straggly thatch of dirty black hair.

"What was it you said, Nephew?" his uncle demanded in careful tones.

208

Julian sighed. "I said that the prisoner had given me a message."

"What message? Where? And how?"

"I have it here, in my pocket," Julian muttered. "It's quite safe. The Englishman passed it to me, through the window."

"Let me see."

Julian made no move to hand the all-important scrap of paper to his uncle. "He promised me five hundred francs for sending it," he said pointedly.

"Poof!" Raoul Poirier disclaimed. "And where would he get five hundred francs in that cell? His pockets were empty when we brought him in here. He lied to you, Julian, you little fool. Give it to me."

"He didn't lie! He said the man who was waiting for the telegram would pay me when he came here."

"Telegram?"

"Oui. He wanted me to send it for him. I consented, for a price. But I knew that it was my duty to show it to you first, Uncle."

"But of course," Poirier agreed, fighting the urge to lift Julian by the seat of his pants and soundly paddle his scrawny derrière. He forced a smile, that made him resemble a hungry tiger instead of a benign uncle. "Very good, Julian, my boy. We will make a good little gendarme of you yet! Now, the paper, yes?"

His nephew drew the paper from his pocket and seemed about to hand it to the inspector when he hesitated, drawing back. Poirier, whose hand had come out eagerly for the paper, muffled a curse.

"What now?"

"The money, Uncle. Maman and I, we could do many things with five hundred francs, *oui?"*

"How much, Julian?" his uncle demanded, resigned.

"A hundred francs?" Julian quoted hopefully.

"Fifty."

"Seventy-five. Not a sou less!" Julian insisted stubbornly, his bright eyes hard and greedy now. Seventy-five francs in the hand was far better than a promise of five hundred. Grownups, he had learned long ago, were not to be trusted to keep their promises.

"Very well, seventy-five, you little shark!" Raoul barked. He reached into his pocket, withdrew several ten-franc notes and a five. "Now, *give it to me!*"

The boy reached for the money, simultaneously dropping the paper to the floor. He knew his uncle only too well, knew how swiftly those stubby fingers could reach out to cuff an ear or tweak painfully at an earlobe. His fingers closed about the money and he was off, a blue streak erupting through the door of the police station, leaving dear Uncle Raoul to grovel on the floor for the precious paper like a beggar after coins on the Champs Élysées.

"Merde!" Poirier muttered. "One day, *cher* Julian, you will go too far!" But his livid expression faded as he smoothed out the crumpled note, written in lead pencil on the white paper that bread came wrapped in, he noted. As he read the contents, his face became tight with concentration, then revealed realization and finally dread. It was, as Julian had hinted, a telegram— addressed to the Prefecture of Police himself, in Paris! Prickles of foreboding raced down Raoul's spine as he digested the import of the words:

INFILTRATION ACCOMPLISHED STOP EVIDENCE SUPPORTS INFORMATION RECEIVED FROM INFORMANT STOP WIDESPREAD CORRUPTION AT LOCAL LEVEL STOP RECOMMEND IMMEDIATE ACTION STOP SIGNED ORCHID STOP

"Mon dieu!" Poirier breathed, his mouth suddenly

dry. They were on to him! He jumped up from the desk and paced. "Lapin!" he roared. "Here!"

Constable Lapin came at a run. "Inspector?"

"Read this!" Poirier barked, hurling the note at the gendarme. He waited impatiently while Lapin read it. "Well?" he demanded, drying damp palms on the immaculately pressed leg of his uniform trousers.

"Who is Orchid, *m'sieu?*" the constable asked, a puzzled frown wreathing his dull-wit's features.

"Our prisoner, back there. The Englishman!"

"Orchid?" Lapin chuckled. "What a name, eh, *mon brave!*"

"It's nothing to laugh at, you stupid fool!" Poirier ranted. "It's obviously a code name! He's been sent here by the Prefecture of Police, don't you see, planted here in Calais to observe and report on the conduct of our department!"

"Non, non, m'sieu, you are wrong!" Lapin disagreed. "Captain Mouette paid us to keep him here, do you not recall?" He grinned. "And paid very we—"

"Exactly!" Poirier cried, exasperated by his stupidity "He *paid* us! It was all part of the plan—don't you understand—to see if we would rise to the bait! And, *mon dieu,* we did! Rouget is a part of it too. We are in grave trouble, Lapin, very grave trouble!"

"Non, non, m'sieu," Lapin disclaimed, waving hands that resembled hocks of ham about in the air, "I beg to point out that it is *you* who are in grave trouble, not I, since I did not receive one sou of the money, if you recall?"

The police inspector laughed scornfully. "True, *mon ami.* But did you not take it upon yourself to lay into the man with your baton when we arrested him? Ah, that's better! Now you do not look so certain of yourself, *hein?*" Lapin's usually florid face was now the color of cheesecloth. "We must think, and quickly,"

Poirier muttered, pacing back and forth and fingering the curling ends of his waxed mustache agitatedly as he did so.

Several minutes passed before he exclaimed, "Ah! I have it!"

Lapin looked up eagerly. "You have? What do we do?"

"We must see to it that the prisoner escapes, *mon ami,*" Poirier murmured, his expression thoughtful.

"Be he will only send the telegraph himself then, will he not?"

"I did not say he would remain free, fool! We will see to it that he escapes . . . and then he is no longer the responsibility of our department! Who is to blame us if an escaped prisoner is unfortunately killed shortly after he escapes, is perhaps found floating in the harbor. You understand my meaning?"

Lapin did. He grinned slyly. *"Oui, monsieur l'inspecteur,* I understand very well!"

The door swung open, and Adam glanced up as Constable Lapin entered the cell carrying a tray of food.

"Here you are. Don't eat it all at once, eh, *Anglais!"*

Adam eyed the bowl of greasy, lukewarm soup and the hunk of dry black bread, but said nothing.

"What's the matter, *Anglais?"* Lapin jeered. "Does ze cat have your tongue, per'aps?" He shrugged. "No matter." Pointedly jingling the ring of keys in his fist, he strolled about the cell, glancing out through the barred window, lifting the tick mattress to peer beneath. "Just a little precaution, you understand, to see if you have any hidden weapons, *non? Mon dieu!* It smells like a pigsty in here!"

"Then leave, Lapin, and take the stench with you,"

212

Adam retorted.

Lapin glowered. "Pah! Poirier has grown soft. If not for him, I would teach you some manners!"

Adam swung off the bunk and strolled toward the constable, wearing a deceptively lazy grin, "Really?" he urged, all ears. "And how, exactly, would you do that, friend?"

Belatedly, Lapin remembered his inspector's warning that the prisoner was really an informant for the commissioner, and quickly backed down, visions of charges dancing in his head. "Never mind how," he muttered, beating a retreat toward the door. "Just shut up and eat!"

The heavy door swung shut, but, as Adam had speculated might happen, it was not locked behind the gendarme.

"Markham, my friend, I believe you've done it!" he congratulated himself, a slow grin spreading from his lips to his gentian eyes. Devilment twinkled in them. Young Julian had run true to form, as had his uncle. He rubbed his chin thoughtfully. But what now? Obviously, he was expected to escape, but what might Poirier have up his sleeve for the "informant" of the Prefecture of Police then? Something not too pleasant, he surmised, fighting the urge to let out a great roar of laughter as he let himself out of the cell, and slipped down the short hallway to the office.

It was, as he had anticipated, quite empty. No doubt Lapin and his inspector were waiting for him beyond the door, pressed up against a dark alley in their inimitable bumbling way. Well, he vowed grimly, they'll have a long wait! They expected me to sneak out the door and barrel straight into their arms, so I'll do the last thing they expect! He cast about him for a suitable tool, finding it in a gendarme's stout baton, or billy club, that hung from a thong on the wall. "Perfect!" he

213

murmured softly. "And rather fitting, somehow, *oui,* Poirier?"

Quickly, he turned back to the cell he had just left and, using the baton as a lever and exerting a bit of muscle and sweat, he forced the bars on the window, clambered up and through it, and dropped to the muddy ground outside. Free now, he dusted himself off and glanced about him to get his bearings. It had worked like a charm! Before Poirier and his cohort realized they had been duped and thought to check the cell, he'd be halfway across the Channel.

"I'm as good as home, Heather, my love!" he murmured under his breath as he sprinted across the mud flats toward the harbor, where the masts of several little vessels made a fretwork of spars against the pale blue, winter sky.

"Come in!" Heather called in answer to the soft rapping at her door. "Oh, yes, Bridie, what is it?" she asked as the little Irish maid, in a crisply starched skirt, whisked in.

"The master sent me to fetch you, mum," she said, the words coming out in a rush. "He said as how you're to go down to his study, if ye will?"

"Why would Uncle Jamie want to see me?" she wondered aloud.

"Well, mum, 'tis not my place to be after sayin' things I shouldn't but I couldn't help overhearin' Carmichael tell Cook that Lord Dennison were here awhile ago, an'—an' askin' fer your hand, mum!" Bridie beamed. "Now, mum, ain't that somethin'?"

"Indeed it is," Heather acknowledged, her heart sinking. "Please tell my uncle that I will join him shortly."

Bridie bobbed a curtsy. "Right you are, mum!" she

agreed perkily.

Heather smiled despite the despondency Bridie's news had stirred inside her. "How are the wedding plans going, Bridie? Have you and Victor set a date yet?"

"Aye, mum, we have, t' be sure. We're t' tie the knot on Valentine's Day." A pretty blush suffused her country-fresh complexion. "I'm ever so happy, mum, an' my Victor, why, he's like a dog with two tails, he is, and waggin' both!"

"I'm glad to hear it—and that everything has worked out well for you, Bridie."

Recalling the gossip she'd heard in the kitchens that the young Captain had promised to ask for Miss Heather, and then up and run out on her, Bridie nodded soberly. "Aye, mum, it has. An'—beggin' yer pardon, mum—I'm hopin' an' prayin' it'll be the same for you."

"Thank you," Heather acknowledged distantly. Bridie curtsied again and left.

Heather took a seat before her dressing table and took up a brush, stroking it through the long, fiery ringlets that spilled down over her shoulder onto the lace collar of her gray morning gown. What answer, she wondered, had Uncle Jamie given to Douglas' request? Approval, no doubt. After all, what was there to disapprove? Douglas was a personable young man, sound in wind and limb, from an old, moneyed and, furthermore, titled, family. What more could any girl possibly ask for, she thought bitterly, glaring at her reflection in the mirror. A wealthy Douglas bird-in-the-hand was worth two heartless, penniless Adam Markham birds-in-the-bush, after all! Adam . . . The very sound of his name seemed to set her teeth on edge these days. She sternly appraised her reflection, irritated by the pallid, defeated-looking creature that

215

stared wanly back.

"It's over, you little fool!" she told that silly, love-sick girl she saw. "Finished! Done with! Put him out of your heart! He only used you, don't you see that, even now? Wake up and face facts, Heather Cameron. Think of yourself. Think of your child. Do what's best for the baby, if not for yourself." The girl in the mirror nodded.

Uncle Jamie smiled as she entered the study. He was pouring two glasses of porter as she crossed the room toward him, and he paused as she rose on tiptoe to kiss his cheek.

"Good morning, Uncle! You weren't at breakfast?"

"No, my dear. I had a visitor." Sandy head cocked to one side, he eyed his niece thoughtfully. Somehow, the fragile, melancholy air that had clung about her like funeral crepe these past weeks was gone this morning. Though she still appeared less than her usual self, there was a resoluteness, a strength about her now, and that encouraged him to believe she might receive his news with other than a point-blank refusal.

"A visitor, Uncle?" she echoed, wrinkling her brow in a puzzled frown, and letting the dear, sweet man enjoy his little surprise.

"Indeed. Young Lord Dennison was here! Rode all the way from Heathlands to speak with me at this early hour on a matter of some importance." His blue eyes twinkled. "Aren't you curious, lass?"

"Of course!" Heather agreed, laughing. "Won't you tell me now what this is all about, Uncle, and stop being so mysterious?"

Her uncle chuckled. "Well, my girl, it would appear the young earl has become quite smitten with Miss Heather Cameron! He asked me for your hand, lass, aye, and very prettily too, setting all his cards on the table. He told me that he's rather more than comfortably off, and that he can provide you with a fine home and all the little luxuries you've been used to, and then some. Furthermore, lass, and what's more t' the point, he told me that he loves you, and that he'd confessed as much to you. He said you'd promised to give him an answer very soon? I couldn't fault him, I must admit. He's done well for himself, Heather. Despite a father who bullied and beat him at every turn in his childhood, and a mother who was far too spineless and clinging, I feared, to raise a son alone after Andrew Dennison passed on, he's grown into a fine young man. You could do a lot worse than marry Douglas, child." He watched her face, but there was not so much as a flicker of change in her expression as he expounded Douglas' virtues. "Well? Have you nothing to say, lass?" He all but held his breath as he impatiently awaited her answer.

She walked across the room to the French windows, a graceful if grave figure in gray velvet and lace. For a few moments, she simply stood there as if entranced by the view, her violet eyes distant as she gazed up the glen toward the ruins of the castle, outlined against the misty morning sky. Then she gave a little shrug, as if to rid herself of some best-forgotten memory, and turned back to face him. She was, he saw with relief, smiling.

"I have a great deal to say, Uncle," she murmured, and there was a gently teasing light in her eyes now," but I believe you are only truly interested in one thing, so I will say it and have done with it! You may tell Lord Dennison that I am honored by his proposal, and having given the matter my utmost consideration, I would be happy to become his wife."

"You would?" His eyes lit up. "Well, I'll be! This is cause for celebration, is it not? I'll pour another glass or two, lass, while you go and fetch Elise and Annabel in here to join us. Och, 'tis a toast we'll be drinking today, my bonny, aye, that it is—to the loveliest bride Moorsedge has ever seen!"

The beaming smile on her uncle's ruddy face almost made the pretense worthwhile, Heather thought numbly as she went in search of her aunt and her cousin. Almost . . .

Chapter Fourteen

Moorsedge huddled like an old gray she-wolf under the blizzard's onslaught, moaning as the wind infiltrated her hallways and rooms, and whistled down her chimneys. Window frames rattled in ancient protest. Timbers and floorboards creaked. Towering pines bowed low before the howling white monster that piled up about their trunks and flung their needled branches hither and thither.

But inside the Hall, fires crackled merrily in every hearth, defying the bitter weather outside, and velvet draperies, securely drawn and fastened, kept in the heat. In the servants' hall old Shelagh, the cook, nodded off beside the hearth over her Fairisle knitting, and Carmichael, in the butler's pantry, took an extra nip of his master's finest brandy to keep out the cold, his old gray head nodding. In a warm bed above the stables, Bridie snuggled up to her brawny Victor, glad of her sweetheart's square-boned warmth and happy not to be in her own cramped quarters in the back attic, which was freezing cold in winter.

Heather stretched sleepily in her cozy leather chair beside the fire in the drawing room, yawning as she glanced at the clock. Almost midnight. She had fallen asleep over her book. She smiled ruefully. She doubted she would be passing her nights reading, had it been Adam she had wed, instead of Douglas. But it *is* Douglas you have wed, Heather, insisted the voice of her conscience, and she sighed. Yes, Douglas was her husband now, though it was hard to believe, and even harder to accept.

They had been married a week ago, just eight days after he had proposed to her. The service had been performed by Rory Markham in St. James's church in the little village of Kirkenmuir. There had been no time to have a new bridal gown made so she had worn Aunt Elise's, brought out from a trunk in the attic where it had been stored all these years, between layers of black tissue to prevent the ecru-colored silk from discoloring. Her cousin Annabel, Heather's only attendant, had looked glorious in a green velvet gown trimmed with fur. Her fiancé, Anthony Winchester, had been Douglas' best man, for Douglas was an only child, with no brothers to stand up for his nuptials.

It had been a bitterly cold February morning, and snowflakes had drifted down about her in the cobbled churchyard, alighting like frosted feathers upon her heavy lace veil, on its trim of cream satin roses and pearls, and upon her bouquet of white chrysanthemums and the rosettes made of white ribbon. Victor, smartly attired in claret-colored livery, had stood, beaming and stiffly at attention, while Uncle Jamie handed her down from the coach. No doubt he'd been thinking about Bridie and about his own wedding day the following week. It had seemed that only minutes later she had been turning to look up into Douglas' eyes as the minister pronounced them man and wife. Douglas had lifted the veil that hid her lovely, pale face and had kissed her. As he did so, the bells in the gray stone tower had pealed a joyous carillon. In celebration of their marriage, it rang out over the glens and heaths, and could be heard by the servants at distant Moorsedge. But there had been no joy in Heather's heart. Despite her radiantly beautiful appearance and the dazzling smile she wore, she felt it had turned to ice!

A wedding breakfast, as sumptuous and elegant as only Aunt Elise, bless her, could arrange in so brief a time, had followed, and then Douglas had bade her a tender farewell, expressing his impatience for her to join him in Nairobi.

"I cannot tell you how it pains me to leave you, my precious Heather," he had whispered, "without so much as a single night to show you how very much I adore you. But there will be other nights, my love— many, many nights. Think of those nights yet to come while we're apart, my darling!"

She had accepted his proposal so late that he had warned her he would have to leave immediately following the reception if he was to reach Southampton and the *Cassiopeia* before the vessel embarked. But her immediate relief that she would be spared the wedding night for a few weeks, at least, had swiftly been replaced by near panic. *You little goose!,* she had said to herself. She'd married Douglas primarily to give her child a name, had she not? Then she must somehow engineer it so that Douglas would have every reason to suppose he was, indeed, the father of her child once her condition became apparent. In short, she must seduce her husband before he left for the station. There was little time to lose!

He had made his excuses to their guests and had retired to a guest room at Moorsedge to change from the handsome gray top hat and tails he had worn so dashingly for their wedding. When Heather had seen him mount the stairs, she had quickly disengaged herself from Squire McGregor's wife, who was still

221

gushing out congratulations between tears and ineffectual dabbings at her reddened nose with a tiny handkerchief. She had followed him upstairs, her heart beating so erratically and loudly that she was certain he would be able to hear it. At the doorway to the guest room, her resolve had almost failed her and she'd hesitated for several moments, hand poised to knock, before taking a deep breath and rapping upon it.

"Come in!" Douglas had ordered from beyond the door.

Her palm suddenly moist upon the doorknob, she had done so.

"Ah, Heather. What is it you want, my dear?" he'd asked.

"Want?" She'd given a nervous little laugh that even to her ears had sounded forced. "Why nothing, Douglas!" she'd murmured. "I was simply wondering if perhaps . . . perhaps you needed some help . . . with your packing?"

"It's all been taken care of, my dear. Nothing for you to worry your pretty head over. Glover is quite efficient, aren't you, Glover?"

"Aye, that I am, sir. At all manner of things," a coarse voice had replied.

Belatedly, she'd realized that Douglas' valet-cum-general-factotum was in the small dressing room that opened off the bedroom, vigorously brushing down his master's coat, and they were not alone as she'd thought.

The pair had chuckled as if over some shared joke that Heather had no part in, making her feel the outsider. Heat and color had rushed to her face, and momentarily she'd been at a loss for words. Douglas, with a sensitivity to her moods that had surprised and pleased her, seemed aware that she'd wanted to speak with him alone, and took action accordingly.

"That's all for the time being, Harry," he'd told the

horrible little man. "Leave us, will you?" Harry Glover had left, giving Heather a bold leer that would have warranted instant dismissal from her uncle's staff but to which Douglas paid no mind.

"It . . . it was a lovely wedding, wasn't it?" she'd commented nervously, unpinning her heavy lace veil and draping it over the tallboy.

"Very." Eyes hooded, he watched her cross the room, noted the way her hands seemed to flutter aimlessly about, as if she were at a loss as to what to do with them. "You seem agitated, my dear?"

"Too much champagne and excitement, I believe," she confessed, managing a tremulous smile and feeling as if she'd swoon with fright at any second. "Perhaps I should sit down for a moment?"

"Of course!" He'd hurried to her side, the very picture of the concerned bridegroom, and taken her elbow and gently pressed her down onto the bed. The contact of his cool, slim fingers upon her arm had almost sent her flying across the room, but she'd forced her emotions under control and had allowed him to settle her comfortably, arranging the voluminous skirts of her bridal gown about her.

"Thank you. That's much better. Won't . . . won't you sit beside me, just for a little while?" Her dark lashes had swept up as she'd gazed beseechingly into his handsome face, and in an unconsciously graceful gesture, she had reached out to smooth back the lock of pale hair that fell forward over his brow. "I know you must be leaving soon, but I'd hoped we might have a few quite moments together, before you did so?" Her voice had trembled.

He had sat beside her, slipping his arm about her shoulders and drawing her against his chest. "Then you shall have them, my dear. How could I deny my lovely bride anything she asked?" He'd grasped her gently by

223

the chin and tilted her face up to his. "You're extraordinarily beautiful! You know that, don't you, my darling?" His sky-blue eyes had roved over her face, lingering on the loveliness of her eyes, dark pools of shimmering amethyst set in an exquisite heart-shaped frame. His possessiveness had been blatantly obvious. "And all that beauty is mine!" he'd added softly, as if to stress what was already so evident.

There had been a trace of something hard and ruthless in his tone. It had disturbed her, but she had decided the edge was caused by the iron control he was exercizing upon his emotions. Surely he must desire her, loving her as he professed to do?

With trembling fingers, she had reached up and plucked the ivory combs and pins from her hair, giving her head a little shake to loosen it. Dark-flame tresses had tumbled down past her shoulders in fiery cascades, vivid and glorious against the satin pallor of her gown. "Douglas, I—" she'd begun huskily, her eyes meeting his.

There had been no doubt about what she'd intended to say in Douglas' mind. It had seemed quite obvious that she was endeavoring to tell him she wanted him! But before she'd been able to do so, he had silenced her with a finger across her lips.

"I know!" Smiling, he had nodded. "Ah, yes, I know only too well! You don't have to tell me what it is you're feeling. Believe me, my dearest, I feel the same! But"— he glanced pointedly at the clock upon the bureau—"I regret that time is against us."

He'd pulled her to him and kissed her full on the lips, one hand cupping the soft fullness of her breast as he did so. With satisfaction, he felt the sudden quick intake of her breath, the quiver that swept through her body, pressed hesitantly to his, as his fingers had fondled a sensitive nipple. Even through her clothing, the impudent crest had hardened, thrusting upward to meet his touch. *So easy,* he'd thought, *so damned easy!* Women are no more complex than the simplest machines. Press the right buttons, pull the right levers, and they respond on cue. It was almost laughable. "Now, my delicious little wife"—he had breathed the words against her burning cheek—"I must, regrettably, be on my way."

"Not yet, please?" she had implored him, her fingers digging into his sleeve. "I couldn't . . . couldn't bear it if you left me now!"

He had disentangled her fingers and kissed her hand, saying simply, "I must!" before quickly striding from the room.

Crestfallen and alone, she had fallen back upon the bed and stared bleakly up at the ceiling. She'd failed! Oh, Lord, she'd failed! How on earth could she hope to convince Douglas that he was the father of her child now—a child that would be born only seven months after their wedding day! Yet despite her awareness of her situation, the fear that had been uppermost in her mind was soon outweighed by enormous relief that her new husband, in his haste to be gone, had not taken her.

Under the circumstances, it had been decided that Heather would remain with her aunt and uncle at Moorsedge until it was time for her to follow Douglas to Africa in a fortnight. There seemed little point in her removing herself and her wardrobe to Heathlands Hall to be with Douglas' mother for so short a period of time. She was vastly relieved about that! Despite what Douglas had told her regarding his mother's delight about their forthcoming marriage, Lady Winifred Dennison had seemed very possessive of her handsome, only son on the few brief occasions they had met, and not at all delighted by the prospect of his taking a bride! So lacking in delight was she, in fact, that she had pleaded a migraine on their wedding day, and had not so much as put in an appearance at her son's wedding.

There was no way out now. She was Lady Heather Dennison, Douglas' wife, like it or not, she acknowledged with a rueful frown. I must try to make the best of the situation, she decided firmly. He knew that she and Adam had been . . . close. He had accepted it. She owed it to Douglas to be a good wife to him in return for his patience and understanding, and she owed it to her aunt and uncle to do so, for their love and caring over the years. She *must* not let them down, not when they were so delighted with the dazzling marriage she had made, and with a man of whom they wholeheartedly approved.

The clock struck the hour. Midnight! High time she made her way to bed! She rose and extinguished the lamps, then pulled the bellrope to summon Carmichael to bank the fire for the night before gathering her dressing robe about her and making her way out into the hall. Aunt Elise, Uncle Jamie, and Annabel and her Tony had gone to Squire and Mrs. McGregor's residence in Kirkenmuir for supper and bridge. They had sent Victor back earlier that evening with the coach and the news that they would pass the night at the Squire's, on account of the blizzard.

Lord, it is freezing out here, she thought with a shiver as she headed for the curving staircase that led upstairs. She had just placed her foot upon the bottom tread when there was a loud hammering at the main door. Who on earth could that be, at such a late hour?

Startled, she waited, expecting the butler to answer it. But Carmichael did not. He was fast asleep, perched upon a stool in the pantry, brandy fumes rising from him along with his snores.

The hammering continued, coupled with loud, angry shouts. Perhaps her aunt and uncle had braved the blizzard after all? She hurried back the way she had come, and unbolted the lock.

The sight that met her eyes when she flung open the door drained the blood from her face. Upon the threshold, snow swirling in a blinding frenzy all about him, stood Adam.

His heavy cape was crusted over with white flakes, and his curling black hair was wet and matted with still more of them. But it was his blazing gentian eyes that held her frozen to the spot! They were so filled with fury they radiated a crackling electrical charge that stung her with shocking heat as he glowered down at her.

"Damn you!" he flung at her, stepping into the hall and slamming the door like thunder in his wake. In two swift strides, he was upon her, just inches away, giving her no time to gather her wits. *"Damn you!"* he breathed again, more softly this time, and she flinched under the jealous fury of his tone. "What madness possessed you to marry that bastard! Answer me, damn you!" he railed, suddenly reaching out and grasping both her wrists in fingers of steel.

"How dare you!" She, too, was furious. Wrenching free of him and facing him, her eyes spit amethyst fire now that her initial shock had worn off, and all the pain and hurt and anger of these past weeks flooded through her. "How dare you force your way in here like this! You deserted me! You used me and left me! I have nothing to answer to you for, Captain Markham, nothing! Leave this house before I have you thrown out!"

227

"You would, would you?" His face a mask of dark fury, he shook his head and advanced upon her. "No. You don't get off so easily, my sweet," he gritted out. "You say I deserted you?" He shook his head. "No. You know bloody well why I left Kirkenmuir—my letter explained everything. Don't deny it, damn you, don't add lies to your faithlessness, or by God, I swear I'll strike you where you stand!" His voice was a roar that shook the walls and struck terror into her heart. "Why, Heather? Tell me why. I loved you!" He grasped her by the shoulders and shook her angrily, her dark-flame hair tossing wildly about them. "Answer me!"

"Stop it! There was no letter from you! Let go of me, you brute!" she panted, trying to tear free of his bruising grip. "You're hurting me, Adam!"

"What could you, of all people, possibly know of hurt?" he jeered, his fingers tightening about her wrist. "I loved you from the first moment I set eyes upon you! I thought you felt the same. I come back and what do I find—that you've married *him!* I could kill you for this, Heather!" The murderous fury in his eyes, his hoarse tone, left no doubt in her mind that he meant what he said, and fear ricocheted through her.

"You've gone mad—you've lost your reason!"

She broke free and fled from him toward the servants' hall, but he sprang after her, knotting his fist over the flowing sleeve of her dressing gown and jerking her back into his arms. The flimsy fabric rent under the strength of his fingers, baring her shoulder. He shook her violently.

"Mad, am I? Yes, by God, I think I am. Mad with grief! If your pretty Douglas were here now, I'd tear him apart, limb by limb, I swear it! God, you're so damned beautiful! All that beauty—wasted!" The bitter words were wrenched from the dark and violent depths of his soul. "You're mine, Heather, not his," he raged,

"No matter whose name you bear, whose ring you wear, you're mine, forever and always!"

Suddenly he grasped her fiercely to him. His cruel mouth, his hard, bruising mouth, came down upon hers, crushing it. Her lips were stained crimson, swollen from the violence of his ardor, throbbing from the pressure of his kiss when at last he tore his mouth from hers. His arms were a band of steel, tight about her slender waist. She clenched her fists and pummeled his broad chest, her cries muffled by his hungry lips as he kissed her with savage passion yet again.

He broke away at length and thrust her from him, still gripping her brutally by one wrist and looking down at her with a reckless and dangerous expression she had never seen before in his eyes, one that sent stabs of fear darting through her. "I'll be damned if I don't still want you, my lovely, faithless witch, even knowing what you are! What do you say, my darling? Once more, for old times' sake? . . ." He smiled mockingly. "If you can sell yourself for Dennison's wealth and title, then you can give yourself to me, who loves you. How much for your favors, Heather? Ten shillings? A guinea? More?" He thrust his hand into his trouser pocket and flung a handful of notes and coins in her face. "Here! Take it all, my lovely. I mean to see the price well spent!"

"What are you saying? Adam, please don't be this way! You frighten me!" she whispered, recoiling as he reached for her.

"Frighten you? Don't make me laugh!" he taunted, each word like the crack of a whip. "You weren't frightened before, were you, angel? Why not? Because you didn't know then that I had no wealth, no prospects to offer you?" With that, he suddenly stepped toward her and hauled her roughly into his arms, striding purposefully toward the drawing room.

"No, Adam, no!" she pleaded, trying to wriggle free and escape him. "My aunt and uncle—they'll be home soon!" She strained against his arms, but his grip was unbreakable, her pleas all in vain.

"Liar!" he scoffed. "The blizzard will keep them in Kirkenmuir until morning, at the very least. Only a lovesick fool would brave this foul weather to reach Moorsedge," he ground out through clenched teeth. "Or a man who was so damned trusting, he couldn't believe his own brother when he told him he'd been betrayed by the only woman he's ever loved!"

Inside the drawing room, he carelessly tossed her onto the chaise, then turned and pointedly locked the door behind them. She quailed before the storm-filled fury in his gentian eyes, backing away as he flung off his cape and the coat beneath, and strode toward her.

"Why so frightened, Heather? You should welcome this!" he mocked, towering over her. "You should thank me for it! You see, I intend to give you a night to remember, my lovely! A night to fill your dreams as you lie, wanting, in your bed, ruing the day you married Dennison!" His gentian eyes smoldered like banked coals.

He knotted his hand in her tumbling hair, wound a length about his fist, and dragged her roughly to him on the chaise, kissing her fiercely, feverishly, despite her struggles to free herself. "Did he kiss you as I kiss you?" he rasped, dragging the torn dressing gown and the silken night chemise beneath it from her body with his free hand, thus baring her rosy flesh to his hungry lips and his feverish touch. He molded the rounded curves of her shoulders. He cupped the fullness of her breasts and fondled them ardently, his breathing quickening against her moist, swollen mouth as he teased the crests to stand erect beneath his fingertips.

"Did he touch you this way?" he demanded cruelly.

230

His hand slid jealously down over the sleek length of her body and across the rounded swell of her hip to cup her derrière, stroking maddeningly as he pressed her against him. His manhood thrust, hard and urgent, against her belly, its heat palpable even through his clothing.

"Did he hold you this way? Tell me, you heartless little bitch, did he—did he?" he whispered raggedly, his breath rasping against her cheek. His hand moved to her belly and swept down, stroking, stroking. Those strong, marauding fingers roughly parted her trembling thighs, brushed aside the fleecy triangle at their joining to bury themselves deep inside her. His intimate touch involuntarily sent fiery darts of desire piercing through her. He watched her face as he caressed her, and triumph flared in his burning eyes as she parted her lips and moaned helplessly, her fingers opening and closing convulsively against the brocade of the chaise. "Look at you! Tell me now that it's Dennison you love, and be damned for a liar! Tell me it's him you want to hold you, touch you, this way! Look into my eyes. Say it, *mean* it, and I give you my oath I'll leave Moorsedge this instant."

"Yes!" she cried, damning her body for its treachery. "Yes! Go, damn you! I—I feel nothing for you!" she denied vehemently, shaking her head.

Yet even her eyes told him she lied. They were alive with desire: dark, moistly luminous. Her voice was husky now, and her struggles had grown noticeably weaker. Her fingers, which had clenched his forearms and then gouged the chaise, now clung helplessly to him, half-caressingly. "Adam . . . oh, Adam!" she cried desperately. "There was no wedding night for Douglas and I! He left for Africa the very afternoon we were wed! There's been no one but you!"

"He never touched you?"

231

"Never. Never! I swear it! Oh, Adam!"

All at once she was in his arms, her fingers twining in his dark, damp curls, her lips covering his dark, scowling face with feverish little kisses. Her slender body arched against his, pressing its soft, rounded form to his hard, masculine lines. "Take me! Hold me! Oh, love me! Adam, I want you so!"

With a muffled groan, he kissed her, held her, touched her as she implored him to do, while placing himself above her on the chaise. Their mouths were brands, flaming torches of consuming passion that came together out of desperation as much as desire, their arms bonds that defied all comers to separate them.

Damn her! She's Dennison's wife! Adam thought. His love mingled with fury, he hungrily stroked the sleek curves of her lovely body as if he'd never caressed her before and as if he feared he might never do so again. He tore the remnants of her garments from her one by one until she lay bare and quivering in his arms. Deep inside, he knew that he should halt this, that he should be the stronger one and leave before he dishonored her. Yet he could not, would not, find the strength or the compassion or the will to let her go! The need to hurt her, to make her pay for what she'd done to him, came first—and the wanting her. God, how he wanted her!

Oh, dear Lord, nothing's changed! I still love him! It's wrong, but it's Adam I love, Adam I'll always love—not my husband! Heather cried silently, drawing Adam's hand to her breasts, caressing his bare, muscled shoulders as she whispered his name again and again.

His mouth, his hungry mouth, covered her breasts, enflaming them with moist heat and circling caresses that sent her pulse singing through her veins, made her blood a raging river of liquid fire that spread tingling heat throughout her: heat that finally centered in that tender, hidden place between her thighs—a throbbing, maddening inferno demanding release. A release that only he could give!

Urgently they loved, their fierce loving matched in ardent fury only by the force of the blizzard that howled and shrieked about Moorsedge. When he gathered her up into his powerful arms and came into her, driving with possessive, jealous fury into her moist haven, she twined arms and legs about him, and kissed him with a desperate hunger that fired his blood still further. In her bittersweet torment, her nails gouged little half-moons from the smooth flesh of his back and arms. Her teeth nipped and gnawed greedily at the tanned cords of his shoulders as if she sought to devour him! He knotted his long fingers in the river of dark-flame hair that spilled seductively about them, and caught her hungrily to him as they cried out their passion in blissful union.

For endless moments of giddy rapture, reality ceased to exist. Their world became the whirling, velvety bubble of sensation in which they floated as one, their vision filled with rocketing explosions of light, their bodies at last rocked on the warm, soothing sea of utter content, the afterglow of their tempestuous joining.

Reality returned but slowly, filtering into their consciousness as the morning light fingers its way between drawn draperies. They lay side by side where they had tumbled, upon the flowered Aubusson carpet before the fire, its flames casting tawny light over their bodies, dewed now with drops of perspiration. He leaned upon one elbow and cupped her face in his hand, his eyes drinking in her exhausted beauty with such a jealous fury she feared she would swoon.

"As God's my witness, I love you, angel!" he said

233

huskly, kissing her with sudden desperation now that their passion was spent.

She stroked his hair, a lump in her throat too great, too terrible to bear. "And I, you, my dearest Adam. Oh, Lord, what can we do?"

They clung to each other, helplessly entangled in their love, filled with despair at the hopelessness of their cause, until with a muffled curse, he thrust her angrily away. She was not his, and the bitterness of that knowledge was like acid in his soul. She could never be truly his. Not now. She belonged to another!

"Do?" he echoed, his tone harsh and cold. "It's a little late to think of that now, Heather, wouldn't you say?" He rose from beside her and reached for his clothing, pulling it on with rigid fingers that fumbled over buttons and buckles. "The time for doing is long past!"

"You said there was a letter?"

His dark eyes searched her face. He nodded.

"I received no letter from you, Adam, none at all. I've had no word from you since you left here on Christmas Eve, 'til now."

"What?" His eyebrows came together in a black bar of consternation as he frowned. Tucking his shirt into his belt, he turned to look down at her. "There must have been! There was a coachman outside the church on Christmas Day when I left for London. I gave him a florin to see it delivered safely into your hands!"

"It was never delivered, Adam," she whispered. "Don't you see? That's why I thought you'd only used me, that you didn't want me, or our child. It was to give the baby a name that I married Douglas. He was kind, you understand, and he said he loved me. After so many weeks without hearing from you, I thought . . . thought I'd never see you again. Adam, believe me, I didn't know what else to do!"

For a second, his expression softened. Then the steel

returned to his eyes. In short, brittle sentences, he told her of his lawyer's letter and of the meeting with Elwood, of coming to on the ferry to Calais—everything that had ensued. "Letter or no letter, you should have trusted me! Isn't trust a part of love?" he demanded. "Damn it, I was fool enough to trust you! All those days I imagined you here, waiting for me, wondering what had gone wrong. I went through hell until I found a way to get back to you and put your mind at rest. And all the while you—"

"That's not fair!" she cried furiously, drawing the remnants of her robe up to cover herself. "I couldn't afford to wait indefinitely." She pressed her clenched fists over her belly, and he nodded, gentian eyes blazing.

"Ah, yes. The child. *Our child,* isn't it? You needed a substitute father, and in a hurry, too, for it to be convincing. Did you once stop to think that it was *my* child you'd be foisting off on Dennison? That I might have something to say about that?"

"As far as I was concerned, you gave up that right when you left here and failed to come back!" she retorted, standing up and pacing furiously.

"I wasn't to blame for that."

"No. You weren't. But how was I to know that? No man could ever understand what I went through—the desperation, Adam, that feeling of being trapped in a blind alley with no way to turn, so few avenues open to me! I couldn't bear to bring a child into this world who would forever be considered a bastard, who would be thought less precious than other children because he lacked that all-magical father's name. These are unforgiving times, Adam. You, of all people, should know that! I did what I had to do—for me and for my baby. It was the best I could do."

When her impassioned speech ended, the fire seemed

to have dwindled out of Heather. She drew her dressing gown about her shoulders and shrugged her arms into it, vaguely astonished to see that the sleeve was torn, for in the ardor and heat of the moment, she had not noticed it before. "Did you ever find out who struck you?" she asked wearily.

"No. But I have my suspicions," Adam admitted, dark eyes crackling with anger.

"Who?"

He smiled wolfishly. "Your husband. Or rather, one of his henchmen."

"Douglas?" Seeing him nod, she frowned. "Nonsense! Why on earth would he do such a thing?"

"To bring about exactly what's been brought about! Somehow, I believe he's tied in to the missing letter. The contents would have told him I was leaving unexpectedly. I think he decided to turn my temporary departure into something a little less temporary. That way, he had a clear field to provide you with a sympathetic shoulder to cry on, and he no doubt added a few choice slurs against my character to bring you to the altar!"

The skeptical expression on her face was blatant. "Oh, come now! Isn't that a little far-fetched? It sounds like one of those wild tales in the penny dreadfuls! 'Dastardly villain attempts to destroy hero to win heroine's love!' I think what happened between you and Douglas in India years ago has colored your judgment of the man! He's nowhere near as black as you've painted him."

He swung about and grasped her by the upper arm. "He told you about India?"

"That the men in your command went beserk, and abused and shot several female prisoners and their children, that you were forced to resign your commission to avoid court-martial, and that because of the

236

scandal your father disowned you." She did not add that Douglas had implied Adam himself had taken part in the atrocity. That much she had never believed. "Yes, he told me. Of course he did! He wanted no secrets between us, you see. He wanted me to understand why there was such hostility between the two of you."

"And you believed him?" Adam asked, his eyebrows arched. He was seething.

She had the grace to appear somewhat uncertain of herself. "No-o-o. Not entirely."

"Thank God for small mercies, at least!" he retorted, his voice dripping with sarcasm.

"You don't deny it?"

"Is there any point?" he challenged her, his eyes hooded. "The truth couldn't alter the way things stand between us, not now. Unless you are prepared to prove you love me, that is."

"How?"

"Pack your bags. Come with me when I leave here."

"Leave? You mean, run away with you?"

His eyebrows quirked. "What else? You say you love me, and since—God help me!—I still love you, what choice do we have? None, if we mean to be together!"

"But I'm Douglas' wife. He's expecting me to join him in Nairobi. No, I can't betray his trust in me! For all that you've no liking for the man, Adam, he loves me. He's shown me only kindness and respect. To learn I had left him for you would destroy him! And what of the shame my aunt and uncle would face if I were to run away with you? They would never again be able to hold up their heads in society. Adam, ask anything of me but this, I beg you! I love you. But . . . I can't!"

"Can't? Or won't?" he demanded harshly. "If you truly love me, who the devil cares what Douglas thinks or feels? Leave here with me tonight, Heather, or regret

237

not having done so for the rest of your life! Choose. Will it be Douglas and your aunt and uncle's good name and approval," he taunted, "or me?"

Silence hung like a heavy pendulum between them. Her pulse pounded in her ears. Her heart fluttered like a wounded bird. Memories of the heartache she had known while waiting for Adam to return, wanting him so, played through her mind. She knew where her duty lay. She had made her choice that day in her uncle's study. But oh, the price it would exact of her. *Please God, tell me the right thing to do!* she prayed. On the mantel, the clock ticked ominously, marking each minute that passed as she wavered, torn between leaving with her love and the honor that bound her to stay.

"You must go without me, Adam, my darling," she whispered brokenly at great length. "I have no choice. I gave up the right to choose when I accepted Douglas' proposal. I can't blindly follow my heart, hurt those who have loved and trusted me all these years. Go, my love! Go quickly, before I can't bear to let you leave!"

He cursed under his breath, his face a stern, unfathomable dark mask, his emotions betrayed only by the throb of a nerve at his temple. "You disappoint me, Heather. I'd thought you were different, that you had the courage to fight for what you believed in or wanted from life. I was wrong! You're a coward like all the rest. Your love is just a matter of convenience, isn't it? Whoever has a larger bank account, whoever offers you greater security, that man holds the key to your fickle heart!"

"That's a damned lie!" she exploded. She swung back her hand and slapped him hard across the face, the anger and hurt—the guilt—inside her giving her enormous strength. The sound of flesh against flesh was like the report of a gunshot. His head jerked side-

238

ways. She glimpsed the marks of her palm and fingers branded in scarlet across his cheek in the second before he caught her by the hair and wrenched her to him.

"Is it?" he seethed. "Then prove it! To hell with duty! To hell with honor, and Douglas be damned! It's not his child you're carrying, but mine. Mine! As God is my witness, if I leave here tonight without you, I'll take it from you by force before I let you name Dennison as the father! For the last time: *Come with me!*"

Numbly, she shook her head. "No." She looked up into his face, and for a second it seemed he might strike her. But at length he thrust her forcibly away, almost hurling her to the carpet with the violence of the gesture.

"All right, damn you," he rasped. "If that's the way you want it, then so be it!" He strode toward the door, turned there, and looked back at her once, just once, his gentian eyes filled with agony and withering contempt. And then, he was gone.

"Adam!" she whispered. "Oh, Adam, no! Come back!" She flew across the room and ran into the hallway, to the front door, battling it open. A shower of snowflakes swirled against her face as she stared blindly out into the howling blizzard. The tears froze on her cheeks in the cold.

Too late! He had gone. And this time, she knew in her heart that he would never return.

Part Two

Africa

Chapter Fifteen

Heather's most vivid impression of her birthplace, on seeing it again after eighteen years, was not the colorful, seething' bazaar that lined the picturesque wharves of Mombasa's Old Harbor, the cries of fruit vendors and water sellers vying in melodious discord to be heard. Nor was it the mélange of people—white-robed Arabs and turbaned Indians, African women in their vivid *kangas,* and colonials in tropical whites—or the scents of spices perfuming the air. It was not the breathtaking sight of the sails of countless shows from the Persian Gulf etched against high-walled Fort Jesus, built by the Portuguese three centuries before and now a prison; not the white minarets of the mosques and cathedrals glittering in the sunlight, not the flowering jacarandas and flaming poinsettias that lined the dusty street. What imprinted itself on her mind was the vast sweep of the pale golden savannah that she and Ellen Reading, who had agreed to come with her as her companion, rode through heading northwest by oxcart toward Nairobi, two days after they had disembarked from the *Achilles.*

The sky was a vaulting canopy of vivid azure, paling to smoke beyond distant mountains that were an ephemeral, misty blue. Kilimanjaro's twin snow-capped peaks were the most beautiful, dominating the scene from the northwest where the extinct volcano rose magnificently on the Tanganyika border of Kenya, like an iced, many-tiered wedding cake.

The early morning light seemed to touch everything with gold. All about the dusty trail along which they rumbled swayed golden grass, waist-high, broken only by low-spreading thorn trees and scattered bush. Off to their left, a herd of zebra paused in their grazing, black velvet noses quivering to catch the alien scents as the oxcart swayed perilously past them. Their stripes of black on white, or white on black, stood out sharply as if painted against the sea of dry amber grass. A pride of perhaps fifteen lions, moving with languid grace, padded in stately fashion, their bellies full and swinging from an early-morning kill, to a small watering hole fringed with grass, blinking amber eyes disdainfully at the noisy cart before lowering massive heads to lap at the murky water like enormous, tawny domestic cats lapping a dish of cream. The cubs, growling and tumbling about their mothers' feet, were swatted into obedience by well-aimed, massive paws. Tiny, delicate gazelles gamboled everywhere, and a sprinkling of bearded black wildebeest moved ponderously across the savannah like rheumy-eyed elders, attendant snowy egrets perched precariously upon their backs, ridding them of vermin. In the distance, the long, elegant necks of the giraffe rose, somehow reminiscent of the elongated necks of the prehistoric brontasaurus as they breakfasted on scrubby foliage amongst the spreading tops of the umbrella trees.

For Heather, it was a vista that never palled. In her excitement she forgot the overwhelming disappointment—and anger—she had felt in Mombasa, the capital of the new British East African Protectorate, when the *Achilles* had docked, and she had learned that Douglas had not come to meet her personally but had sent Thomas Worth, one of his district officers, instead.

"I'm very pleased to meet you, Mister Worth," she had murmured, tight-lipped, after the man had introduced himself and had explained that he was to escort them from Mombasa to Nairobi, Kenya, "but I fail to understand why my husband could not have come to meet me himself?"

Thomas Worth, a man of medium height with a pleasant, weatherbeaten face and twinkling blue eyes, had shrugged and appeared embarrassed. "You must understand that your husband, as Governor, is an extremely busy man, Lady Dennison. The journey to Nairobi from here is almost three hundred miles, and would require that he spend precious time away from his duties. He reluctantly felt it advisable to send myself in his place. He extends his fervent wishes that you will have a safe and not too uncomfortable trip."

"Did he now?" Mrs. Reading had commented, grimly pursing her lips, her displeasure at her charge's cold welcome to her future home evident in her expression. "That was decent of him!"

But Douglas' lack of consideration had not been Tom Worth's fault. The dear man had done everything in his power to see that they were both made welcome and comfortable, Heather reflected. He had taken rooms for them at the Mombasa Grand Hotel, it transpired, and had speedily arranged for their trunks and boxes to be transported there, while they had ridden in an open carriage through the teeming narrow streets. When they were safely installed at the shabbily elegant Grand Hotel, he had said that he would be honored if they would join him for dinner in the dining room that evening, and join him they had. Tom Worth had proved very likable, if strangely reticent to discuss her husband, though he had not been unwilling to discuss any other facet of life in Kenya that she might choose to inquire about.

After two days for the women to rest and recover from their long sea voyage, and to adjust a little to the African climate, which was blistering in this month of March, they had set off in the cool, sweet air of dawn for Nairobi, on the Athi Plains below the Kikuyu foothills. And here they were, rolling across the savannah in an oxcart, oxen being more hardy than horses in such a clime, and better able to handle the rough, rutted tracks.

The sunrise had been spectacular! Mangrove swamps, choked with tangles of tree roots visible above the muddy ground, had bordered the sometimes seemingly nonexistent road they traveled for the early hours of that first day, as did coconut palms and cashew trees. The gleaming green water had been alive with the shimmer of wings touched with glorious flame-light whenever waterfowl rose into the air in breathtaking, feathered clouds. Pelicans and cormorants, salmon pink flamingoes, and ducks had added their vivid plumage to the wheeling and dipping, crying multitudes of them darkening the sky momentarily. It was like a scene from a surrealistic painting, the birds silhouetted against rose and tangerine skies and gold-bordered, creamy clouds, the fiery orb of the sun bursting over the horizon beyond and igniting the tips of their wings and tails with fire.

But once away from the coast, they had left the mangrove swamps behind and the vegetation had grown steadily less as they entered the vast grasslands, or savannahs, farther inland. Behind the cart came the native bearers, four magnificently strong Kikuyu tribesmen that Tom Worth had brought with him from

Nairobi. With apparently effortless grace and amazing sense of balance, they bore the enormous bundles of tents and groundcovers, upon their heads. Tom kept up a stream of easy conversation, alternately chatting companionably with his porters and with the women, to whom he pointed out sights he thought might interest them, or various forms of wildlife. During the heat of midday they rested. Tom erected an awning for their shade, suspending it from one side of the wagon and then deftly lighting a small fire and boiling a billy-can of water, poured from a canteen, in order to brew tea. Fresh fruits—luscious, sweet mangoes that Heather had never tasted before, but loved immediately— bananas, crackers, and dried strips of meat comprised their luncheon, along with steaming mugs of the inevitable tea.

"You may transplant an Englishman to any far-flung corner of the globe, ladies. You may threaten him with any number of dangers, and he will deal with them all, and remarkably well. But he must have his cups of tea at regular intervals, or the British Empire will crumble!" Tom remarked with a wry smile, and the women laughed and nodded their agreement. The tea tasted delicious, ridding their throats of the dryness caused by miles of dusty travel and the heat, the *endless* heat that danced and shimmered in waves over the tall grass all about them.

While they ate, seemingly alone in that endless savannah, a Masai warrior, or *moran,* appeared from nowhere, with several sleek cattle herded before him. He was very tall and moved with the superb self-assurance of one who belonged there, on the savannah, as the lions belonged. His hair was fashioned into a pigtail and coated with a reddish clay. His body gleamed with a red-black luster where it was not covered by his only garment, the red cloth or *shuka* he wore knotted at one shoulder. In his fist he carried a spear, long and slender with a broad tip. He moved past them with a harmonious grace that seemed born of the land of which, by birthright, he was a part, ignoring the group beneath the awning completely.

Tom Worth jerked his enamel mug in the warrior's direction after he had passed on. "A Masai warrior," he volunteered. "His *manyatta*, his village, must be nearby. The Masai count their wealth according to the number of hump-backed cattle they own. They drink only blood, drawn from the live beasts' veins and mixed with milk, for their sustenance."

The glorious golden light had already begun to fade when they moved on. The savannah took on a stillness that was deceptive for creatures were stirring and flexing muscles relaxed from the day's sleep, preparing to hunt when darkness fell. It came with a purple suddenness that Heather was to recognize in only a matter of days as peculiar to Africa, that brief, breathtakingly gaudy sunset. Then the fiery sun seemed to drop abruptly over the edge of the world and disappear. In the fading amethyst dusk, as the porters emptied their bundles to pitch tents for their camp, thousands of insects could be heard, droning in the long grass. Numerous furry brown moths, drawn by the gleam of the lanterns that Tom Worth had lit, filled the air and hurled themselves into the hot glowing flames as countless sacrifices. Seeing them, Heather was reminded sharply of Adam who had, one snowy afternoon in Scotland when they'd lain replete in each other's arms, likened himself to a moth, drawn irrevocably and recklessly to her radiant beauty. A lump formed in her throat. If only it were Adam here with her now, showing her his Africa, the Africa he loved, through his eyes. . . . She fumbled in the darkness for the tiny crystal unicorn he had given her that fateful Christmas

Eve, and then held it tightly to her breast, like a child drawing comfort in the night from a beloved doll. Despite his hurtful, hateful words, she still loved him.

She and Mrs. Reading, or Ellen as Heather had come to call her during their voyage aboard the *Achilles,* shared a tent. While the older woman quickly fell asleep, Heather lay awake, watching the shadows of the insects through the sloping, white canvas walls. She could not sleep, she was so filled with excitement at her new and breathtaking surroundings, an excitement that was inevitably tainted with sadness at the loss of her love.

Somewhere in this vast, savagely beautiful land, did Adam stare up at the glittering night sky of indigo velvet spangled with myriad stars, and think of her? Did he long for her, want her, as she longed for and wanted him in the cold of the African night? As she had longed for and wanted him on countless nights aboard ship, when she strolled the silent, shadowed decks and stared out at the midnight blue Indian Ocean, in which the stars had swum and danced like silvery shoals of flying fish? She closed her eyes tightly, willing herself to remember the way his slim, tanned fingers had felt as he'd caressed her body, the sweet-fire heat of his lips as he'd kissed her, the delicious sensations that had pooled and swirled like warmed honey in her veins when he'd made love to her. Why must she torture herself with her memories! Soon she would share Douglas' bed. She *must* forget Adam! But would Douglas arouse the same, wonderful feelings inside her that Adam had—or would his touch leave her as cold and unmoved as his few emotionless kisses had left her? Tears stung her eyes. She was trapped, trapped in marriage to a man she cared nothing for, a man who aroused no desire in her whatsoever! She had vowed to try to be the best wife she possibly could, but oh, she was so afraid that trying would not be enough! Trying could not ignite the spark of physical attraction and desire between two people. That depended on an almost magical alchemy, some elusive element of heightened awareness and electricity that could not be brought about: it simply *was*.

She lay in darkness, hopelessly enmeshed in her fears and doubts, until the harsh, grunting roar of a male lion, the beast securing his territory, ricocheted through the black night, bringing her thoughts sharply back to the present. Soon after she slid down into a deep, exhausted sleep.

Four days more brought them onto the Athi Plains. From time to time, they passed native villages composed of round mud huts thatched with dung and grass, or the loaf-shaped dwellings of the Masai herders. Bare-breasted women wearing wide, pretty collars of intricately woven beads and skirts of indigo or red native cloth, were hard at work in most of these villages, pounding couscous grain with tall wooden pestles while their menfolk hunted. Village dogs came out, barked half-heartedly at the newcomers, then flopped down under shade trees to sleep once more, their tongues lolling. The blue smoke of cooking fires rose into the hot morning air, and the throbbing message of the gourd drums passed the news of the white women's arrival to the next village. There, still more little black children, quite naked, would escape the watchful eyes of the old grandmothers and run out to watch them pass, shouting the Swahili greeting, *"Jambo sana! Habari ya leo?"* The youngsters liquid brown eyes were bright with curiosity, their thumbs were tucked shyly into their mouths. Heather and Ellen, enchanted with the little ones, gave them the remaining mangoes in their packs and rationed out the last of their sweets, black-and-white striped peppermint "humbugs" that Ellen had brought with her in a tin from England. The children had a sweet tooth, so broad smiles followed the women on the last stage of their journey along the banks of the Athi River to Nairobi. Tom mentioned that a railway was being built to link coastal Mombasa with inland Nairobi and Uganda, but was some years to completion. As it was, the plains were much like the savannahs they had traveled the previous four days, seas of golden grass and low, dense bush and thorn trees; home of the eland and impala, the giraffe and wildebeest, the zebra and the cheetah.

Shortly before dusk the day before, Heather and Ellen Reading had looked where Tom Worth, speaking very softly, had bade them, and they had glimpsed a pair of tawny ears poking above the grass. They had followed his pointing finger to a lone gazelle, quietly grazing several yards away. "Watch, and be still," he had murmured.

Suddenly, an amber streak burst gracefully from the tall grasses as a spotted cheetah sprang toward the gazelle. The gazelle leaped nimbly away, dainty hooves flying, yet she was no match for the predator. With fluid grace, the cat became an effortless machine, a mere stripe of speed and tawny color, swifter than the swiftest arrow unleashed from a bow, as she ran down her prey. The lithe motion of forelegs and backlegs blurred into one flying stream of gold unburdened by the forces of gravity as the distance between the hunter and the hunted irrevocably closed. The gazelle went down without a sound, her neck instantly and painlessly broken as the cheetah took her in powerful jaws. Only a single smear of blood stained her coat, where the female cheetah's claws had dug in

251

for purchase.

"Quick and clean," Tom Worth had commented as the cheetah, after resting briefly to regain her wind, had daintily begun her meal, "and necessary. Not like the ivory poachers who kill for greed and gain, and leave all but the tusks or the skins of the animals they kill to rot! She killed only to live."

Heather and Ellen had echoed his sentiments. When the cheetah was done, she had vanished again between the tall grass. Vultures and storks had come to finish what she had begun, and when they had picked the bones clean, the jackals and hyenas took their place. With doglike short yelps and loud crunchings of their powerful jaws, they finished the cleaning job, keeping at it long after dark fell. By the next morning, the gazelle had been totally absorbed, not so much as a bone remaining. Clean. Efficient. *Right.*

They reached Nairobi at midafternoon of the fifth day, and at once Heather was struck by the incongruity of the place. The whitewashed residences were markedly British in appearance despite the heavily fronded coconut and date palms that towered exotically over them and over the few native mud huts that lined the dusty main street. One building, bigger than the others, caught Heather's eye.

"Is that Douglas' residence over there?" she asked, suddenly nervous.

Tom shook his head. "No, that's the hospital, Lady Heather. Some of your husband's clerks and assistants live here, in these houses, but Lord Dennison's official residence is farther on, in the hills above Nairobi that are known unofficially as the White Highlands. Most of the Europeans have made their homes there, where the climate is cooler, you see."

"And what do they do for a living?"

"They've started farms or plantations, for the most

252

part. The red soil here is good for planting coffee and tea, or sugar cane and so on; and the rainfall is sufficient too." He smiled as she nodded gravely, her beautiful face animated by her keen interest in her surroundings. "I expect you're anxious to see your husband again, and your new home, Lady Heather. We have a carriage to take you the rest of the way. It wouldn't do for the Governor's wife to arrive on an oxcart, would it now?" His blue eyes twinkled merrily.

"I suppose some people would think not," Heather agreed with a smile. "But for myself, I found it rather fun these past five days! Thank you, Mister Worth. You've been a perfect escort, and a most entertaining companion."

"The pleasure was mine, madam." For a fleeting second, something dark and stern was in his eyes, but it was as swiftly gone. "If you should need me—if there is any way at all in which I may be of service to you in the future—please do not hesitate to ask, Lady Heather."

"Why, thank you, Mister Worth. I shall do so, I promise you, if the need arises," she acknowledged warmly.

And soon after, they were jouncing up a curving driveway lined with date palms and purple-blue jacaranda trees in full bloom. It was flanked by lush lawns, exotic gardens, and the outbuildings of Douglas' white-walled governor's residence, the size and appearance of which put her in mind of a petty sultan's palace, a comparison that amused rather than overwhelmed her at the thought of being mistress of such a place!

Douglas came out at once to greet her, handing her down from the carriage himself although houseboys and servants hovered eagerly at his elbow, eying their beautiful new mistress with delight.

Early that morning before setting out on the last leg

of the journey, Heather had donned a gown of pale green muslin, and she had set a jaunty wide-brimmed straw hat made gay with trailing green ribbons atop her upswept auburn hair. Now, with a frilled parasol shielding her from the fierce sunlight, she appeared as fresh and tempting as a cool dish of sherbet, or an oasis in the desert.

"At last!" Douglas murmured. "You are here!"

"Yes," she agreed, surprised to find herself glad to see him, despite her doubts of the past few weeks. "I've missed you, Douglas, my dear," she fibbed, firm in her determination to make the best of her situation from the outset.

"And I you, my darling! I can't believe you're here at last! I expect Tom has told you how it pained me that I couldn't come to Mombasa myself to meet you, but we've had some trouble with the native headmen recently, and I had to deal with it myself. Damn it all, Heather, welcome to Nairobi!" With that somewhat astonishing comment, he swept her into his arms and kissed her breathless in front of everyone.

When Heather, gasping in surprise at his ardent greeting, had recovered, she looked up, pink-cheeked, to see a circle of grinning faces—white and black and brown—watching them. Tom Worth nodded to her in a dismissive gesture, and strode off toward the stables. After she had stammered a greeting to one and all, Douglas introduced her to the company as his bride and their new mistress; then he led her up the steps and inside the house. Ellen, relieved that the reunion with Douglas had gone so well, followed.

Cool, high-ceilinged rooms led off a long marble hallway. Big-game trophies adorned the walls, zebra and antelope, kudu and impala heads stared, glassy-eyed, down at Heather as she passed. An assortment of native weapons—painted shields of stretched animal

254

hide, broad-tipped spears, and the like—were arranged strategically on the walls. The furniture was of light and airy natural rattan, the settees pillowed with pretty green and blue brocade of a distinctly Indian, rather than African, motif. Tall Oriental vases stood in shadowed corners, as did carved idols with grotesque faces, obviously ancient pagan African gods and goddesses worshiped before the conversion of the majority of the native population to the Moslem faith or to Christianity. This was a far cry from the staid and fussy Victorian drawing rooms of England, and she loved the airy spaciousness of the residence immediately.

Douglas rang for tea to be brought, and she and Ellen sipped it from dainty bone-china cups while Douglas described his duties as Governor of the area.

"It appears I shall be a lady of leisure," Heather remarked with a smile when he was done, "what with so many servants?"

"Your servants, my dear. Yours to instruct in the way you wish your new home to be run."

"I caught a glimpse of the hospital in the village on the way here. Perhaps before too long I shall be able to see what needs to be done there, in the way of changes, as you suggested?"

"All in good time, my dear," Douglas promised, smiling indulgently. "For now, I believe your time will be amply occupied by your duties as my wife and hostess. There is little by way of entertainment in these parts as yet. The farmers and plantation owners hereabouts look upon me to provide them with civilized divertissements. We have dinners, balls, and some polo and cricket when the weather permits. Some of the wives even enjoy accompanying their husbands on safaris to shoot big game." He came across the room and squeezed her hand and kissed it benignly. "You'll be far too busy running my household to worry about the hospital for quite some time."

"But I'd hoped that—"

"Patience, Heather, patience!" Douglas cut in sharply. "You really should endeavor to curb that obstinate streak, my dear, and heed your husband. Believe me, I know best. The hospital can wait." He walked to a corner and tugged once on a braided bell-pull. In seconds, a black servant appeared, clothed in a flowing white robe.

"Ngudu, see your new mistress and her companion to their apartments."

"Ndio, Bwana," the servant murmured.

Douglas turned to Heather, assisting her to stand. "I have taken the liberty of arranging a small dinner party for this evening, in honor of your arrival, my dear. I trust you are not too exhausted from your travels? Everyone has been dying to meet you!"

"No, no, of course not," Heather insisted. "A bath and an hour or two to rest, and I shall be as good as new."

"I'm happy to hear it." He drew her across the room, out of earshot of Ellen Reading. "Tonight will be our wedding night, in effect, my dear," he said with a fond smile, drawing her fingertips to his lips and kissing them. "Wear your most dazzling gown. I want my guests to be astonished and green with jealousy at the radiant beauty I've made my bride!" His sky-blue eyes glowed. "You will permit me this one evening of husbandly conceit?"

"Of course," she agreed readily. "I want very much to make you happy and proud of me in all ways, Douglas." Her violet eyes were earnest, her sweet face gravely beautiful.

"You will, my dove. You will," he reassured her.

Chapter Sixteen

The rooms that the servant, Ngudu, led her into were whitewashed and vast, cool caverns after the heat outside. The first of the two was a sitting room, furnished with a low chaise, a desk and chair, and a rattan rocker. A surprisingly modern water closet opened discreetly off it. The second was the bedroom, with a wide, brass bed shrouded in white mosquito netting that hung from the ceiling. A paddle fan whirred softly overhead, impelled, Ngudu informed her in excellent English, by a small boy, seated cross-legged outside on the long verandah that fronted the apartments and which was reached by tall French doors curtained with filmy white cloth. Beyond the verandah were gardens, lush and filled with giant greenery and enormous scarlet hibiscus blossoms.

"If you should want for anything, Missie Bwana, you will ring, yes?"

"Yes, thank you, Ngudu."

The man bowed his head, smiled, and left her alone.

To her surprise, Heather saw that while she had taken tea with Douglas, her trunks had already been brought to her rooms and the contents unpacked, her gowns shaken out and hung in the huge cupboard built into one corner of the room. Ruefully, she saw that not one was not in urgent need of pressing, and she pulled the bellpull as Ngudu had suggested to summon help. As she waited for it to arrive, she selected a dinner gown, one of lavender *mousseline de soie* caught up at the hem in tiny tucks held by narrow black velvet ribbons. She decided she would wear a matching narrow velvet ribbon about her throat to offset the gown's daring décolletage. The dainty amethyst pendant earrings that Uncle Jamie had presented her with last February on her birthday would be her only jewels, other than her slim golden wedding band. Amethysts were her favorite gems; they brought out the color of her violet eyes.

A light tap upon the door signaled the arrival of a servant. She bade whoever it was enter, turning to see a statuesque young native woman standing there. Her short black hair stood out in a becoming halo all about her face, which was smooth and brown and gleamed as if oiled. Her features—flashing dark brown eyes with a feline slant, a long sculptured nose, and full, sensual lips—were incredibly beautiful. For a few seconds, Heather was struck speechless as the woman glided across the room to stand before her, her grace that of a lithe cat, hips undulating, long shapely legs outlined against the indigo cloth of the flowing garment she wore fastened under her arms and falling in graceful lines to her bare feet. Her shoulders were bare too, smooth and gleaming as if also oiled, their rich velvety dark brown accented by the heavy bangles—they appeared to be gold—that adorned her upper arms.

"I am Dalila, Lady Heather. How may I serve you?" she asked. Her voice was husky, a perfect partner to her dark, sensual beauty.

"I shall need this gown pressed, if you will, and water to bathe."

Dalila inclined her head. *"Ndio,* Lady Heather." She bent gracefully and gathered the voluminous folds of the lavender gown into her arms. "Will that be all?"

"Yes, thank you." Heather paused. "You speak excellent English, as does Ngudu. Where did you learn my language?" she asked, curious.

"I am from Malindi, on the coast. I learned at the missionary school there, where I was raised by a minister from Newcastle, in your England, after my parents were stolen by Arab slave traders."

"Slave traders! But I thought slaving had been outlawed years ago?"

"On paper, yes, Lady Heather," Dalila acknowledged with a faintly mocking smile. "In reality, it is not so. The Arab slavers have raided my people's coasts for centuries, and continue to do so."

"I see," Heather murmured, shocked. "And Ngudu?"

"Ngudu learned your tongue because he wanted to, as he does in all things."

"I see. Thank you, Dalila."

The young woman moved in her svelte fashion toward the door, then turned and hesitated, looking back over her shoulder. "Your father, he was also a missionary here in my country many years ago, yes?"

Startled, Heather nodded. "Yes, he was, a medical missionary to the Congo in the northwest."

Dalila smiled, revealing pearly white, even teeth. "Alexand-er Camer-on, yes?"

"Yes. How did you know?"

"Ngudu."

"Ah, yes. I see."

"Ngudu said that he and your mother were not like the others that come here, to Africa. They did not try to interfere with our people's ways. They wanted only to heal. For their sake, you are welcome here."

"Thank you," Heather murmured, somewhat astonished. "I shall also try only to help, not interfere."

"It would be wise," Dalila agreed softly, then left like a dusky shadow, sliding through the barely opened door without a sound.

Hot water arrived, borne in pitchers by numerous other curious servants, and a hip bath too. Heather bathed, relishing the cool water and fresh, light floral scent of the soap. On the journey here from Mombasa, she had been forced to wash using precious water from the canteens, a sketchy business at best. A bath was a luxury in this land where every drop of water was precious, and she reveled in it, spilling it over her body in cooling trickles.

Later, feeling clean and refreshed, she turned down the counterpane that covered the bed and slept for several hours on crisp white sheets that smelled of sunshine, waking to find the room heavily shadowed. She rose, yawned and stretched, and walked to the French windows, drawing aside the filmy curtains and looking out into the darkened gardens.

The air was hot, heavy, filled with the earthy, tangy scent of plants drenched with night-dew. But the hibiscus that she had seen earlier wafted no perfume to her nostrils. She recalled vaguely that Tom Worth had said a few African flowers possessed perfume, their brilliant coloring having been considered adequate by Mother Nature to ensure pollination without need for the attraction of a scent. The moon, full and golden as a round, ripe tamarind growing on some towering celestial tree, was suspended above the hills. A warm wind from the east riffled the palm fronds, carrying with it the night-roar of a distant lion, splintering the darkness with the message that here, he was lord. A faint stirring movement in the shadows of the verandah startled her. Eyes adjusting to the gloom, she saw that the little boy who manned the paddle fan still crouched there, the cord held limply in one hand, his head lolling on his chest. She bent down and gently shook his shoulder.

"Go to bed now, child," she urged. "It is late."

He murmured something, eyes round and frightened as he gaped up at her.

"It's all right. Go!" She smiled and made a sign with her hands to show someone sleeping.

He understood her gentle tone and her gesture if not her words, nodded and scuttled away, rubbing sleepy eyes as he went.

Ellen Reading came to her room then, and helped her to dress and arrange her hair, chattering on about how lovely her own quarters were, and what a grand place Lord Dennison's residence had proved to be.

"There's almost an army of servants for the house, not to mention gardeners and grooms and so on!" Ellen exclaimed.

"Yes, so I gathered," Heather acknowledged absently. "How do I look?"

Ellen appraised her critically. "Breathtaking! Absolutely breathtaking!"

"Really? Douglas has given me instructions that I'm to look my most dazzling tonight. I'm to turn his friends green with jealousy!" She pursed her lips and wrinkled her nose, dark-flame ringlets stirring upon her bare shoulders. "I hope I don't disappoint him."

"Is the man blind?" Ellen demanded with a snort. "My dear, you could do that clothed in a sack, I shouldn't wonder! Oh, the conceit of the man!"

Heather laughed. "Now, Ellen, give Douglas a chance, do. This is but our first evening here."

"And tonight, your wedding night, in effect," Ellen reminded her.

She need not have done so. The knowledge had been hovering at the back of Heather's mind all day, thrust there countless times in her determination not to dwell on it. "Yes," she agreed, voice barely above a whisper.

"Do not give way to panic, my dear," Ellen urged, her gray eyes concerned. "How can Douglas not desire you, when he obviously loves you so very much? Come tomorrow, you'll laugh at your fears. And, when a month has passed, you can announce to your husband that he's to become a father, and everything will work out."

"Yes, I suppose so," Heather said doubtfully, thinking it would take a far more gullible man than Douglas appeared to be to believe it. Her mouth felt suddenly dry, and a horrible feeling of dread made her stomach turn over. How could she explain, six months from now, the birth of a healthy nine-month-old baby? Perhaps . . . perhaps it would be better to tell Douglas the truth, throw herself on his mercy? He loved her, didn't he? Maybe he could find it in his heart to forgive her, to accept the child as his own? The night Adam had returned to Moorsedge flooded back to mind. She heard his voice, cold and angry as he spoke about the child: *I'll take it from you before I let you name Dennison as the father!* She sighed heavily. Was there to be no end to this? "I hate to deceive Douglas. This deception goes against my nature, Ellen."

"I know, dear. But it's necessary in this instance."

"Necessary, perhaps. But excusable . . . I'm not so certain."

Ellen shrugged. "What's done is done. For now, you had best put on a charming smile, and join your husband. He instructed me to tell you that your guests will be arriving soon."

With a last glance at her appearance in the cheval mirror, Heather left the room.

*   *   *

The dining room was lit by several sparkling crystal chandeliers. Over forty guests, all attired in evening wear as if this were a formal dinner in the heart of London society, were seated at a very long, highly polished table laid with fine china, crystal, and silver, and cut-glass bowls of bright blossoms. Potted palms added their cool, fronded greenery to the elegant high-ceilinged room. Discreet black servants robed in flowing white moved silently about bearing trays and dishes to and fro. Conversation ebbed and flowed all about Heather like a sea.

Douglas appeared enormously complacent about the impact she had made when introduced to his friends and associates, and he favored her with intimate little smiles from the other end of the long table, smiles that caused the more tactless of the guests to nudge each other and wink knowingly. For the most part, they were planters or farmers, gentleman farmers who merely oversaw the working of their land, but left the actual cultivation to African laborers and foremen. It was a pleasant enough gathering, but from time to time Heather had to stifle a yawn as the guests talked incessantly of crops, the insect pests that damaged them, and the constant need to oversee their native workers, whom they obviously held in low esteem.

They adjourned to another room for cigars and brandy, and one of the planters' wives, a Sophia Whiting, if Heather's memory served, entertained the company by playing the piano and singing the popular "I Dreamt That I Dwelt in Marble Halls"—a singularly appropriate choice, Heather decided, hiding an amused smile as she looked about her at the vast room with its airy white walls and arched doorways! Enthusiastic applause followed Sophia's rendition.

"Do you sing, Lady Heather?" asked the planter

called Gerald Atkinson.

"A little," she confessed.

"Would you honor us with a song?" he persisted.

"Oh, yes, do!" exclaimed his plump wife, and the others chimed in insistently.

"Very well," Heather agreed reluctantly. "If you'll play for me, Mrs. Whiting, I should be delighted."

She sang a few bars unaccompanied, and then Sophia Whiting picked up the melody and accompanied her. The song she sang was a haunting Scottish ballad, of Bonnie Prince Charlie's escape from his enemies by boat to the beautiful Isle of Skye, and there were tears in many of the women's eyes when she was done.

Douglas came across to the piano in the hushed silence that followed her singing. He bent his blond head and kissed her gently before all, murmuring, "That was simply lovely, my dear. I had no idea that you were so accomplished."

The others echoed his praise. Flushed with pleasure, Heather accepted their compliments, then excused herself after a few minutes to slip away from the crowded drawing room and venture outside into the cool of the gardens.

The shrubberies were a fairyland of light, as if tiny stars had fallen to earth and become snared in their branches. The "stars" were, she realized, fireflies. She gratefully drank in the cool, sweet air, glad to be away from the stuffy gathering of single-minded, boring people. By comparison, London society seemed far from dull, not in light of the monotonous existence she believed would unravel endlessly here. *The hospital will keep me sane!* she thought, trying to be optimistic. In a few weeks, when I have settled in, I will broach the subject with Douglas again. . . .

She sensed suddenly that she was being watched by

someone behind her, and the hairs at the bare nape of her neck rose in response to that awareness. She whirled about to see a figure in the scented shadows of the Madagascan jessamine bushes.

"Who's there?" she demanded. "Show yourself!"

The dark silhouette of a man separated itself from the darker mass of the foliage, stepping into the puddle of light that spilled from the residence doorway. It was Adam. He wore a broad-brimmed bush hat that had seen better days, a band of leopard skin about the crown. His white shirtsleeves were rolled up to the elbow, the tail of his shirt was tucked into the belt of his trousers, the buttons were unfastened to midchest. Against his hip, Heather glimpsed a wicked black revolver in a leather holster, and she noted the rifle slung casually over his shoulder, as if he were accustomed to carrying it. His knee-length boots were soundless in the grass as he strode slowly toward her.

"You! What are you doing here?" she cried, shaken to the core.

Arms akimbo, he chuckled softly, infuriatingly. "Not even twenty-four hours, and already you're beginning to sound like your husband, my lovely!" he mocked, amused. "That's hardly a warm greeting for a man who has been loitering here in the garden for the past three hours, hoping he'd see you!"

In the shadows, she caught the flash of his teeth as he grinned, and she knew without seeing them that his gentian blue eyes would be alive, dancing with devilish laughter. She said nothing, her heart hammering too madly in her breast to permit speech had she thought of anything to say. The old, familiar fluttering in the pit of her stomach began anew at the sound of his voice.

"What? Has dear Douglas forbidden you to speak?" he taunted, coming closer.

"Of course not," she retorted. "Why have you

come here?"

He shrugged. "Several reasons. To pay my respects to the Governor's lovely bride, perhaps? Or to visit with an old and very *dear* friend?" His tone left her in no doubt of his meaning. He laughed softly again. "Or perhaps simply to infuriate our esteemed and pompous Governor! The last time I was here, he had me seen off the premises at gunpoint!" He paused, and the smile faded from his face. "And then again, maybe it was concern that brought me here. Concern for you—and for my child." His gaze shifted to her belly. The elegant line of the lavender gown was still smooth and flowing, unmarred by any outward sign of her condition, and he frowned.

"You needn't be concerned about either of us, I assure you." She flared, tossing her head. "Although a fortune-hunting coward in your opinion, Captain, I'm quite capable of taking care of myself." His cruel parting words that night at Moorsedge still smarted, for she knew at heart he had been right. She *had* been too cowardly to go with him as she had longed to do; although she had told herself that it was her duty to remain Douglas' wife. However, she had no intention of admitting that to anyone, least of all to Adam. "I don't need your concern, nor does *my* child!"

"Don't be a stubborn little fool! Be intelligent enough to accept friendship when it's offered. You're alone, in a foreign land. You never know when you may need friends." Perhaps sooner than you think, my lovely, he added silently, and his expression was filled with foreboding.

"And you would have me consider you a . . . a *friend?* After all that has happened between us? Oh, Adam, surely you know that's impossible!" she cried, her violet eyes filled with anguish.

"Ah. Then you still care?"

"I didn't say that!" she muttered indignantly.

"What you leave unsaid tells me more than words," he whispered harshly. "No! Don't turn away! Look at me!" he hissed, and she spun around to face him. "When I left Moorsedge that night, I was angry, determined never to see you again. I intended to leave you to Dennison's tender mercies. But I heard you'd arrived here in Nairobi today, and damn you, I couldn't stay away! I had to see you again, to see if I still felt the same."

"And?" she asked in a whisper.

"Don't you know the answer to that?" he demanded roughly. "God help me, nothing's changed! I know you for what you are, but I still want you!"

With a start, she realized that he was scant inches from her now, that his breath fanned her hair and mingled with her own. His scent was full in her nostrils: alive, warm, and irresistibly male. If he wanted, he could reach out and touch her in a single, swift move, and she would be powerless to escape him. . . .

"Heather! Where are you?"

It was Douglas' voice, calling her from the doorway.

"Coming!" she called back. To Adam she whispered fiercely, "If I truly mean anything to you, you'll leave here now, before he finds you here!"

"I'll go," he agreed reluctantly, his tone tight and controlled, "though I'm itching to throw you over my shoulder and carry you off!" He saw her face grow pale in the moonlight, and scowled. "Don't look at me like a terrified rabbit, my love. I won't. Not tonight, anyway! Listen carefully, before he comes," he continued urgently. "I'm setting out from Magadi on the first of May, taking an expedition northwest into the Congo. I talked with Robert Elwood in London after I left Kirkenmuir that night, and I'm going after the diamonds. Leave Douglas and come with me. We'll find them together!"

"That's impossible," she said flatly. "Now, please, go!"

"I'm on my way, damn it, woman!" he growled, fighting the urge to shake her senseless. "Just remember. If anything should happen to make you change your mind and leave Douglas, have Ngudu bring you to Magadi. I'll be there until May, but I won't wait forever, Heather. You've got two months. After that"—he shrugged—"I'm leaving, and who knows what the Congo will bring?"

Another day, another time and place when he had urged her in a similar fashion to meet him, flashed before her eyes. "But I won't change my—"

"Who knows what the future holds? You'll come if things go wrong here—promise me that much!" he commanded urgently, his gentian eyes heated in the gloom, "or I'll stay here and let your bloody husband find us together, and to hell with the consequences!" For a second, he seemed torn, and she knew it would take very little for him to do just that.

"I promise," she agreed hurriedly. "Go, now, go quickly!"

He seemed about to do as she had urged him, but at the last second he reached out and hauled her roughly to him, his hard mouth covering hers in a heated, ardent kiss that left her weak and trembling in his masterful embrace. She looked up, wide-eyed, into eyes as turbulent as a stormy sky in the fleeting second before he melted silently into the shadows of the foliage and was gone.

And not a second too soon, she thought shakily as she saw Douglas strolling across the lawn to meet her, immaculate in his tropical whites. Her lips still burned from Adam's kiss, and she wondered dazedly if his mouth had not left some outwardly visible mark upon them that Douglas would see.

"What are you doing out here all alone?" he asked.

"Enjoying the night air," she lied easily, giving him a smile and slipping her arm through his. "The nights are so deliciously cool."

He nodded, seeming convinced. "Several of our guests are preparing to leave. I think it is proper that you should see them off?"

"Of course. I was about to come inside when you called."

After the Whitings, the Atkinsons, and the others had left, she remarked to Douglas that she was still a little tired from her long journey and thought she would retire for the night. Douglas, smiling, kissed her forehead fondly after she had excused herself to their remaining guests, all men, with whom he was drinking.

"Run along, my dear. I'll join you shortly," he urged, the picture of a concerned and affectionate bridegroom as she headed gracefully for the doorway.

His guests grinned and winked.

"You lucky dog, Dennison, to have a fetching little baggage like that all to yourself!" she heard one man mutter as she went. "And as your wife, to boot!"

"She's far too lovely for the likes of you, old chap!" another bantered.

"Hear, hear!" agreed a third.

"Gentlemen," Douglas said with a grin, "I agree!" He raised his glass and offered a toast to his absent bride.

Heather lay in the wide double bed as tense as a board, waiting with bated breath for her bridegroom's footsteps in the marble hallway outside her room. She wetted her lips nervously and brushed aside the voluminous folds of the mosquito netting to peer for the hundredth time at the tiny clock upon the bedside table. It was almost midnight! Somehow, two hours had gone by since she had excused herself to their wedding guests and made her way to bed.

Douglas had seemed very much the ardent bridegroom anticipating his wedding night when she had told him she intended to retire. Indeed, he had winked at the male guests who remained and had promised he would soon join her in such a wicked fashion that her face had flooded with crimson color. When then, had he not done so? Oh, lord, let him come soon and get it over with! She felt no eager anticipation at the thought of Douglas' making love to her, not as she had with Adam. It was simply an unpleasant duty she must learn to bear. She must will herself to submit to her husband's desires, she told herself firmly, but that didn't help much. With a gulp, she forced her thoughts away from what was to come and thought instead of other things.

Lady Heather! How very grand it sounded, and how beautiful Douglas' residence was! The white, high-ceilinged rooms were a welcome haven after the fierce sun outside, and the cooling currents of air, stirred by the wooden paddles of the numerous ceiling fans tended diligently by little African houseboys, were like delicious, refreshing breezes.

The vast rooms, almost without exception, opened onto shady verandahs with pretty rattan furniture, delightful places to rest and enjoy their various views. The lush gardens about the house were filled with the riotously colorful blossoms Douglas had described weeks before at Heathlands Hall, and with trailing or fronded greenery that cascaded down high walls. There were spacious lawns on which peacocks strutted, emitting their harsh calls as they spread their jeweled tails like multieyed fans; and there were immaculate lawns where poloplayers upon well-schooled ponies, or cricket players in spotless white, no doubt competed like overgrown schoolboys.

It was clear that a life of languid luxury and delight might be hers as the Governor's wife, should she choose to accept such a lot . . . but she could not. Ever since Douglas had mentioned, back in Scotland, that he was concerned about the running of the area hospital under his jurisdiction, she had nurtured the hope that he would keep his promise to allow her to inspect it, and to spend at least a portion of her time in making suggestions and in giving practical assistance for its improvement. That goal had filled her thoughts while aboard the *Achilles*. Indeed, that and the child she carried had been the only inducements that had persuaded her to follow Douglas to Africa as planned! If only he would keep his promise and allow her to have some say in the running of the hospital, she believed she could be reasonably happy as his wife—at least, far happier than she had expected she could ever be again . . .

The bedroom door opened then, and Douglas lurched in. To Heather's dismay, the smell of liquor hung about him, and she knew by the bright glitter in his eyes and the high, unnatural color to his cheeks that he was quite drunk. Despite the sticky heat of the night, she pulled the sheet up to her chin and tensed.

"So, there you are, my little bride!" he exclaimed, staggering to the bedside. "Are you eagerly awaiting my ardent attentions, my dove?" The jeering quality in his voice was not lost on Heather.

He tried to thrust aside the netting, but succeeded only in getting entangled in its folds in the process. He cursed, grasped the mesh by the fistful and tore it from the ceiling, tossing it aside. "There! Now I can see you better," he slurred, sitting beside her and removing his coat, then his collar studs and shirt, and flinging them after the netting. He hauled off his boots and stretched out beside her, wearing only his trousers. Despite her dismay, she saw that his body was well muscled, smooth and pale gold, and his chest was forested with curling golden hair.

He grinned as he wrested the sheet from her and made to embrace her, for she shrank from his touch. "No, Heather. There'll be no false modesty tonight," he threatened, his speech somewhat indistinct. "You're my wife, and don't you ever forget it! My every wish shall be your pleasure, you understand me?"

Sick at heart, she nodded, steeling herself to yield to his caresses and embraces as he toyed with the wealth of her fiery hair spilling across the pillows. Was it seeing Adam again so suddenly that gave rise to the feeling of revulsion that swept through her when Douglas touched her? No. It is simply that he's drunk, she told herself silently. That is what repels me, for until this moment I had thought of him as an extremely attractive man, despite my lack of feeling for him.

She sucked in a horrified breath as his fingers strayed to the ties of her silk nightgown, closing her eyes as she braced herself for his touch upon her breasts. Yet he did not unfasten each button as a tender bridegroom might do. Instead, he knotted both hands in the delicate fabric and yanked it from her body, leaving her quite naked upon the bed and trying desperately to cover herself from his glittering eyes, even as she reeled from the shock of his assault!

Oh, Lord, where was the tenderness and shared passion he'd promised her? she wondered, feeling faint with fright and sickened by his roughness. But barely had she recovered from her shock when he made a lunge for her. She cried out and rolled away from him, springing off the bed and to her feet, and flying toward the door. Douglas staggered after her.

"Come here, bitch!" he growled. "Don't pretend

you're outraged, for there is no need of pretense with me!" He laughed triumphantly. "I know bloody well you're no innocent chit. I knew it before we were betrothed, my love, if you recall?"

Silently, shamed to the core, she nodded.

"Then I'll enjoy some of that passionate nature now, miss. As your husband, Heather, my dear girl, I demand it! Don't cringe away from me in false modesty. Wipe that look of disgust from your lovely face this instant and stand over there by the lamp so that I may admire your naked beauty." He leered at her and waved her toward the lamp.

"Please, don't ask this of me, Douglas, I can't—"

"I'm waiting, Heather," he cut in, his cold voice filled with menace.

Sick at heart, she stood where he had commanded, her hands shielding her breasts and womanhood from his eyes.

"Hands by your sides, my dear. I'm your husband, remember? You may have no secrets from me."

Cheeks burning, she dropped her hands to her sides. For moments that seemed endless, his gaze traveled over her, lingering on the full, high curves of her ivory-pale breasts surmounted with small, shell-pink nipples, and the flaming triangle that surmounted her thighs. Her glorious hair spilled about her shoulders, its warm dark-flame hue contrasting sharply with her creamy flesh. But his eyes were not filled with desire when he looked upon her; she sensed that even in her deep shame. Instead they seemed peculiarly cold, as calculating as those of an appraiser of fine art assaying the worth of an expensive, but not coveted, piece.

"Charming," he murmured at length. "Quite charming. Turn."

She did so, fighting the urge to be violently ill. The clock ticked off what seemed like endless minutes as she stood, her back to him, in the all-revealing light of the lamp. An eternity passed before he spoke again.

"The face of an angel, and the body of Aphrodite," he murmured softly. "Little wonder your captain could not keep his hands off you! Did you enjoy those afternoons in Adam Markham's bed, my dear?" he demanded. When she made no answer, he sprang to his feet, crossed the room, and spun her about by the shoulder to face him. "Did you? Answer me!"

"Yes!" she whispered.

"As I thought," he murmured, his sky-blue eyes glittering strangely. He traced the outline of one of her breasts with his fingertip, smiling when he saw that his touch caused her skin to rise in gooseflesh, the nipple to pucker in revulsion, involuntary reactions he assumed were those of desire. "For all that innocent loveliness, you're no better than a harlot at heart, as are all women. Does my touch please you?"

"Of . . . of course. You're my husband, Douglas," she stammered, unable to meet his eyes.

He grinned. "Ah. Am I not lucky to have such a dutiful wife—albeit she's a liar! Admit it, Heather, you feel nothing but contempt when I caress you, isn't that so? It's Adam Markham's hands you long to feel caressing your body, not mine. It's him you hunger for, not me, isn't it?"

"No!" she cried, her tone heated in protest for she knew at heart she lied. "I feel nothing for Adam, not anymore, I swear it! Please, Douglas, won't you give me the chance to prove that I'll be a good wife!"

"How? Upon that bed?" he demanded in jeering tones. "No, I think not! I've no desire to make love to a woman who imagines she lies with another even as I make love to her. You see, I thought when I proposed to you that I could forgive you your affair with Markham, Heather, so great and consuming was my

274

love and passion for you. But in these weeks since last I saw you, my passion has regrettably cooled. Reason has returned. The thought of your fresh innocence having been sullied—used—by that adventurer, of you having given yourself to him freely and eagerly countless times, fills me with disgust!"

Speechless, she gaped at him. "What are you saying?" she whispered, her tone strangled.

"Is it really so hard to understand? I'm saying that I've decided you'll be my wife in name only, my dear. That you may sleep here alone each and every night, and contemplate the wages of your past sin. Ours will be a loveless, passionless marriage!" He smiled, as if he had made a vastly amusing joke. "Well? Have you nothing to say before I leave you . . . alone?"

"Yes!" she flared, amethyst eyes alive and brilliant with anger, "I have a great deal to say! You're quite right. I didn't love you when I accepted your proposal. But I swear to you, Douglas, that I intended from the first to be a good wife to you, the best I could possibly be. I hoped that in time, I'd come to love you as I believed you loved me. That . . . that is all."

She did not appear as broken and humbled as he'd planned, and the triumph that had flared in his glassy blue eyes wavered. "All!" he rasped. "Isn't it enough that you accepted my offer of marriage while still panting after your Adam? You little slut!" So saying, he struck her across the face with his open palm, spinning her to the ground.

Her hand flew to her smarting cheek. "How dare you! You have no right to strike me!"

"I have *every* right, my dear. As you said, I'm your husband! Your cuckolded husband, but your husband nonetheless!" Douglas threw back at her. "And however you may have disgraced me with your wanton behavior prior to our marriage, you will not forget that you're my wife—ever again! If you do, if I hear so much as a *whisper* that you are seeing Markham—or any other man—I shall beat you until you are unable to stir from that bed for a month, as is my right! Do you hear me? You'll be above reproach, or regret it!" There was a sick, excited blaze in his eyes now, as if the threat gave him sadistic pleasure.

She got to her feet, her violet eyes hurling shards of indigo glass at him. Outraged, she tossed her fiery mane over her shoulders, uncowed despite the angry red mark upon her cheek. "You have known what took place between myself and Adam since before we became betrothed. Why, then, did you court me so ardently? Why did you ask my uncle for my hand?" she demanded, quivering with outrage.

His smile wavered. "I had my reasons, none of which need concern you, *Lady* Heather," he retorted with heavy sarcasm. He shoved her aside and flung open the door, looking back at her over his shoulder as a smile curled his lips. "It's a great pity that exquisite body will be wasted, my dear. Despite your whoring, you're very beautiful," he murmured as his eyes raked her from head to toe. "What a shame I can find no pleasure in you, knowing many others have sampled your charms before myself, especially that bastard Markham. Good night, my dear. Sleep well, won't you?" With that parting cut, he left the room before she could fling a denial in his face.

What use would further protests have been? He was far too drunk to listen to anything she might have to say, she thought dully. Mechanically, she set about righting the room, which was a shambles; then she poured water from the pitcher onto a cloth to bathe her cheek. For all that Douglas had not made a fist when he'd struck her, there would be a bruise there in the morning, she knew. A dull ache began in her temples presaging a headache, not from the blow but from her upset. She poured herself a glass of tepid water, and then drew a fresh nightgown from her dresser drawer and put it on. Returning to sit upon the bed, she drank the water.

Would Douglas remember his behavior in the morning, she wondered? Had he meant all that he'd said, or had it been mainly the liquor talking? Surely he would never have married her if he truly felt as he said he did? It was difficult to see him as the same man who had asked her to do him the honor of becoming his wife just a month ago! Then he had been romantic, respectful, correct in his behavior—in short, everything that Aunt Elise and Uncle Jamie had desired in her future husband. Could they have been so wrong? Could *she* have been so wrong? But then, she thought wearily, the nagging headache becoming an insistent, throbbing monster, was the blame his alone? Surely any man would feel rage, disappointment, and jealousy upon learning the woman he loved had given her innocence to another? But then, knowing of her affair with Adam all along, *why* had he asked her to become his wife in the first place? It didn't make sense! Oh, Lord, what had she unwittingly gotten herself into?

And what, a nagging voice asked, could she do when it became obvious that she was carrying a child—a child that even a fool could guess was Adam's? And Douglas was no fool. She recalled his hate-filled face when he'd said Adam's name and she shivered.

Chapter Seventeen

She awoke the following morning feeling exhausted and upset. Her head throbbed, and vicious cramps made her double over in agony.

Later, while dressing, she discovered blood on her clothing. A miscarriage, she thought at first, I am having a miscarriage, brought upon by her upset of the night before! But it was not. The flow was not unusually heavy, and her cramps gradually subsided to a dull ache. Her monthly inconvenience had finally recommenced, she realized, after being absent for two, almost three, months, and she was stunned to the core. Dear God in Heaven, she had married Douglas for nothing!

Her knees trembled in reaction to that shocking knowledge, and she felt suddenly dizzy and weak. Abruptly, she sat down upon a stool to recover her composure, her mind in turmoil. It was little wonder she had experienced few symptoms other than the cessation of her monthly—no swelling of her belly and breasts, no further sickness in the mornings since her bout with pneumonia. She wasn't carrying Adam's child; she had never been carrying Adam's child! The relief she should have felt, however, was peculiarly absent. Oh, she knew that now she would have no reason to fear Douglas' anger, no need to explain herself. But a part of her had wanted desperately to have Adam's baby, had ached to have some part of him that neither Douglas nor anyone else could take away. Now she would have nothing. No marriage. No husband with whom to share the little triumphs and disappointments of life, perhaps to gradually learn to love and cherish. No child—not Adam's and certainly never Douglas', unless he relented. Overwhelmed with confusion and bitter disappointment, she flung herself on the bed and wept. Mrs. Reading found her there later when she came to help her make her toilette prior to breakfast at nine.

"Whether you believe it or not now, it's for the best, my dear," Ellen said sadly after Heather had told her the news and had hinted at what had occurred between Douglas and herself the night before. "He would never have forgiven you for carrying Adam's child! His hate for the man has already been transferred in part to you, I do believe. Give thanks, Heather, that he'll not have an innocent babe to vent his anger and hatred upon!" She gazed with disapproving eyes at the livid bruise upon Heather's cheek, soaking a cloth in tepid water to bathe it. "That monster!" she exclaimed, horrified that Douglas had struck her Heather, "And to think I once urged you to marry him! How can you ever forgive me, my dear?" Her eyes were filled with concern. "You must rest quietly in bed today, and I shall bring you a powder to help you to relax. I'm sure a tray can be sent from the kitchens if you're hungry. Perhaps some tea, and a few slices of those mangoes you so enjoy?"

"That sounds lovely, Ellen," Heather murmured, drying her eyes.

She allowed her companion to take charge, to fuss over her and spoil her as she had done since Heather was a child. Something inside her cried out to be

279

cossetted and cared for, especially after the night's events. She felt wounded, scarred deep inside, where her hurts were unseen. She found herself longing for Annabel's bright smile, for Aunt Elise and Uncle Jamie's loving company. Her wrenching, aching loneliness bordered on physical pain.

But life went on. She could not go back, could never go home again, she knew. And her spirit, though outwardly fragile, inwardly adapted to change and adversity, growing stronger in the process.

After a few days in bed, she rose and took on her role as mistress of the household, instructing the servants in the manner she wished their duties to be done. She was firm but fair, and they soon came to respect and love her. As Heather's days in Nairobi turned to weeks, and the weeks into a month, their Missie Bwana won their hearts.

Shortly after coming to the decision to make the best of things, Heather made up her mind to confront Douglas and to suggest that they try to act civilly toward each other. He had been avoiding her, and the situation threatened to become intolerable. She found him in his office, deep in conversation with one of his clerks, a slender youth with dusty blond hair and delicate features. From the first she had sensed that this young man had resented her presence in the household. His name was Philip Whiting, and he was the son of the planter, Edward Whiting, and his dowdy wife, Sophia, who had played the piano on the night Heather had arrived.

"Please ask Mr. Whiting to leave us for a few moments, Douglas," she said quietly. "We must talk."

"On the contrary, my dear," Douglas countered, a faint smile wreathing his lips, "I don't see that we have anything to talk about." His handsome face was mocking, superior, as he looked down at her.

"But *I* do," Heather insisted. "Mr. Whiting, would you step outside for a moment, please?" With a sulky nod, the youth left and Heather turned to face her husband.

"Douglas, this state of affairs has got to end! We're married, like it or nay, and for the smooth running of this residence, we must endeavor to behave congenially, at least, toward each other."

"Must we?" He sneered. "Why?"

His reply took her aback.

"For appearances' sake, if nothing else," she hinted, knowing Douglas put great store in appearances. "You know how servants talk! Soon the plantation will be abuzz with the gossip that you and I are not on good terms. Do you want your friends to whisper about us behind our backs? I know that I've disappointed you in some ways, Douglas, but couldn't we at least try to put the past behind us and start afresh? Won't you forgive me for what took place before I knew you? We could become friends, if nothing more." In truth, she didn't give a jot for what the servants thought of her and Douglas, but she desperately wanted to close the yawning gulf that separated them, in the hope that something, however small, could be salvaged of the remnants of their marriage.

"I'm afraid not, Heather," he replied coldly. "To be honest, my dear, I can't even bring myself to look at you without seeing you with Markham. You can't imagine the distaste that wells up inside me, that my own wife should have— Well, I've tried to be forgiving, but I've found there's a limit to a man's capacity to forgive or forget. No, we must go on as we are. I must learn to accept that you were what you were. Nothing can change that, and so a normal relationship is quite impossible between us. While you, my dear, must learn to live with your shame, and with the knowledge that the estrangement between us is your doing, yours alone."

After that, Heather had tried gamely to make the best of things. On the occasions when Douglas' friends—the planters and farmers and their wives, the district officers under his command, or the occasional visiting dignitary—came to the residence to dine or to take part in the polo games or cricket matches, she was a charming and attentive hostess. Guests invariably complimented her on her smoothly run household and her graciousness, not suspecting the pain she carried inside her.

For despite her animosity toward Douglas, his words had taken root. Raised strictly in accordance with the unbending morals of the times, Heather felt a deep sense of guilt over her passionate affair with Adam. Her guilt was sharpened by vivid memories of the pleasure she'd found in his arms, and at times by a compelling urge to run away, to go to Magadi and join him. This last feeling was so violently at odds with the shame she felt, if confused her utterly! April was flying past. Soon it would be May, and Adam would be gone! At the moments when Heather allowed herself to think of this, despair swept over her. To go running after Adam was as good as admitting that she had made a mistake, had failed. She'd made her bed, and now she must lie in it . . . alone!

Her husband's undisguised and frequent insults, his sly innuendos added to her shame. He's right, she acknowledged secretly. However much I may try to deny it, this hatefulness between us—my unhappiness—is my own doing. The greater responsibility for the failure of our marriage must be laid at my door.

Douglas did nothing to lessen the burden she carried as the weeks passed; rather, when they were alone, he added to it by casting reproachful glances at her and by making frequent pointed comments designed to question her fidelity to him.

"Tom Worth seems to be spending rather too many afternoons here, my dear, and rather too few in the bush where he's supposed to be acting as liaison between the tribesmen," he observed one evening as they sat silently in the vast drawing room, he reading some papers he had brought from his office, she working on a needlepoint fire screen she intended to send to Aunt Elise for a Christmas gift. Ellen had retired to her room to read, obviously finding the unrelieved tension between them disturbing.

"Tom? He's been helping me with the household accounts. As you know, he has a head for figures, which I do not," Heather replied, somewhat defensively. She enjoyed Tom's company. He filled a void in her life, for she needed companionship other than Ellen's; and his gentle chivalry and his many kindnesses and his obvious respect and admiration of her had restored, at least in part, the self-esteem that Douglas had so effectively damaged. Indeed, Tom's visits had become the high points of her week. She did not want to give them up. And I won't, she decided obstinately. Douglas can go hang!

"Just be sure that accounts are all he's 'helping' you with, Heather," Douglas remarked pointedly, and her face filled with high color.

She tossed her needlework aside. "How dare you insinuate that Tom's visits are anything other than what they are!" she had cried.

But Douglas only gave her a sneering smile and added, "There's no smoke without fire, my dear! Just keep in mind that you are my wife, and that you will remain so until 'death do us part.'"

"Why?" she said hoarsely. "Why keep up this pretense? You don't love me!"

"It is not a question of love, my dear, but of possession. You're my wife—as this chair is mine, or that painting on the wall is mine, you see? Get any notion you might have of leaving me out of your pretty little head, Heather. I'm not a pleasant man when I'm angry, and I would be *extremely* angry if I had to chase after you and bring you back by force." With that threat, he returned to his papers.

She had not seen Tom since that week, and when she swallowed her pride and asked Ngudu, who knew everything that went on in the residence and the surrounding area, if he had seen Mister Worth lately, he told her, "Bwana Dennison has sent Bwana Worth to Mombasa, Missie, to work for the Governor there."

"I see. Mister Worth told me nothing of this."

"I do not think Bwana Worth knew of it himself, not until the last minute," Ngudu volunteered, his brown, gold-flecked eyes sliding uncomfortably away from hers.

"When will he be back?"

"Next month, it is said. Perhaps the one following?"

"I see," Heather murmured thoughtfully.

That was the first time she suspected the turn Douglas' possessiveness might take. She began to realize the power his position as Governor gave him over the lives of those under his command. It was that same week that she began to suspect that Douglas had a mistress.

As the weeks passed, her suspicion became a conviction. Every afternoon, Douglas took to his apartments and gave instructions that he wished to rest and was not to be disturbed—not an unusual order, since Heather herself often napped during the hottest part of the day. But on one occasion an emergency arose, and she was forced to summon a servant to fetch Douglas.

"No can do, Missie Bwana! Bwana say no wake him, I no wake him! Bwana very damn' bloody mad, yes, yes!" Zahur, the houseboy, a tall Kikuyu lad, shook his woolly head so vigorously she wondered with faint amusement whether he would break his neck in the process, or if his eyes, rolling so much that the whites were very evident, would fall out.

"Very well, Zahur," she said firmly, "I shall wake him myself."

But before she rapped upon Douglas' closed door, she caught soft laughter, and the murmur of voices—two voices—within. Quickly, she left without disturbing her husband, but she was irritated and very curious.

Over the next few weeks, her curiosity grew until it became unbearable. One afternoon, lying restlessly upon her bed, her thoughts turning as always to the afternoons when she had lain in Adam's arms as she watched the fan paddles lazily rotate above her, she decided to find out just who was whiling away the afternoons with her husband.

What a hypocrite he is, she thought as she made her way down the hallway and out through a side door, weaving a path between the lush shrubbery to the verandah that fronted Douglas' apartments. He had forbidden her Tom's innocent companionship; yet he thought nothing of having a mistress here, in his bed, under her very nose! Silently, she went up the verandah steps. Filmy curtains billowed from the open French windows, and the sound of muted voices reached her, one Douglas', the other so low she could not identify it. She edged forward, pressing up against the wall as she went and craning her head to look inside the room.

The bed lay in half-shadow, its gauzy netting having been drawn despite the fierce heat of the noonday sun. Douglas lay on his side, his back to her. From what she could see, he was unclothed, a rumpled sheet thrown

285

carelessly across his hips as he embraced his mistress. From the low pitch of his voice, he appeared to be murmuring endearments to the woman who lay curled beside him. There was a tinkle of glass as she saw him reach for the drink that stood on the low table beside the bed, then soft laughter as Douglas and his lover shared some intimate joke.

Contrary to what she had expected, she felt no jealousy whatsoever to find him with another, but she did experience a twinge of regret. If things had only been different, if she had never met Adam, perhaps they could have had a good marriage, she and Douglas, a productive and fulfilling life, and yes, children too. If not for her . . . Tears blinded her and she wanted to run away, to hide, to give way to them. But she stood as if rooted to the spot, fascinated and, yes, ravenously curious about the identity of Douglas' companion. Was it the cook's daughter, precocious little Tabia, that black, svelte beauty with seductive dark eyes and pointed, dark-nippled breasts like dusky papayas? Or that sultry tigress, Dalila? Or perhaps one of his clerks' dowdy wives, eager for any diversion in this languid, steaming climate that stirred the blood and brought ancient, savage passions roiling to the surface? She would wait and find out. . . .

Not many minutes passed before Douglas rose from the bed. Padding naked to the bureau, he took a cigar from the humidor there and lit it. As she watched him exhale a stream of fragrant blue smoke, his companion threw back the netting and swung from the bed to pad barefoot to his side. Her eyes widened in horror and disbelief as she saw that person petulantly tug the cigar from Douglas' lips and toss it into the spittoon across the room, then kneel and curl pale, slender arms about her husband's lean hips, laying a downy cheek against her husband's muscular thighs, while Douglas muffled a strangled groan of passion. Heather gasped. His companion—his *lover*—was none other than—

"Philip Whiting!"

She had cried the name aloud, and the clerk gave a small shriek and leaped to his feet, burying his face against Douglas' chest to hide as she stepped between the French windows, revealing herself. For a moment, she was too stunned, too incredulous to react. But as the import of seeing two of them sank home, she could find only amusement in the sight of the delicate clerk desperately clinging to his handsome lover—her own husband!

"Get out of here!" Douglas barked, whether to his paramour or herself, she neither knew nor cared. He then flung the weeping youth aside and reached for his trousers. Philip, with a great howl, snatched at his own clothes, gathered them up, and fled the room, Heather's mocking laughter ringing in his crimson ears.

All the humiliation she had experienced at Douglas' hands, the shame and self-pity, vanished in that instant. It was suddenly clear why he had married her though he had known of her passionate love affair with Adam. He was using her as a *cover* for his own indiscretions while he let her go on thinking it was disgust at her wantonness that kept him from her bed. He had done that to ensure her silence! Rage filled her, igniting furious amethyst sparks in her eyes.

"You hypocrite! You damned hypocrite! What was it, Douglas, that sent you flying to England in search of a wife? Tell me!" she demanded. "A whisper of scandal that had to be publicly disproved? Was that it? I was never intended to be more than a convenient front, a cover for your own indiscretions, was I? And you said you could not bear the thought of my wantonness! Oh, how blind I've been, how very naïve! But then, that

287

suited your purpose admirably, did it not?"

"Breathe a word of this and you'll be sorry, I'm warning you!" he threatened, stalking toward her, his handsome, bronze face livid.

"I?" she queried. "Why should I be sorry? What can you do to hurt me that you haven't done already? Make public my affair with Adam before we were wed?" She laughed, and it was a harsh, bitter sound even to her ears. "I don't care anymore! Create a scandal. Say what you will, Douglas, my darling husband. Everyone will sympathize with me for having once known another man's love when they learn of your . . . fondness . . . for your own sex. Whereas your reputation will be quite destroyed, your position here taken from you, if I breathe but a single word. Our Queen is a great woman, but above all, Douglas, she's a prude! I warrant she'd not turn a blind eye to her governor keeping a boy lover! Or do you believe you are elite, above the courts, that you would not be convicted and sentenced to hard labor?

"For myself, I don't give a jot about your peccadilloes, not one jot! But I won't let the fact that you have preyed upon my guilt, used my feelings of shame against me these past months, go unanswered!" She shook with the fervor of her anger.

He had grown white about the lips beneath his now-mottled tan, and his visible apprehension gave her enormous pleasure. "You will be silent, Heather. You are my wife. I forbid you to speak a word of this!"

"You *forbid* me?" She laughed. "No, Douglas, that Heather's gone! I'll never cower in shame before you again! I'll not suffer as I have these past months, believing I alone was guilty for the failure of our marriage. If you would buy my silence, you must make some reparation for the pain and blame I have suffered. If you do not, I shall denounce you!"

"What is it you want?" The words came out as more of a snarl than a question. Indeed, they seemed torn from his lips.

"Not so very much. I must think about what I shall do. Meanwhile, I want you to give me free rein in overseeing the running of the hospital, and I want your sworn word that you will never come to my room, never threaten or strike me again. In return, I will say nothing. To all appearances, we will be deliriously happy together! Man and wife." A mocking smile hovered about her lips as she awaited his reply.

"Very well," he said heavily at length. "You shall have all that you ask."

She inclined her head, then turned away, stepping back out onto the verandah. The humid, jessamine-perfumed air was sweet to her nostrils after the cloying air of her husband's room. She drew in a cleansing gulp of it before she crossed the verandah and descended from it, heading through the gardens and toward the stables, in search of the head groom. When she found him, she ordered the open carriage to be brought around to the front door.

"I shall be taking a drive. To the hospital," she added, her tone revealing her immense satisfaction. That done, she swept inside the residence to dress for her outing.

On her entrance she all but collided with Philip Whiting. He was dressed now, yet his eyes were red and swollen with weeping. He shrank back against the wall when he saw her, and lowered his eyes. Silently, his slender body shook with fresh sobs.

"You may have him, Philip," she said softly. "You may have him and gladly, for I have never loved him, though we are married."

"You are not . . . not angry, Lady Heather?" he stammered, his green eyes with the thick, gold lashes filled with disbelief now as well as tears.

"Angry?" she echoed, her fine eyebrows arched. "No! Rather, I'm relieved that the deceit Douglas has practiced upon me these past weeks is finally at an end. I can again hold up my head." She reached out and squeezed the youth's arm comfortingly. At her gesture, the expression in his eyes turned to amazement. "It is not for me to judge the actions of others, Philip, to say if what they do is right or nay. Nor do I presume to judge you. We are, none of us, without faults. I am guilty of more than many others, I'd wager! But, please, be careful, Philip. You're very young, and my husband is a great deceiver. He uses people as if they were merely possessions, toys for his own amusement, as he has used you to serve his desires. He will cast you aside without care or thought when he has tired of you. Decide now what you will do when that day comes, as it must."

"No! You're wrong, Lady Heather!" the youth protested. "That isn't so! Doug—Lord Dennison—he loves me, I know it! You're just jealous because he wants me and not you!" His lower lip quivered, yet his eyes blazed.

"For your sake, I hope—I truly hope—that you're right." Heather murmured, shaking her head. There was pity in her violet eyes as she left the clerk staring after her and swept down the hall.

Chapter Eighteen

The Nairobi hospital, a rectangular building set at the far end of a dusty street lined with towering coconut palms, was run by a harassed, but seemingly dedicated, doctor named Ian Fairchild. This physician appeared dumfounded to find the Governor's wife before him, offering her services as a nurse. He shook his head in disapproval.

"My regrets, Lady Dennison, but I have no tasks suitable for a lady such as yourself to perform. If you are seeking charitable work for which to volunteer your services, might I suggest you leave the nursing to the native girls I have trained, and try the mission school instead?" His weary gaze slid scornfully away from her indignant face, instead traveling down over the cool, elegant picture she made in a morning gown of gray and white striped linen, the closest garb she'd found to a nurse's uniform in such a hot climate. With undisguised amusement, Ian Fairchild then stared at a patch of mildew on one badly whitewashed wall where blue-armored flies buzzed half-heartedly.

"Nonsense," Heather argued firmly. "In London, I was a second-year student nurse at the Nightingale School in St. Thomas' Hospital. Hard work does not make me swoon, I can assure you, nor does the sight of blood or dirt or of anything else for that matter. This is the nineteenth century Dr. Fairchild! We women are proving what we've known all along but men have refused to acknowledge, that we are able-bodied, intelligent, and far from helpless individuals who can contribute to the world in which we live, and contribute well. The nursing profession has gained enormous respect in the past few years. Those who pursue nursing are dedicated and well trained. Think of me not as a lady, if it troubles you to do so, Doctor, but as a nurse, first and foremost! Now, do you still insist you have no 'suitable tasks' for me?" Her expression was challenging. Fists on hips, Heather defied him, her violet eyes dancing brightly. Dr. Fairchild had seemed harried but sincere initially, however, in Heather's opinion, his sincerity was diminishing by the second. She fancied she could discern a faint odor of spirits about him now. His stained shirt and rumpled trousers, his stubbled cheeks and bloodshot eyes were not, perhaps, the result of a sleepless night spent devotedly caring for a patient as she had sympathetically first imagined. At the moment she wondered if they were signs of a frequently intemperate disposition.

"I do," he said in answer to her question. "Now, if you will excuse me, Lady Dennison, I must be getting on." To his mind, it was clear that she was dismissed. He turned away, heading for the door, but Heather stalked after him.

"Why?" she demanded, angry now. "This hospital of yours is scarce worthy of the name! The floors are filthy, the walls need scrubbing, and the flies . . . I'm sorry, Doctor, but I can't believe you're not in need of help here—dire need! The place speaks for itself."

"Be that as it may, madam," Fairchild said tersely, "I cannot accept your offer of assistance."

She snorted. "Cannot?"

"Cannot," he repeated, running a weary hand through his graying brown hair. "I must be blunt with you, Lady Dennison. Shortly after your arrival in Nairobi, your husband came here and expressly forbade me to allow you to do work of any kind in the hospital."

"Ah," Heather murmured, suddenly understanding, "he did, did he?" She smiled grimly. "Well, I do believe you will learn very soon that our dear Governor Dennison has had a recent change of heart! I shall return in the morning with my husband, and he shall tell you so himself."

"Certainly, Lady Dennison. Then I shall look forward to your visit."

With a curt nod, she swept from the hospital and out into Nairobi's dusty streets.

Squinting as her eyes adjusted to the brilliant late-afternoon sunlight, she lifted her skirts from the dust and started across the street to the spot where she had left Ngudu and the carriage in the shade of a date palm. She found the Kukiyu in conversation with a man who, when he turned at hearing her approach, turned out to be Tom Worth.

"Heather! You're looking lovely as usual!" he greeted her.

"Why, Tom, how marvelous it is to see you! What are you doing back in Nairobi? I had heard you were in Mombasa, and were to stay there indefinitely?"

"That is so, Heather," Tom agreed. "Your husband sent me there to work in the Mombasa office." He grimaced. "I returned only to submit my resignation to Lord Dennison. I'm done with being a district officer, you see."

"Your resignation?" She sighed and her lovely face grew solemn. "Are you certain that's what you want to do, that you won't stay on? I've missed you these past few weeks, Tom, and I have looked forward to your return. Your friendship has been one of the nicest things about Africa."

"And your friendship has been important to me, Heather. Which is why Douglas sent me to Mombasa. I rather fancy he didn't care much for our friendship." He grinned reassuringly. "Please, don't be concerned. I have far more exciting prospects than that of being a district officer. Adam Markham, a fellow who lives in Magadi and who fancies himself an explorer, has asked me to go with him into the Congo. Between you and me, it's a treasure hunt we'll be setting out on!" He winked. "Or a wild-goose chase!"

But of course, she realized, April was almost over! Adam had said he would have his expedition ready to depart on the first of May. That was only two days from now! "Ah, yes. The Tears of Agaja! So, Adam still means to follow his dreams," she mused aloud; then she flashed Tom a warm, wistful smile. "I'm glad, for both of you." And envious, she added silently, a long-buried dream of her own resurfacing to tug at her heart.

Tom frowned, then nodded. "Ah, yes, you knew Adam back in England, I believe?"

"Yes. I knew him . . . quite well," she confessed, feeling her cheeks pinken under Tom's blue-eyed scrutiny. "Well, if you'll excuse me, I really should be on my way. Good luck to you and Adam, and God be with you both."

"Wait!" he called after her. "Won't you let me ride with you, since we are headed in the same direction?"

"Of course! What could I be thinking of? Tie your horse to the rear of the carriage, Tom, and we'll be off," Heather declared, unfurling her frilled parasol.

A small herd of elephants were grazing on the low,

spreading trees and scrub vegetation of the plains as the sturdy carriage approached in a cloud of red dust. They extended gray trunks in its direction as if waving, then turned and ran, thundering across the savannah raising still more rust-colored dust clouds in their wake, their small taseled tails dangling ridiculously against their enormous, baggy, wrinkled rumps. A calf trumpeted in panic, then lumbered speedily after his mother, and Heather smiled, glancing across at Tom seated beside her. She saw that he was laughing too.

"The wildlife here more than makes up for the inconveniences, doesn't it? I never tire of looking at the creatures or the scenery."

"You were born in Africa, I seem to recall?"

"Yes. My parents were medical missionaries, Alexander and Isobel Cameron. I was born in Jinja, on the northeastern shores of Lake Victoria. My father was killed when I was only a few weeks old. My mother stayed on, trying to carry on the work he had started, but she contracted a fever when I was two, and died soon after. Ellen Reading was Mama's companion. She brought me back to England, to my father's brother, Jamie Cameron. My aunt and uncle raised me."

"The Camerons? Yes, I've heard of them—and great things too. You must be very proud of the work they did?"

"Yes. I've always wanted to follow in their path." Her jaw tightened suddenly, and determination glinted in her lovely eyes. "And I shall do so."

The residence was dozing in the late afternoon heat when Ngudu drove the carriage up to the front stairs. Heather bade Thomas Worth a warm farewell and again wished him luck before going inside and heading directly to her apartments.

Douglas would be preoccupied because of Tom's

295

resignation, no doubt, nonetheless, she decided to tackle him at dinner on the subject of her working at the hospital. That should *thoroughly* unsettle my digestive system, she thought ruefully, shaking her head, but then she decided that this day had been an unsettling one in many ways. Her discovery of Douglas with Philip filled her mind again, sending a flood of renewed indignation surging through her. Imagine! He had never intended that their marriage should be anything more than a sham, nor had he ever intended to permit her to work at the hospital, despite his promises. His orders to that awful Dr. Fairchild proved as much! Why? she wondered. Had he believed her working at the hospital might reflect unfavorably on himself? Or had he feared she might make friends of the Europeans in Nairobi, friends who would be her allies if his true nature were discovered? That seemed probable. At any rate, to have let her carry the burden of guilt regarding their relationship all these weeks was cruel, unthinkable!

She rang for water and bathed, then washed her long, dusty hair, briskly toweling it dry. Cool and refreshed, she lay down in a loose, thin wrapper to rest prior to dinner. Her eyelids drooped. Relaxed and drowsy, she idly dreamed in the few seconds that preface sleep.

Slumber had almost claimed her when she heard hammering at her door, so forceful the wood bulged inward from the jamb and the walls trembled. A religious tract that was attached to the whitewashed wall shuddered and fell, the glass shattering.

"Open up!" Douglas bellowed. "Open up before I break this blasted door down!"

She sprang from the bed and snatched up a vase from the bureau. "Go away, Douglas!" she cried. "I warned you never to come to my room again, and I meant every word I said! Take one step inside here, and the world will know of your peccadilloes!"

"Will they? Ha! I think not!" Douglas sneered from beyond the door. "I've been thinking over your little blackmail scheme, and it won't work! I won't let you ruin everything I've worked for here, you little bitch. Open the door, this instant!"

"Never!" she refused defiantly, her face paling.

More thunderous knockings. Then a loud crash finally made the lock give and the door exploded inward, reeling on broken hinges. Douglas stood on the threshold, a liquor bottle in one hand, a riding whip in the other. He all but fell through the broken doorway, grinning malevolently. He set the bottle down upon the nightstand and lurched unsteadily toward her.

"I warned you on our wedding night what would happen if you so much as looked at another man, didn't I? But you've not only disobeyed me today, you've tried to bring me to heel with your rash little threats. For both, you must be punished. You must learn who is your master!"

"What other man? You're mad!" she cried, backing away as he lumbered across the room toward her.

"And what of Thomas Worth? What about your little rendezvous with him in Nairobi this afternoon?" He chuckled nastily. "Don't bother to deny it, Heather! I already know the truth. I saw the two of you riding cozily home together, you see."

He slapped the riding crop across the palm of his left hand in a menacing gesture she knew he enjoyed. "First I shall teach you a lesson you will never forget, and then—why, then I shall claim my rights as your husband!" He leered as her lovely face paled to the color of chalk. "Ah, you seem surprised, my dear? Do you think me incapable, less than a man? I shall prove you wrong!"

"Take one step, Douglas, and you'll regret it!" Heather warned, the heavy vase brandished above her head.

"No, Heather, it's *you* who'll have regrets!" he gritted out, then stepped toward her.

She hurled the vase at his head, using all her strength, then looked about her for another missile for he had stepped nimbly aside to avoid the first, which shattered against the wall opposite. Heart pounding, she snatched up a hairbrush from the dresser, then a porcelain pin box, then a book, flinging them at him in quick succession. She was breathing rapidly now, eyes hectic, cheeks flushed, breasts heaving. Her damp, curling, dark-flame hair tumbled in disarray about her shoulders.

With a roar, Douglas lunged forward and swept the remainder of her belongings from the dresser. The crystal unicorn, given to her by Adam on Christmas Eve, along with his avowals of love, flew through the air and fell with a splintering tinkle to the floor, shattering into a million tiny shards. Her anguished, wounded cry was abruptly silenced as he sprang at her.

She ducked and attempted to run under his outstretched arm, but even as she sprang for the door, his fingers knotted cruelly in her flying curls and he jerked her painfully back into his grasp. His grip on her hair was so painful tears filled her eyes. Her scalp seemed afire! But then she knew pain of a different sort for Douglas wrenched the flimsy wrapper down to bare her shoulders and back, and he dealt her sensitive flesh one burning cut after another across the back with the riding crop. Involuntarily, she screamed, trying to wrench herself free. But his fingers only tightened unbearably in her hair, twisting and pulling mercilessly. Another cut from the crop, and a haze of crimson agony filled her vision with blood red.

"You . . . bastard!" she sobbed. "You cowardly *bastard!* You're no man, whatever you say, to treat a woman so!" She flailed her clenched fists at his head, his chest; struck out at his groin with a vicious knee, her breath labored and now mingled with sobs provoked by outrage as well as the stinging pain of her shoulders and back.

"Shut up!" he hissed, and flung her across the bed, falling upon her to pin her down with his weight. "I'll teach you now that I'm man enough for you, my lovely slut!"

When he reached for the fastenings of his clothing, she screamed—screamed as loud and as long as she could, the sound torn from a throat long since gone hoarse. He laughed and thrust aside the front of her wrapper; then he tore free the knotted sash at her waist. She lay bare beneath him briefly before he covered her body with his own. She recoiled in disgust as he clenched her chin in his fist and kissed her wetly, the sour smell of liquor and lust filling her nostrils until she felt that she would gag if he did not cease his foul kisses. His hand stroked downward over her heaving body to cover the tangle of curls that surmounted her thighs. She gave a great twist, seeking to throw him off balance, but his weight and his strength were too great.

"No-oooo!" she cried, her voice ending in a sob as he forced her thighs apart.

He laughed mockingly. "Go ahead, Heather darling, scream as loud and as long as you wish! I'm master here, remember, and I've given orders that we're not to be disturbed—not on any account."

Sick with disgust, she tensed, sensing the moment had come, that he would now take her, brutally and forcefully. But to her relief, he could not. His manhood had failed him. With a sob of fury and shame, he raised his clenched fist above his head. Heather's eyes widened in horror, then closed as she waited for the rage-filled blow to land. Every muscle taut, every nerve screaming, she strained to roll aside.

But then, quite how she did not at first realize, the weight was gone. She opened her eyes and dimly saw Douglas' astonished face suspended above her before she heard a solid crack like the sound of a shot. He hurtled backward.

Tom Worth stood over him, breathing hard. His kind face was a scarcely recognizable mask of fury, his knuckles were grazed and bleeding. He hauled Dennison to his feet and punched him a second time, then flung him to the floor. Douglas groaned once and then lay quite still. Blood was trickling from his nose and mouth as a result of Tom's ringing punches.

Muttering a curse, Tom picked up the riding crop and broke it across his knee. Heather gathered up the counterpane about her as he swung about to face her, his blue eyes enraged. Belatedly, she glimpsed Ngudu at his back, his dark face concerned, his brown eyes sliding discreetly away from her in respect for her modesty as she sat up.

"Say the word, and I'll kill him!" Tom hissed, fists clenched at his side.

"No, Tom, you mustn't! Leave him there. He's not worth hanging for!" Heather declared bitterly.

They all turned as Ellen Reading hurried into the room.

"What on earth? . . ." she cried. "I heard screams!"

"That bloody Dennison took a whip to Heather," Tom explained through gritted teeth. "That bastard!"

"No!" Ellen cried, hurrying to Heather's side. "My poor, dear child! Where did he hurt you?" An anguished cry and an unladylike oath came from her when she saw the angry red weals rising across

300

Heather's back and shoulders.

"Her injuries must wait, I'm afraid, Mrs. Reading," Tom cautioned. "First, Lady Heather must decide what she intends to do, and she must do so before Dennison comes to. Heather?"

"I tried so hard to be a good wife to Douglas. Ellen, Tom, you know that. I did everything in my power, to no avail! He didn't want us to have a good marriage, or even be friends. I was a fool to think I could change anything. I won't stay here another day," she declared in a low voice, "not one! Take us away from here, Tom, I beg you! We'll leave, Ellen, this very afternoon! Go quickly and pack your bags. I'll see to mine."

"But where will we go?" Ellen asked, her face suddenly aged by worry and concern.

"Where I should have gone long before," Heather said bitterly, choking back the sob that welled in her throat. "To Adam!" And the devil take Douglas!"

She suddenly felt that a great weight had been lifted from her shoulders. Her heart sang with joy, and for the moment all pain was forgotten. Her decision was *right*. She knew it! Duty, propriety, and convention be damned! Henceforth only she and Adam counted. She loved him so, loved him with a fierce, sweeping tenderness that flowed into her. A warm, golden light had penetrated the darkness of her soul, chasing away the cold and frightening shadows of her marriage to Douglas.

"Yes, to Adam, in Magadi," she repeated, her violet eyes aglow with radiant inner light. "If he'll still have me, I'll go with him to find the Tears of Agaja!" She smiled. "Trying to do my duty at the expense of my own happiness was wrong. I'll make his dreams my dreams. We'll follow them together! . . ."

*   *   *

301

There were enormous butterflies in her stomach when she rode through the village of Magadi the next morning, heading toward Adam's bungalow that lay on the western shores of Lake Magadi, after having spent the night at Tom's little house in Nairobi. What if Adam's feelings had changed in the past two months? What if he no longer loved her? What if, for some reason, he had already left? Apprehension nibbled away at her elation like a small but greedy mouse, its effect far more painful than the throbbing welts that crisscrossed her back.

Fruit and water sellers ran alongside their horses, thrusting bananas and plantains under their noses and demanding in strident tones that the bwana and the missie bwanas buy their wares. Tom tossed them a few shillings and good-naturedly told them to go away, Ngudu echoing his commands in sterner tones.

Native fishermen were wading chest-high in the blue waters of the lake, setting enormous fish traps of reeds, while boys herded hump-backed cattle, staring at the little cavalcade as it passed. Farmers tended fields of ripened corn, or hoed and weeded their patches of fonio or millet. Women wearing skirts made of orange cloth, carried baskets of grain upon their heads, from the farming patches taking them back to the village, meanwhile the children squatted beneath an enormous baobab tree and listened to the ancient grandmothers tell tales of how the hyena first came to have such a peculiar gait and was able to laugh, or why the leopard has spots.

Adam's bungalow was a long, low building set on short stilts above the ground. Beyond it, the lake shimmered like sapphires, reflecting the sky's glorious blue, and the distant mountains seemed wrought of mother-of-pearl. The bungalow's walls were constructed of native stone and local woods, the roof of thatch. All about it towered lovely African tulip trees, alive with scarlet and flame-colored blossoms, and flowering yellow acacias. Three steps led up to a long, shady verandah which a native girl was industriously sweeping when they rode up. Ngudu called to her in Swahili and she nodded, smiled showing sparkling white teeth, and ran inside.

Adam appeared through the doorway minutes later, buttoning up his shirt, his black hair attractively rumpled. It appeared they had awakened him from a nap. He looked at them, frowned, then strode quickly down the steps, going straight to Heather's horse.

"What happened?" he snapped, his gentian eyes dark with concern as he looked up at her.

In faltering tones, she told him, as simply and as briefly as she could. His jaw hardened. His fists clenched. "He hurt you. Damn him!" He swung about, his expression murderous. "Get down, Tom!" Give me your horse! I'm going back to Nairobi. I've a score to settle with that—"

"No, Adam, please don't!" she protested, alarmed by the blazing anger that raged in his eyes. "I've left Douglas for good. I won't be going back to him, whatever happens." She looked down, toying with her horse's reins, embarrassed. "I want to be with you . . . always . . . if you still want me," she murmured, her voice so low it was almost a whisper.

The anger in his expression faded. *"Want* you!" He threw back his dark head and laughed, incredulity in his eyes. "What took you so bloody long to leave him, that's what I'd like to know?" he demanded gruffly, swinging her down from her horse's back and into his arms. "You've got some explaining to do, my girl—and it'd better be good!"

She laughed shakily, knowing that behind his stern façade was the Adam she loved. "It's . . . it's a long story," she said softly. "About pride and mistakes and misplaced loyalties."

He nodded, and his dark, sensual gentian eyes gazed down into her face. "You can tell me later, sweet," he murmured huskily for her ears alone. "Right now, talk is the last thing on my mind. . . ."

In his office at the Governor's residence in Nairobi, Douglas Dennison was pacing back and forth like a man possessed. The livid bruises on his jaw and the split lip, which had swelled grotesquely, gave an ugly cast to his handsome face. There was a crooked appearance to his nose now, and the rusty stain of dried blood in one nostril was the legacy of Tom Worth's fists. His sky-blue eyes were crackling with anger as he looked at the circle of district officers standing uncomfortably before him.

"Damn you, I want her found!" he ranted. When he pounded his clenched fist upon the desk, Philip Whiting flinched nervously as if he had been struck. "Adam Markham's abducted my wife. I want them both found and brought back here, understand?"

Edward Whiting, Philip's father, stepped forward. Taller and far stockier than his son, he glowered at Dennison, his expression ugly.

"If you want Lady Heather back, then go after her yourself, damn you! In my opinion, she's better off with Markham. And I'm warning you, Dennison, stay away from my son, or as God's my witness, you'll regret it!" His massive fists, clenched at his sides, were flexing and unflexing with his anger.

"Father, please don't—"

"Shut up, Philip! Get your things together. You're coming home with me. We'll see if a stint in the army can make a real man of you, give you some Whiting backbone, boy!"

"No!" Philip protested, white about the lips now. "I'm not coming home, Father. And I'm not joining the army!"

"You'll do as you're bloody well told, you disgusting little sissy," Whiting snarled. He spun about on his heels and stormed from the office.

"I'm afraid Whiting's right, Governor," one of the District Officer's said when he had gone. "If you want Lady Heather found, you'll have to go after her yourself. Your domestic problems are a private matter—nothing to do with the department. You're on your own in this, sir." The others muttered their agreement.

So, Douglas thought, looking around the circle of closed faces, the rats are leaving a ship which they judge to be sinking! I'll show them! Yes, I'll show them!

"Get the devil out of here then, blast you!" he growled, and to a man, they left, all save Philip. His lip curled back in a sneer, Douglas eyed the youth. "Well? Aren't you going to run home to dear Mama and Papa?" he jeered.

Philip shook his head stubbornly. "No. You need me here."

Douglas grunted noncommittally, a faraway expression in his eyes.

"You do need me, don't you, Douglas?" There was a desperate note in Philip's voice now, and there was uncertainty.

"What? Ah, yes, of course I do, Phil, of course," Dennison agreed absently, and the youth smiled a fawning, eager smile that sickened him.

Douglas' mind was not on Philip, nor was he thinking of the desertion of his district officers. His

305

thoughts were filled with images of Heather and Markham together. Of the two of them sharing little jokes about him, deriding him. They'd not laugh for long, he vowed. Heather was his wife, his possession. His! She'd not run off with Markham and make a fool of him, not without paying for it, that little bitch!

He'd find them and kill them both first.

Chapter Nineteen

"Adam, hold me!" she whispered. "I can't believe I'm really here with you at last. Hold me, hold me tightly, so that I know you're real!"

She had awakened minutes before, dreaming she was back at the Governor's residence and that Douglas was after her, instead of here in Magadi, curled safely in Adam's arms, in Adam's bed, in Adam's bungalow on the banks of Lake Magadi, beneath the flowering tulip trees and the stars.

They had made love blissfully, hungrily, before falling into an exhausted but sated sleep, limbs tangled, heads resting side by side upon the pillows, dark flame against jet black. But the dream had frightened her terribly and she had awakened, trembling, to darkness and fear.

"I'm here. I'm real. And I love you, angel. Love you, love you . . ." Adam murmured soothingly, his deep voice husky with passion and sleep. His dark head dipped as his lips trailed over her rounded shoulder and down, to nuzzle the satin flesh of her breasts with little caresses and kisses that sent quivers of renewed longing flickering through her loins. "Now and for always, my love! Nothing will part us ever again, I swear it!"

Knowing his touch, his nearness were the only things that could make her feel safe and loved and cherished, he drew back the sheet that had covered them, and took her in his arms. The feel of her body, round and warm and seductive in his arms, filled him with renewed desire.

She laced her fingers in the crisp black curls that clung to his nape as his lips grazed up the column of her throat to cover her mouth. Ardently she clung to him, swept away on a warm tide of desire that she wished would never end. The feel of his lightly furred, masculine chest pressed firmly to hers, her breasts crushed beneath its broad, rough strength, his wonderful, strong arms embracing hers, filled her with vivid explosions of delight. His lips and tongue tip explored the velvet of her mouth in a way that made her pulse suddenly leap like a gazelle bounding across the savannah.

"Now, Adam, please, take me again! It's been so long I feel I can never be close enough to you!" she cried out desperately when he paused in his kisses.

"Soon," he promised. His warm breath fanned her cheek. "I intend to spend the rest of the night reminding you just how close we are, my love. . . ."

Her fingertips drifted down across the tanned width of his shoulders, relishing the powerful feel of corded muscle beneath smooth flesh while he stroked her body, first lazily, then with increasing ardor, learning each curve, each plain and tiny hollow anew. His wiry, powerful hands were so very gentle, even upon her most sensitive parts. She gasped in delight as he tenderly parted her thighs and stroked their velvety inner columns, gliding higher and higher until he teased the soft cluster of curls that shielded the font of her womanhood from his touch.

Delicately, with a lack of haste that both delighted

308

her and drove her to the brink of madness, he plundered her womanhood, a gentle pirate taking treasures freely offered, gladly given. His gentian eyes were aflame with burning desire when at long length he eased himself onto her. The moonlight that spilled through the open window touched his curling ebony hair with blue-silver, and it gleamed on the sweat that filmed his muscular shoulders as he bore her down into the feather mattress beneath his weight. The pale, shimmering light was also reflected in his eyes, and they became alive, fierce, smoldering with passion for the woman in his arms, the woman in his heart; the woman he had longed for, hungered for, each long, empty night and endless day since he had left her in anger weeks ago at Moorsedge.

He had feared he would never again hold her, love her, possess her. He'd felt that his unrequited love and desire would consume him, would plant seeds of bitterness in his soul, seeds that would grow and choke him, that would encase his heart in strangling overgrowth which could never be penetrated by any other woman. But now, miraculously, she was here, eager to be his, imploring him to show her with his body how deeply he cared for her, and offering herself as proof that his love was returned.

The real world had no meaning for them then. It ceased to exist. Their world became one of trembling delight, of sensations too wondrous to describe. Their endless giving and taking transcended physical boundaries, until they neither knew nor cared who gave and who took, for they were one, joined, inseparable, moving swiftly then slowly; blazing ardor alternating with gentle passion as they soared ever higher to the rapture that beckoned them, beaconlike, to a point just beyond.

With whispers and kisses, with touches and long,

drawn-out sighs, they loved, her slender legs cradling his lean hips, her arms embracing his chest and back, her whole body warm with surrender and love. With endearments and caresses, with grace and fluidity of movement and gentle yielding, they moved together in age-old rhythms. His flanks tautened, rippling with muscle as he claimed her, filled her with his throbbing hardness. His powerful arms were corded, yet tender, in their embraces. His mouth was bold, arrogant—masterful in possession and love. Draining her of doubt and fear, he replaced both with a raging fire that swept through her and consumed them both.

The trembling deep inside her built unbearably. It became a spinning, fragile orb of exquisite delight that grew and grew for endless, blissful moments before shattering and showering her with pleasure.

"Oh, dear God, Adam, my love!" She sobbed his name aloud in her rapture, her fingers locking convulsively over the tanned flesh of his forearms as she soared into bliss, her nails branding him with deep little crescents.

At her joyous cry, drops of perspiration sprang out like dew upon his brow and shoulders. He felt the storm inside him gather, build, become a relentless, raging crescendo of sensation that could not be halted, could no longer be denied! Gathering her into his arms, he thrust deeply once more, his lips heatedly covering hers as the tempest burst, exploding through him. He groaned in delight, then lay quite still.

Later, lying side by side, fingers entwined, his dark head pillowed upon her breasts, they fell asleep again. This time, Heather's sleep was deep and dreamless and endlessly sweet.

She awoke in the still, cool hour before dawn, to find

Adam already awake. He leaned upon one elbow, his other palm pressed flat against her belly. He'd been watching her as she slept, her face bathed in the fading moonlight that shimmered through the window.

"When?" he whispered, and she knew he was asking the question she had dreaded—about their child, the child that had never been.

She rolled away, turning her back to him, unable to find the words.

"Heather?" Taking her shoulder, he firmly turned her back to face him. "I asked you when the child will be born?"

"Never!" she whispered, her lower lip trembling.

His black eyebrows rose. "Never?" A black and terrible anger filled his face. "What did that bastard do to you to make you lose my child?" he asked in a strangled voice so filled with grief and rage it tore at her heart.

"No, no!" she whispered urgently. "He hurt me, yes, but I didn't lose the baby. There was no baby to lose. You see, I was wrong. I was never with child, Adam! Ellen said it can happen, that a woman who's under great duress can sometimes have reason to believe she's having a child, when in reality she's not."

He swung off the bed and strode to the window, staring out at the starlit lake, his stern, handsome profile etched black against the charcoal sky beyond.

"Then you married Dennison for nothing? This whole mess . . . was for nothing?" he said at length, his tone heavily laced with bitterness.

"Yes."

"Christ!"

She flinched at the forcefulness of his tone. Then silence yawned, like an abyss, between them, neither able, in those endless, painful moments, to find the right words to bridge it.

"I was destroyed when I learned I wasn't carrying your child, Adam. Despite everything, I'd desperately wanted your baby—to love, to hold. Oh, yes, it would have been a part of you, a part that no one could take from me. You must believe that!" The tears in her eyes caught the moonlight and glistened.

"When did you find out?" he asked curtly, unmoved by her emotion.

"The morning after I arrived in Nairobi."

"And still you stayed with him for two more *months!*" His gentian eyes flared in the meager light as he suddenly stalked to the bedside, reached out, and grasped her wrist. He towered over her. "Damn it, I don't know whether to kiss you—or kill you!" He spoke so low she had to strain to catch his words. His silhouetted body was tense. "Tell me the truth," he demanded, "the whole truth! Did you come here because it was me you wanted or escape from Dennison?"

"What?" she cried, taken aback by his cruel words. "How could you ask me that! You must know it was because of you. I could have had Tom take me to Mombasa, bought passage on a ship home to England if all I wanted was to escape Douglas!"

"Then why the wait?" he demanded, his jaw clenched, his fists balled at his sides. He strode across the room, away from her, as if he feared he would strike her if he did not put distance between them.

She slipped from the bed and padded barefoot to stand before him, reaching up to press one palm against his chest. The tension in him crackled against her skin. "Believe me, I never stopped loving you, Adam, not once, not even for a second! But . . . I was a coward! I'd married Douglas, and I was afraid, even after I first suspected what he was really like, to admit I was wrong. Like an ostrich, I buried my head in the

312

sand and foolishly hoped everything would work out. The pain I was feeling inside seemed somehow just, as if I deserved nothing better from life. My upbringing had taught me only that succumbing to one's desires was wrong, and yes, there was enormous guilt inside me because of our affair, Adam! Douglas guessed that, and he used it against me."

"How?"

In brief, brittle sentences, she told him, ending with her discovery of Douglas with Philip Whiting. As the tale unfolded, much of the dark anger faded from his face.

"It was as I first suspected," Adam said heavily when she was done. "He was only using you. With a beautiful young bride, few would suspect his homosexuality. And there was an added bonus: marrying you would keep you from me. He would finally be able to get even with me. If he read the letter, he must have known that I loved you and intended to ask for your hand."

"You knew about Douglas' homosexuality?"

"How could I help but know! When we served together in India, he made little attempt to be discreet, nor did others like him."

"Why didn't you tell me?" she cried, aghast.

He shrugged. "He was your husband, Heather. Whatever I said, I knew your loyalty would compel you to defend him. There seemed little point . . . and I was furious that you'd married him."

In hurt and anger, he'd struck out at her by remaining silent, she realized, her eyes filling with tears. "Oh, dear God, Adam, what fools we were! I to have blindly—stubbornly—insisted on remaining with Douglas instead of doing what everything within me cried out to do! And you—"

"And I to have left that night without you," he said fervently. "I should have followed my instincts and

313

carried you off, whether you liked it or not! Come back to bed." He'd noticed that she was shivering, so he drew her back to the warmth of the bed, stretching out alongside her.

"That time at Moorsedge, when I told you about the atrocities Douglas said you and your men had committed in India, you refused to defend yourself. I'd always thought that was because you still felt some guilt about what happened, for being unable to prevent what your men did. But it wasn't so, was it? What Douglas told me about India was nothing but lies!"

Adam nodded grimly. "The true story is quite different, believe me!

"You see, there was a bugler attached to my company—a handsome, fair-haired lad of fifteen. From the first, it was plain to all of us that Major Dennison was . . . attracted to the boy." Heather bit her lip and nodded, and Adam continued, "Most of us knew where Dennison's sexual preferences lay, but we turned a blind eye and minded our own business so long as the parties involved were willing. In this instance, the boy was not. He came to me, and asked me to help him. Douglas' advances had scared him, you see. He was in awe of the man, and didn't know how to fend them off.

"I went to Dennison and warned him in no uncertain terms to leave the boy alone. He laughed in my face, told me to mind my own damned business. The lad— Paul, his name was—was brutally seduced by Dennison one night while I was away, against his will. I found him shortly after dawn on my way back to camp, swinging from a tree. His own belt was knotted about his throat. He'd hung himself the evening before. God! The senselessness of the boy's death left me blind with rage! I went to Dennison's tent and thrashed him to a pulp! I would have killed him with my bare fists if

Tom—Lieutenant Tom Worth, he was then—hadn't pulled me off him!

"Dennison recovered in due course, and he started court-martial proceedings against me for striking a superior officer. I didn't give a damn! But my father, Colonel Charles Markham, did. He demanded to know what had occurred, and when I told him in private, he insisted I make public what Dennison had done. He threatened to disown me and cut me out of his will if I allowed the court-martial to proceed without clearing the Markham name. But I couldn't. You see, the code was too deeply ingrained in me."

"Code?"

He nodded. "The blasted officers' code of honor, the unwritten code by which we all lived! I could no more inform on a fellow officer, albeit that officer was Dennison, than I could my closest friend, no matter what he'd done. Father was livid. He arranged for the court-martial proceedings to be quietly dropped, and for me to discreetly resign my commission. He brought pressure—how, I don't know, but Father had his connections—upon Dennison to resign his own commission too. But Father never forgave me for allowing the Markham name to be tarnished by the scandal that surrounded that incident. Not 'til the day he died." Adam shrugged. "Perhaps I was wrong. If I'd had the gift of foresight, if I could have known then what far-reaching consequences my silence would have on my own life and on yours, I would have acted differently. But I did what seemed right to me at the time, which is all any man can do."

"And once you left the army, you came to Africa?"

"Yes. I'd heard there was money to be made in gathering new strains of orchids and introducing them into London, you see. I'd hoped to use my interest in these plants to amass a tidy fortune, and to do some

315

exploring into the bargain. During those years I kept up correspondence with my brothers, Hunter and Rory—we'd always been close—and they told me our father never mentioned my name, nor did he allow others to mention it in his presence. As far as he was concerned, I no longer existed. He succumbed to thrombosis shortly after and died, without going back on his decision."

"My poor Adam," she murmured, stroking his face, which was dark and bitter at the memory.

"After I'd been living in Magadi for a year or two, I heard Douglas had been appointed Governor of Nairobi, and I wondered how long it would be before he slipped up. He did exactly that last year. Rumor was rife in the White Highlands that our beloved Governor was overly fond of his little houseboys. He panicked, apparently, and rushed off to England in search of a beautiful, desirable wife to use as a cover—"

"And he believed he had found her in me," Heather put in. "No doubt he saw an opportunity to get even with you once he learned we were lovers. He would take me away from you! That monster!" Of a sudden, the darkened room seemed no longer a delightful haven for their lovemaking; it was sinister and threatening. She shivered. Remembering the hatred on Douglas' face when he'd struck her, she reached blindly for Adam.

Sensing her fear, he gathered her tightly to him and kissed her, brushing the deep, heavy waves of dark hair from her pale little face with a caressing hand. "Don't be afraid," he murmured. "Dennison is in the past. It's just you and I, sweet, from now on. And I won't let anybody, not Dennison or anyone else, hurt you again, believe me!"

"I do, Adam," she acknowledged. "I do! It's just that I keep seeing his face in my mind! He's completely

316

ruthless, you know that. He never thought of me as a person, not once, not even at the beginning. I was an object to be acquired and then possessed. He'll not sit back and let you take me from him, Adam, I know it! He'll come here!"

"Hush, my love. Let him come, if he will! Ngudu has promised to find me the extra bearers I need for the expedition. By this time two days from now, we'll be gone!" He cupped her face in his hand. "I was only waiting for you to join me before setting off, hoping against hope you'd come, hating you yet loving you when the days passed and you didn't!" he told her. "From now on, it's you and me, together. I don't intend to let you out of my sight!" He grinned down at her, and was rewarded by a smile.

"Don't worry, Captain Markham," she murmured softly, tracing the line of curling black hair down over his chest and his firm stomach with her fingernail, "your own shadow will seem distant henceforth, compared to the way I intend to stick by you!"

"Amen!" he murmured as he drew her to him, laughter glinting in his gentian eyes.

They set off on horseback a little after dawn two days later, headed for the vast lake two hundred miles to the north, Lake Victoria, named years before by its discoverer, John Hanning Speke, for his beloved Queen. Across that vast inland body of water lay the Congo, and hidden somewhere in its steaming jungles, the Tears of Agaja!

Heather rode sidesaddle alongside Adam and Tom Worth, while Ellen Reading, who had no great fondness for horses, alternately walked or rode a feisty mule, which she had christened Jezebel on account of its faithless inclination to leave its rider sitting in the

317

dust in the middle of the trail rubbing a bruised bottom. The Kikuyu porters—some trusted friends of Adam, others recruited for the expedition by Ngudu—followed the horses, bearing their bundles effortlessly upon their heads in the manner that had so amazed Heather when she'd journeyed from Mombasa to Nairobi.

The sky was an endless ceiling of blue above them, punctuated only by cloud masses of fluffy white cotton. The distant mountains shimmered in pale mist or lavender haze. The glinting golden grasslands were abounding with wild game and bird life: zebra and giraffe, and the most dangerous animal of all, the Cape buffalo, as well as the pretty gazelle and the purple-patterned topi.

They camped each night under the stars, the roar of nearby lions and the snuffling of zebra reverberating in their ears. Adam and Heather shared a tent, while Ellen and Tom each had one. The bearers preferred to sleep out in the open inside the circle of campfires, rolled into blankets, while one of their number stood guard in case a lion should attempt to drag one of them away while he slept, a rare, but not unheard of, occurrence. If either Ellen or Tom found the lovers sharing a tent shocking, they did not remark upon it. Perhaps they felt Adam and Heather had suffered enough, had been separated far too long. For Adam and Heather the nights were sheer bliss. They spent them exploring each others needs and desires with that tender devotion known only to those truly in love.

By the end of two weeks, over two hundred miles of grasslands, the Great Rift Valley—a cratered lunar landscape with crocodile- and hippo-filled Lake Beringo at its heart—and the Masai Mara territory lay behind them. They had reached the Mara River which fed into Lake Victoria, the source of the White Nile.

It was dusk as they neared the river, a gleaming green serpent that twined its way between sloping banks littered with pebbles and white sand, or pursued a tangled course through swampy land ripe with those peculiar upside-down trees, the baobabs and mangroves. Lyre-horned Ankole cattle grazed the grasslands beyond the swampy banks, sleek and fat.

The tall, magnificent Watusi tribespeople, some seven feet in height, came from a nearby riverside village to greet them, calling the traditional Swahili greeting, *"Jambo sana! Jambo sana!"* as they approached.

Adam and Tom went forward first with the bundle of tradegoods, greeting the red-robed Watusi headman or *kabaka* with the respect and gifts befitting his rank. The headman, in turn, introduced his sons and his wives, a bevy of bare-breasted, brown beauties who wore heavy golden bangles about their upper arms and skirts of flowing cloth dyed with indigo about their hips. Though not strangers to European males, it was obvious that white women were unfamiliar to them, and after greetings had been exchanged, the women of the village crowded about Heather and Ellen, curiosity in their dark eyes as they studied the Englishwomen's clothes coloring, hair, and everything about them. In anticipation of this event, Adam had given Heather and Ellen little gifts to hand out: strands of pretty beads and small round mirrors, combs, and sweets for the children. While they dispensed these, strings of precious cowrie shells were given by Adam to the chief in exchange for the use of three dugout canoes. These sturdy vessels were to carry them down the Mara and thence across the lake, over twenty-six thousand square feet of water, to the tip of the area known as the Congo to white men, to the natives as Kinshasa, on the opposite northwestern shore.

That night they feasted with the *kabaka* and his villagers in the open, and the air was filled with the heavy fragrance of lush blossoms and ripe fruits and the smoke of the cooking fires. Roasted goat meat and fowl, yams, rice, and fish taken from the river, along with bananas and mangoes and the sweet, milky white flesh of the coconut, were set before them in gourd dishes arranged upon woven mats.

Seated cross-legged upon exotic leopard skins, Adam on one side of her, Ellen on the other, Heather ate hungrily as she watched the graceful dancing of the women entertaining their guests. The fierce, arrogant dancing of the young warriors followed. They enacted past battles, brandishing shields and spears, their ebony faces frighteningly painted or masked, the vivid plumes of their headdresses bobbing and fluttering as they moved. A thrill of excitement ran through Heather as the tempo of the throbbing tobala drums increased to frenzy-pitch. The dancers' pace quickened perceptibly until the throng before her melded together into one whirling, stamping, and crouching mass. They were partnered by leaping shadows cast by the flaring torches. The frantic rhythm of the drums stirred something ancient and savage in Heather's soul, causing the blood to pound in her ears, her heart to leap in answer to its throbbing, insistent call. *Life is too short,* they seemed to say. It is to be lived to the fullest. Love and live today, for tomorrow may never come!

And when the women again rose from their places in the circle and beckoned her to join them, she ignored Ellen's astonished expression and did so. Matching their swinging, graceful movements, she rolled her head from side to side, doing so with wilder and wilder abandon until the pins and combs that had bound her hair were lost and it sprayed about her shoulders in a curtain of dark-fire as she flung herself from side to side. Her lips were parted and moist, her eyes hooded as the passion the music stirred in her roiled to the surface and carried her on its wild heartbeat. She was a goddess, the queen of some lost and ancient tribe, dancing a seductive dance of magic power, a dance of enticement that would irrevocably bind the warrior she desired to her. Its sacred power would fire his blood until he hungered for her—her alone—all the days of his life, blind to the charms of others! The message was there, in the wanton, uninhibited undulating of her hips in time to the drums; in the sensual swell of her breasts as they thrust against the cloth of her blouse; in the erotic movements that gave new excitement and allure to her prim garments even as they concealed her lovely body. The message was there in her half-closed eyes, her sultry, pouting lips ... *I dance for you, Adam, my beloved, no man but you!*

Adam watched, transfixed, the urge to take her sweeping through him with jolting force. Uttering a low growl, he was on his feet, striding between the dancing, smiling women to her side before the decision to move had actually registered on his conscious mind. Their gazes met, and a thrill ran through them both at the hunger each saw mirrored in the other's eyes. She waited, breathless, until he stood before her. Unsmiling, he grasped her wrists and dragged her roughly against him, kissing her with savage passion before all. Then he lifted her into his arms and strode swiftly away, carrying her back to the shadows of their little camp outside the village. The villagers' whoops and yells of approval rang in his ears, coupling with the wild, throbbing beat of the tobala drums.

"You're a fever in my blood, lovely witch," he breathed raggedly as he ducked under the tent flap with Heather still carried in his arms. "Every minute of my every waking hour is filled with desire for you. Your dancing drove me to madness!"

"It was intended to," she confessed huskily. "The beat of the drums stirred something buried deep inside me that I couldn't deny. I wanted you—want you!—as never before. Come, my love, take me, have me! I'm yours!" As she spoke, she unfastened her blouse then her skirt, fingers trembling on each button and hook; then she knelt before him clothed in only the splendor of her cascading hair. What little light there was gleamed on the ivory pallor of her rounded shoulders and pearly breasts, it caught the amethyst sheen of her eyes.

His manhood surged. With bated breath, he silently undressed and towered before her, tall and straight as any palm. She drew him between her hands and caressed him, aware of his sudden quick intake of breath at the seductive brush of her fingertips, of the thickened quality to his breathing.

"You're beautiful," she whispered, "a man perfect in every way! If it's wicked to want to touch your maleness, to pleasure you as you've pleasured me with your touch countless times, then I must be wicked. Nevertheless, I will not deny us, Adam!"

Whispering her desire for him, she caressed his strong, straight thighs and flanks, stroked his throbbing manhood until his fingers knotted in her mane of tangled hair, and he groaned in torment. He grasped her by the shoulders and pressed her down to the groundcover, parting her thighs and plunging deeply inside her with a hoarse cry that was almost animallike. His hands were everywhere at once, hungry, searching, fondling her velvet breasts until the nipples rose rigidly against his touch, becoming hot points of exquisite pleasure-pain that drove her to the brink of madness!

"Dear God in Heaven!" she cried as rapture

enveloped her in a white-hot, roiling blast. Her nails gouged his back, drawing blood. She threw back her head, eyes closed, lips parted, as she surrendered to the fiery explosion. In almost the same second, she dimly heard Adam's roar of release, felt him drop, exhausted, to her side.

The thump-a-thumping of the village women, who were pounding couscous grain with log pestles, woke them the next morning, as did their singing in rhythm with their work.

"Bwana Markham!" came Ngudu's voice from beyond the tent flap. "It is past daylight already. We must be leaving soon."

"Coming, Ngudu," Adam called. He brushed Heather's nose with a wake-up kiss. "Come along, sleepyhead, time to wake up."

She rose, washed, and dressed, and in less than an hour their camp had been packed up by the bearers, who indulged in good-natured bantering as they worked, finally lashing the enormous bundles with rope. When the canoes had been lowered into the green water of the river, farewells to the headman and his people said, they were ready to go.

"Isn't this exciting?" Ellen exclaimed, donning a broad-brimmed straw hat from which a veil was suspended completely covering her head and shoulders. Looking at her, Heather thought of a beekeeper about to inspect a hive. "Imagine, to see Lake Victoria again after all these years! It is reputed to be one of the largest lakes in the entire world, you know?" Her gray eyes sparkled at the thought of the adventure that lay ahead of them, making her appear much younger than her fifty or so years, and Heather laughed.

"If only dear Annabel could see her Ready now,

she'd never again dare to call you stuffy!" she said.

Mrs. Reading snorted. "Stuffy? Is that what that little minx called me? Why, I'll have you know when my husband was alive, we had some fine high jinks, I can tell you!" She sniffed, a plump-breasted, indignant little bird whose feathers were thoroughly ruffled. "Dear Arthur was such a rascal! Once, we even went ice-skating with him clad in only his long, woolen winter drawers. I had wagered he wouldn't dare, you see, and so he just had to prove me wrong. He was a great one for bets, my poor, dear Arthur!"

Heather's mouth formed a perfect O in shock as she tried to envision prim Mrs. Reading skating with a man clad in only his long johns! She sighed heavily. No. It was such an outlandish notion she could not imagine it at all!

Her shock seemed to delight Mrs. Reading, who sniffed again. "You see, my dear, it just goes to show that you cannot judge a book by its cover. Stuffy, indeed!" She sailed off in her festoons of net and her long, sensible navy skirt and white blouse, leaving Heather staring after her.

Chapter Twenty

After two days and two nights, they had left the Mara River behind and had crossed the blue mirror of Lake Victoria where native fishermen laid reed nets to catch fish, and pudgy hippopotami wallowed in great numbers amongst the papyrus reeds. Here they saw crocodiles sunning themselves on the banks of the lake, and beautiful crowned cranes, their golden crests like the helmets of ancient Roman centurions, wading in the marshy water. Before the hard, relentless orb of the fiery African sun had fully come up the next day, they were on the last leg of their journey and were entering the Ugandan Ituri forests. The three narrow, dugout canoes they had traded from the Watusi were lowered into the muddy Ituri River, and they were on their way. Ahead, the Ituri joined the serpentine Congo River, and the dense jungle and her mysteries beckoned!

Heather and Mrs. Reading went into raptures of delight at the sight of scores of elegant flamingoes stalking fish, their breathtaking salmon pink plumage afire in the first golden rays of the morning light. They exclaimed over the emerald- and sapphire-bejeweled feathers of thousands of water fowl dabbling tails-up amongst the water-lily platters. The smaller forest elephants had left the jungle by the score to bathe in and drink from the river channel. Their spoor was everywhere on the marshy ground, and their trumpeting filled the air. Ears flapping like great sails, they drank and played.

Above rose the mysterious, constantly mist-shrouded Ruwenzori mountain ranges. In the native tongue *ruwenzori* meant rainmaker, but this range had also been called the Mountains of the Moon by the ancient geographer, Ptolemy, who first suspected their existence. At their highest altitudes, they were the home of strange, towering plants and below was the jungle sanctuary of gentle, vegetarian gorillas. The lowest slopes were clothed in rice paddies and wild plantains, while higher up the light green of bamboo forests swathed the mountainside like a broad bright sash. In a fleeting break in the heavy veils of mist, the morning sun shone dazzlingly through, revealing the vast, sparkling white peaks of the snow-capped ranges for a rare and breathtaking moment that would remain forever imprinted on Heather's mind.

Some of the bearers rode in the first canoe with their camping goods, while the second carried Heather and Adam and Ngudu, and the third Thomas Worth and Ellen Reading, the remainder of their bundles, and three more of the bearers. The natives sang as they bent their backs, their bodies glistening with sweat and alive with the magnificent rippling of muscles beneath smooth, oiled ebony skin. They propelled the canoes swiftly through the water. Their song, raised in melodious and deep harmony, served to keep the paddlers in time while it tunefully dispelled the almost eerie silence of the jungle that rose, a curtain of creepers, grasses, and ferns, on either side of the gleaming ribbon of green river.

The water surrounding the small, light crafts was

326

filmed with a scum of minute weeds now, and the
paddles made a rhythmic sucking sound followed by an
emerald splash as they broke the surface. The lush,
steaming undergrowth seemed peculiarly alive, breathing with a humid, humming respiration of its own. In
large part this was due to the lazy drone of the hordes of
minute midges that hovered above the water in silvery
clouds, and to the monotonous buzz of iridescent blue-
green flies which were in a gluttonous quest for blood, a
quest that the women, by means of the veils suspended
from the wide brims of their hats, were mercifully
spared. From time to time, the snarl of a leopard, its
sleep disturbed by their intrusion, would splinter the
hush, then all would fall eerily silent once again.

Heather looked up, yearning for a glimpse of the
glorious saffron and rose African dawn that had
greeted her upon rising and leaving the tent that
morning, but there was no sky to be seen through the
tunnel of foliage that met high above them. Rather, the
meager light filtering through that canopy of leaves
and creepers imbued everything with a hazy yellow-
green hue, much like that one saw upon opening ones
eyes when swimming underwater in some English
pond. The effect was a disturbing one, and more than a
little claustrophobic.

In some of the distant treetops she spied great, gaudy
blossoms, crimson or bright yellow-green, that on
closer inspection proved to be parrots. From time to
time these colorful birds took flight, their raucous
chatterings and squawks rupturing the preternatural
hush as they soared to other roosts, flirting vividly with
their feathers. There were genuine blossoms too; tiger-
striped or spotted yellow, white or mauve orchids
blooming delicately in cloudy sprays from the rotted
bark of trees. Much to Ellen's surprise, Adam
explained casually but knowledgeably that they were

called epiphytes, or air-grown orchids. When she asked him how it was he knew so much about orchids, he grinned.

"Orchids have long been a hobby of mine, not to mention the source of my livelihood for the past few years. My mother became fascinated with orchids when she was out in India with my father, in the years before her death. I suppose her interest communicated itself to me." He laughed at her surprised expression. "Ah, yes, Ready, I don't seem the type, I know!" he admitted. "But you'd be amazed by the variety of people who cultivate orchids as a hobby. We're not all bumbling, scholarly types, or spinsterish matrons, not by any means! Orchids growing is all the rage in Europe now. Why, the price those plants could command on the London wharves is astronomical! You see, the origins of shipments of the plants are kept secret by the commercial growers, to put hobbyists at a disadvantage in their cultivation! Someone who possessed a map that would show their location, or the location of any orchids anywhere, could expect to make quite a tidy sum if he sold it." He winked down at Heather. "If we don't find the Tears, I'll continue to explore strictly for the purpose of finding orchids, and I'll sell the maps. I could make us a considerable fortune that way. What do you say to that, sweetheart?"

Looking at Adam, his bush hat with the leopard-skin band set at a rakish angle, his disreputable off-white safari shirt unbuttoned to the waist to reveal a broad, sun-bronzed chest, and a rifle angled casually across his shoulder, she had to admit he looked capable of turning anything to his advantage. He certainly looked neither scholarly nor spinsterish, not smiling that wicked, engaging smile, but he could be a big-game hunter, or a wicked ivory poacher! "It sounds wonderful!" she agreed. But then, anything he suggested would sound wonderful to her! She envied him his ability to dream, his devil-may-care attitude toward life that made each day a rousing challenge to be accepted with eagerness. Why could she not be more like him, reckless and adventurous, instead of requiring some steady, definite goal, some purpose in her daily life?

Giant crimson or purple-blue bugles dripped down between the tangle of liana vines. Beautiful orange cannas flared flamelike amidst the green, while lovely African violets peeped shyly from the lush grasses. Swarms of pretty butterflies flitted from vine to vine in the green and amber light, and it was as if the tissue-paper, rainbow-colored petals of the bougainvillaea had been wrested from their stalks by a capricious wind and set to flight. The chatter of monkeys, alarmed by the presence of Man in their midst, was echoed by the oozing, squelching sound of the hippopotamus that heaved its massive gray bulk up from the muddy bottom of the river to wallow amongst the papyrus reeds that grew beneath the swampy banks. The massive beast gazed at them in stupefied curiosity as the canoes glided swiftly past. Upon the muddy banks lay crocodiles, prehistoric relics armored in gray-green, slyly masquerading as numerous beached and lichened logs.

They continued through the wet greenery, never catching so much as a glimpse of the sky above and rarely seeing anything that could be recognized as a tree, so festooned with creepers were all growing things. Heather had the impression that they were moving through some brooding dream, the warm, ripe smell of decaying vegetation rank and full in their nostrils, the dripping air pressing in close about them. All too soon her clothing was soaked with perspiration;

her hair was wringing wet. Ellen, seated in the canoe behind her, seemed just as uncomfortable, while Tom Worth cursed softly under his breath and rubbed ineffectually at the welts from the fly bites that blotched his bare tanned skin where shirt, jodhpurs, and boots had not protected him.

The riverbanks steamed as midday approached. The chatters, whooping and squawks that ricocheted endlessly in the treetops far above them diminished as the jungle life settled down to rest during the hottest part of the day. Still the paddlers bent to their task. Still the three swift canoes carried them onward, and Heather wondered if their journey through the foamy, weed-coated muddy water would ever end. She dozed from time to time, leaning against Adam, her head cradled upon his chest. Occasionally, waking with a start, she found little different about the jungle they were traveling through, save that the light had become a fraction dimmer, darkening to deep green as the day wore on.

Night came at last, and the booming chorus of the bullfrogs became deafening. The canoes were dragged up onto the riverbanks, and several campfires were lit about a small clearing, which soon became smoky because of the wall of vegetation ringing them in. Before it was quite dark, Ngudu took two of his men and plunged into the forest, returning shortly after with several large birds that they'd snared, the fowl dangling by their feet from the men's fists. The bearers proceeded to pluck and roast these birds over one of the fires.

As they sat about the campfire, eating the fowl along with some of the provisions from their packs, Heather saw that numerous pairs of slanted topaz eyes gleamed at them through the darkness, and her heart gave a quivery little leap of fear. There were leopards out there, in the pitch blackness, close enough for her to reach out and touch! Would they dare brave the campfires to attack, she wondered apprehensively. Her only answer was the angry, spitting snarl of a great cat. In the wet black night it sounded very close, and she thanked God for the crimson glow of the fires that did, indeed, keep the jungle cats at bay.

"How much farther?" she asked Adam, and he in turn put the question to Ngudu, who grinned, teeth flashing pearly white in the firelight.

"Six, seven suns," Ngudu promised cheerfully. "Then we come to place of Agaja's treasure."

"I like your optimism, Ngudu," Adam said with a grin. "Let's hope what old Robert Elwood told me can be relied upon, and that my calculations are correct." He frowned. "It will be a hit and miss project at best, since we're dependent on the memory of an old man for what happened many years ago, but I'm certain we can find it!" In the firelight, his dark blue eyes shone. He wiped the perspiration from his forehead with the battered broad-brimmed hat, and grinned at the circle of eager faces watching him. Delving inside the open front of his shirt, he withdrew a seamed map, which he unfolded, jabbing his finger at a circle inked upon it as he held it up to the light of the fire for them to see.

"Elwood said he became separated from Stanley's main expedition, and then he was found by friendly natives and returned to civilization. Using the distance between the two points, where he became separated and where he was found, and calculating the speed he must have traveled—I figured his sickness in my calculations—I decided the treasure must be hidden within this area." He pointed to the map. "Tomorrow, we'll be here"—again he jabbed his finger at the paper—"on the perimeter of that circle. Elwood recalled that the place was backed by a small clearing,

331

and that he could hear the roar of rapids nearby. The entrance to the cave where the treasure is hidden is guarded by idols, half-human, half-leopard."

Heather nodded. She was not overly convinced, though with all her heart she wanted Adam to find his treasure. Despite the cut marks that he made at regular intervals with his machete on trees lining the river, the jungle always appeared the same to her, day after endless day of vines and creepers. How he hoped to tell where the circle ended or began was a mystery to her! She sighed wearily, scratching at a swollen, throbbing bite on the back of her hand. The heat was oppressive. It steamed from the ground morning, noon and night. Only in the hours before dawn did the jungle become cool, and then the coolness was so extreme, it made one's teeth chatter. She had discarded all notions of proper female attire yesterday, had shed her numerous, sweltering petticoats and camisole and stays, only donning them again at night for sleeping. It had been cooler by day wearing only her blouse, the sleeves rolled up to the elbows, and the skirt and boots and pantalettes, but not much cooler.

She glanced across at Ellen, ashamed of her own irritable mood, for the older woman's face seemed very drawn. Once or twice that day, Heather had seen Ellen close her eyes and pass her hand across her brow as if overcome by a spell of dizziness. Lord, Heather prayed, I hope she isn't coming down with jungle fever! Although Heather had passed out quinine to all of them, including the bearers, she had no medicine to combat jungle fever, that same lethal fever had killed her mother years before, not too many miles from here, in the village of Jinja on the northeast tip of Lake Victoria.

Sleep eluded the travelers for the greater part of that first night. Stinging insects found their way through the folds of mosquito netting and their bites swelled and itched miserably. The heat within their canvas prisons became intolerable, and when fatigue finally overwhelmed them, Heather's rest was fraught with dreams and fears, and was filled with the lithe, shadowy specters of strange wild beasts, half-man, half-leopard, savage natives wielding spears, and vines that curled around her like sinuous snakes and squeezed the life from her body. And all the while the wild throb of tobala drums beat a frenzied tattoo.

On the third day the muddy Ituri River narrowed and became no more than a trickle that disappeared into the undergrowth, choked by vines and reeds and roots. Ngudu gestured them out of the canoes and the bearers leaped to the reedy banks, raising their massive bundles, or the heavy canoes, to balance them precariously on their heads before setting off after Ngudu, who was hacking a path through the vines with a wicked-looking machete. Adam took up his own machete and went ahead of the two women, widening the path, while Tom, shouldering a rifle, and the last two bearers, carrying the third canoe, brought up the rear.

Their arduous trek on foot through the jungle made the first three days seem like a Sunday outing, for along with the creepers, snakes as wide as a man's thigh or upper arm hung suspended from the trees and slithered through the oozing wet foliage about their feet. Redbacked, poisonous frogs leaped from leaf to dripping leaf, and enormous lizards slithered into the undergrowth when they passed. Insects swarmed and hummed and flashed iridescent wings everywhere. The air was alive with them. The leafy ground teemed with them. They attacked with startling accuracy, the bites swelling and itching painfully beyond the curative powers of the calamine lotion that Ready had, with her usual foresight, brought along. Looking at the others, their faces blotched with pink lotion as was her own, Heather had the wildest desire to laugh. Only Ngudu and the bearers seemed unaffected, for their bodies had long since become immune to the stinging flies' bites.

That night, when their supper of wild fowl and crackers and hot tea had again been prepared by the ingenuous Ngudu, Heather went to Ellen's tent to call her to the campfire to eat. There was no answer! Feeling apprehensive at what she might find, she ducked under the flap and crawled across to the woman. A single touch to her brow, and Heather knew that the jungle fever she had feared had become a reality. Ellen's body was burning!

"Adam! Come here, quickly!" she called, lighting a lantern. He came at a run, ducking his head under the tent flap.

"What is it?" he demanded, his handsome face concerned.

"Ellen. She's been taken ill. Jungle fever, I think, though I can't be certain."

"Damn it, no!" He shook his head regretfully, his shoulders sagging; then he shrugged. "I'm afraid there's nothing else for it. We'll have to turn back. She doesn't have a hope unless we can get her out of this infernal jungle. At first light, we go back the way we came."

"No-oo," Ellen protested weakly, her eyelids fluttering open. "Mustn't! You've ... come too far ... waited too long. Leave me. Be ... be all right tomorrow. Promise!"

Adam crouched down and squeezed her shoulder reassuringly. "Don't fret. I won't jeopardize your life for a few paltry diamonds. They'll still be here another time. You've been a grand soldier, Ready darling, but we're going back."

"'Ready darling,' indeed, you young rogue!" Ellen

334

muttered, smiling wanly.

"What's up?" Tom asked, coming to the tent.

"Ellen's ill," Adam explained. "We'll turn back in the morning, Tom. She doesn't have a chance, not without medicines and proper nursing."

"Now, look here, Adam old chap, you're not going back!" Tom protested. "You've come too far and waited too damned long for this. I'll go back with Ellen, and take half of the bearers with me. You, Heather, Ngudu and the rest can go on—and be sure you find those bloody diamonds! I need my share to start some sort of business. Truth is, I've had it with pushing a pen for the Foreign Office!"

"I can't let you do that, Tom!" Adam cut in angrily. "You've put just as—"

"Shut up, Markham, there's a good chap! Ellen has the constitution of a horse. She's a tough old bird, bless her, and you know it! We'll be fine."

"Shouldn't I go with you? I have some nursing experience. I can take care of her," Heather suggested.

"Do you have any knowledge of tropical fevers?" Tom asked.

"No, but—"

"But nothing! I'm a fair nurse myself, though not such a pretty one as you, I admit." He winked. "I'll take care of our Ellen as if she were my own sister, I promise. Go on with Adam, Heather. I won't hear another word."

"You're certain you don't need me?" Heather agreed doubtfully, glancing at Ellen.

Tom shook his head, and he and Adam went back to the campfire to tell Ngudu and the others their decision.

As the men left, Heather heard Ellen mutter, ". . . Tough old bird, indeed!" She smiled through the tears that filled her eyes, and bathed the older woman's brow with a handkerchief dipped in a little of the precious fresh water from the canteens, saying sadly, "You weren't so tough after all, were you, my old darling?"

It would be so hard parting with Ellen, Heather thought, half-determined to talk Tom into letting her go back with them. The older woman had cared for her like a mother these past eighteen years. Surely she owed it to her not to let her be nursed by strangers? But what about Adam? Who knew what dangers lay ahead for him in the Congo's mysterious depths? Her place was at his side, wherever he might decide to go, whatever he might have to face, come what may. "You and I, together," he'd said. Her choice was clear.

"I hope you understand that I'm not deserting you, Ready," she whispered, "but I love Adam. I won't let him go on alone!"

Chapter Twenty-one

It was a sad leave-taking the next morning when their little party split up.

Tom and Ellen and half of the Bantu bearers were to go back the way they had come, to the mission at Kigali where Tom assured Heather, there were Belgian nuns, nursing sisters who would know how to care for Ellen. The sick woman was lifted gently into a crude hammock made from a blanket and slung on a long pole. It was to be carried between two of the bearers, which necessitated leaving some of their equipment behind.

As Heather watched them go, Ellen's hand waving feebly as they disappeared between the vegetation, she wondered if she would ever see her dear friend and companion again. She could not bear to think that Ellen, who had been like a mother to her since she had lost her own dear Mamma, might succumb to the fever and die. Adam, standing beside her, sensed her fears and hugged her comfortingly.

"Pull yourself together, sweet," he ordered sternly. "Your Ready would be the first one to scold you for the thoughts going through your head right now. Ellen spent several years living only a few miles from here, and never succumbed to the fever. If anyone can survive it, she can. She'd be furious to see those tears in your eyes."

"She would," Heather admitted, smiling bravely through the watery mist. She dried her eyes on her knuckles and took a deep breath. "I'll be all right now, I promise."

He nodded, bent, and kissed her. "That's my girl! Come on, let's get going. Ngudu. *Safari!*"

Drawing strength from his reassurances, she smiled and started after him to the canoe.

They traveled miles along the winding river, in some places as broad as fifteen miles from bank to bank with numerous small islands sprouting above the muddy water, in others little more than a wide stream, bordered on each side by walls of dense forest.

Toward late afternoon, the riverbanks and marshes were the gathering place for countless varieties of wild animals that left the jungle and came to the water to drink. There were dainty forest antelope, elephants, and even a troupe of noisy baboons that jumped from rock to rock and shrieked at the other animals in a great display of ferocity. They decided to make camp early that night, since they had made good time that day, and Adam pointed to a relatively dry, open spot that appeared perfect for their needs.

The bearers dragged the canoes high up onto the sloping banks and Heather scrambled out. Her clothing was soaked with perspiration, and her long hair, pinned up beneath her broad-brimmed hat for coolness, was sodden. She announced that she intended to bathe herself and rinse out her clothing. She could hear the sound of running water nearby, and the forest springs and pools were crystal clear. Unlike the muddy river which teemed with crocodiles and hippos and all manner of water snakes, these were perfect for bathing.

"Your clothes won't dry, not in this humidity," Adam warned her.

"I don't care," she declared obstinately, "At least I'll feel clean! There's a stream somewhere nearby. I can hear it." In a determined manner, she took soap and a linen towel from her pack, and then headed off across the fern-carpeted ground.

"I'll come with you," Adam decided. "It's not safe to wander about alone." He gave instructions to Ngudu, then slung his rifle over his shoulder as she led the way, guided by the sound of burbling water, to a small pool formed by a sparkling, crystal-clear spring that bubbled down amidst rocks and ferns, only a few hundred feet from their camp. The sound of the bearers' conversation carried to where they were, yet the lush foliage—huge, heart-shaped leaves and creepers, wild banana trees and lianas—gave a semblance of privacy to the tiny emerald pool. She peeled off her sodden outer clothing, her nose wrinkling in distaste as she plunged the garments into the water, then thoroughly scrubbed them on a convenient rock until they were cleaned to her satisfaction. That done, she draped them over a broad banana leaf to dry.

"Turn your back," she instructed Adam pertly as she reached for the ribbon fastenings of her undergarments. Clad in only a filmy bodice and pantalettes that reached decorously to her knees, she was an incongruous sight amidst the tropical vegetation.

Adam's eyes gleamed wickedly. He snorted and shook his head, setting aside the rifle and reaching for the buttons of his own shirt. "Turn my back? Not a chance, my lovely," he refused with a grin. "There'll be no need for modesty, since I'll be joining you!" His gentian eyes were twinkling. "We'll be the new Adam and Eve in our own Garden of Eden. Just cross your fingers and hope we don't encounter the legendary serpent!"

She sighed, exasperated but grinning nonetheless. "It's not the serpent that I'm worried about, Captain Markham," she said teasingly. "It's you!" Mischief danced in her violet eyes as she waited until he lifted his shirt over his head, then shed her own remaining garments with amazing speed and, bare now, ducked quickly under the water before he was completely undressed.

"Spoilsport!" he muttered, feigning a scowl. Slowly and deliberately, he unbuckled the belt of his trousers, yanked off his boots, and peeled off his last remaining garment. Blushing furiously at his boldness, she turned away, his roguish laughter ringing in her burning ears. Hearing a splash, she turned back to him, believing he had dived into the water, but it was a ruse, she saw, for Adam still stood on the banks, tanned and quite naked, his superbly muscled torso and strong, straight legs dappled by the fading light that filtered down through the treetops above.

Fists on hips, he threw back his jet-black head and roared with laughter as her eyes were drawn irresistibly to his tumescent maleness for a few, fleeting seconds, before she hurriedly looked away. "My word, Lady Heather, could it be you are nothing but a shameless voyeur?" he asked accusingly, laughter in his voice.

"I'm no Peeping Tom," she spluttered indignantly. "Your lecherous behavior is disgraceful, Captain, quite disgraceful!" But the little twitch at the corner of her delightful mouth denied the sincerity of her words. She broke down and giggled, and with a grin he poised, then dived, clean as an arrow, into the pool, surfacing seconds later with his black hair slicked, seal-like, against his fine head.

Arching forward, he swam alongside her and drew

her into his arms. She lay back in his embrace, reveling in the sweet coolness of their hidden pool, in his kisses, and in the arousing pressure of his powerful arms about her bare body. Their breaths mingled. Their tongues touched. Their mouths joined.

Nearer, he drew her, until the sleek, curvaceous wet length of her was pressed firmly against his hard, wet body. Her shell pink nipples tingled and tautened as he rubbed his hairy male chest against them, reaching lazily to cup one perfect ivory breast in his tanned hands and fondle it sensually, aware as he did so that her breathing had quickened against his lips. He could feel the frantic beat of her racing heart under his fingertips, could almost see it wildly fluttering against her breast as he lowered his damp, dark head to taste the sweetness of her flesh, like a hummingbird sipping sweet nectar from a rare and enchanting blossom.

"My little orchid, my precious, wild orchid," he breathed, cupping her breasts in his large hands and kissing and caressing her between endearments. "No jungle blossom was ever lovelier than you, my sweet!"

He looked up, and saw on her face an expression of transported delight. Her dark-flame hair tumbled in wanton abandon about them both, the ends furling and swirling upon the gleaming water like delicately fronded water weeds. Her eyes were closed, her head flung back exposing the graceful arch of her creamy throat and the lovely, fluid angle where her swanlike neck joined her slender shoulders. With a groan, he pressed his lips against the little hollow there, where the flutter of her pulse was visible, clasping the dimpled globes of her bottom to draw her still tighter to him. Again, he kissed her, until her senses reeled and little cries broke, birdlike, from her lips. His gentian eyes smoldering darkly with desire, he lifted her tenderly astride his hips, making love to her there and then in

341

the water, while the harsh hoots and squawks of the parrots and the shrieks and chatters of the monkeys reverberated through the treetops above their gleaming pool, and the dying sun colored the water blood red momentarily before it slipped over the edge of the world.

Silent save for the sound of their breathing and her languorous sighs, they moved together without haste, tenderly savoring each other, too caught up in the watery web of their delight for speech now. Theirs was the language of touch, of taste and scent, more eloquent than words. Only at the last did she utter a single, drawn-out sob of joy that rent the silent jungle bower momentarily before the silence fell anew between them. It seemed, as rapture claimed her, that she was whirling in the velvet blackness of infinite space, where brilliant milky galaxies curtained endless highways into eternity and moons spun in dizzying orbits about kaleidoscopic planets; and she floated, weightless and unfettered, to her own appointed place in the spangled heavens, to become one with the pulsing, brilliant stars. . . .

Dimly, she became aware that he had lifted her, was carrying her out of the water and to the lichened, velvety rocks that cradled the tiny emerald pool where they had loved. In lush grass, he gently set her down and, taking up the linen towel, dried her damp body inch by tender inch. Her lashes fluttered as she opened her violet eyes to dusk's indigo shadows and to his face, so darkly handsome, poised above her.

"Wonderful," she whispered, her face radiant in the gloom, still filled with the shattering emotion of their joining. "So wonderful!" Her eyes darkened, and her fingers closed about his arms as fear edged its way into her bliss. "Tell me it will never end! That we'll always be together!"

"Always," he vowed. "As long as we have breath left in our bodies, we'll never let anything—or anyone—part us again."

"But what of Douglas?" she asked, her voice breaking as she said her husband's name.

"To hell with Douglas!" Adam growled, features taut and angry. "We'll go away together—far, far away, where no one will know that you were once his wife. You'll be mine, as you should have been from the first!"

"But we could never be married, not as long as Douglas is alive. We would be living in sin. Our . . . our children could never carry your name."

His jaw hardened. "Would that be so terrible, as long as they're certain of their father's love and protection? It's people that dictate what's right and what's wrong, my love. They are that mysterious 'they' we answer to for so many things. Should we live our lives by their plan, or our own? We'll give our children something better than a place in society—pride, and a sense of themselves. And we'll be married in every sense of the word that matters. Our union will be founded solidly on love and a deep commitment more binding than any legal scrap of paper!"

"But Douglas isn't a man to give up easily, Adam," Heather whispered. "If he should come after us—find us!—he would kill you, kill both of us, I know it!"

"Hush," Adam cut in sharply, his eyes stormy and turbulent. "He won't come after us."

"But he hates you! He tried desperately to keep you from your appointment with Robert Elwood that time. And he wed me while knowing you intended to return to me. Surely that proves he would stop at nothing!" she cried.

"It's a hatred of long standing, Heather, as well you know. If his intent was to kill me, he could have done so long ago in India."

"I suppose you're right," she admitted doubtfully. Adam seemed so certain, but she wondered why his reassurances did not put her mind at rest? Did she, perhaps, know the workings of Douglas' mind far better than Adam?

They dressed and Adam hoisted his rifle onto his shoulder. Hand in hand, they made their way back toward the flickering red glow of the campfires that ringed the camp Ngudu had made.

A thunderstorm, a frequent occurrence in the region through which they traveled, woke them the next morning. The crackle and rumble sounded as if an angry god were hurling thunderbolts across the heavens. From time to time, great flashes of blue-white lightning lit the muddy river with an ethereal, bright light. Then, the rain came, in soft patters and splatters that bounced off leaves in huge droplets at first, then heavier, until it became a drumming, roaring sheet of water that was deafening. Adam and Heather huddled in their tent under an oilcloth, coughing as smoke from the fires they'd built in the clearing when the downpour first started, in an attempt to keep dry, rose in choking clouds in the close confines. Nearby, Ngudu, Ewasu, Sau and the other bearers did likewise.

It rained solidly for two hours, and then as suddenly as the storm had started, it stopped, but its roaring sound was still ringing in their ears long after it was done, accompanied by the steady drip-drip of rain falling from the leaves. They all crawled out from their tents.

"Better we place guards, Bwana," Ngudu advised. "Big rain come, then after, plenty of animals everywhere in forest. Very dangerous!"

"You're right, friend," Adam agreed. "Ewasu, come with me. We'll bag something for the pot. Ngudu, place a guard and take care of Missie Bwana for me."

Adam and Ewasu left to go hunting, and Heather, with Ngudu's help, managed to hang their sodden tents and bedding over stripped poles. They lit several fires underneath them in an effort to dry them out. The results would be smoky at best, but if they did nothing, mold and mildew would quickly line the canvas. Fortunately, the ground was only damp despite the recent torrents of rain that had fallen. Heather surmised that the layer of humus, of rotting leaves and grasses, that carpeted the forest floor acted as a filter for the rain. If not, their campsite would have been a muddy morass.

Their tents seen to, Ngudu and Heather set about building a cooking fire and then hung a billy can of spring water over it to boil for tea. Ngudu drew a knife from his belt and whittled sharp points on several sticks. On these, the game the hunters caught, all going well, would be spitted for roasting.

The water was boiling, the fire was glowing hotly, when Ngudu noticed that Sau, the bearer he had assigned as their guard, was gone. He took up his spear and motioned to the others to remain. "Missie Bwana, you stay here, by fire. I go look!"

Heather nodded and Ngudu padded silently across the tiny clearing, headed toward the spot where he had last seen the Bantu youth, Sau. Several minutes passed, and there was nothing but silence, broken only by the lazy drone of insects stirring after the rain. The jungle was a beautiful, if disturbing, place, she reflected. The lush walls of vegetation seemed filled with menace, dangers she could only guess at, and she felt at times as if countless unseen eyes were watching her. Yet she could see no one, and she shivered, hugging herself

345

about the arms. It was another world here, a world far removed from the drawing rooms of London's Mayfair and Windsor Square, or even the slums of Whitechapel with its gin shops and unfortunates and public houses. Would she prefer to be back there, living an orderly life and attending teas and soirées and at-homes with her aunt and cousin? Never! she thought with a shudder. Here, every day was an adventure! Moreover, here she was where she had longed to be—with Adam.

A sudden spitting snarl carried from the direction in which Ngudu had gone, and she started, hands flying to her breast in alarm. *Leopard!* The wild cats abounded in the jungles of the Congo, and Adam had told her that they possessed great cunning. Were Ngudu and the bearer, Sau, in danger? Lord, she couldn't just sit here and do nothing if they were! If only Adam had left her one of his revolvers, or a rifle to defend herself . . . Still, what good would that have done? Ladies were not expected to be able to shoot, and so she had never learned to use a firearm. Cursing her female lot in life, she snatched up a flaming brand from the fire, holding it gingerly by the, as yet, unburned end, and ran across the clearing in the direction of the ferocious snarl she had heard, ignoring the bearers' shouts.

The jungle seemed even eerier once she had left the clearing, not so dense as it had been farther inland from the river, but a thick tangle nonetheless. She brushed aside hanging lianas and thick ferns, ears cocked, trying to get a bearing on the direction from which the sound had come. A sudden ululating, agonized scream rent the air, sending the parrots and monkeys above her into noisy confusion, and chilling the marrow in Heather's bones. She gasped in horror and started to run, blundering into rotting tree stumps and tripping over creepers as she flung herself headlong in the direction of that awful sound.

346

"Stop!" The command rang out, and Heather abruptly halted, frozen in place by that single word. Ahead, she saw Ngudu, spear in hand, crouched beside a bloody bundle of rags that had feet and arms, yet did not appear human.

"Oh, my God, Sau!" she whispered, the blood draining from her face. And then she followed the direction of Ngudu's eyes, and saw what it was he was staring at so intently.

Above her and to her left, a leopard crouched upon a tree branch, coiled to spring and spitting fiercely deep in its throat as she gingerly turned her head to look at it. Her eyes came into contact with tawny golden eyes that glowed like twin topaz coals. Their hypnotic, unwavering gaze, paralyzed her. She could not move, could not look away! Perspiration sprang out upon her brow and upper lip. Her bowels churned with fear. The cat was watching her . . . waiting . . . ready to spring! One leap was all the beast needed, just one!

"No move, Missie!" Ngudu said softly. "Stay still . . . still. . . ." With slow, easy moves, he raised his spear to shoulder height.

Heather did as bidden, too terrified to move even had he commanded it. She seemed rooted to the spot, those beautiful, dangerous golden eyes boring into her, into her very soul, draining her will to move, her will to flee, with their power. And then, so suddenly and swiftly her scream caught in her throat, the leopard was still no more, but airborne in a single, lithe leap.

She looked up, and death—her death—was mirrored in those golden eyes, in the roaring mouth, in the cruel fangs revealed as the snarling animal sprang.

But then, the leopard seemed suspended in midair. By some miracle it defied gravity momentarily, before it crashed heavily to the ground, breaking through the foliage. She was dimly aware that the long, black shaft

347

of Ngudu's spear protruded from the beast's throat. Great gouts of blood stained its magnificent spotted breast, pooling on the ground beneath as the leopard gave a low growl, twitched its tail and massive paws once, then lay still.

A roaring sound that had nothing to do with wild cats began in Heather's ears, and she swayed dizzily, overcome by the closeness of her escape and near to swooning. Ngudu stepped over the leopard's body and squeezed her shoulder, looking a little gray himself beneath his smooth blackness. He grinned, revealing white teeth, and said shakily, "Lucky Missie Bwana listen good! One more step! . . . He made a slashing motion across his throat that she understood only too well.

"*Asante!* Thank you, Ngudu! You saved my life!" she whispered, overwhelmed with gratitude.

Ngudu nodded. "Sau not so lucky. The *chui,* leopard, drag him from camp. This one," he added, jerking his head toward the animal's body, "was wounded by hunter's snare. See? No can hunt good. Man more easy meat than antelope!"

"Woman, too!" Heather said with feeling. "Poor Sau!"

Ngudu nodded grimly. "This place plenty danger. Sau lazy. He no keep eye for *chui*—but *chui* keep good eye for him, *ndio?*"

"*Ndio,*" Heather agreed.

Ngudu hefted Sau's bloodied body over his shoulders, and together they went back to camp. Shortly after, Adam returned. The brace of guinea hens and the small antelope carried by the bearers was as evidence that their hunting had been good. His relaxed expression dwindled and was replaced by a thunderous scowl when he heard what had taken place during his absence. He turned on the bearers, gentian eyes crackling and dark with anger, then swung back to Ngudu. "Tell them if I catch them slacking off while on guard again, I'll feed them to the damned leopards myself, understand?" he snapped.

Ngudu nodded. "I tell them, Bwana," he promised solemnly.

"And as for you," he barked at Heather, "When Ngudu tells you to stay in camp, you stay! You were safe by the fires, you little fool!"

"But I—"

"But nothing, Heather!" he cut in angrily. "The first rule of thumb out here is to obey orders given by those who know what they're doing. You certainly don't damn it!" With a curt nod, Adam turned on his heel and strode away from them, down to the river, leaving Heather gaping after him.

"Bwana afraid for you, Missie, and what happen to Sau make him feel very bad," Ngudu said softly. "When afraid, he come angry."

Ngudu was right, Heather knew, and so she nodded but said nothing.

Adam stayed well away from her for the remainder of that day and an air of gloom hung over the camp. The bearers, sobered by their friend's death, moved quietly about the clearing, eyes downcast and averted from the telltale mound of earth on its perimeter that revealed Sau's final resting place.

It seemed they would not take to the river that day, but would remain where they were. Heather busied herself in darning the rents in her and Adam's clothing while sitting quietly with Ngudu, who was trying to teach her more words in Swahili, which was the lingua franca throughout much of eastern Africa, while he cleaned and resharpened his spear.

"You know Bwana Markham very well," she observed as she sewed.

Ngudu nodded. "We are friends, Missie Bwana," he added, and there was pride in his voice. "I have met many Europeans, but only Adam Markham reached out to offer me his hand. Only him treat Ngudu as equal, a man like himself, for all that the color of my skin is black, and not white as is his. He was this way from the very first. I was happy to work for Governor Dennison so that I can watch over Missie for Bwana Markham."

"Watch over me?" Her brows arched in surpirse.

"*Ndio,* missie. Bwana Markham, he tell me the woman he love marry Dennison. He afraid for you. I tell him not to worry, Ngudu take care nothing bad happen Missie Bwana. If Bwana Worth no stop him that time, Ngudu kill Governor!" He grinned, blood-thirstily, relishing the thought. "Perhaps better that way, maybe."

Heather nodded mutely. "You have no liking for the Europeans in your country, do you, Ngudu?"

Ngudu hesitated, then shook his head. "No, missie. Too much greedy white man come here. He say he help my people, but only help hisself come rich!"

"Not all of them are like that," Heather pointed out. "The medical missionaries mean to help your people, Ngudu."

"No, not all. But too many that way! They come, and they divide the land of my people like antelope meat, so much for this white man's king, so much for that. But this land belongs to the black man, not the white! Who is he to say how we must live?" Ngudu asked grimly, and Heather had to acknowledge that perhaps he was right. How long would it be before Ngudu and others who felt as he did rose up and revolted against the whites, reclaimed their land and independence, and with it the freedom to rule Africa as they saw fit? She had no idea, but she was certain that day would come.

That night was the first since they had been reunited that Adam did not reach for her in the darkness once they were inside their tent. They slept apart, on opposite sides of the groundcover, inches that might have been miles separating them. Only in the gray hours before dawn did his arms curl around her and embrace her gently as before. Relieved, she realized that he had reconciled his anger at her, and she gladly melted into his arms.

On rising, they saw that during the night, Sau's grave had been disturbed, the body dragged away by hyenas or jackals. The bearers went into the jungle in search of his remains, but they returned with only bones, picked clean and white, not a single shred of flesh left upon them by the beasts and the black columns of ants that were everywhere. There was no sign of his skull. Adam looked from the pile of gleaming bones to Heather, and there was no need for him to speak his thoughts aloud. Do you see how final death is, how fragile we are? his eyes said. Do you see how swiftly this savage land reclaims and absorbs her own?

Silently, she vowed that never again would she think she knew best and disobey orders. Her very life depended upon following them.

Chapter Twenty-two

The feeling that they were being watched, which she had first experienced in the clearing, grew stronger over the next two days. Once or twice, when the sensation of eyes boring into the back of her neck was particularly strong, she turned quickly and searched the jungle, her gaze rapidly shifting from creeper to creeper, vine to vine, in an attempt to spy the unseen watchers. She imagined once that she caught a glimpse of a tiny elfin face, then immediately scolded herself for such fanciful notions, for when she looked back again, there was nothing but foliage, or perhaps a curious monkey peering at her through the lianas. Was the steaming heat affecting her mind, she wondered? Finally, she could contain herself no longer!

"Do you ever feel as if there's someone out there, watching us?" she asked Adam a little hesitantly, afraid he would laugh at her and blame her fancies on an overactive imagination, for she had always prided herself on being down to earth and of a practical nature.

To her surprise, he did neither. Instead he said seriously, "We are being watched. We've been watched every step of the way since we entered the forest two weeks ago."

"By whom?" she demanded indignantly, astonished that he should confirm her suspicions so casually, without even hinting to her that someone had them under surveillance.

"The Twa people."

"Twa?"

He nodded and grinned. "Perhaps you've heard of them. They're Pygmies—little people no taller than four-and-a-half feet even at adulthood."

"Pygmies! Are they dangerous?" she asked breathlessly, curiosity mingled with apprehension in her lovely, violet eyes.

Adam shrugged. "Let's hope not. They have a reputation for being peaceful folk, but since the Belgian colonists began mining copper not far from here, near the Tshopo Falls, I've heard rumors that the Twa have grown hostile to Europeans."

"Why should that be?" Heather asked, flexing her stiff back and fanning her hot face with her hat. "Surely the missionaries can't have inspired any fear in them?"

"It's not the missions. It's because the Belgians use forced African labor," Adam said, his lips tight, "and natives that are . . . recalcitrant, shall we say, often find themselves minus hands or feet by way of punishment."

"No!" Heather cried, blanching in horror. "But that's brutal—unthinkable!"

"Yes. Is it any wonder the Twa tend to steer clear of white men, under the circumstances?"

"No, of course not! I don't blame them," she agreed with feeling.

Ngudu shipped his paddle and let the canoe glide, unmanned, through the gleaming green water while he rested briefly. Adam took up his paddle to spell the head bearer. He matched his strokes to Ewasu's, the

353

pair of them moving as one.

"Twa people are hunters, Missie Bwana," Ngudu said. "Not like Bantu, who are farmers, tall men like Ngudu who live outside this forest. Bantu, he think he master of Twa people. He make Twa catch game for him, and he give arrowheads and plantains and yams to Twa in trade. Twa sometimes obey Bantu, sometimes not. Twa small, but got his own mind, *ndio?*" Ngudu tapped his woolly head to emphasize his point.

"I see," Heather acknowledged with a smile. "I wish we could meet them, Ngudu! Do you think they'll show themselves?"

"Maybe," Ngudu acknowledged with a grin. "Maybe not. Twa people very shy!"

Despite Ngudu's doubts, Heather's wish was granted that same afternoon, soon after they had again pitched camp for the night on the banks of the river, where rubber, mahogany, and ebony trees grew in abundance. They were seated cross-legged about the fire, drying out their belongings after the customary fine, but soaking, shower that fell each and every afternoon now, waiting for their supper of guinea hens and antelope meat to roast over a smoky fire.

Heather looked up and saw a small man, wearing only a skirt of leaves about his protruding belly, standing hesitantly at the edge of the bush. He appeared ready to take flight and dive back into the forest at the least provocation on their part. He was, as Adam had said, certainly no more than four-and-a-half feet in height, yet perfectly proportioned, his woolly dark brown hair close-cropped, his complexion a deep gold, his lively, inquisitive features undeniably elfin. In one hand he carried a small bow, and in the other a brace of short arrows, the tips encased in a folded leaf. Curiosity sparkled in his brown eyes as he stared fixedly at Heather—so fixedly she began to feel a little disturbed.

Ngudu stood and went to greet their guest. He welcomed the Twa in the Kingwana tongue, which resembled Swahili so closely that Heather was able to understand a few words. After a quite lengthy conversation, Ngudu turned to Heather. By the twitching of his lips, she got the impression that the tall Kikuyu tribesman was trying hard not to laugh. "This one is named Mbaka. He welcomes you, Missie Bwana, to the forest of the Twa people! He says he has gifts for you from his people, and he wishes you to go with him to his village, where a feast has been readied in your honor."

"For me?" Heather squeaked. "Why me?"

"Your hair, Missie!" Ngudu divulged. "Twa people believe fire belong to the spirit of the forest. It keep them warm. It cook their meat. It is good. They see the fire color of your hair and believe you are forest spirit, *esumba*. They wish to honor you."

Astonished by this revelation, Heather took a few seconds to digest it. She looked across at Adam, and when he raised his eyebrows approvingly, she smiled and nodded. "Tell Mbaka I would be honored to visit his village."

"I've always suspected that you were a goddess," Adam teased as they set off between the trees a few minutes later in the wake of the little Twa man, accompanied by Ngudu as translator, and Ewasu, his younger brother, the other bearers having been left behind to guard their camping goods. "No woman could be as beautiful as you, and not have some unearthly power!"

"Oh, you!" Heather scolded, laughing nonetheless.

Mbaka led them deeper into the jungle where brilliant flowers flaunted enormous, vivid blossoms and to a small clearing. Dotted under the trees were

355

several low, mound-shaped huts made of vine frameworks thatched with huge mongongo leaves. Naked children swarmed everywhere, climbing vines, yelling and laughing, apparently fearless and completely carefree. Bare-breasted women, wearing bark-cloth aprons and carrying doll-sized babies in antelope-skin slings upon their hips, looked up from their cooking. But as the white "giants" entered the village, all activity halted. Every man, woman, and child turned to stare at Heather. Even the curly-tailed yellow dogs, which had remained curiously silent even at the strangers' approach, stopped their scrapping and looked expectantly toward them.

"Do something goddesslike," Adam suggested out of the side of his mouth, his gentian eyes twinkling. "They're waiting."

"What?" Heather asked. Nonplused, she ventured to direct a nervous smile at the expectant circle of people.

"You're their goddess," Adam reminded her. "You'll think of something, no doubt!"

She nodded and raised her hands, feeling an utter fool even as she did so. *Jambo sana! Habari ya leo!"* she greeted them in a clear, ringing voice, and swept off her veiled hat, letting her glorious, dark-flame tide of hair stream over her shoulders.

It was the perfect move on her part. The Pygmies fell back, eyes round with astonishment, mouths agape.

"Ya! Madami esumba! Madami esumba! Ya! Ya!" The murmur began, then swelled until it became almost deafening in volume. Then the little people ran off to their huts, returning with precious iron arrowheads and cooking pots, woven mats and hunting knives, lovely carvings fashioned from ebony wood, a sulky green parrot in a wicker cage, a little brown monkey and more, which they heaped at her feet before backing respectfully away. Obviously the assortment

356

of goods were intended as gifts!

"Asante. Asante," Heather murmured, inclining her head graciously to all as she admired their offerings. She held out her arms to the monkey, and it chattered noisily and eyed her calculatingly before leaping onto her shoulder and playing with her hair. The Twa grinned and exchanged approving comments amongst themselves. Heather smiled too. She liked their pixie faces and the warm welcome they had given her, the modest way the Twa maidens shyly looked down at their bare feet when she glanced at them, and the frank curiosity in the dark eyes of the toddling infants who had probably never seen a white woman before, let alone one possessed of flaming red hair such as her own!

Mbaka led them to a place heaped with leopard skins and calabashes of food, indicating by a gesture that they should be seated. The feast, of roasted *mboloko*— a variety of small antelope, and chicken cooked in palm oil, nuts, yams, and plantains—was set proudly before the guests in gourd calabashes or on banana-leaf platters. Treated as if she were truly a goddess, or a queen at the very least, Heather was served only the choicest tidbits. After they had eaten, dancing followed. The Pygmy women circled the male dancers, some beating upon small skin-covered drums while others played shrill whistles or flutes. The male dancers' actions cleverly simulated an elephant hunt, with one brave fellow chosen to play the part of the elephant, his arm extended before him like a trunk.

"They can't possibly hunt elephant, not small as they are . . . can they?" an incredulous Heather whispered to Adam as they watched.

"Don't let their size fool you," Adam responded. "They're excellent hunters. What they lack in size, they make up for in cunning. They sharpen their spears to razor edge and then hide in the forest beside the path that the elephants take to water. When an elephant is but inches away, a fearless hunter darts forward and thrusts his spear up, into its belly, then the others rush forward and finish the wounded animal off. To hunt game for their pots, they string long nets of nkusa vines between the bushes and trees. The women assemble in a line several hundred yards away and make noise, beating on pots and hollow-log drums and moving steadily closer to the nets. The game tries to flee, and is tangled in the net. The Twa can then shoot it with their bows and arrows, or simply slit the throats of smaller creatures."

"And are their arrows really tipped with poison?"

"Sometimes, yes!" Adam confirmed. "And a fast-acting poison, at that. One of Stanley's men was shot by a Pygmy arrow when he explored this area last year. According to all accounts. The man died in less than a minute! They dip the arrowheads in poison, then dry them over the fire to make them safer to handle. Believe me, sweet, we're far safer with the little Twa as our friends than our enemies. Thank God for that fiery mane of yours!"

The dancing continued far into the night, and finally Heather's eyelids began to droop. The little monkey, curled in her hat like a tiny babe in a miniature cradle, was fast asleep. At last, when the moon hung high over the jungle, and a sprinkling of glittering stars darted tiny points of light through the treetops, the feast was over, and the little chief, Mbaka, led them to huts that had been specially built by the women for the guests. The huts, Heather was relieved to see, were far larger than those of the Twa. Apparently their enormous size had been the cause of much giggling amongst the Twa women as they had constructed these "giant" residences. Inside, more mongongo leaves lined the dirt floors of the huts, which had first been cleanly swept. The chief wished them a good night, and left them.

"Come here, *madami esumba,*" Adam whispered once they were alone, reaching for her in the pitch darkness of the hut. "I've never made love to a goddess before!"

"Then be certain that you do so with proper respect for my position," Heather cautioned him teasingly.

"That won't be difficult, since I already adore you, my sweet!" he retorted, and tenderly undressed her.

They lay facing each other in the hut's close confines, breaths mingling. Adam ran his hand through the silky mass of Heather's hair, stroking her throat lingeringly before moving his hand down to caress her rounded shoulder. "Forest spirit?" he breathed. "Love goddess is more like it!"

She sucked in a shivery breath as he drew his hand across to fondle her breast, gasping as his fingertip flicked ever so gently across her nipple before moving down over her rib cage and sensitive belly. His gentle, feathery caresses tickled, and she giggled softly and writhed under his delicious torment. "Stop it, you great, lecherous brute, or this hut will come crashing down about our ears, *madami esumba* inside or no!" she protested.

"Let it!" he breathed as he gathered the delectable, squirming, seductive length of her into his arms and kissed her. His kisses, as always, were promises of the delight to follow, and her mouth clung ardently to his, teasing and nibbling in the ways she knew gave him pleasure. Soon, his breathing quickened, became husky with desire, his arms tightened about her. She could feel the hardness of him thrusting arrogantly against her flat belly, and the low growl that broke against her lips when she pressed her softness hungrily against him, molding her curves to his body, imparted his urgency to her. He parted her thighs with a tender mastery that sent further anticipation sweeping through her in a hot flood, then poised for one fleeting moment above her, his weight resting on his elbows.

Moonlight fell like pirate silver through chinks in the hut's leafy thatch, sapphiring his black hair, glinting in his smoldering dark eyes like tiny, silvery flames as he murmured her name. She felt the thrust of him against her, at once so velvety soft and yet deliciously hard, as his manhood plunged deeply inside her, and she cried out as gloriously they became one, the savage fires of their passion sweeping through them like wildfire out of control. There was no languor to their loving that night, but a hungry, tempestuous seeking of release on both their parts. The blissful ache deep in her loins quickly built to a tender torment that pulsed and quivered in answer to his deep thrusts, his caresses, his kisses, his whispered endearments. When release came, the force of it left her stunned and breathless, as if lifted and borne aloft on a tidal wave of delight, hurled at last—at last!—onto the golden isles of rapture. Exhausted, their bodies heavy with satisfaction, they lay tangled intimately together in the rosy afterglow, limbs loosely entwined.

"Let me sleep for a while, you insatiable minx," Adam murmured moments later, brushing his lips against her nose. His tone was fondly exasperated.

"Insatiable? Me?" she retorted softly. "It's you who are insatiable, Adam Markham! How can *I* sleep when you persist in toying with my hair?"

"Toying with *your* hair! Rot! It's you, minx, tugging mine!"

"Nonsense!" Heather protested sleepily. "I never touched you!"

A low chatter came from above their heads then, and Heather giggled. "I do believe I've found the culprit," she whispered, reaching out in the darkness to find the little monkey. "Come here, you little rascal!" The monkey came to her, snuggling into her arms like a child. "Oh, Adam, I do believe he misses his mother," Heather cried softly. "He's clinging to me so!"

"Whether he misses his mother or no, I'm not sharing this hut with that damned monkey. Out with him!" Adam said sternly.

"Oh, but Adam—!"

"Out! A *ménage à deux* is one thing—a menagerie *à trois* quite another!"

"Oh, very well," she grumbled. With a heavy sigh, she deposited the little monkey outside the hut's low, round opening, and then settled down in Adam's arms, her head cradled on his broad chest, the beat of his heart even and comforting in her ears. In minutes, she was deeply asleep.

Adam lay awake, stroking her hair as he stared thoughtfully into darkness. They had already entered the circle of land that he had designated as the area where Robert Elwood must have glimpsed the fabled Tears of Agaja years before. Tomorrow, they would be near the Tshopo Falls—and Elwood had mentioned that he could hear the roar of a waterfall where he stumbled upon the treasure! The excitement Adam had been containing these past days of journeying down the Congo and through the jungle was building. His dreams were within reach. A sultan's ransom in diamonds awaited him! The woman he loved lay, exhausted from his loving, in his arms. What more could any man ask for?

A childlike, pitiful whimpering began beyond the hut's opening. It was interspersed with angry chatters that sounded like scolding. He tried to block his ears—and heart—to the sounds, and he succeeded—briefly! After a few moments, he could stand it no more. He gently lifted Heather's head from his chest, crawled to the opening, and hefted the monkey back inside in one large hand. The ungrateful beast gave him a nasty nip on the palm by way of thanks. He cursed with feeling as it sprang away from him to cuddle once more against Heather, then ruefully shook his head in the darkness. "Can't say I blame you, you wretch!" he muttered, and lay down again to sleep.

The morning air was golden green and hazy when they awoke and left the hut, light streaming down from above them into the clearing and making rainbow arcs in the mist that steamed from the ground. Already the insects had begun their incessant droning, and the raucous laughter of some tropical bird ricocheted through the treetops. Yet the Twa, a noisy laughing people just the evening before, were curiously silent and gloomy this morning. They moved about their village with the air of a people oppressed. The children huddled by their mothers as they cooked the morning fare of pounded manioc, made into a form of gruel. The men squatted on their haunches in small groups, disconsolately whittling their short arrows. Adam and Heather exchanged glances. Something was obviously wrong, but what?

The answer was apparent when Ngudu appeared, carrying a young Twa boy in his arms. Behind him came Mbaka, tears rolling down his dusky gold cheeks. He was mumbling incoherently. Behind them was a woman with a babe riding in a sling upon her hip, obviously the boy's mother, and with her was a young girl, her front teeth filed to points as beauty and fashion decreed for Twa maidens of marriageable age, possibly the boy's older sister.

"What happened?" Adam asked.

362

"Mbaka's son," Ngudu supplied, indicating the still child in his arms. "He play with other children at their *bopi,* their playground. He fall from tall vine. The others come to him. They tell him to stand, to wake up. He does not. Mbaka says it is the rainbow that has caused this. That the rainbow is evil, and takes shape of water serpents to eat the children of the Twa!"

At once, Heather was all brisk efficiency. She ordered Ngudu to carry the child into her hut, and after Ngudu had done so, she asked him to have the villagers bring water to her. Then she set about examining the limp child. There was a nasty cut on his temple that needed cleaning, and under it a dark bruise, but other than that, she could detect no further injuries to the lad. His arms and legs were unbroken, his back too. She pressed her ear to his little chest. No heartbeat was audible, none whatsoever!

She yanked the child to a sitting position and shook him several times. In the tent doorway, Mbaka began to mutter angrily under his breath at her rough treatment of his son. "Keep him back, Adam," Heather flung over her shoulder. "Somehow, I must get the boy's heart started again!"

Lowering the boy back upon the leafy carpet, she slapped him hard across one cheek, then again on the other. Mbaka's furious mutterings increased tenfold.

Adam stood before the hut, rifle at the ready, while Heather vigorously massaged the child's chest, arms, and neck. Mbaka watched anxiously as she listened again for a heartbeat. Nothing! *Oh, Lord, help me!*

"*Bolozi!*" the little chief declared querulously, over and over again. "*Bolozi!*"

"What the devil is *bolozi?*" Adam asked Ngudu.

"Evil eye," the Kikuyu translated. "If not rainbow serpent that do this, Mbaka blame child's sickness on the evil eye of an old woman in the village."

363

"Evil eye, my foot!" Heather muttered from inside the hut. "It was the fall that caused this. Here goes!" She curled her fingers into a fist, and brought them down against the lad's chest, once, then a second time. The sound of her flesh violently meeting the boy's was loud and threatening in the hush. "Come on!" she gritted out. "Beat!"

Mbaka cried out and shouldered his bow, nocking an arrow against the string. Around him, his hunters did likewise, until a circle of Pygmies, their bows strung with poison darts and aimed at Adam and Ngudu, surrounded the hut. Their expressions and their angry mutterings boded ill, for all their diminutive stature, and inwardly Adam groaned.

"Do something, and quickly, love! They're turning ugly out here!" Adam said in a low voice, his fingers straying slowly but surely to the safety of his rifle.

Again, Heather struck the child with her knotted fist, immediately pressing her ear to the lad's chest, praying for, *willing* his heart to commence beating again.

Sweat beaded Adam's brow as his gaze traveled the circle of ferocious elfin faces, every one hostile now. Silence yawned like a bottomless void, he and Ngudu on one side, and the hostile, suspicious Twa on the other. Seconds stretched, became minutes, an eternity.

"I've got it!" Heather exclaimed. "His heart's beating again, strong and steady!"

"Thank God!" Adam muttered. "Quickly, Ngudu, tell Mbaka his son is going to be well again, and let's get out of here."

Ngudu did so, and the change that came over the Pygmy chief was more magical than the power of his *madami esumba.* He threw himself down on his belly at Adam's feet and clutched him about the boots, mumbling his thanks over and over.

"Adam, the little boy is waking up now." Heather's

364

voice came from the hut.

Sure enough, the Twa lad was coming to. His long-lashed eyes fluttered open, and he murmured something. At once, the woman whom Heather had correctly guessed was his mother rushed forward, thrusting past Heather to envelop the lad in her arms. Tears of joy trickled down her cheeks as the child sat up and rubbed his eyes as if awakened from a deep sleep. Mbaka came to Heather and prostrated himself at her feet, babbling incoherently.

"He say *madami esumba's* magic is strong indeed, stronger than water spirit and *bolozi,*" Ngudu explained. "He says you are great goddess, Missie Bwana, and that Mbaka will never forget *madami's* healing of his son."

"Tell him to get up, and say that I'm very glad I was of help to his child," Heather murmured, embarrassed by the headman's outpouring of adoration. "Tell him also that it was *knowledge,* a knowledge of the white man's medicine, that saved his son, not supernatural powers. Explain to him that the missions can heal or help many of his people, if he will only trust them."

"I try," Ngudu promised with a shrug of his shoulders and a broad grin, "but I do not think Mbaka will believe me!"

The water she had ordered had been brought to the hut, and she deftly bathed and bandaged the boy's wound with strips torn from her chemise, advising his mother through Ngudu's translations that he should rest for a day or so, and play quietly. Feeling shaky in the wake of her triumph, she tottered outside to where Adam waited.

"I do believe your knowledge saved our lives," Adam said, his admiration obvious. "Well done!"

"Don't praise me, it was all luck!" Heather whispered, a delighted smile curving her lips, her amethyst eyes dancing with merriment.

"Luck? You mean, you didn't learn how to revive him at that nursing school? It wasn't the 'white man's knowledge'?"

"Not on your life!" she confessed, grinning as she saw his mouth drop open in disbelief. "I had no idea whether what I was trying to do would work! But when it did, I couldn't pass up the chance to convince the Twa that the European medical missions can help them." She shrugged expansively. "Besides, my idea worked, didn't it? Rather well, too! I prayed that a severe shock to his system might jolt his heart into functioning again, and so it did. Sometimes, Captain Markham, it pays to be practical."

He grinned broadly. "Point taken, Lady Heather!"

They left the village in triumph amidst the farewells of the happy Twa people. Laden with gifts wrapped in woven grass mats or heaped into calabashes, they headed back to the site where they had made camp the afternoon before. The little monkey rode upon Heather's shoulder, chattering all the while and daintily accepting the tidbits of fruit she offered him, his tiny fingers reaching greedily for each morsel.

At the clearing by the river, Adam brought up short and cursed, thoroughly and at length, causing Heather, who had rarely heard him use such language in her presence, to gape at him.

"Damn it all, look!" he snapped, fury in his eyes.

Bearers, tents, bundles, trade goods, and clothing were gone! Except for the ashes of the fires they had lit the day before, it was as if their camp had never been.

Chapter Twenty-three

Adam strode to the center of the clearing. He crouched down and sifted the ashes from the fire through his fingers. "They're cold," he muttered, then rocked back on his heels and looked about him. "Last night would you say, Ngudu?"

Ngudu felt the ashes and nodded. *"Ndio, Bwana."*

"Damn it!" Adam growled, tossing the handful of ashes aside. "What the devil do you think got into them? What made them take off like that?"

"They've been uneasy since Sau's death, Bwana. My people are simple people, with simple beliefs. They were afraid that since the leopard killed Sau, Sau would now be one of them. I believe they feared last night that his spirit had come back to haunt them in its new leopard shape. Look!" He squatted on the ground, and pointed to the spoor of a great cat, each enormous paw print clearly preserved in the mud of the riverbank. The tracks were everywhere. "You see, Bwana? *Chui* here, and here, everywhere about the camp! It was a big one too, Bwana. The spoor is fresh and deep. That is why they left. They were afraid!"

"Bloody superstition and ignorance again! Add disease, and together they'll be the downfall of Africa, mark my words," Adam muttered. "Lord! I can see now why they ran off, but did they have to take all the blasted equipment? I didn't expect that of them!" He swept off his bush hat, and ran an angry hand through his unruly black hair. "Thank God I have the rifle and my revolver and a few cases of shells left! All going well, we can still make it out to Kigali with what we've got."

"You mean we have to turn back?" Heather asked. "Oh, surely not? We've come too far for that, Adam!"

"What choice do we have? The porters have run off with everything else: dry provisions, clothes, tents, ammunition—the lot! How are we to hunt? Where are we to sleep. Be realistic, Heather, we couldn't last forty-eight hours without those packs, what with the mosquitoes and the flies. Not to mention the big cats!"

"I find the bearers, Bwana," Ngudu offered. "Ewasu and I, we find them, bring everything back bloody quick!" He grinned.

Adam frowned, deep furrows forming between his black eyebrows. "You mean split up? Not a chance! It's too damned risky. You're no more accustomed to these jungles than I am, Ngudu."

"*I* choose men to go with you and Bwana Worth," Ngudu said stiffly. "These men no good. He afraid. He run away. He take everything! He bring shame upon Ngudu. I find him, Bwana, I find him good!" His smooth black face was no longer relaxed and good-humored, but indignant and filled with wounded male pride. He appeared grim, angry, and vengeful. "Ewasu, my brother!" He exchanged a few rapid words with the other bearer and then turned back to Adam. "It is agreed. We go now. You and Missie Bwana wait here two, three days, no more. We will return."

After a pause, Adam nodded, although obviously reluctant. "If you're not back by then, we'll come looking for you."

Ngudu snatched up his spear. "We will be back, Bwana."

Adam clasped the Kikuyu warmly by the shoulder, his gentian eyes solemn and earnest as he looked into the bearer's stern black face. "Take care, my friend," he murmured softly.

The head bearer nodded and grinned wickedly, a trace of his former good humor returning. "It is not Ngudu you should worry about, Bwana, but those worthless jackals I go to find, *ndio?*"

Adam laughed. *"Ndio,"* he agreed.

"Allah be with you, Bwana," the bearer said simply.

"And with you both."

"Safari!" Ngudu shouted, and he and Ewasu set off, waving to Heather as they strode past her before plunging into the jungle in search of the missing bearers.

"They'll be back, you'll see," Adam reassured her, seeing the anxiety etched in her face. He slipped his arms about her waist and pulled her back against his chest, resting his chin on the crown of her head. "A finer man never lived than Ngudu, black or white. If he says he'll be back, little madami, he will."

Mbaka and several of his wives arrived soon after, apparently having heard of their plight by some means unknown to Heather. The little women carried sheafs of mongongo leaves with them, and in less than three hours had erected them a sizeable hut. Heather was deeply touched by the gesture, and she delighted the Twa women by showing her eagerness to learn how the huts were constructed. They proved to be willing teachers. Amidst much laughter at their beloved madami's clumsiness, the hut was built in time for Adam and Heather to take shelter during the afternoon showers. They also brought gifts of food and stored it

369

neatly inside the hut, along with the other gifts the villagers had presented to her.

The monkey, which Heather had named Mackintosh after a wizened little gardener once employed at Moorsedge, kept them amused with his chattering and his lively antics. He leaped about the hut emitting wild bursts of sound that seemed to mock the poor green parrot in the vine cage. "Look at me, I'm quite free!" Mac seemed to boast, "while you are not!"

"Malicious little devil," Adam remarked, nodding at the monkey. "I'd swear he was crowing about his freedom."

"You would say that," Heather retorted, settling herself comfortably against Adam. "I do believe you're jealous of Mac, and the attention I give him. He's never acted maliciously to me."

Adam snorted. "Try putting him outside the hut tonight, and see how tame he is then!" He pointedly eyed the bite mark on his palm.

"You must have frightened him," Heather insisted. "Poor baby!"

As if he understood, Mac edged along her shoulder and nuzzled up to her neck. He gently stroked her face with tiny fingers, making low clicking sounds in his throat as if crooning, meanwhile eying Adam craftily over Heather's shoulder. With unerring instinct, he guessed that the man had dark intentions in his soul when it came to monkeys!

The sunset that evening was glorious, bathing the river in ruddy light until it flowed blood red between the muddy banks. The sky was streaked with feverish flame, cerise and gold, the dying sun a fiery globe that was cupped momentarily by the snowy peaks of the breathtaking mountain ranges, staining them rose-colored, before slipping behind them.

Animals padded from the jungle to the river to drink

or bathe. From the hut's concealment, Heather and Adam saw lovely, crested, white herons stalking the reeded banks in search of fish. They watched the antelope and the small forest buffalo pick their way daintily to the water to drink, observed the hippos heave themselves out of their muddy wallows and bask in the mellow evening sunshine, like fat ladies sunning themselves on the sandy beach at Brighton. Meanwhile the crocodiles continued to play their monotonous game of let's-pretend-we're-logs, although one occasionally slithered down the riverbanks, entering the water with a great splash, to float, submerged save for its cunning, ever-vigilant eyes and its nostrils. Elephants came to the river too. Giant ears flapping, they filled their trunks and shot water over their calves and themselves. In the long grasses, the leopards awaited their turn, blinking lazy golden eyes and yawning.

Soon the moon rose, a sliver of silver in a deep violet sky spangled with hotly glittering white stars. The nightly humming of the insect orchestra began. The snarls of jungle cats, hunting, ruptured the ordered buzz, as did the uneasy twittering of birds roosting in the dense crowns of the creeper-laden trees, high above the jungle floor.

"Are you still awake?" Adam whispered in the shadows.

"Yes," Heather replied. "I can't sleep. I was thinking about Ngudu and Ewasu. Are you sure they'll be all right?"

"Of course."

"But what of the Belgians? If they should find them, they might force them into one of the labor gangs in the mines!"

"Don't even think it. Ngudu's too clever to allow himself to be caught by them," Adam said firmly, squeezing her hand. His tone brooked no arguments, and she was reassured by it.

"What is it that the Belgians mine?"

"In this area, copper mostly. To the northeast, gold. To the south, industrial diamonds. All revenues go to King Leopold, who established his *personal* claim to the Congo about fifteen years ago. The Belgians use native labor to do all the mining, and elephants to transport the ore and haul away the trees when they clear the jungle. They have the only elephants in Africa that have been domesticated, by Europeans, like those used in India."

"And the Tears of Agaja?"

"They're near here somewhere. Call it wishful thinking if you will, but I know it!" he murmured. There was a trace of certainty in his tone. "We'll find them."

"And afterward, when we have the diamonds—what then, Adam?"

"We'll return to London, and you'll start proceedings against Douglas for a divorce."

"Divorce him?" She laughed, a bitter little laugh. "Do you know how difficult that would be? A wife can't simply divorce her husband, not in this day and age! I would need proof of his adultery to divorce him, or at the very least his agreement to swear that such adultery took place."

"Then we'll have to see that *he* divorces *you.*" Adam grimaced. "Much as I hate to see your name dragged through the courts, my love, we'll do whatever we must do to set you free."

"He'd never let me go, not to be with you, not in a hundred years. I know him!" Divorces were almost unheard of. They were rarely granted, and when they were the cooperation of both parties involved was required. Douglas, Heather thought with a chill of foreboding, would be far from cooperative.

"As a last resort, there's always blackmail."

"He and Philip?"

"Why not? He's never balked at using people. Perhaps it's time someone turned the tables on him?"

"We couldn't do that, Adam. Think of the people who'd be hurt if the truth came out! Douglas' mother . . . Philip's parents . . . our families. In striking out at him, we'd hurt innocent people too."

"Then we'll go away, as I told you once before." He cupped her face in his hands and kissed her. "Come what may, we'll be together, I give you my word."

"You say that with so much conviction, make it sound so simple! I want more than anything to believe it will work out, truly I do! But you see things through rose-colored spectacles, Adam. You want the diamonds; therefore, you feel you cannot possibly fail to find them. You want me, and so you can't conceive that for us, there may be no happy ending. Be realistic, please, my darling?" she implored him. "See things as they really are. Douglas will put up a fight, I'm certain of it. He'll say terrible things about me—about us. The scandal could drag on for years, with him blocking the divorce at every turn. What will that do to our families—to our lives and to the way you feel about me?"

He snorted. "For God's sake, Heather! Do you still have so little faith in me that you believe anything Dennison could possibly do or say would make one iota of difference to the way I feel?" His tone was harsh, laced with bitterness. "Does it mean nothing to you when I say that I love you?"

"Of course not!" she insisted hotly. "It means everything to me. But passion can fade. What we have—is it strong enough to withstand those pressures? Will it last?"

"Passion is only a small part of love, Heather. What I

feel for you goes beyond passion. Haven't you realized that yet? I want to be with you always. I want to share my name and my life with you. I want to love and cherish you, rich or poor, in sickness or in health, until we grow old together. I want to watch the children born of our love grow, to know that they're a part of us. Does that tell you how I feel? Does that still your fears? We're as strong as the love we feel for each other! Our love is a fortress in which we're secure as long as the walls—as long as we—stand fast. I've desired many women before you, Heather, but I've never loved them as I love you. Never!" He gathered her into his arms and kissed her again. His warm lips were filled with tenderness, and she shivered as she felt tremors overtake his body—tremors of emotion. The love that filled him flowed through his lips, the gentle touch of his hands, to fill her very soul.

They didn't make love that night, but instead lay quietly together, embracing, confiding their hopes and their fears until sleep claimed them both. The relaxed intimacy they shared during those hours somehow bound them closer than their passionate lovemaking had.

Heather awoke first the next morning, vaguely aware that something was wrong. What that something was dawned on her slowly. Mac's lively chatter was missing! The little monkey had left the hut at some point during the night. She hurriedly fastened her clothing, only loosened for sleeping since she had no clothes to change into now, and then ducked through the low, round opening and crawled outside.

At first, she couldn't see him. The clearing was deserted, as they had found it the morning before. But then a burst of excited chatter greeted her from across the clearing. Mac swung by one hand from a low branch overhanging the river, engaged in his perpetual gymnastics. Laughing and relieved that he had not returned to the jungle as she'd feared, she started toward him, scolding him for having run away. Mac responded with equally stern tones, jumping up and down as she approached. She saw his bright, dark eyes flicker from her to a log floating downstream, and she guessed his intent the instant it was born.

"Don't you dare, silly Mac!" she chided, edging toward him. "You'll be carried away. Come here, baby . . . come to me." She held out her hand to the monkey as if offering him a piece of fruit, but Mac was not tricked by her ploy. With a scream of indignation that she would try such a transparent ruse on him, he leaped for the floating log and clung to it, baring his teeth in a triumphant grin. The log bumped once against the banks, then began to edge out, into the flow of the river itself.

"No!" Heather cried, throwing herself onto her belly on the muddy riverbanks, and straining to grab Mac before he was carried away. Too late! The log gained momentum and slid out of reach. Mac's cries were now filled with alarm, rather than triumph. They tore at her heart. He ran pitifully back and forth along the log, whimpering like a frightened child. His chocolate eyes, now round and enormous with terror, beseeched her to help him. "I'm coming!" she screamed. "Hang on, Mac!" *The canoe!* She'd go after him in one of the dugouts!

She scrambled to her feet and swung about. Boots sliding in the oozing mud, arms windmilling for balance, she scrabbled wildly for purchase in the fleeting second before she realized she was going to fall. She toppled backward into the muddy Congo with a single, panic-filled scream, hands grasping for some purchase—a tussock of grass, a low-hung branch, *anything*—before, like Mac and his log, she swirled into midstream, and out of reach of all handholds.

Farther along the riverbanks, the crocodiles blinked, stirred, and watched with keen interest as the strange white creature thrashed in the murky water. . . .

It seemed to Adam that he heard Heather's voice, screaming frantically for help. Her cries came from the bottom of a deep, black well.

He fought his way through cobwebs of sleep to wakefulness. Relieved to find he was in the hut, he was convinced that the terrified cries he had heard had been but a part of his dreams. But then he rolled over, and saw that the place beside him was empty. The golden-green light spilling through the *mongongo* leaves dappled the place where Heather had lain. A frisson of fear slithered down his spine, raising the hackles at his neck. God in Heaven, *had* it been only a dream? In seconds he was up and through the hut's opening, on his feet and striding rapidly across the clearing, casting about him for Heather. Not a sign of her anywhere!

Sweat sprang out, like blood, upon his brow. He turned this way and that, drawing the revolver from the holster at his belt as he did so. Where the devil had she gone? There was no sign of her! Had she wandered away from camp, or had someone taken her away? God damn it, which way should he go?

As he was about to plunge into the jungle in search of her, he heard a thin scream, carried from the direction of the river. The sound knotted his gut with apprehension. A half-dozen strides brought him to the water's edge. Far downstream, he glimpsed a pale hand above the chocolate water, an arm clothed in white, flailing frantically! The churned mud on the riverbanks told the story.

Shoulder braced against the stern of the canoe, he

hefted it down the muddy banks and into the river, then sprang inside and took up the paddle, using it to thrust the dugout away from the banks. He cleaved the water with strong, even strokes that carried him swiftly into midstream. The current aided him then, for at this point it was rapid; and the narrow canoe glided like a swift snake through the muddy water toward her. That pitiful arm and her bobbing head grew closer by the second as he strained muscle and sinew to force ever greater speed from the canoe.

"Come on, you sluggish bastard, *move!*" he gritted through tight lips.

Every second brought Heather closer to death! The cords in his neck, his arms, his shoulders stood out. They were knotted ropes under his tanned flesh as he strived to reach her. His palms and fingers were slick with sweat, and it streamed down his face and bare back. Yet he was heedless of the salt that stung his eyes, blind to anything but his goal. His existence had been telescoped into a single, narrow tunnel: the water between Heather and the canoe was all. He could hear a galloping, a hammering thump, a roaring in his ears. He was dimly aware that this frantic clamor was his heartbeat. His breathing came in short, painful rasps.

Pull! Pull! Pull!

The water flowed back strongly, evenly with every stroke of the paddle, but not fast enough! The craft's movement was painfully slow. He felt that it moved through some sucking, dragging mire instead of mere water.

Fifty feet. *Sweet Jesus Christ!*

Forty feet. *Faster, damn it, faster!*

Thirty feet from her, he sensed movement on both sides of the canoe. He saw the gray-green of a powerful, leathery tail thrash the surface of the water, caught an elongated snout cleaving smoothly through the current like the prow of an ancient, lichened barge. Simultaneously, Heather spotted the crocodiles bearing steadily down upon her. Her frantic screams fired him with reservoirs of strength and energy he had not known he possessed. Like a man crazed, his desperation gave him superhuman strength, and at last he drew the canoe alongside her. Sweat blinding him, the canoe lurching, he reached out, his fingers clawing for and finally knotting in the cloth of her blouse. He hefted her bodily from the water and half over the side, gasping for breath. Respiration was now a heaving agony that tore at his throat, his lungs.

Like a beached fish, Heather sprawled half in and half out of the canoe, her skirts still trailing in the water, her long, tangled hair streaming. She was coughing and sobbing and shivering with exertion. Fighting the swift current had drained her strength. She was too exhausted to haul herself all the way into the canoe: he was too played out to help her all the way in.

And then, a long head like that of some prehistoric monster reared up out of the water, massive jaws redly agape, throat a crimson cavern, teeth a pointed palisade of doom.

"Damn you, *no!*" Adam roared. The cry, wrenched from somewhere deep inside him, spewed forth as if torn from his soul. He grabbed for the paddle, and with all his remaining strength, plunged it straight into the center of that crimson cavern that yawned like the pit of hell before him. The crocodile thrashed about, the paddle wedged in its throat. Its whiplike, powerful tail lashed, churning the brown water and rocking the narrow craft dangerously; then the disabled beast swam awkwardly away.

Adam hefted Heather up against his chest and dragged her bodily down into the bottom of the canoe.

378

His limbs weak and ashudder with strain, he drew greedy, hungry breaths into lungs that were afire. Then, head bowed, shoulders slumped over, he rested on the crosspiece of the canoe, feeling strength seep back into his body.

He raised his head wearily and turned Heather over. With her tangled, wet hair limp about her ashen face, she appeared quite lifeless. Adam wept then, wept at the futility of his struggle to save her, wept because he believed he had lost the battle he had waged against distance and time.

Then Heather retched. Muddy water spewed from her mouth, followed by a choked sob. Relief swept through him. *Alive!* Thank God, she was alive!

Only then did he hear the roar of the falls ahead: the Tshopo Falls, a cataract that plunged madly over sheer, rocky cliffs into the foaming torrents of the Congo.

Chapter Twenty-four

The canoe glided inexorably onward to the falls, and without a paddle with which to steer her, Adam could not hope to alter their course. Forthing white water flecked the muddy brown of the Congo now, and the roar of the falls became deafening as the canoe hurtled toward the rim of jagged rocks that topped the cliff. Huge, conical reed baskets had been set on poles and lashed between the rocks across the edge of the precipice by daring native fishermen, to trap the fish hurled over the foaming rapids.

Heather struggled to a sitting position, then realized instantly the dilemma they were in when she turned to look ahead. Adam's face was grimly set, his eyes narrowed as they met her own.

"What can we do?" she cried hoarsely as the canoe raced onward, riding swiftly on the rampaging current now, its pointed prow rearing violently from the water.

"Pray," he ground out. Then there was no time for further words, for the canoe was careening rapidly toward the jagged teeth of the rocks, jerking to left and right as the crosscurrents battered it. "Jump for the traps," Adam yelled above the roar of the falls, flicking the spray from his face. "Hang on!"

Ashen, she nodded and crouched in the bow, waiting for the moment. "What about you?" she shouted over her shoulder as he reached out to steady her in the lurching craft.

"I'll be right behind you! Ready! Go-o-o . . ." he replied, but his words were carried away in the rushing of the water.

Adam pushed her, and for one dreadful moment Heather saw the foaming water below and thought she would be pitched, headlong, into it. Then she was slammed full-force against one of the huge basketwork fishing traps she had glimpsed. Instinctively she grasped it and hung on grimly, feeling the water rushing over and past and around her body. The torrents sucked at her full skirts, threatening to tear her from her precarious handhold and drag her over the falls. Flinging her hair from her eyes, she saw Adam jump. As he did so, the canoe was flung against one of the rocks. It bucked high into the air, clipping his brow as it arced back down and slammed into the water, broken in two. A thin spray of red erupted from Adam's streaming black hair. The water flowed pink momentarily, before the stain was quickly washed away by the creamy froth. Heather screamed again as the force of the water lifted his limp body up and tossed it over the falls like a rag doll. He disappeared beneath the foaming, angry water below, as did the shattered halves of the canoe, and she could see him no more. Her desperate cries were drowned out by the roar of the rapids.

Sobbing, Heather clung to the reed basket, fighting the pull of the water. Her limbs were weak, trembling, their strength gone, and her body felt bruised and achy. Nonetheless, she managed to hoist herself halfway into the basket and to hook her arms awkwardly through the slats as if she were in a sling. The current battered her against the fishing trap's hard ridges, again and again.

There she hung for what seemed an eternity, drifting in and out of consciousness, and from time to time uttering feeble cries for help. The will to live, the determination to hang on, *somehow,* was surprisingly strong at first, but it ebbed as the minutes stretched into hours, and finally her exhausted body yearned to give up the fight.

She was so tired . . . so very, very tired. Her arms felt as if they had been wrenched from their sockets. How easy it would be to simply let go, to let the busy water take her as it had taken Adam. They would be together then, and without him, she didn't want to go on living. Death would be quick, probably painless . . . welcome.

She came to from one of her lapses into pain-free oblivion to feel tiny fingers touching her cheeks, to hear Mac's pitiful whimpers somewhere nearby. She opened her eyes, swollen from being so long in the water, to see the little monkey perched atop the fishing trap beside her, his round, brown eyes filled with terror as he peered into her face. Through cracked lips, she whispered his name, trying to comfort him. The little monkey chattered nervously, twisting back and forth. He seemed to want to cling to her, but was afraid to release his hold on the basket to do so. Her voice seemed to calm him, however, for after some moments he settled down and fell silent.

Heather had welcomed Mac's incessant chatter, for it had helped her to block out her fears for Adam. *Oh, my love, where are you?* she wondered, feeling sick to her stomach. When she closed her eyes, she could see, in her mind's eye, the awful red spray that had erupted from his head, the head-over-heels arc his body had described in the air as if motion were slowed as he was hurtled over the falls. Could he have survived the tumble through the raging cataract to the ferocious water that roiled about the treacherous rocks below, wounded as he was? Could anyone have hoped to survive it? Heather's grief surfaced, swelling inside her and filling her with pain too deep and wrenching to bear. When she gave way to huge, agonized sobs, the awful sound of her weeping disturbed Mac. He shrieked in terror and edged fearfully away, and though she knew he was afraid, she could not stop.

She judged it to be midafternoon by that time. The sky was a darker blue above the treetops that lined the Congo, actually blue and white like the delft ware in Aunt Elise's Welsh cabinet at Moorsedge. She jerked her head up, forcing herself to stay awake, and was suddenly aware of laughter and voices—native voices —calling to each other across the wide rapids. With difficulty, she managed to turn her head, and she saw that dark figures were gathering on the distant bank— women in brightly patterned silk *kangas* balancing huge baskets upon their heads. She heard the shouts and singing of children at play. With a groan of pure agony, she managed to untangle one stiff arm from the reed basket, moaning as she moved. She waved feebly at them. "Help! Please, help me!"

Whether the native fisherman heard her cry, or whether he was paddling his dugout canoe across the falls simply to retrieve his catch, she was never to discover. She was only aware that suddenly she was looking into the startled eyes of a tall, black-skinned man, who had expertly maneuvered his canoe alongside the fishing trap to which she clung, angling it crosswise against the raging river. He called to the others, and scant seconds later she was being carefully lifted and lowered into his canoe.

How the native fishermen steered their long dugout canoes so expertly to and from the riverbank against the fierce current was little short of miraculous, for no amount of experience could possibly lessen the hazards of their method of fishing. As they neared the banks, she saw several more such canoes pulled up onto them, others just setting out for the traps, and still others returning with their catch, silvery tails slapping in the bows of these. The fisherman told someone to hold his canoe, and then he swung her up in his strong arms and carried her to a spot beneath a tall acacia tree, where he put her down. He grinned at her, and said some words she did not understand.

"Asante!" she whispered. "Asante." He obviously understood her thanks, for he nodded, then turned and spoke rapidly to another native man who turned and ran off.

Native women milled about her then, offering her dry clothing—one of their own vividly patterned silk *kangas*. Too weak to worry about modesty, she allowed them to peel off her sodden garments and wrap her in the wide dry length of silk, fastening the cloth under her arms instead of about her hips as did they. Another length of cloth was draped warmly about her shoulders, for despite the steaming heat, she was obviously chilled. As warmth and feeling gradually returned to her aching arms, she tried to explain to the women, using frantic hand motions, that she had not been alone in the canoe, that Adam had gone over the falls.

"One more," she repeated, pointing to herself. "Canoe . . . boom!" She mimed the canoe slamming into the rock, and Adam's body hurtling over the edge. They smiled politely and nodded, yet their eyes were blank. "You have to understand me—you must!" she cried, almost in tears because of her frustration.

At last, a young native woman in a violet-blue skirt indicated her understanding. She and one of the younger fishermen hurried off, and then Heather fell gratefully back down to the woven matting her rescuers had spread out beneath her, offering a prayer of thanks that she had been understood.

The pair returned some time later, little Mac perched on the native girl's shoulder. He leaped onto Heather's shoulders and clung to her, chattering joyfully. Despair swept through Heather as the import of the pair's act sank home. They had found only the little monkey. There had been nothing, not even a body, at the base of the falls. Numbed by grief, she sat there, dazed, not aware at first that her rescuers had fallen silent. When she looked up, she saw that they were staring down the rise in the direction of a white man who was riding up it toward them. From the apprehension mirrored in their dark eyes, it appeared he was not someone they were pleased to see.

When he reached them, he swung his pudgy body down from the back of his scrawny horse, carelessly tossed the reins to a nearby native, and strode across to her. Pudgy fists planted arrogantly on his ample hips, he looked down at her, his small, black eyes shining like wet currants in his fleshy, ruddy face. His portly belly spilled over his wide black belt, straining the yellowed white cloth of his shirt. His immaculately polished black boots gleamed.

"Madame Dennison, is it not?" he asked in heavily accented English. "We 'ave been expecting you, madame—though per'aps not in this manner!" He gestured toward the falls.

"Expecting me?" she echoed, her tone incredulous. "How could that be?"

"Later, I will explain to you, madame, but for now, allow me to present myself. Hercule Cigale, *à votre service, madame!*" He clipped his heels smartly together, and made her a half-bow. "Now, we must see you properly taken care of, must we not? These black devils haven't tried any of their witch-doctor mumbo jumbo on you, have they?"

"Certainly not! They've been very kind to me!"

Cigale grunted noncommittally, and barked an order to some of the native men gathered around. They fled without hesitation to do his bidding, and Cigale smiled pompously at Heather's arched brow. "You must show them who is master 'ere, you see, or they are impossibly lazy and *stupides!* These Wanegi, they already know that M'sieu Hercule Cigale is a man to be respected!" His currant eyes gleamed nastily.

What a pompous toad of a man, Heather thought silently. She wondered how he commanded the obedience of the gentle native people who had been so kind to her. Not because they respected him, she suspected. She had been about to explain about Adam and to demand that Cigale organize a search party for him, but some sixth sense—perhaps a trait of her Celtic ancestors?—cautioned her not to. The native girl had said she had found no one at the base of the falls. Surely if Adam were found later, the Wanegi would care for him, would tell him what had become of her.

The native men returned then, bearing a hammock slung over a long pole to form a litter much like that which Ngudu and the others had fashioned for Ellen Reading when she'd fallen ill with jungle fever. Despite her protests, Cigale bent down and, wheezing heavily, lifted her into the hammock. Two of the fishermen hoisted the poles over their shoulders while Cigale awkwardly remounted his sorry horse. With a wave of farewell for her rescuers, Heather was carried down the gently sloping hillside, back the way Cigale had come.

The dense jungle had been cleared here, she saw, and all vegetation replaced by huge, barren tracts of land

386

that scarred the red earth like great, raw wounds. Huge open-pit mines, their inner walls cut in series of steplike "benches" from which the ore-containing rocks were removed, spiraled from top to bottom of a yawning hole. Hand wagons filled with enormous rocks veined with copper and traces of silver and gold, were being laboriously hauled up the spiral ledges by sweating native laborers, while at the surface waited large wagons drawn by oxen. The beasts would pull the rocks to the nearby mill for crushing and smelting.

Closer to the jungle, trained elephants, each with a small native boy perched on its broad back, were hauling away the fallen timber to clear yet another area for still more mining. Several of the older beasts had half-grown calves harnessed to them, obviously in an attempt to teach the younger animals the tasks they would perform when grown. Signs of digging were everywhere, and in the distance was an ugly slag heap of mining waste, an unlovely contrast to the distant, misty mountains beyond. From afar she saw native laborers, clad in only loincloths, toiling in the murderous heat under the eagle eye of a white foreman who slapped a wicked-looking bullwhip against the polished leather of his boots and viciously urged them on.

The scene was one from another, sadly not-too-distant time, when the Arab slave traders had come to the mighty Congo Kingdom in search of lucrative "black ivory"—slaves—and marched them by the hundreds of thousands to the coast, wrenching them from their beloved land and families forever. But this is 1889, Heather told herself, incredulous. Such medieval treatment couldn't exist in this enlightened age, could it? Then she recalled what Adam and Ngudu had told her a few days before, that King Leopold had claimed vast regions of the Congo as his own, personal colony, that the natives were forced to labor in the Belgian mines against their will and terrible punishments meted out to those who refused to comply. A frisson of foreboding trickled like icy water down her spine. What kind of monsters was she soon to find herself amongst? And what, she wondered uneasily, had Cigale meant when he'd said they had been expecting her?

The surface of the ugly copper mine was soon left behind, the Wanegi natives straining to carry her up slopes carpeted with lush green grass to what appeared to be a settlement of some kind atop the hillside. Sure enough, as they drew closer she realized that there was actually a quaint little town sprawled across the rolling land, very European when viewed from a distance.

They entered the town of Stanleyville, named by King Leopold after Henry Stanley, the journalist turned explorer who had charted the Congo River. They were passing through what appeared to be the native quarter. A market was in progress as they made their way through the dusty square. Conically roofed thatched huts were clustered under papaya and lemon and orange trees. Avocado trees, guava and hibiscus bushes were everywhere, their fruits or flowers arrayed for sale on woven mats spread out on the dirt. Gay scarlet hibiscus blossoms decorated the woolly black heads of the bare-breasted native maidens, while the matrons seemed to favor the fragrant blooms of the exotic ginger plant, carved-ivory necklaces or elephant-hair bangles for their ornaments. White mounds of grated manioc and tobacco leaves and yams, heaped in reed baskets, were being haggled over by native vendors and purchasers. Plantains and bananas, leopard skins, elephant tusks, spears and arrowheads, and monkey meat were likewise being sold or traded. The dickering was loud yet amicable, the natives calling to each other or deriding a price offered in singsong local dialects.

They moved on through the native quarter without stopping, led by the pompous Hercule Cigale, who cursed, in furious French, at everyone who got in the way of the little cavalcade. Heather, thanks to Nanette, Aunt Elise's French maid, understood what he was saying only too well, and she found the European quarter a complete contrast to the primitive, but colorful, native section. The colonial-style bungalows she had glimpsed at the foot of the hill lined narrow and dusty little streets that were nonetheless charming and set out in an orderly fashion. Boasting thatched roofs and long verandahs, the dwellings lay, cool and white, in the afternoon sunshine that streamed through shady red-leaved mango trees, the flowering jacaranda, and the lofty palms that lined the main street. They passed a small cathedral and approached what appeared to be an official residence of some kind.

As if he had read her thoughts, the pompous Hercule Cigale reined his horse to a walk, turned in the saddle and said, "The residence of the governor-general, madame." He made a flourish toward the red-tiled building with a small, chubby hand. "I am certain Governor Mauricier will be delighted to 'ear you 'ave been found."

"Found?" She frowned. "Then Adam survived? He's been here, looking for me?" she cried eagerly, rocking the hammock as she abruptly sat up.

"Adam? I do not recall anyone by that name, madame. On the contrary, it was your 'usband, M'sieu le Governor *Dennison,* who came here to Stanleyville in search of you."

389

She sank back, staring blindly at the blue and white sky above. Not Adam. *Douglas!* As she had always known he must, given the type of man he was, he had come after her. And now, he had found her!

Adam's eyelids fluttered open. He stared above him at a patch of blue, blue sky, in which a crimson angel hovered, dancing on air.

This is it, Markham, he thought wonderingly, *You're dead, damn it all!* Strange, that. He'd never imagined crimson angels. Heavenly white-winged, golden-haloed angels, certainly, but crimson? Maybe these were Purgatory's angels? If so, he was in the right place! He attempted a wry grin, but the effort cost him. Pain filled his skull with galaxies of stars that rivaled the angels in psychedelic colors and sent comet-tails of agony shooting through him. Hell! If this was death, then he didn't think much of it. Pain was as real and unpleasant here as it had been during life!

He squinted against the brilliant light, focusing his vision on the creature above that, like a brilliant, frilly tailed butterfly, shimmied and bobbed in the warm current of air coming from somewhere above him. *That's no angel, Markham, you damned fool! It's Polystachya cuculatum.* The botanical name jumped into consciousness from some source buried deep in his mind, but was instantly dismissed. Couldn't be, not crimson like that. That variety of orchid didn't have crimson coloring. *Angraecum eichlerianum?* That full throat and lip, those frilly, caudate lateral sepals and petals—what the hell was it?

Frowning, he sat up, listing a little to starboard as he did so. He definitely wasn't dead after all. When he drew his hand away from his brow, dark, sticky blood stained his fingers. His clothes were sodden, and due to their wetness, the ground under him was little better than a muddy wallow. He scowled, straining desperately to remember. How and when had he been wounded? Lord, what the devil was wrong with him? He couldn't even remember who they were supposed to be fighting! And where was his horse? His saber and service revolver? He looked down at himself, at his mud-stained and blood-spattered white shirt and trousers. He wasn't even in uniform! Christ! Sweat sprang out on his brow, huge beads of it. More dampened his palms. In agitation he raked his hand through his streaming hair and looked about him.

The crimson orchids he had thought were angels bloomed profusely above his head like enormous captive butterflies, chained by their delicate stems to a rotted tree stump that, peculiarly, had a face, the leering face of a she-demon, or so he imagined, half-woman, half-leopard. The ceiling of dense jungle overhead was penetrated by a single arrow of golden light that fell through a small patch of blue and white sky, the only break in the leafy canopy. The raucous laughter and whoops of tropical birds and the constant chatter of monkeys—God, how he loathed monkeys!—provided a louder background to the incessant drone of insects. From somewhere nearby came the dull roaring sound of water, rushing, crashing, tumbling over rocks. He staggered to his feet and started forward, lurching toward the sound. He had gone no more than two unsteady, weaving paces before he turned back, and looked the way he had come, his dazed vision falling once more on the spikes of brilliant orchids.

Gentian eyes narrowed, he lurched back toward them, cupped one of the vivid blooms in his hand. A

391

woman's face flashed into his mind. *Lovely.* Exquisite face—too beautiful to be real. Skin like magnolias. Eyes the deep, velvety violet of pansies. Hair the color of dark copper, gleaming like red wine through fine crystal in candlelight. Body—oh, lord, perfection! Flawless breasts, sleek line to waist and hips and thighs . . . He cursed under his breath. Her name! Surely he'd remember such a lovely vision's name? And why had seeing the orchids brought her face back to him so vividly? He rocked back on his heels as a wave of vertigo swept over him, then angrily shrugged it off. He plucked several of the crimson orchids with parts of their stems intact, and turned back toward the sound of the water nearby, brushing aside a curtain of vines as he went.

When he exited the jungle, he gaped at the drama and splendor of the falls above him, the foaming pool below. In wide-eyed amazement, he reached up to touch the livid bruise upon his brow. His clothes were still wet. Had he taken a fall through that foaming white cataract and somehow dragged himself out and into the jungle? Did that explain his situation? It had to. It was the only explanation that made sense. Where to now? It might be risky to stagger around in the open, not knowing where he was or whether the enemy might be nearby, whoever they were. . . .

He started at the sound of voices, and quickly ducked back into the jungle so he could see who was coming without being seen himself. As he watched, he saw a dark-skinned, bare-breasted young woman in a long sarong of deep blue cloth clambering down the rocks alongside the falls. She was accompanied by a young native man. The frown on Adam's face deepened as he watched them skirt the frothy pool, peering anxiously among the rocks, obviously searching for something as they called to each other in a tongue he did not understand. Their short, woolly black hair and features identified them as African, rather than Indian. This further mystified Adam. He sank back down, crouching on his heels to wait until they moved on. Something peculiar was afoot here, and he didn't trust himself to move on until he had figured out just what it was. . . .

Chapter Twenty-five

Heather awoke to the reedy trill of cicadas from a nearby garden, and to the monotonous whirring of a paddle fan. She opened her eyes, startled at first to see shrouds of mosquito netting all about her like a vast spider's web in the gloom. The feel of the bed beneath her was strange, alien after so many weeks of sleeping outdoors. Long gray shadows mottled the walls, and for a second she thought she was back in Nairobi again, in her apartment in Douglas' residence.

Her heart gave a horrible lurch at the thought, before memory came flooding back: Stanleyville. Hercule Cigale. Governor-General Pascal Mauricier. Oh, yes, she had met the smooth, elegant Belgian governor on her arrival at his residence, prior to being shown to her present accommodations, and she had liked him even less than Cigale, she recalled with a shudder of distaste. Like Cigale, Mauricier had sidestepped her guarded questions about Douglas, implying that he would answer them over dinner that evening, and insisting with the utmost solicitation that she should rest and recuperate from her ordeal for the time being. But what, she had wondered, was to be explained that could not be covered by a few simple words. What necessitated their evasive behavior?

That question still perturbed her after what appeared to be several hours of sleep, judging by the amethyst sky framed by her window. Yawning and wincing as she stretched muscles that still ached abominably, she tossed aside the single sheet that had covered her bare body, brushed aside the netting, and crossed the room. French doors led out onto a small, semicircular balcony with a black wrought-iron railing. It overlooked a shadowed garden below, she saw as she stepped out onto it. From the darkened shrubbery, the heady, sweet perfume of Madagascan jessamine rose pungently on the humid night air, and silvery moonlight gave a sheen to the film of perspiration that had dewed her body while she slept, dappling the lawns with silver and gray. She could not see the little town or its townsfolk, for her room had only a view of the distant jungle and of the looming, darker silhouette of the mountains beyond.

Despite the slowly rotating fan, the humidity billowed against her face like moist flannel as she stepped back inside. Almost square in proportion, the whitewashed walls of the room were quite without paintings or decorations of any kind. Other than the massive, old-fashioned fourposter bed, there was only a washstand and a heavy chest of drawers, an oval mirror fixed to the wall behind it to serve as a dressing table. The lovely old red-tiled floor had seen better, cleaner days, she thought absently, noting as well the cobwebs in the corners and the slut's wool peeping out in great drifts from under the bed. She wrinkled her nose in distaste as she ran a finger across the top of the chest. Whoever attends to your housekeeping, Governor, should be shot! she thought absently.

Before Heather had fallen asleep, Mauricier's sullen-faced black servant had brought her a jug of hot water, a basin, soap, and fresh linens, setting them on the chest. The water had long since cooled; nevertheless, she busied herself in making a sketchy toilette, forcing herself to concentrate on each task as it needed to be done, for only in that way could she deny the worry and grief that filled her mind. *One step at a time, Heather,* she told herself. Yet Adam's name throbbed through her mind, despite her determined efforts to the contrary. Memories of his handsome face, of his dear, twinkling gentian eyes and his unruly, crisp black hair, filled her mind and her heart with a nagging, gnawing ache that could be postponed but not relieved.

Nevertheless, she felt refreshed when she had washed, and having no other garments, she wound the crimson silk *kanga* about her once more, then raked her fingers through her heavy hair in lieu of a comb. There. What now? she wondered. Do I sit here and meekly wait for someone to come to me? No. Wondering about Douglas—whether he was presently in Stanleyville, what his mood might be, what he intended—was simply too nervewracking. She preferred to find out what was going on, ugly though the knowledge might be. Of one thing she was completely certain; she would not willingly return to Nairobi with her husband. She would not go back there where his word was law and he could abuse her at will. She thought of the poor women who had stumbled into St. Thomas' more times than she'd cared to count, beaten and bloodied by their husbands. It had horrified her that those women had returned to the monsters who used them so cruelly, yet return they did, seeming, in some perverse way, to believe they deserved no better from life. She had no intention of joining their sorry numbers! Heavy of heart, she slipped from the room, closing the door softly in her wake.

A long corridor, a beautifully molded balustrade of

polished mahogany along one side and numerous closed paneled doors along the other, led away from her room, which was at the far end. The corridor overlooked the tiled entrance hall that she remembered from her arrival. In the center was a fountain in the shape of four dolphins, water cascading from their mouths to a round stone pool beneath. Fronded, potted palms basked, green and waxy, in the light of a glittering crystal chandelier. Small, fringed Turkish carpets warmed the mirror-polished tile floors with their vibrant colors. It appeared that Mauricier had not stinted himself in regard to the appointments of his lower residence, and for a fleeting moment she wondered at the contrast of the exotic elegance below and the Spartan chamber to which she had been taken.

The hallways leading off the entrance were no less fine. Portraits of King Leopold of Belgium; of Henry Stanley, the journalist and explorer; and of former Stanleyville governors-general adorned the walls, their forbidding expressions well illuminated by the light of the many tall candles that burned brightly in the brass sconces set on the walls. Where was everyone? she wondered as she padded down the corridors. So far, she had not encountered a single servant, or anyone else, a strange occurrence in such a large residence.

She paused before a door that was slightly ajar, for she could hear low voices from within. She lifted her hand to knock, but then let it fall to her side. Whoever was in the room was speaking in French, and she understood every unpleasant word.

"Stick to what it is you do best, Cigale—managing your grubby little mine." It was Mauricier's drawling voice, an edge of irritation in his cultured tone. "I will take care of Madame Dennison, never fear."

A second voice, obviously Cigale's, replied, but he spoke so rapidly and softly Heather could not make out what it was he'd said.

Mauricier cursed. "Women! Can you think of nothing else? There are more important things at stake here than women, *n'est-ce pas?* With your share of the diamonds, you could buy yourself a harem of willing sluts, you fool!" A thud followed, and again Mauricier cursed. "Get that damned ape out of here, Cigale, before I wring its scrawny neck!"

A fierce burst of chatter erupted from within, and Hercule Cigale cried out in alarm. *"Sacre-bleu!* That wretch! *Merde!* He bit me!"

Heather was about to turn and hurry back the way she had come when Mac suddenly sprang through the door and landed on her shoulder, curling his tail and his small hands tightly about her neck. She let out a startled "Oh!" and the door flew open. Pascal Mauricier stood there, looking suspiciously down at her. At his side stood the chubby mine manager Cigale, rubbing at his hand where Mac had bitten him and scowling like a ferocious pig.

"Why, Madame Dennison! What are you doing here?" Mauricier demanded in perfect English, his pale blue eyes narrowed in his sharp-featured face.

"I—I awoke a short while ago, but I couldn't find anyone to send to you, Governor. I heard voices and was about to knock when"—she shrugged and lifted Mac down from her shoulder—"this little fellow leaped through the door and surprised me!" She shot the governor an innocent, dazzling smile and cast a stern eye on her furry pet. "Shame on you, Mac! You're a rogue for scaring me so!"

"Forgive me," Mauricier murmured, his composure quite restored by her guileless expression. "My servants are an idle lot, at best. It is likely they have sneaked off to the native quarter yet again for one of their heathen bacchanals. Cigale, go to the kitchens and see if the cook has gone with them. Madame, won't you take my arm?"

Accepting, her expression giving no clue to what she had overheard, she allowed him to lead her down the hallway to the dining room.

Apparently the cook had not disappeared along with the remainder of the household, for shortly after Mauricier seated her at one end of a long, polished table exquisitely set with china and sparkling crystal and ornate silverware, dinner was served. To her surprise, Heather found she was famished, and she ate eagerly of everything set before her: consommé, crêpes stuffed with mushrooms and served with a delicately seasoned sauce, and tender breast of chicken marinated in wine and served hot and golden on a bed of fragrant, spicy rice.

Mauricier watched her with an amused smile as she ate, unaware that he was also the object of covert appraisal. This second appraisal improved her first opinion of the governor-general not at all. Though he was a striking man in his own way, with his long, elegant features and straight dark-blond hair, the unpleasant twist to his thin, pink lips suggested a streak of cruelty that his excellent manners and apparently congenial mood could not negate. Imagination on her part? She didn't think so.

A silver coffee pot and two tiny cups and saucers, a board of cheeses—a rarity in Africa where dairy cows succumbed so readily to the tseste fly—and fresh tropical fruits and crackers, stood in readiness to complete their meal. She offered to pour the coffee for Mauricier, but the governor-general declined with a wave of his hand, indicating he would prefer another snifter of cognac instead. She poured herself a cup, adding a small quantity of sugar, and stirred it slowly, watching the governor as she did so from beneath a silky fringe of dark lashes, and thinking how incongruous it was to sit here gowned in only this vivid length of red silk, her shoulders bare, her hair flowing to her waist, not knowing whether Adam, her beloved Adam, was alive or dead, having no choice but to play out this charade of normalcy. *Would you care for some coffee? A little more chicken, perhaps, my dear madame? Oh, really, I couldn't, not another bite!* It made her want to scream with hysterical laughter, like one gone quite mad!

"Now, madame. You have rested and dined," Mauricier announced, his voice cutting in on her train of thought as he leaned back in his chair and inspected his manicured nails, "and I would hope that you are feeling quite recovered from your frightening ordeal. It is time now to discuss what we can do for each other, *oui?*" He cocked his dark-honey-colored head to one side, brows raised inquiringly.

"I'm afraid I don't understand you, Governor Mauricier?"

"Pascal, my dear lady. Since we are to become . . . partners . . . you must call me Pascal," he insisted. "And I shall call you? . . ."

"Madame Dennison," Heather replied softly, meeting his piercing light eyes with a level glance quite devoid of any amusement.

Mauricier inclined his head, acknowledging and accepting that challenge. "As you will, madame. But I would caution you to refrain from angering me unnecessarily by any further little ploys. I am not a man to put up with the foolish games that your sex indulges itself in playing."

Heather's chin came up stubbornly. Anger sparkled in her violet eyes so that they glittered like amethysts. "And I am not one to put up with those played by men, *m'sieu.* You obviously have something to say. Then

400

please, say it, and cease this beating about the bush. I am a forthright woman, and I respect the same trait in others."

A slight smile played about his lips, but he said nothing for several moments, taking a sip of his brandy and leisurely savoring its rich bouquet. When he began, the veneer had slipped away, the pretense of charm had fled. His voice was crisp, direct, hard. Without the silkiness it had possessed moments before, it was distinctly threatening. "Your husband arrived here in Stanleyville three days ago, madame—and a very angry, unpleasant fellow he was too, I might add. He told me that he was searching for his lovely bride of only a few months, a foolish creature who had run away with her lover, one Captain Adam Markham. Dennison possessed a quite violent temper, as I'm sure you are well aware, madame; and it was obvious to me that he intended to find you both—at any cost."

He paused and watched her lovely face in the candlelight, but no flicker of emotion crossed her exquisite features, nor was any reaction betrayed in her remarkable eyes. Dennison had not lied when he'd described his young wife as lovely, Mauricier thought, but he had gravely underestimated her if he had truly imagined her to be foolish! The keen intelligence in her eyes was unmistakable, and her poise was extraordinary under the circumstances. Grudging admiration flared in his own eyes. "Ordinarily," he continued, "I would have had little interest in or sympathy for a man who could not control his own wayward wife. But your husband, in his anxiety to enlist my aid in finding you, offered me an incentive to find you and Markham that I could not ignore.

"He told me, madame, that your . . . lover . . . knows the whereabouts of a priceless hoard of diamonds that has been lost for over two centuries, a treasure trove which has come to be known as the Tears of Agaja, as I'm certain you are well aware. In the past, many have searched for the diamonds, myself among them. But to date, they have not been found. Rumors have abounded regarding the treasure. Some say that the diamonds will never be found, for they do not exist, are no more than a romantic legend. Others swear that they are real, but they are guarded by a tribe of fierce warrior women, descendents of the female warriors of King Agaja's royal army. Supposedly he sent them after the Oyos who had stolen them, and they now stand guard over his treasures. Others speak of fabulous creatures, half-female, half-leopard, the spirits of the ancestors of Agaja the King, who protect what rightfully belonged to him. How much of this is fact, how much fiction, only one man knows—the only man who has ever seen the treasure and returned to tell of it: Robert Elwood. Your husband told me that Adam Markham had a meeting with Elwood some months ago in London, and he is certain that Markham is now able to determine the location of the Tears. Is that so, madame?"

His question, posed sharply after such a long discourse, startled her, yet she recovered swiftly. "If I knew, do you truly believe I would tell you, Governor?" She smiled, but the smile never reached her eyes. "I am many things, but a fool is not one of them, I can assure you."

The governor-general laughed softly. "I did not for a moment presume that you were, *chère madame!* I merely hoped that if I dealt with you in a civilized and *forthright* manner"—his pale eyes gleamed—"you might perhaps respond in kind, and I would be able to spare you any unpleasantness. Unfortunately, it appears that you intend to be difficult, that gentle means will not be possible."

"To exactly what 'unpleasantness' do you refer?" Heather asked. Her slender fists were clenched beneath the table, and a sudden lurch of fear snaked through her belly at his words. But no hint of her response showed in her expression as she looked across the gleaming table at Pascal Mauricier.

"I have decided to allow you—oh, say, twenty-four hours?—to find your tongue and tell me what it is I wish to know. If you are still obstinate after that time, I shall send a runner downriver after your husband, and have him brought back to Stanleyville. Perhaps the two of us will be more persuasive, yes?"

She laughed in his face. "Call up an army if you wish, *m'sieu*," she said in a firm, controlled voice. "It won't make a shred of difference. I know nothing of the diamonds' whereabouts."

"Come, come, I find that very difficult to believe! A beautiful young woman like yourself, and you expect me to believe you did not inspire your lover's most intimate confidences? Now it is you who are attempting to play me for a fool, my dear! However, I have made further provisions should you refuse to cooperate," Mauricier continued, his tone silky again. "Whilst my runner is gone, I have decided to permit Hercule Cigale and some of his friends to apply their . . . unique . . . methods of persuasion upon the young captain."

For a second, her violet eyes flared and a flicker of emotion crossed her face. "Adam?" she queried, her voice little more than a breathless whisper.

"Certainly 'Adam,' madame! The Wanegi are a simple people. It took no great effort on my part to learn from them that you had tearfully revealed that you were not alone in your canoe before it was swept over the falls. While you slept, a search party was organized, and the captain was happily recovered." He smirked, his smile that of a complacent cat that has just devoured a particularly plump and succulent canary. "And if, by some unhappy chance, your captain's extreme discomfort will not persuade you to talk, then we shall be forced to try those same methods upon your lovely self to see if perchance your lover is more talkative than his mistress."

He stood and came around the table to where she sat, picking up a loose dark-flame curl and winding it about his finger, then laughing delightedly as she jerked her head away in anger. "It would be a great pity to destroy a creature as lovely as you. But, as I told Cigale earlier, such a priceless hoard of diamonds can buy many women, equally lovely and far more eager to please. Twenty-four hours, madame!"

Across the room, where he perched nervously upon one of the sconces, Mac whimpered in fear, and then hid his face beneath his tail.

Chapter Twenty-six

Adam groaned and rolled over, blinking in disbelief against the brilliant light as he saw a dusky-gold face with peculiarly pixielike features grinning broadly inches from his own.

Oh, lord. First angels, now damned little cavorting pixies, he thought, disgusted with himself. *The old gray matter is definitely not what it used to be, Markham,* he muttered ruefully. The ache in his skull was still there, though it was not as severe as it had been earlier— which was when? The sky appeared light now. Daytime, certainly. But what day? Had he been out cold for one night, two, or more? He still had no recollection of where he was or of when or how he'd come to this place.

"Blast!" he growled, and sat up, cradling his head in his arms. The pixie danced around him, gesticulating wildly, jerking a wickedly sharp, short spear up and down in a way that was decidedly risky, if not downright threatening.

"Put that down, there's a good lad," Adam requested. But when the pixie kept doing his jiggling dance, Adam's head swam. "It's a hallucination, damn it!" he cursed. "Cut that out!"

"Madami esumba! Madami esumba! Ya! Ya!" the pixie yelled over and over, like one demented.

"Madami esumba to you too, my friend," Adam repeated, grim-faced. He staggered to his feet, lurching unsteadily. He was, he soon discovered, considerably taller than his little friend, who reached only to his rib cage. He started across the curling fern carpet toward the jungle, but the pixie ran after him and tugged at his shirt, pulling him back.

"Madami esumba!" he cried again, pointing toward the falls.

"Yes, I know, damn it. I went over them, didn't I?" More wild gesticulations on the short fellow's behalf. Adam sighed heavily and crouched down, peering into the pixie's face, astonished by the fierce scowl he found there, the fury in those bright dark eyes. He pointed to himself. *"Madami esumba?"*

The little man shook his head vehemently, so Adam pointed toward the falls. *"Madami esumba?"* he asked again. Again, a vigorous shaking of the small man's woolly head. Nonplused, Adam rocked back on his heels, shrugging his confusion.

With a sharp click of exasperation, the pixie snatched up a twig and quickly scratched something in the dry earth between the ferns. Adam peered at it when he was done. Two figures, one a man, the other obviously a woman, rode in a canoe atop the falls. The pixie pointed to the man, and then to Adam. He pointed to the woman, and muttered wearily, *Madami esumba."*

"Ah! Now I see." Adam shrugged again. "But I'm sorry, my friend. I haven't the foggiest idea of where, or even who, your *madami* is."

His tone seemed to communicate something to the little man, who began scratching in the earth once again, this time etching a little stick figure on horseback.

"She's gone for a ride with that chap?" Adam suggested, making the motions of a rider. He felt as if he were taking part in some weird and peculiar *Alice in Wonderland* game of charades, and that like Alice, he would soon wake up to find it had all been an extraordinary dream!

The pixie was so furious at this response that he jumped up and again did his angry little war dance, his bark-cloth apron flapping dangerously. He brandished the spear in his fist and jabbed it at a tree trunk. *"Madami esumba—aaggh!"*

His meaning was obvious this time. *Madami esumba,* whoever the woman was, was in danger of her very life from the fellow on horseback! Adam nodded vigorously, hoping to show he understood this time, for it was obvious the little fellow considered him to possess less intelligence than the village idiot!

The man stopped, jabbed his hand toward himself. "Mbaka," he said slowly and distinctly, and jabbed again. "Mbaka!"

Adam pointed at him. "Mbaka?" Seeing the fellow nod, Adam grinned. "I'm delighted to meet you, Mbaka." He pointed to himself. "Me, Sahib Adam Markham. Now, I'd love to stay and chat, but I really don't have the time!"

He swung about and took to his heels. He would have made it too, had Mbaka not barked a single command. All at once, he saw more pygmies, many more, springing up all about him like weeds amidst the tall grass. *Christ Almighty!* The short bows in their hands were already nocked with arrows and held at shoulder height, preparatory to firing!

Inwardly, Adam groaned. He pulled up short. "Now

then, there's no need for you to get nasty, is there, Mbaka? If it's that important to you, damn it, I'll stay put!"

Apparently it was, for in that moment the whole lot of them jumped him! In his groggy condition, Adam went down easily under their numbers, feeling like Gulliver when he was overwhelmed by a small army of Lilliputians. Grim elfin faces were the last things he saw before one of the little people clubbed him with a hefty rock. "Lord, not again!" he thought disgustedly as he spiraled down into starry blackness once more.

He awoke to find daylight streaming down through the thatched roof of a small, mound-shaped hut. Bowls of food and gourds of fresh water had been placed at his elbows, and a tiny maiden with alarmingly sharp, filed teeth was seated patiently beside him, either his nurse or his gaoler, he decided. She smiled as he turned his head, and gestured toward the food.

Wincing, he sat up, realizing as he did so that he was ravenous. He wolfed down the food the little elf woman had indicated, showing her with grunts and appreciative nods that it was good. And it was! Roasted antelope meat, tender fowl, manioc bread, ripe bananas—food fit for the gods! Why were they feeding him, treating him like a guest, he wondered? They'd seemed far from friendly earlier, when they'd jumped him! A horrible thought leaped to mind. Good God! Was it possible, with those sharpened teeth, that these fierce little people were perhaps . . . cannibals? He groaned, cradling his head. "You're to be tonight's entrée, Adam, you bloody fool!" he told himself.

Adam? Was that his name? He momentarily cast aside his fears regarding the elfin people's dietary habits. Adam . . . what? Adam Rivière? Now, why did that name jump onto his tongue? Wrong. His mother's maiden name. Something else. Adam . . . Adam *Mark-*

ham. Yes, that was it! He said it several times. It felt right. It *was* right! Shamefaced, he felt his eyes fill with tears. Thank God, his memory was coming back! Exhausted with the sheer effort of remembering, he slumped back onto the blanket of leaves, and sunk immediately into a deep, healing sleep.

It was dark when he awoke, and he felt much improved, almost like his old self. Some memory had returned as a result of that second hefty whack to his skull, he decided, but his recollections were still fragmented and unsatisfying for the most part.

His name. He still knew it, he realized gratefully. God, he'd wept like a blasted baby on remembering that! He also remembered snatches of his service in the dragoons in India ... and coming to Africa. He remembered Dennison! And each time he picked up the orchid plants he'd found down by the pool—someone had put them beside him in the hut—a vision of that same, lovely auburn-haired woman flashed into his mind, accompanied by disturbing images of the two of them together ... intimately together. Was she his wife? His mistress? Surely he should remember *her!* He loved her. That much he knew!

His hands started to shake, and perspiration dampened his palms. Angered, he stuffed his hands beneath his head, where he wouldn't have to watch them flutter aimlessly in the moonlight, absently touching the goose-egg lump just above his temple as he did so. His headache had settled down to a dull throb, which worsened when he tried to remember, but he refused to stop doing so. Could it be that something terrible had happened to the woman—something so terrible that his healing mind refused to yield up the truth? Some instinct, some gut feeling, told him he was right.

He turned to the hut's low, round doorway at the

sound of voices, tensing for a few seconds before a familiar face appeared in the aperture.

"Tom! Thank God you're here!" he exclaimed. "Do I have a story to tell you!"

Heather paced restlessly back and forth in her room at the end of the hallway, seething with anger and frustration. Despite her protests and her struggles, Pascal Mauricier and that pudgy toad, Cigale, had forced her back here after she'd refused to provide the governor-general with the answers to his questions. Her twenty-four hours were almost up, and the door was locked. She was their prisoner in every sense of the word, yet she knew nothing that could help them, despite what they believed! She must come up with a plausible lie about where the diamonds might be hidden—or escape and try to free Adam. She wondered if they really had him. She doubted it, but she couldn't be sure. What was she going to do?

She crossed the room, the folds of the silk *kanga* rustling noisily with the abruptness of her movements, and she stepped through the French doors out onto the balcony. No. She could not jump. The balcony was far too high, and there was little below to break her fall, only a few small shrubs and some lush greenery. Besides, she had no head for heights! Even the Whispering Gallery in St. Paul's Cathedral in London had made her feel dizzy and nauseous, much to Annabel's disgust. She turned back into the room, sighing heavily, and went to perch upon the bed, her hands clasped loosly in her lap, her head bowed. There seemed nothing else to do but wait. Pascal had promised—or threatened—to return this afternoon, to see if a night and a day spent locked in her room, without food or water or bedcovers for warmth during the night, had persuaded her to abandon obstinacy. He'd be here soon. Perhaps by then she could formulate some plan. . . .

"This is a fair pickle we're in, hmm, Mac?" she said thoughtfully.

The little monkey cocked his head to one side, his bright eyes inquiring.

"Come here," Heather urged, but he evaded her outstretched arms and scuttled under the bed, reappearing seconds later with a tuft of slut's wool perched nattily upon his fuzzy brown head like a bizzare hat, another clinging to his tail. Despite her despondency, she could not help laughing, but her laughter soon ceased and her expression became thoughtful. Hope flared in her eyes. She had an idea! It was by no means foolproof, but its simplicity just might serve, in a pinch. "What have we got to lose?" she wondered aloud, not heeding the unwelcome answer that clamored in her mind: *everything!*

Hercule Cigale tossed the stub of his cigar into the brass spittoon in the corner of the entrance hallway; then he looked furtively about him. *Bien!* That snake, Mauricier, was nowhere in sight, thank God! He would be certain to object most heatedly to what Hercule was about to do, were he aware of it, but Cigale would make certain he did not find out. It should not be too difficult to persaude Madame Dennison to keep her lovely mouth firmly shut—after all, did he not have her lover safely under guard? *Certainement*. And there were any number of exquisitely painful ways Capitaine Markham could be made uncomfortable if *madame* were to mention what he had done. . . .

He skulked at the bottom of the stairs momentarily before starting up them two at a time, his pudgy body moving with deliberate stealth. At the doorway at the end of the long hall, he pressed his ear to the wood and listened. Not a sound. It appeared *la belle* was sleeping yet. A sly smile puckered his fleshy mouth. Even better. The element of surprise would be on his side. He felt a stirring against the buttoning of his jodhpurs and his smile deepened. His tiny, black-currant eyes gleamed. *Mon dieu,* it had been a long time since he had so lusted for a woman! The excitement he had felt at having his first little blackbird slut had, long since, waned. He had wearied of the whimpering, terrified dark lovelies who shrank from his touch and shuddered with revulsion when he lowered his corpulent white body onto their writhing blackness, begging him to let them go. He had tired of their woolly hair and heavy features. *Vraiment,* he longed for the soft, silken caress of Madame Dennison's beautiful, long auburn hair, for the ivory pallor of her lovely, smooth skin. He wanted to squeeze her voluptuous breasts in his eager hands. . . .

His palms sweating, he unlocked the door as quietly as possible. More sweat beaded his upper lip as he quickly stepped into the room. But his expectant smile turned to a furious scowl when he saw that the room was quite empty, the French doors leading onto the balcony ajar.

Cursing foully, he lumbered across the room, out through the French doors, and craned his head over the wrought-iron balcony. *Mon dieu!* How had she done it, unless she could fly! He flung around and barreled back out onto the landing, along it and down the stairs two at a time, squealing loudly for Mauricier as he went.

When she was certain he had gone, Heather slithered out from under the bed, slut's wool festooning her head as it had Mac's shortly before. She held the little monkey clasped tightly to her bosom, and he gave an indignant chatter as she drew the clamped hand, with which she had kept him silent, away from his mouth. Tiptoeing quickly, she went out onto the landing and looked down over the carved balustrade to the hallway below. Good! Cigale was nowhere in sight!

She all but ran down the stairs, without incident reaching the elegant foyer where water splashed musically from the dolphin fountains. She was headed for the grand double-doored entrance, and freedom, when voices froze her. She looked about, frantic, seeing no hiding place other than a large potted palm at the foot of the stairs. Heart throbbing like a drum, she slipped behind it, pulling the fronded greenery close about her. Pressing Mac to her breast once more, she trembled there, scarce daring to breathe, as Pascal Mauricier and Hercule Cigale came racing from somewhere into the hall. They stopped scant inches from where she hid.

"And I'm telling you, fool, she cannot have escaped! Did you search the room?"

"I . . . well, I—"

"Did you?"

"No," Hercule confessed lamely.

A torrent of ripe French curses followed, and Heather winced. The two men started up the stairs, and Heather closed her eyes and prayed. Her pulse seemed deafening in her ears, loud and insistent. *Oh, please, God, don't let them find me. . . .*

"You may come out now, madame!" snapped Pascal's voice, like the crack of a whip on the silence. "Your little game of hide-and-seek is now over, *n'est-ce pas?*"

Fool! she upbraided herself. Of course, they could see her from the upper landing as easily as if she had sat by the fountain in the very center of the hall! She broke and made a run for it, hair and bare legs flying as she

413

raced for the entrance door. But Mauricier moved with the speed and grace of a snake, leaping down the staircase three steps at a time. Before she reached the door, he stood before her, cutting off her escape. She shrank from him, but Hercule hovered at her back. Trapped! She wetted her lips nervously.

"You estimated that fool correctly, madame," Mauricier said silkily, amusement in his tone, scorn in his eyes as he looked at Cigale. "But do not make the mistake of underestimating me! I am quite a different proposition, I assure you. The little monkey, if you please!"

He held out his hands and Heather reluctantly relinquished Mac to them. He means to leave me quite alone, she thought miserably, without even little Mac for companionship. He thinks that that will break my spirit, persuade me to talk, but it won't—it won't! she vowed hotly.

But she had gravely mistaken Mauricier's intent, underestimated the depths of his cruelty. He grasped little Mac by the throat, and squeezed. Mac's eyes bulged. He gave a strangled, pitiful whimper, and then Mauricier casually flicked his wrist. There came an audible snap as he twisted the monkey's neck, breaking it under those long, manicured and elegant fingers with less compunction than if he had squashed a scorpion underfoot, while he smiled and watched horror glaze and incredulity fill Heather's eyes. Mac's body dangled limply in his grasp for a second before Mauricier tossed it casually to the floor, amusement wreathing his pale pink lips.

"*Voilà, madame!* Your little friend is no more! Life is such a fragile thing, *oui*? Here one minute, and quite gone the next . . . It is so for little monkeys—and no less true for us, you understand?" He reached out and splayed his long fingers across her throat, noting how pale she had grown now, how bright her violet eyes were with unshed tears. The soft flower of her lips quivered. The pulse in her throat throbbed violently against his touch. "The diamonds, madame. Where are they?" he demanded softly, his tone almost caressing.

"Monster!" she whispered, wincing as his fingers tightened, squeezed. "Monsters—all of you!" His face began to spin like a catherine wheel in her vision, his cruel pink mough becoming an endless, mocking loop, his pale eyes flattening out into glittering bands of silver. The roar of her pulse was a hurricane howling in her ears. Blackness nudged between the bands of spiraling, whirling colors and her lungs felt close to exploding. But then, even as she felt herself plummeting into oblivion, he released her. She swayed dizzily, feeling hot blood flood her cheeks and replace the dark murkiness, feeling her scalp tingling, feeling the places where his fingertips had prodded deeply into her throat begin to ache sickeningly.

"Enough, madame?"

Weakly, she nodded, loathing herself for her compliance, her cowardice. How she would have loved to spit in his eye, to toss her head defiantly and vow that she would rather die than tell him anything, had she possessed the knowledge he sought. But . . . pain was a powerful persuader! She rubbed her throat, the gagging feeling still strong.

Mauricier chuckled. "Very well, madame. I believe I have adequately made my point. But just in case you still harbor some doubts in your lovely breast that I mean business, I believe it is time now for you to see your Adam. Cigale! Have my carriage brought around. Madame and I are going to make a little visit to the mill. Come along, *chère madame.*"

With a mocking bow, he grasped her elbow and jerked her forward. Like a puppet with wooden limbs,

Pascal controlling the strings, she stumbled outside into brilliant, blinding sunlight framed by ragged palms, seeing over and over again in her mind's eye Mauricier's slim, elegant fingers coiled about little Mac's throat, and the careless twist with which they plucked the life from his warm, furry body. . . .

The mill was set on a rise above the open-pit mines. Great flumes carried the "flurry"—the water and rock-particle waste that remained after the smelting process—down the chutes and to the Congo, where they were discharged. Wagons loaded with ore were everywhere, mules or oxen in the shafts. A small enclosure, palisaded with sharpened timbers like the slave barracoons of the last century, held several black laborers, thrown inside for some disciplinary measure or other, she judged. Off to one side, set apart from the other buildings, was a large hut with the word *"Danger!"* painted upon it in glaring red letters. A sudden small explosion rocked the ground and startled the scrawny carriage mule, causing it to fight the traces momentarily as they drew up before the mill. The loud blast jerked Heather into alertness. Explosions? Then the hut must contain explosives, she guessed.

She had no time to ponder more on this, for Mauricier had jumped nimbly down and was now extending his arm to help her from the carriage. Still holding on firmly to her elbow, he propelled her inside the mill by a side door, Cigale puffing after them.

The air smelled awful inside the mill, and there was dust and deafening noise everywhere, the sound of grinding rocks and the hiss of the smelter predominant. Sweating black laborers toiled in the hellish heat on every side, the loud cracks of a whiplash and the snarled curses of an overseer audible despite the clamor and din of the mill. Pascal thrust her before him to another door, outside of which a tall, brown-haired white man stood guard, a rifle hooked casually over one shoulder.

"Has he given you any trouble, François?" Pascal asked.

"None, *m'sieu le governor*— not since last night, that is!" The pair exchanged knowing smiles, and Heather's mouth felt suddenly parched with fear. It had been no bluff, she realized with a sinking heart, a knot of dread uncoiling in her belly. They had Adam. There, in that very room! Her joy in learning that he was actually alive was bittersweet. He had been at the mercy of Cigale and his friends. What awful things had they done to him?

"Open up. We have brought *m'sieu le Capitaine* Markham a visitor," Mauricier said with a smirk, and behind him Cigale sniggered as the one named François unlocked the grilled door.

Mauricier gave her a little nudge in the small of the back, and she toppled forward. The room was obviously used as a cell—perhaps for the holding of those recalcitrant laborers that Adam had told her of, prior to their removal to the cattlelike wooden pen that she had glimpsed outside. The hard dirt floor was unrelieved by furniture of any kind, but the pairs of iron shackles bolted securely to the stout wooden walls were reminiscent of the days when coffles of slaves had been marched to the coast from these savage parts. Against the wall, a man sagged in his chains. His wrists were manacled cruelly above him, his head was bowed. His formerly white shirt front was stained now with rusty streaks of dried blood. A whimper broke from her lips. She started forward, arms outstretched to him. "Adam! Oh, my God, Adam, my darling, what have they done to you?" she whimpered.

But the man who raised his bruised, battered face to hers was not Adam. It was Tom Worth!

* * *

417

"Mauricier's given me five minutes alone with you, Tom. Can you hear me?"

"Yes . . . you didn't tell them I wasn't Adam?"

"No. I—"

"Then don't. Let . . . let them go on thinking they have him."

"I don't think they'd believe me anyway."

She lifted the hem of her *kanga* and attempted to wipe some of the blood from his poor, swollen face. Those monsters had beaten him terribly, she noted, tears brimming in her eyes. "Adam might very well be dead," she told him, her voice breaking. "I—I haven't seen him since our canoe went over the falls. He hit his head, Tom, and disappeared."

"He's not dead, old girl." Tom managed to grin through his swollen lips as joy flared in her eyes. "He hit his head when the canoe broke up and was swept over the falls, but he somehow managed to crawl up onto the banks below, by the pool. He was wandering around in a daze when Mbaka—the pygmy chief, remember?—found him. Couldn't recall a blasted thing about where he was, or what he was doing there. He thought he was back in India, for God's sake!"

"Is he all right now?" Heather asked hesitantly, ashamed of the relief she had felt to see it was not Adam before her, and of how glad she was to know that he was alive and safe, even if injured.

Tom nodded. "Just a bit disoriented still, and he has a whopping headache. He kept mumbling on about crimson angels and pixies, of all the bloody things!"

"Thank God! But what are you doing here?"

"After I'd taken Ellen to Kigali, she urged me to go after you and Adam. She was nicely on the mend, and I decided I might as well. I'd been tracking you for days when I ran across Ngudu and Ewasu. They told me that the bearers had spooked and run off with the supplies,

418

and that they'd left you and Adam camped by the river while they went to get everything back. When they returned, you'd gone! We later found Mbaka—and Adam—at Mbaka's village. Mbaka told Ngudu he'd seen one of the Belgians take you away, and that he was afraid for you. Adam was still a bit groggy, so Ngudu and I came looking for you. We had no reason to suspect that the Belgians might be on the lookout for us with other than friendly motives, and so we hiked down into Stanleyville as openly and boldly as you please. That wretch, Cigale, and some of his men, jumped us. Straightway it was obvious they thought I was Adam. Ngudu escaped."

She nodded. "Douglas is out here somewhere, Tom! He came after Adam and I, as I feared! Mauricier and the others found out about the diamonds from him. I think he promised to split them with the Belgians if they helped him to find Adam and myself. But Mauricier's no fool. He knows if he can force us to tell him the whereabouts of the diamonds, he can have them all to himself. They won't let either of us go, Tom, unless we tell them what they want to know. And we can't! Even Adam has no idea where they're hidden. He has simply determined from Elwood's recollections, the area where they might be. What on earth can we do?" she cried, anxiety mirrored in her violet eyes, the strain of the past hours betrayed by the faint lavender shadows beneath them.

"Keep up the pretense as long as we can," Tom said grimly, wincing as a cut on his lip opened and began to bleed anew. "We're worth nothing to them dead. So long as we're alive, they'll figure there's a chance we can tell them something worthwhile, don't you see? With luck, Adam's even now figuring out a way to get us out of here, old girl. Hang in there, and keep your chin up!"

She smiled valiantly. "I'll try. But . . . what of you,

Tom? You can't take much more of this. Why, look at you!" One of his eyes was blackened and closed, and deep, angry cuts crisscrossed his kindly face. Dark bruises showed through the open collar of his shirt.

He laughed, but the laughter ended in a painful bout of coughing. When he was done, his voice was hoarse. "I think they broke a rib or two, damn them." He groaned. "I'll hold out for as long as I can; then I'll tell them what they want to hear." There was now a determined sparkle in his one good eye.

"Tell them? . . . Ah, I see," she amended, sudden understanding in her voice. "What—"

"Your time is up, madame." Mauricier's sharp voice came from the door.

"Coming," she snapped, then turned back to Tom. "I have to go, Tom. I'll—I'll be thinking of you, hoping you're all right."

"I know. Kiss me before you leave. Mauricier's watching."

She slipped her arms about his shoulders and kissed his cheek, the tears that had brimmed in her eyes spilling over now. "Please, take care."

"I will," he promised. "Adam's a lucky young dog, you know. I only wish that kiss had been intended for me, old girl."

"But it was, Tom," she murmured. "Just for you! You're the dearest, kindest, *bravest* man I've ever known."

He was still grinning his painfully lopsided grin when she left the cell.

Chapter Twenty-seven

Back in her "room" in Mauricier's ornate mansion, Heather paced restlessly, arms folded over her breasts, a knot of anxiety in the pit of her stomach that nothing could dispel. Her fears for Tom, and for herself, were too great. They blotted out idle or casual thought. They blotted out hunger and thirst too. She had been given no food or water since the evening before, but she had no desire for them.

Was Adam, as Tom had said with such conviction, even now undertaking an attempt to free them? Lord, she hoped so! She lay down upon the lumpy, massive bed, now devoid of sheets and mosquito netting, indeed of anything that would contribute to her comfort in any way, as was the remainder of the room. Beneath her was only the bare, stained tick mattress. She stared up at the mildewed ceiling, the dampness making grotesque monsters and strange greenish maps against the whitewash. From somewhere distant, closer to the jungle, the slow throb of native drums began. The pounding seemed to keep time with the building throb in her temples.

She closed her eyes, recalling the night she and Adam, along with Tom and Ellen, had been feasted by the Watusi, and a different throb of the drums had sent her pulse leaping, stirring her desire for Adam. Was he thinking of her now, in much the same way she thought of him . . . with an aching, longing pain? Did he fear for her very life, as she did, for her own and Tom's? He must! He loved them both—her as the woman of his heart, and Tom as a friend. Oh, how she wished she could spare him the agony he must be feeling now. . . .

She sat bolt upright as the door flew open, the latch slamming back, gouging the wall, and dislodging a shower of plaster. Two of Mauricier's sullen black servants stood behind a leering Hercule Cigale in the doorway.

"Madame, you are cordially requested to accompany me below. *M'sieu le governor* awaits your lovely presence at a little entertainment he has arranged just for you. *Vous comprenez, madame?"*

She stood, cloaking herself in her dignity and the tattered remnants of her courage. Head erect and proud, she nodded coolly. *"Je vous comprends bien, M'sieu Cochon!"* And with that she swept past him, drawing aside the hem of the *kanga* so that it would not brush him as she went, as if it were a grand ball gown and he were refuse that might soil it.

Cigale's face flushed with anger. "Go ahead, madame, call Hercule a pig, if it amuses you. But be warned. It is I who will laugh last!" He snickered. "You will not enjoy it when your lovely naked body is spread beneath that of a 'pig' such as myself, I think, no? Nevertheless, I *shall* lie with you. You may cry out and plead and fight me all you wish, madame. You see, that desperation—that fear—is what pleases me the most, *hein?"* His voice had become thick and breathless with lust, and his currant eyes glittered, hot and wet and black. "Soon, you will beg this 'pig' to let you go, but I will not. Never, madame!" He reached out a hot, damp little hand, his intent to fondle her breast with his chubby, sausage-link fingers. Yet the instant she realized his intent, she stepped back, out of his reach, placing herself between the two servants. To her surprise, she noticed that they appeared to be hiding smiles as they each took one of her elbows and propelled her out of the room and down the landing, a seething Cigale puffing importantly along in their wake.

She was taken to the dining room, where she and Mauricier had shared that farcical dinner the first night. Mauricier was seated at one end of the polished table, a platter of delicacies spread before him, wine in a tall, green bottle beside them. He dabbed at his pink lips delicately as she was brought in, then rose, the very epitome of a cordial host greeting a welcome guest. *He's relishing every minute of this!* Heather thought as he smiled and offered her a mocking half-bow. Her indignation turned instantly to trepidation as she realized for the first time that Tom was also in the room, as was the guard named François. Tom's wrists were bound tightly behind him, and a second rope had been looped around his throat in a slip knot, the end of it securely lashed over one of the wrought-iron sconces that branched out from the wall. Even the flickering amber light of the candles could not disguise the dark bruises that mottled his poor, weathered face.

"Now, *mes enfants,* we shall begin our entertainment!" Mauricier announced. "François, are you ready?"

"Oui, m'sieu," François agreed with a broad smile, stepping forward from the shadows. A vicious bullwhip dangled from his fist, and he gestured menacingly with it in Heather's direction, his smile widening still further as he saw the horror in her eyes. "First, the *capitaine,* madame, and then, if he still remains obstinate and will not talk, the governor has promised

423

me that I may try the lash upon your lovely back. Personally, I hope the *capitaine* says nothing!" François smirked, his eyes devouring every inch of flesh the saronglike native *kanga* exposed.

Heather started forward. "Stop it! Adam can tell you nothing! Neither of us can! He has no more than a vague idea of where the diamonds might be hidden, I swear it! Please, don't—don't hurt him anymore!"

"Heather, be qui—" Tom commanded, but his words were abruptly cut short by the whistling crack of the rawhide lash as it snaked through the air and cut deeply into the flesh of his bared back. His body lunged violently. "Ah! You bastards!" he gritted out, his face contorted with agony. His body sagged, but the rope about his throat tightened, and he was forced to jerk himself upright or be strangled.

The one named François stepped back, and coiling the whip for a second lashing, raised it slowly above his head.

"No, please, Governor Mauricier, make him stop! I'll do anything you ask, anything, if you'll only let him go, I beg you!" Heather cried, breaking free of the two servants and springing toward the governor. "I can't stand any more of this!" She drew up short before him. "I—I'll tell you all that I know, if you promise— swear—that you'll let us go?"

"But of course, madame," Mauricier promised glibly, "that goes without saying, *oui?* Have a glass of this excellent Burgundy, my poor little madame, and compose yourself before you do this so difficult task!"

To his surprise, and Heather's own, she eagerly accepted a glass of the blood-red wine without hesitation, draining it in a single quaff, and then gasping as she set the glass clumsily upon the table. "I'm ready," she said shakily.

Mauricier's eyes gleamed with triumph as he saw the

apologetic and beseeching glance she shot the captain across the room. He nodded, leaning back, the tips of his fingers meeting beneath his chin.

"First, I'll need a map of Stanleyville, *m'sieu,*" she said firmly, speaking with the confidence of one who has made up her mind at long length and who is determined to stick to her guns.

"No, Heather!" Tom groaned imploringly from across the room. "For God's sake! Don't—don't do this!"

"I must. I have no choice," Heather said firmly. "You mean more to me than any diamonds, Adam. Far, far more."

"You shall have your map," Mauricier agreed. "Cigale?"

Grumbling, his fat henchman waddled off in search of one. While they waited, Mauricier rose and stalked across to where Tom stood, bound, against the wall. His head was sunk as far forward on his chest as the rope would permit. Mauricier grasped his brown hair and jerked his head up, looking him full in the face. "There is no accouting for a woman's tastes, is there, François?" he murmured. "I do believe the lady's husband was far more pleasing to the eye than this fellow. He had a homely face even before you . . . rear-ranged his features, *oui?*"

"It is not men's faces that women care about, *m'sieu.* Believe me, I know!"

The two laughed at their crude little joke; then the door opened and Cigale strode importantly in, to spread the map upon the table before Heather.

Heather swallowed, nervous as she scanned the map. There was the river and the falls, where she had been found. Over here was the site of the open-pit mines, the mountains beyond. There, the native quarter . . . What she was looking for had to be in the area between them,

425

as near as she could judge. Lord, she hoped so! If not . . .

"The captain showed me a map very much like this one many times over the past few weeks. It was given to him by Robert Elwood himself. Correct me if I'm wrong, but at the time of Elwood's disappearance into the jungle, Stanleyville was much smaller than it is now, little more than an outpost, yes? Adam told me he believed the diamonds were buried in a hidden cave, in what was still dense jungle then, right about . . . here." She stabbed her finger at the spot she had chosen upon the map, and looked at Mauricier levelly.

Mauricier came around to her side and followed where she was pointing. "There?" he exclaimed. He snorted in derision. "*Impossible!*"

"Why is it impossible, *m'sieu?*" she asked innocently.

"Because that spot, my dear madame, is buried under the accumulation of years of slag!" Mauricier barked, visibly irritated now.

"Slag?" she echoed innocently, eyebrows arched.

The governor-general sighed impatiently. "Yes, yes, the rock waste from the mines. The smaller parts are mixed with water and drained into the river. The larger boulders and waste products are heaped here, on this very spot." He smiled nastily. "Come along, my dear lady, you'll have to do better than that!"

Heather shrugged. "I didn't know, *m'sieu,* and I'm very sorry I've pinpointed a place that does not meet with your approval," her tone was heavily laced with sarcasm, "but that's where Adam said he expected to find the cave, opposite that little curve in the river, you see? I can't change that simply because it's inconvenient for you, can I?"

He stared at her searchingly, hoping to detect some indication that she was lying. Yet, her cool, calm amethyst eyes met his unwaveringly, and it was obvious to everyone in the vast room that the governor was of half a mind to believe her.

Suddenly, they all swung about at a muffled roar from Tom. "Bitch!" he yelled, so convincingly that Heather herself was taken aback by the vehemence in his tone. "You damned, treacherous bitch! I told you to say nothing, *nothing* do you hear me!" He fought against his bonds, as if determined to free himself and leap at her throat.

That was the final proof Mauricier needed. He chuckled softly, triumphantly. "Take him back to the mill, François. Let the poor fool be for the time being. I do believe he has suffered enough one way or the other tonight. First from your lash . . . and secondly from the treacherous 'lash' of his lovely mistress' tongue!"

"No, Adam, please . . . I didn't mean . . . I only wanted to help you!" Heather sobbed beseechingly as they untied Tom and François dragged him away. She ran after him, pleading with him to forgive her, yet the door closed on her outstretched arms, leaving her alone with Mauricier and Cigale, weeping copious floods of crocodile tears!

"Come, come. Perhaps he will forgive you, in time, madame—certainly long before that mountain of slag has been carted away by him and a gang of my blacks! Meanwhile, you must amuse yourself elsewhere. Cigale?"

"Oui, m'sieu?"

"She is yours."

"No!" Heather shrieked, her triumph of moments before forgotten at this fresh threat. "You gave your word! 'Tell me,' you said, 'and you and your lover will go free'!"

Mauricier smirked. "You must be mistaken, madame? I recall no such conversation—but then, my memory is notoriously poor, you understand?" He rose

427

and made his way toward the door, pausing as he held it ajar. *"Bonne nuit, Cigale.* And to you too, Lady Dennison, a very entertaining good night!"

Adam and Ngudu wriggled forward on their bellies through the long grass, then parted it to look below. Moonlight and starlight dappled the foliage all about them. Below the gentle rise, the open-pit mines yawned blackly against the lighter earth like gateways to hell. Toward the mountains, the slag heap made a darker, ugly mountain against the indigo sky, and nearby the elephants snorted and snuffled in their corral, disturbed by the frenzied beat of drums from the native quarter of Stanleyville on the next ridge.

"All set?"

"Ndio, bwana," Ngudu agreed. "First, we find Bwana Worth, and then we split up, yes?"

"Right. Let's go!"

They rose and sprinted across the open ground toward the mill, keeping low. Halfway to it, Adam jerked Ngudu back and down. Again they dropped to a crouch, using the shadows of a small hut for concealment. "Someone's coming!" Adam muttered by way of an explanation, and he saw Ngudu nod in the gloom.

Sure enough, there was someone—the guard François, jerking Tom along by the rope looped about his neck like a dog on a leash!

"Get going, you! And while you're at it, think of your woman in the bed of that fat pig, Ciagle, tonight, eh? He is not a gentle man, *m'sieu le capitaine*—not gentle at all, I'm afraid. But then, per'aps madame will discover that his coarseness and roughness please her, yes?" There was a burst of raucous laughter, then a curse. *"Non, non,* you fool! Do not try to fight me, or you will be sorry, yes?" François' voice was tight and angry now.

Adam's jaw was clenched so fiercely that Ngudu wondered fleetingly if the bwana's teeth would crack! He started forward, but Ngudu tapped his shoulder, gesturing that he would take the guard from behind, and then Adam could attack from the front. Adam nodded regretfully. The Kikuyu had earned recognition among his people for his skills as a hunter, and he knew he could not hope to match Ngudu's stealth. Sure enough, like a shadow, Ngudu slipped from concealment and padded silently across the open ground, closing in behind the pair. François was in the rear, chivvying a shuffling Tom toward the mill with nudges in the back from the barrel of his rifle.

Losing sight of Ngudu, Adam edged around the corner of the jerry-built hut in order to see. Starlight caught the sheen of the word painted in glaring red on the hut's front wall, above the door. *Danger!* The grim scowl fled from his face. He grinned broadly and eased over to the door, finding it secured only by a small and fragile padlock. With a snort of disgust, he drew a skinning knife from his felt, inserting it into the loop of the lock. Two or three quick sawing movements with the knife blade, a little pressure from his wrist, and the metal loop snapped. He quickly slipped inside the hut, darting a hurried glance over his shoulder in the direction Ngudu had gone. The guard was still hustling Tom along, snarling a curse every now and then to keep him going, and once Adam heard Tom groan with pain, the sound grating on his ears. Damn those Belgian bastards! They'd pay for what they'd done to Tom, he vowed, and pay well! And if they'd harmed a hair on Heather's head—well, that was a thought he couldn't bear to dwell on!

Lumpy bundled and barrels littered the hut's

interior, and an acrid odor filled his nostrils. Fumbling cautiously in the darkness, Adam found what he was looking for: a neat bundle of cylinders, each about a foot in length. He carefully withdrew several sticks, each one like a long, fat cigar. He sniffed. Dynamite! The Belgians used it for blasting, obviously. And so would he, he thought grimly, reaching about him in search of fuses. Finding them, he tucked the cylinders inside his shirt and quickly left the hut.

He exited in the nick of time, for at that instant Ngudu sprang from the darkness onto the guard's back, toppling him forward with a heavy thud. The rifle slithered from François' hand and skittered away across the dirt, out of reach. As Adam sprinted toward them, he heard Tom give a low whoop of relief.

François had managed to rid himself of Ngudu, and was about to struggle to his feet when Adam exploded from the darkness in the opposite direction. The Belgian never knew what hit him! A sharp, meaty crack resounded as a fist connected with his jawbone, and he slammed back down to the ground with a startled, "Oof!"

As Tom waited impatiently for Adam to cut him loose, his swollen face was one broad grin in the starlight. His hands freed, he lifted the noose over his head and hurled the rope aside.

"Damned glad to see you and Ngudu, Adam old chap!" he said fervently. "Thought for a moment back there it was curtains for me and Heather, but she came through like a trooper, a real trooper, bless her!" He looked down at the guard's sprawled form and gave him a hefty kick in the ribs. "I owe you that, François my friend." He laughed, then winced as his laughter sent sharp pain radiating out through his abdomen from his cracked ribs. "I only—damn, it hurts!—I only hope he enjoys it as much as I have!" he panted.

"Heather's not hurt?" Adam asked, the steely gaze of apprehension in his voice marked now.

"Frightened, yes, but not hurt. Or rather, she wasn't when they carted me back here. We'd better get a move on and go after her though, old chap. There's a fat slug by the name of Cigale that has some very nasty plans in store for her tonight!"

"Not we. I'm going after her alone, Tom. No, damn it, don't argue! You know bloody well that in your condition you'd be more of a handicap than a help! Where is she?"

"The governor-general's residence. It's the white building at the end of the main street. You can't miss it."

"Right. Ngudu, you do what you have to do in the native quarter, then get this fellow back to camp, got it?" Adam demanded, retrieving the rope François had lost in the scuffle and coiling it about his body.

Ngudu grinned, his teeth pearly, his eyes white in the blackness. "Got it, Bwana!"

Adam nodded. "Then it's all set. We'll meet you back there—all going well," he added, grim-faced, as he turned to go.

"For God's sake be careful," Tom urged.

"Don't worry," Adam said, lightly tapping his chest where the three cylinders were hidden inside his shirt. "I've more than enough insurance!"

With that, he started down the hillside at a lope, headed toward Stanleyville on the next rise. Ngudu saw that Tom was settled comfortably beneath some thorn bushes, and with a promise to return shortly, he quickly followed Adam.

Ngudu slipped in unnoticed amongst those gathered in the marketplace of the native quarter.

431

In the center of the open area, a huge fire crackled and blazed, its writhing flames leaping, like tortured spirits, high into the air and illuminating the rapt black faces of those congregated about it.

An old man clad in a swishing skirt of leaves, whirled and danced around the fire. His glowing eyes reflected the light and they also seemed afire, red and evil as if lit from within! A collar of leaves circled his neck, and his headdress of dancing white cockerel feathers swayed to and fro with the violence of his gyrations. The clicking chatter of the snake-bone rattle in his fist provided a jarring counterpoint to the pulsing, urgent throb of the skin drums: the loud *papa* drum; the softer, slower tempoed *maman* drum; and the light, frenetic patter of the *bébé*. The priest's rippling black torso gleamed with palm oil and sweat as he spun like a dervish, shrieking imprecations to his unholy lord. In his other hand, he brandished a long, green snake, and as he whirled and chanted to the frenzied rhythm of the drums, he caressed the snake, held it aloft with great adoration and reverence, screaming to the people to pay homage to the symbol of their snake god, beloved Damballah, and to rise up and throw off the heavy yoke of their white taskmasters.

As he moved amongst the dancers, he rubbed the wriggling serpent across the glistening bare breasts and the flat, black-velvet bellies of the women as they undulated and writhed, snakelike, before him; now standing, now slithering over the ground in their passion. His people, needing little urging, joined their maddened chants to those of the priest, participating eagerly in his crazed ritual, their shadows leaping and jumping grotesquely about the blazing fire.

The young maidens stripped off their *kangas* to dance naked, caught up in the spell of the voodoo magic. The warriors of the village tugged the maidens

432

violently to them, falling upon them and coupling savagely with them in the dirt in accordance with the lascicious rites of their pagan gods. The grunts and cries and moans of their ritualistic matings filled the firelit clearing and penetrated the dense shadows beneath the trees.

It is good, Ngudu thought. The cruelties that the Belgians had heaped upon the people of the ancient Congo Kingdom had ripened the laborers for what he meant them to do. The ritual that he was witnessing would hone their hatred to the keenness of a spear! A carefully chosen word, an impassioned plea added to those already offered by the voodoo priest, and dissension would explode like the swollen carcass of a rotting *kudu,* spilling its poison everywhere!

He would bide his time and wait for a lull in the frenzied rites. When the time was right, he would step forward and urge them to rise up and to overthrow the Belgians with the power of their numbers.

Chapter Twenty-eight

Heather sprawled on the lumpy bed where Cigale had tossed her, thrusting aside the curtain of her tangled hair so that she could see. The pudgy Cigale smiled and slowly unbuttoned his shirt, laughing aloud as her lip curled in disgust when his flabby torso spilled from the confining cloth like an avalanche of lard.

"Do you not like what you see, little madame? No matter! I like very much what I see, yes? And soon, I shall see more. Come *chérie,* come to Hercule!" His extended arms were of a corpselike pallor, and like his fingers, they more closely resembled grossly over-stuffed sausage links than human limbs.

As he advanced, slowly so as to relish her growing panic and to enhance his own anticipation, she felt an acid flood of nausea rise in her throat at the thought of what he meant to do to her. *No.* She would not submit without protest, not to this sadistic buffoon. She licked her lips and waited until he was so near her that, should she have by any flight of insanity wished to, she could have reached out and touched his wobbling, fish-white belly. A strange calm swept over her as she looked up into his leering face. I'm going to fight him, she vowed, I'm going to make him regret this night, so that even if he wins, it won't be without cost on his part!

As he leaned over her, she suddenly drew up her legs, then jackknifed them with all her strength against the bulging front of his jodhpurs. A howl of agony that was scarce human whined from between Cigale's lips. Then he doubled over, clutching himself, doing a little fat man's dance of pain in tiny circles before her. She scuttled backward off the bed, and laughed, warming to the challenge. She had always been stubborn, willing to dig in her heels and stand up for what she believed, but she had never before fought tooth and nail. However, the past few days of Mauricier's smooth menace and Cigale's foulness had caused her to toss her reticence aside. She'd done exactly what her dear cousin Annabel would do under similar circumstances, and it had paid off! In fact, there was every chance it might do so again, she decided, filled now with hope.

Before Cigale's "dance" ended, she sprang across the room and kicked him hard, first on one knee just above the cuff of his boots, and then the other. He yelped, and before he could recover from this second attack, Heather shoved hard at his mountainous belly and sent him sprawling across the bed. He lay there on his back, like a beached white whale, unable to rise and come after her for he was trapped under his own weight, his sausagelike arms and legs wriggling frantically to find purchase. While he was struggling—a turtle on its back—to roll over, she sped to the door. But it was locked, the key tucked snugly in Cigale's pocket, she remembered belatedly, flinging herself about to face him again.

"Now it is my turn, little *tigresse,*" he panted as he succeeded in standing. He lumbered toward her like a heavy-bottomed clown she had seen once in a toy shop, the kind that always bobbed back upright when you knocked it down.

She laughed throatily, amethyst eyes sparkling. "First, M'sieu Cochon, you have to catch me!"

He lumbered after her, but each time he made a grab for her, she ducked or sidestepped and ran across the room, until Cigale was all but spent from chasing around and around after her, like a dog chasing its own tail. Perspiration stood out in great gobs upon his balding head, and his few wisps of hair were plastered wetly down. His fleshy upper lip dripped rivults of sweat and he was wheezing badly, his complexion now a heated crimson. Heather wondered with fierce, savage joy if he might succumb to apoplexy or congestion of the heart and drop dead at her feet!

He came at her again, moving slowly now, every breath a whistling torture that, under far different circumstances, would have filled her with concern. Just as slowly, she retreated. He barreled forward suddenly, and she backed off, realizing too late that he had engineered her flight and was forcing her out onto the railinged balcony. He chuckled as she looked about her, wide-eyed.

"The tables are turned now, are they not? Tell me, little redbird, can you fly?" he asked, and sniggered. His hot, black little eyes devoured her, greedily noting the way her rounded breasts heaved against the slippery silk of the crimson *kanga,* and then roving down the long and exquisitely bare length of creamy thigh revealed where the cloth was hiked up against the wrought-iron rail.

She shrank back against the railing, wondering if she could hope to kick him again or if she might duck under his arm before he grabbed her. But he was not so rash this time. Arms outstretched, for his own protection as well as to grab her, he kept on coming, and all at once his arms were closing about her. His foul little wet mouth, reeking of garlic and sour wine, was

436

lowering to smear itself over her lips. He ground his pudgy hips hard against her own, little snuffles and grunts of pleasure breaking from his lips as he finally tried to kiss her. Her fists beating like pale birds against his chest, Heather silently wailed for help. To her astonishment it came—and from a surprising direction!

A fist whizzed past her cheek from beyond the railing—a marvelous, oaken fist that was firmly attached to a wiry tanned arm! The knuckles slammed into Cigale's forehead with the force of a miniature battering ram. Cigale tottered, circled once, and then dropped like a speared bull elephant.

Open-mouthed with amazement, Heather flung herself around.

"Adam, it's you!" she exclaimed, smiling into a pair of twinkling gentian eyes. "Oh, thank God! Another minute, and it would have been too late!"

He had climbed all the way up now and was perched astride the railing, grinning wickedly in the starlight at her astonished expression.

"How's that for timing, hmm?" he demanded. "I'll bet your paunchy Romeo over there thought it was the wrath of God striking him for his wickedness!" His grin faded. "How are you, love? He didn't hurt you, did he?"

"No." She smiled an embarrassed little smile. "In fact, I rather believe I hurt him!"

He nodded. "I'm relieved to hear it," he said softly. There was hunger in his gentian eyes as he looked down at her, relief in his voice.

Without further words, she knew that he had been as worried about her as she had about him. His expression said it all.

"Much as I'd love to show you how damned glad I am to see you, we've no time, angel. We have to get away from here, and fast! All hell's going to break loose

437

in a few minutes," Adam promised grimly, stepping over Cigale's obscenely unconscious body in all its half-naked glory.

"But Tom is—"

"Tom's already been taken care of. Ngudu and I saw to that. Don't worry. By now he's probably back in Mbaka's village swilling banana beer to dull the ache of his cracked ribs and the lash stripe across his back!" As he spoke, he drew a length of coiled rope over his head, lashed one end firmly to the railing, and gave it a sharp tug.

"Mbaka's village?" she echoed.

Adam nodded. "Yes. Your little chief found me after I crawled up onto the riverbank. He's proved a damned good friend, thanks to you, *madami esumba!* There." He tossed the free end of the rope over the balcony. "Madame, your ladder! Shall I go first?"

She nodded, biting her lip. She had no head for heights, but if shinnying down that rope was the only way she could escape, she would do it.

"Arm over arm, don't look down, don't rush, got it? The governor and his pals are up to their eyeballs in wine right now. They're celebrating having forced you and Tom to 'talk.' Take all the time you need."

Adam went first, sliding down the rope a few feet, then waiting until it steadied before signaling Heather to begin her descent. "Your turn!"

She grasped the rope, closed her eyes, scrambled over the balcony, and then dropped. Her arms felt as if they were being torn from their sockets when she let them bear her entire weight. She paused until the rope had ceased its dizzying spiraling. Then she opened her eyes and did as Adam had instructed. Hand over hand, she climbed down, her fears quickly forgotten. Her beloved Adam waited for her below, waited to take her away to safety, far away from this horrid place! She felt his hands steadying her as she dangled only a few feet from the ground; then she let go, dropping safely into his strong arms.

Instantly, she flung her arms about his neck, burying her face against his chest and drinking greedily of the dear, familiar, comforting scent and feel of him. Emotion poured over her, through her.

He grasped her chin and roughly tilted her head back for a hurried, too brief, kiss. His lips tasted like heaven!

"Adam . . . oh, Adam! Oh, Lord, I was so afraid! I thought you were dead . . . I thought they'd—"

"Hush now, angel," he murmured, cutting the rope free and coiling it about his waist once more, "I'm fine! Let's—"

An angry shout came from above them, and they craned their heads upward to see a groggy Hercule Cigale lurching over the balcony, clutching his head, and shaking a furious, chubby fist in their direction.

"Mauricier! They're below! They're escaping! 'Urry!" he screamed.

"Your fat friend has a big mouth, love," Adam said grimly, drawing a narrow cylinder from inside his shirt, "but this should shut him up! Cigale, isn't it?"

She nodded. Adam drew a match from his pocket and struck it hurriedly, touching the flame to the fuse that dangled from the stick of dynamite. It sputtered, hissed, then caught, the red glow traveling steadily upward.

"Cigale! Here, *mon ami,* catch!" he yelled in French. Then he tossed the dynamite onto the balcony, alongside the fat man. It landed behind him, hissing still like a miniature snake, a thin spiral of smoke rising from the fuse.

In the fleeting second before Adam grabbed her hand and yelled at her to run, Heather caught a glimpse of Cigale's panic-stricken moon of a face, his tiny eyes enormous, his complexion greenish in the starlight, before he plunged headfirst over the balcony railing squealing with terror like a stuck pig!

They raced down the darkened, dusty street as far as the cathedral; then Adam pulled her down in the concealing shadows, placing himself over her on the ground. In that same moment, the governor-general's residence exploded with a ground-shaking blast, like a carelessly ignited box of fireworks on Guy Fawkes' Night, the flash of the blast illuminating the narrow streets and bungalows of Stanleyville with its brilliance! Debris arced through the glowing red, golden and orange sky in graceful showers—splintered timbers and chunks of masonry. Fiery sparks sprayed in confettilike fountains over the thatched bungalows, touching their dry thatched roofs with tiny, glowing cinders that quickly caught flame, crackling and building into eager, licking tongues that traveled swiftly as smoke billowed in great black clouds everywhere.

Men—some dressed, others in their underwear—ran from the bungalows, yelling and screaming. Confusion reigned supreme as the flames leaped from one roof to the next, their greedy appetite sparing nothing.

Adam let out a whoop as the crackle of the flames, the dull roar of the burning residence, and the angry shouts of the miners were joined by another harsh sound—the strident buzz of a rioting mob. Brandishing flaming torches above their heads the blacks stormed into the European quarter from the native quarter on the far side of the little town.

"He did it!" Adam roared with obvious relish. "Ngudu's incited the natives to rebel! Time for us to leave here, sweetheart. They might mistake us for Belgians in the confusion!"

Smoke stinging their eyes and burning their lungs,

the pair broke cover and ran, almost barreling full-tilt into a staggering Governor-General Mauricier as they went. Gone was the elegant, though sadistic, man Heather had known. His scorched clothes and singed eyebrows and his strangely cropped hair were blatant testimony to his narrow escape from the exploding residence. His expression became a contorted mask of fury as he spied them hovering in the middle of the dirt street.

"After them, you fools! The town is done for! Leave it! Don't let them get away! *Vite! Vite!*" he bellowed, hurling himself toward Adam.

Adam thrust Heather behind him and sprang to meet Mauricier, fists raised.

"Come on, you oily bastard! You wanted to meet Adam Markham? Well, here I am, friend!" he goaded him. "Let's see how brave you are when you're fighting a man instead of a woman!"

With an oath, Mauricier lunged, ramming a fist at Adam's belly. Adam sidestepped with virile grace and flung about, chopping the governor smartly across the back of the neck. Mauricier's knees sagged; then he recovered and feinted a right, jabbing viciously with his left. His knuckles caught Adam squarely on the tip of the chin. Adam reeled back momentarily, flicking his head to clear it before recovering and lunging forward. His speedy recovery took Mauricier unaware, and Adam was on the Belgian before he had time to gather his wits, slamming punch after wicked punch to the governor's now battered and bleeding face. Finally Mauricier could no longer stand, and when Adam, breathing heavily and flexing bruised, bloodied knuckles, released him, he slithered to the ground without another sound.

"Adam! They've seen us!" Heather cried.

In response to Mauricier's frenzied shouts, a party of

men had stopped fighting the fire with useless wooden buckets. Adam and Heather turned and fled, feet pounding the dusty street as they bobbed and weaved through the angry mob of rebellious native laborers who were brandishing machetes and spears and knives. Their anger, their hatred was as acrid on the thick, smoky air as the choking stench of the fire, and Heather knew the Belgians would be fortunate indeed if they escaped with their lives this night.

The buildings gave way to sparse open land then. Ahead lay the mill, some scattered outbuildings, and the corrals, the flames licking at their ruins like eerie spirits doing a pagan dance—yet another testimony to Adam's particular form of "insurance"! Still they ran.

"Adam, I can't go much farther!" Heather sobbed, clutching her side.

"Hang in there, sweet, we'll make it. No, not that way," Adam whispered urgently when she turned toward the lower terrain. He steered her past the smoking rubble of the mill and upward, toward the jungle. From here, the sky above Stanleyville was lit with a fierce red-orange glow, they saw, as they darted hurried glances over their shoulders.

"If only we had horses," she panted, hurrying to keep up with his long, loping strides as sounds of a howling pursuit floated up the rise on the darkness behind them. "Then we could outdistance them easily!"

"Horses? Ah, but we have something far better than lowly horses for you, my girl!" he promised, and there was laughter in his tone now.

"What?" she demanded doubtfully.

"Elephants."

Chapter Twenty-nine

"You can't be serious!" Heather whispered hoarsely, disbelief in her voice. Her eyes were as round as saucers. "You *did* say 'elephants'?"

"Elephants!" Adam confirmed, a wicked grin tugging at his lips in the starlight despite the seriousness of their situation. "You must remember—those enormous creatures with the baggy gray pajamas and the big ears? Stay here!"

He ducked under the corral posts and moved stealthily toward the massive beasts. In the shadows, they loomed like rounded black mountains against the indigo night, their odor pungent on the steamy air. She saw Adam's silhouetted figure edge cautiously toward one of them, a great beast that could not shy away as the rest of the herd—already unsettled by the explosions and now by his presence among them—had done, since it wore an iron fetter on its massive foot. And the reason it wore that fetter, she realized belatedly, was because this elephant was a rogue, difficult to domesticate, unlike the other relatively docile cows. The beast trumpeted loudly as she caught Adam's scent, and she shied away blowing noisily, her trunk extended like an upraised arm to ward off attack, her enormous ears like giant sails flapping to and fro in her agitation.

The low, even murmur of Adam's voice carried to where Heather crouched, and she crossed her fingers and prayed that it carried no farther. Her heart was throbbing so wildly she feared it would burst from her breast! She watched as Adam burrowed in his pockets, before extending his arm to the elephant, whose gray sides were scarred with the marks of cruel beatings. She doubted that an animal so badly mistreated by her handlers could ever be calmed quickly and easily. But to her surprise, she heard a contented, juicy, snuffling sound and she knew he had given the animal something to eat—a stalk of sugar cane, perhaps, or manioc—as a bribe. She held her breath as Adam uncoiled the rope from about his waist, and speaking softly, soothingly, flung it over the elephant's back, knotting it securely under its belly. Then, miracle of miracles, the elephant lumbered down on its forelegs at Adam's low command, and he was scrambling astride her, his fists knotted in the rope reins as confidently as the hands of any Indian *mahout!*

"*Allez!*" he commanded softly. "*Allez, ma belle!*" The elephant rose, attempting to obey his gentle command. But after only two paces, the chain and fetter pulled her up short. She emitted an outraged squeal, then Heather heard the dull grinding of chains followed by a loud chink as the fetter snapped in two. Soon a massive black mountain, its head bobbing, swayed ponderously toward where Heather crouched in the shadows of the corral.

"Didn't I always say I had a way with females? Your steed, my lady!" Adam quipped, flourishing his hand and smiling down at her from a great height. He then ordered the elephant down.

"You're mad! Utterly insane!" Heather whispered

fiercely. Nonetheless she scrambled, with his help, astride a back as broad as a barge.

"Who cares as long as we escape?" Adam retorted with a grin. *"Allez!"*

As if sensing the urgency of their plight, the cow elephant heaved herself to a standing position, whereupon Heather let out a little squeak of dismay. The back of an elephant was much higher off the ground than she had ever imagined, but she hung on grimly as the cow lumbered forward and, like a horse with the bit between its teeth, speeded up.

Flattening the sturdy corral fence like matchsticks the elephant burst through it. Squealing and trumpeting as she tasted the freedom that might be hers again, she barreled toward the safety of the jungle that ringed the mines. Small bushes and stands of long elephant grass were crushed as the beast fairly scrambled along, her giant ears flapping back and forth like sails and creating a considerable draft for her riders. Adam turned to look at Heather, and in the moonlight that spilled down between the trees, she caught the roguish sparkle of his eyes and the glint of his white teeth. "How's this for a lark, love? Damned good fun, if you ask me!"

Her unladylike response was never spoken because a bullet suddenly whistled overhead.

"Stay down and hang on!" Adam yelled, quite unnecessarily since Heather was already hanging on for dear life and staying down to avoid the bullets flying past them. "Here's where it gets rough! Come on, Mamma Jumbo, you old darling, get up there!"

With gunfire to spur her on, and the yells of her hated former masters acting as goads, the frightened elephant needed little urging. Clinging grimly to the fragile rope Adam had looped about the beast's body for purchase, and lurching precariously with her lumbering, rapid

445

gait, the unlikely trio literally thundered up the slight grade toward the jungle.

"Tell me something, Adam?" Heather screamed as they ducked to avoid the low-hanging branches that were visible too late in the darkness.

"What?" Adam flung over his shoulder, whooping as they flattened a low thornbush that had momentarily blocked their path.

"How do we stop her?" Heather yelled back.

"Stop her?" There was a pause. "I'll be damned if I know!" Adam confessed in chagrined tones. "I hadn't given *stopping* any thought!"

"Don't you think it's about time you did?" Heather shrieked.

"I think it's already too late for that, sweetheart," Adam bellowed ruefully. "Jump!"

She glimpsed, in that second, moonlight glinting on foaming white water far below, and she realized that Tshopo Falls lay at the bottom of the cliff toward which they were speeding. She jumped, leaping blindly for safety, and felt the tremendous impact as she landed on a tuffet of thick, rough elephant grass. The sprinkling of stars she saw were in her mind, rather than above her in the sky. Then all went black. Seconds later she opened her eyes to see Adam bending over her. She groaned.

"Our gallant steed turned in the nick of time! We could have stayed aboard her, but I didn't dare risk it. She's probably gone clear to Nairobi by now. Are you hurt?" He held out his hand to help her up.

"I don't think so. Just winded. Ow!" She winced as she stood, ruefully rubbing her bruised bottom.

He grinned. "Ah! So that's where you landed!" He clicked his teeth regretfully. "I'd love to massage it for you, but quite frankly, my sweet, we don't have the time! Here they come!"

446

Sure enough, they could make out the light-colored shirts and trousers of the Belgian miners, white blurs against the night, and here and there the bobbing glow of a torch carried aloft steadily came up the grade toward the cliff edge. Upraised, angry voices were growing closer by the second!

Hand in hand, Heather and Adam plunged blindly into the forest, tripping and stumbling and forcing their way through tangled vegetation. It was hard going, and their flight seemed endless. Daring a glance over her shoulder, Heather saw the wavering glow of the torches coming up fast behind them; then she frowned in puzzlement when she turned to see more torches ahead. Dear God, surely they weren't surrounded?

"Almost there!" Adam rasped, racing toward the lights with Heather gasping to keep up.

"Almost where?" she sobbed, a stitch cramping her side.

"Here!" Adam yelled as they reached the flaring torches. To Heather's astonishment, she saw the pygmy chief, Mbaka, holding a flaming brand aloft in one fist, while many of the little hunters of his village who were scattered between the bushes did likewise.

"Get ready, Mbaka!" Adam ordered.

Mbaka nodded and signaled to his fellows. Adam indicated that Heather should crouch down and stay still as the torches were hurriedly extinguished.

The hue and cry the Belgians had set up grew louder by the second; crashes, curses, and yells filling the jungle now. Heather's heart pounded so loudly she was certain they must be able to hear it. Still their pursuers came closer, closer, drew level with their hiding place, then—

"Now!" Adam barked, and the pygmies sprang into action, raising their *nkusa* vine nets—over three

447

hundred feet in length—at the very instant the Belgians reached them! Their pursuers were soon hopelessly entangled in the long, heavy folds. The Belgians struggled fiercely to escape, but to no avail. Adam threw back his head and roared with laughter as their livid curses turned the air blue. "That should keep them busy for a while, don't you think?" he asked Heather, laughter in his voice. *"Asante,* Mbaka, my friend! Let's get going!"

Led by little Mbaka and his victorious, cunning hunters, Heather and Adam quickly reached the safety of the pygmy village, hidden deep in the bowels of the jungle, where the Twa women waited eagerly to hear if their men had been successful in freeing the beloved *madami esumba.* Seeing that she was unharmed was occasion for a celebration, and soon the wild throbbing of their drums beat, like a racing heart, in the silent, steaming night. Tom and Ngudu and Ewasu were waiting there for them, Heather saw with relief, and a joyful reunion followed during which vivid descriptions of their various escapes were amusingly recounted, Adam's drawing the greatest laughter with a description of Hercule Cigale's expression when he had tossed the stick of dynamite at him and urged him to "Catch!"

"Well, that should do it!" Adam declared, satisfaction in his tone. "We should be safe here, at least until daylight. If we couldn't see to find our way, it's a safe bet the Belgians won't be able to see to find us, *if* they ever manage to escape from the net!"

Clutching the stitch in her side, Heather nodded and flopped down at his feet. "Thank God!" She gulped, drawing deep, greedy breaths. "I couldn't have gone another yard!"

Adam laughed softly, then harder, until he was forced to clamp his hand over his mouth to control the deep chuckles that threatened to spill out.

"What in the world is it you find so funny?" she demanded, irritated by his merriment. To him, their near escape from death had been nothing more than a game, a madcap prank that he had enjoyed enormously, she realized indignantly.

"You!" he answered her question. "The expression on your face when I said we were going to escape by elephant! It was priceless, my love! *Punch* would have been delighted!"

She snorted in disgust. "Isn't there anything you take seriously, Adam? We were almost killed back there, and you find levity in the situation? You're quite incorrigible. A hopeless case!" She shook her head in exasperation.

Still grinning, he drew her to him, gave her a smacking kiss full on the lips, and hugged the breath from her. "And you, my darling girl, take life far too seriously! Laugh when you outfox Fate, love! Spit in her eye when she plays a dirty trick on you! Roll with the punches and come up smiling. That's the only way to survive."

"Hmph!"

He smiled, then attempted to muster a serious expression. "Ah, well, since we're safe for the time being, would it be appropriate now to see to your injuries?"

"Injuries?" she echoed suspiciously.

"Yes, your bruised—"

"That's not necessary, thank you!" she retorted waspishly, cutting him off. "There's a time and a place for everything, and this is neither the time *nor* the place!"

"Wrong," he disagreed. "Any time's the time, and anywhere's the perfect place—for two people in love! Don't be such a prude. Where does it hurt, my poor,

449

wounded angel? Won't you tell 'Doctor' Adam, and let him make it better?"

From his tone, she knew that he was grinning lecherously, wickedly, though she could not see his face in the darkness. Confound him! This wasn't at all the tender reunion she had imagined they would share after they'd both so narrowly cheated death. Infuriated, she lashed out with her foot and caught him on the knee above his boot, eliciting a startled yelp from him. "Lay a hand on me, and you'll lose it!" she hissed.

His low, maddening chuckle made her face flame. "You forget, my sweet—I *enjoy* living dangerously! By jove, you're quite a tigress when you're angry, aren't you? Magnificent! I'll have to make you angry more often!"

"I'm warning you! . . ."

His masterful lips silenced her. Although she struggled at first, irritated by his brashness and his devil-may-care attitude, she soon realized that resistance was useless, and in short order, he lifted her into his arms and strode with her to the hut they had shared the last time they'd visited Mbaka's village. Dropping her onto the leafy groundcover, he sprawled alongside her.

Without preamble, he lustily thrust the flowing folds of the crimson silk *kanga* up to her waist and fondled her bared thighs, laughing softly as her furious mutters became none-too-convincing protests, then reluctant sighs of pleasure. Her rigid body, straining against his arms, grew still and heavy; expectant. With one swift flick of his wrist, he unknotted the sarong. It slipped easily away from her body, and he turned his ardent attention to her lovely full breasts. As he cupped them in his warm hands, he found that her nipples had already firmed impudently without need of his caresses, and he tasted them one by one,

450

with greedy relish.

"Damn you!" she wailed, knotting her fingers in his hair as his delicious love play, contrary to her wishes, sparked her own desire. "You're a lecherous devil, Adam Markham!"

"And you, my sweet, are sounding more like a trooper every day! It's obvious I'm going to have to take you . . . in hand," he muttered against her warm, velvety skin, darting his tongue-tip against the tingling crests of her firm breasts while his hands stroked the curves of her derrière. "Like it?" he demanded teasingly, grinning in the darkness as she gasped.

"No-o-o," she insisted with little conviction. "I hate it!"

"Bloody little liar," he retorted fondly, sliding one hand down to nestle against the soft curls between her slender thighs. "You know you do. . . ."

All the pretense became impossible then, for her body melted under his intimate caresses, becoming warm and pliant in delicious, though reluctant, surrender. The ticklish, maddening craving that tantalized her senses became a roaring, ravenous beast. It demanded satisfaction; it would not be denied or delayed. Eagerly she clasped him, drew him to her, guiding his manly hardness to that aching tenderness between her thighs.

"Patience, love," he breathed against her cheek. "There's no need to hurry."

"Now it's your turn to shut up, Adam Markham," she whispered fiercely, a tigress to the core now in her passion.

With a delighted, astonished chuckle, he gathered her into his arms and enthusiastically obliged her.

The next morning, Adam lazily opened one eye to

find Heather sitting, knees bent, her head resting upon them, watching him sleep. Sunlight streamed in narrow bars through the *mongongo* thatched roof, touching her long dark-fire hair with light that glowed a deep, rich crimson, like candlelight shining through fine sherry, the coloring bringing to Adam's mind the orchids he had discovered while stumbling about near the Tshopo Falls. Little wonder that the exotic blossoms had struck a forgotten chord in his cloudy mind and he had remembered her, for she was exquisite, as rare and lovely as any orchid. . . .

"My crimson angel," he murmured, reaching out and tugging at a long curling ribbon of her fiery hair to draw her to him. She rested her head upon his bare chest, and he could feel the flutter of her lashes tickling him there as she blinked rapidly. "I do believe I shall name my find after you; Markham's Crimson Angel. Has a nice ring to it, don't you think?" He grinned down at her proudly, but upon receiving no answering smile or comment from her, his own expression became serious. "You're quiet this morning, love. Not feeling ill, are you?"

Still silent, she shook her head.

"Look at me!" he commanded. She reluctantly raised her head. "What is it? Was it something I said— or did? God, woman, I can't stand it when you turn those sad, violet eyes on me! Out with it! Tell me what's wrong? Where's my fierce little tiger-woman of last night, hmm?" he teased, chucking her beneath the chin. To his alarm, a great sob escaped her.

"There! That's exactly it! I just knew it!" she managed to mutter accusingly between sniffs, "I just knew you'd make fun of me this morning. Men! You're all alike! You say I have nothing to be ashamed of in wanting you as badly as you want me, but afterward it's an entirely different story, isn't it, Adam Markham?

452

Then it's time to make fun of me! *Tiger-woman!* It's all your fault. I was a proper, modest young lady until I met you, and now look at me! I'm so confused. Some— somehow, you've turned me into something I'm not, ha-half woman, ha-half—half lusting *animal!*"

A great snort of laughter burst from him. "So that's what's bothering you, is it? Don't be bloody ridiculous, sweet! I was just teasing you. Believe me, I wouldn't change you for the world! There's no sin, no shame in you wanting me, Heather, just as I want you, whatever you might believe to the contrary. If you're worried about what others would think if they knew you were a warm, passionate, giving woman, then don't. The only person you have to answer to for your actions is yourself." He grinned. "And me, of course! We needn't give a tinker's damn what anyone thinks of us." A peculiar expression suddenly crossed his face. "Half-woman, half-animal?" he repeated belatedly.

Some memory or vague impression, something stirred by what she'd said earlier still nagged in his mind. For a few moments, he fell silent and thoughtful, racking his brain for the memory that had flitted so tantalizingly within reach, then had slipped away. He replayed their conversation in his mind, and suddenly slapped his palm hard against his brow, a look of incredulity in his shining gentian eyes. "I've been a bloody fool! Of course, by God, that's it! You've done it, sweet!" he exclaimed, his excitement building as he quickly shrugged into his shirt and hauled on his boots.

"What? What did I do?" Heather asked, her fine brows arched in obvious puzzlement, her embarrassment temporarily forgotten.

He swept her up in his arms and strode from the hut into the open, twirling her around and around several times in his arms before he lowered her dizzily to the ground.

"What did you *do,* you funny, adorable creature?" he roared, gentian eyes glowing. "You told me where to find the Tears of Agaja, that's what!"

"The diamonds?" she breathed.

"The diamonds," he confirmed. "A fortune in uncut diamonds—and soon they'll be ours!"

"What's all the ruckus?" Tom demanded, striding across to where Adam and Heather were giddily hanging on to each other, still laughing. The Twa stared at the trio, open-mouthed.

"I know where they are!"

One glance at Adam's face told Tom just what "they" were. "Good Lord! The diamonds?" Seeing Adam nod, he swept off his hat and scratched his head. "By jove!" His merry blue eyes were sparkling with excitement, their brilliance incongruous when coupled with the livid bruises and healing cuts he sported. Heather had doctored them earlier that morning, before Adam awoke. "Where?" he demanded.

"Close by the pool at the base of the falls. When I came to after 'shooting the rapids', Markham-style"— Adam paused and grinned—"I dimly recall seeing what I believed to be a tree with a demon face carved into it. Naturally, feeling the way I did at the time, I thought it was just a figment of my imagination, but now I'm convinced it was one of—"

"—the idols that Elwood told you of!" Tom finished excitedly, his grin becoming a grimace of pain as he moved too quickly and his cracked ribs pained him.

Adam nodded. "Something Heather said brought it back to me. We're on the right track, Tom, I'm certain of it!"

"Well, man, what the devil are you waiting for? Get going," Tom urged. "I'll find Ngudu and Ewasu and we'll follow you down at a slower pace. I'm afraid I'm not up to charging through the jungle at breakneck speed today. Sorry, old chap."

"I understand—but don't be too damned long about it, Tom," Adam warned with a rueful smile. "I don't know if I'll be able to curb my curiosity for long!"

"Why try?" Tom asked, glancing from Heather's rapt face to Adam's, both alight with the thrill of discovery. "If the cave's there, then for God's sake take a look. You've earned it, after all!"

Adam gave Heather a hug. "We have, haven't we?" he acknowledged, looking down into her shining eyes. "Thanks, Tom!"

"Rot! Just watch how you go, there's a good chap. I'm not up to another rescue just now, if it's all the same to you!"

Pausing only to take up his rifle, grab a machete and sling canteens of fresh water over his shoulders, Adam set off, Heather close behind.

From Mbaka's village to the base of the falls was a distance of only three miles or so, yet the dense jungle they had to hack through made the way seem closer to twenty, even though the terrain they covered sloped sharply downhill. Almost two hours had passed before they neared the spot, having taken several wrong turns en route, and their clothes were now sodden with sweat, their arms crisscrossed with scratches.

"Not much farther now," Adam promised. "I can hear the falls from here, can't you?"

She nodded agreement, wondering meanwhile how Robert Elwood must have felt years ago when he'd stumbled from the jungle half out of his mind, racked by fever, drawn by the sound of water, and babbling deliriously on about hidden caverns where diamonds winked their promise of untold riches. According to Adam, he'd been close to death when friendly natives had found him, and it had been little wonder that few had believed his tale.

"What was it that made you believe Elwood had really found the diamonds?" she asked, curious, hurrying to keep up with Adam's long, loose strides.

Expertly swinging the machete to left and right as he hacked through the curtain of lianas, muscles bulging like knotted cords under the cloth of his shirtsleeves, he answered, "I did my homework—checked out some of the details Elwood recalled, the name 'Agaja' for one. A king by that name really existed in Western Africa in the 1700s. It was believed by his people, the Fon, that he was the descendant of a human princess and a leopard. His people were at war with the Oyos for several years—it's all on record—and he really did have a royal army that consisted in part of women warriors. Since all of this was true, it followed that much of the rest of the tale was also, don't you see? Most legends contain a fair helping of truth, along with the superstition and elaboration that's been added to them over the years. I figured there might well be a cache of priceless diamonds hidden somewhere in the jungle—perhaps not the king's crystallized tears, romantic though the legend sounds, but real nonetheless." He halted suddenly, his dark head cocked. "Did you hear that?"

Heather strained her ears. "The waterfall? Yes, I can still hear it."

"No. Not the falls. I thought I heard a shot."

She listened intently, but heard only the roar of the distant falls, and the squawks of parrots and the chatter of monkeys that had become commonplace to her. She shook her head. "Nothing."

Adam shrugged. "Imagination, probably," he decided before they carried on.

Less than a half-hour later, they suddenly came upon a tiny clearing in the jungle. It was walled by great mountains of boulders and by mahogany, ebony, and rubber trees.

"This is it," Adam breathed, so softly she had to strain to catch his words.

There is an eerie silence about this place, as if no one has been here for many, many years, Heather thought. And little wonder. The fallen boulders, obviously the result of a landslide some years ago, made the clearing inaccessible save from the jungle, as they had reached it, or from the treacherous foaming pool at the base of the falls. The huge, spreading crowns of the trees met above in a leafy canopy, yet beneath them the ground was bare, only an irregular little patch of blue and white sky peeping through. Across the clearing she spied vivid crimson blossoms spilling down from a rotted tree trunk.

"Crimson angels!" Adam breathed.

Even as Heather caught sight of the orchids, Adam was striding eagerly across the clearing toward them. She raced after him, a jittery sensation in her belly. Excitement, yes, excitement was part of it, but mingled with it was the brooding, melancholy quality the clearing imparted to her.

Adam came to an abrupt halt before the sprays of enormous frilly orchids, his eyes riveted to the "tree" from which they grew. As he had thought, it was no tree. A carved wooden idol leered at them from between the foliage and vines and exquisite blossoms, its face that of a creature half-leopard, half-woman, the illusion enhanced by the fuzzy, spotted lichens that overgrew it. Adam looked about him, then exclaimed, "There's another one!"

Sure enough, there were two idols, both lurching drunkenly under the weight of two centuries of vegetation, the second invisible to Heather until Adam swung the machete and hacked the lianas from it. Between the idols were heaped several large boulders, flung there by a landslide that had occurred long before.

"The entrance to the cave must be under that lot," Adam said, jerking his head at the rubble. "Let's find something sturdy we can use as a lever."

With the aid of a tree branch and the machete, the largest boulder was rolled away, then the smaller ones were laboriously hefted to the side, one by one. For Adam and Heather, time stood still, so eager were they. His shirt was soaked with sweat by the time a small, dark hole, obviously once an entrance, showed through. He scrabbled at it, clearing the earth and fallen leaves and grasses away until it was large enough for them to crawl inside. Then he took up a fallen dried branch and lit it for a torch.

"Well, here goes! Are you game, my love?" he asked, a tremor to his voice, his hopes and his dreams mirrored in his glowing gentian eyes.

"Just try to stop me!" she replied immediately, her own voice peculiarly husky.

"That's my girl!" He gave her a quick, light kiss, a brief hug, then dropped to his knees and crawled inside the cave.

Chapter Thirty

The air inside the tunnel was stuffy, fetid with the smell of something unpleasant that Heather couldn't define. The torch hissing and smoking and at times threatening to extinguish itself, they crawled on hands and knees through slippery mud for what she guessed must be at least forty feet. She experienced a horrible claustrophobic feeling as the cave walls pressed in about them and at times she feared she would scream, but suddenly the tunnel opened up and they could stand, although with heads bowed. A welcome current of fresh air entered the cave from a hole in the ceiling above them, and looking up, they glimpsed bright blue sky through the opening. Farther on, the cave became a vaulted passageway. Furtive rustlings and leathery whispers suddenly filled the darkness, coupled with small squeaks and stirrings.

"What—what's that noise?" Heather whispered, not certain at all that she really wanted to know.

Adam swung around and held the flaming torch above their heads. "Bats," he answered, his voice surprisingly loud and echoing, "there must be billions of them in here. Look!"

High above their heads, the cavern ceiling was filled

with the horrid creatures, their eyes glinting like red-glass beads in the light, their hideous, nightmare faces sending shudders and crawling sensations through Heather.

"That's quite enough, thank you," she whispered weakly. "You can put the torch down now." It was bad enough that the bats were there, so close, but Heather had no desire to look at them any longer. Belatedly she realized what the source of the unpleasant smell was—the sticky, loathsome substance that they were wading through.

The cave tunnel began to slope sharply toward the bowels of the earth then, and sliding and slipping in the darkness, they followed it down to? . . . Apprehensive of what they might find beyond, Heather scuttled after Adam, not letting him get any farther than a comforting six inches ahead of her at any one time!

Soon, the tunnel came to an abrupt end, opening out into a vast cavern. Adam plunged recklessly forward.

"Good God!" he exclaimed. "Look at that!"

He turned the torch slowly so that she could see, a flare of light lurching lopsidedly over the craggy cave as he did so.

Reaching from ceiling to floor of one of the cavern walls was an enormous, carved ebony mask, festooned now with cobwebs. The scurrying spiders that fled the revealing torchlight gave the impression that the mask was a rotting skull, alive with maggots, rather than an inanimate object carved by man. The noble brow was wide, the long nose broad and wide nostriled, the face handsome and commanding. But the mouth was thick lipped and stern. From the sightless eyes, water dripped in a continual stream, draining into the mask from the damp cave ceiling and trickling through these small holes into a small pool that had been hollowed into the rock below by centuries of dripping water.

"Agaja, the King . . . weeping through eternity for his beloved!" Adam said softly, awe in his tone. "I wonder where the—"

Suddenly Heather let out a terrified shriek as something hurtled toward her out of the darkness, missing her by no more than a fraction of an inch! She'd felt a rush of air upon her skin as it passed, and then had heard a metallic clang as whatever it was landed at her feet.

"What the devil!" Adam swung about, hurrying back to her side. The torchlight revealed a rusted spear. Following its shaft, they found a skeleton huddled at Heather's back, the bones collapsed in an untidy pile, obviously shaken loose from where they had rested by this intrusion. The pelvis still boasted an apron of rotted leopard skin. Wide golden bangles loosely encircled the bony wrists and ankles, and the grinning skull sported a mane of long dull-black, kinky hair.

"My God! What Mauricier told me was true!" Heather, still trembling violently, cried. "The treasure *was* guarded by the women of Agaja's royal army!"

"And up until quite recently too, by the looks of it— at least until ten years ago. This skeleton isn't thát old." He swung the torch around, and its light caught the yellowed bones of two others. "Poor devils! The landslide that sealed off the cave must have entombed them alive."

"But Agaja's warriors couldn't have existed here for two centuries!" Heather argued. "It's not possible!"

"No," Adam agreed. "Perhaps their descendants intermarried with the local people, and some of the daughters of each generation were sent here to guard the secret hiding place of Agaja's treasure? Who knows! Their secret, whatever it was, has died with them. Now, the diamonds! It's damned hard to see anything with only the one torch. Where do we start?"

"I would have thought that would have been

461

obvious, Captain Markham," she teased, "given your romantic imagination."

He frowned, then brightened and shot her a broad grin that in the meager light made him appear as Heather imagined a roguish pirate might look. "Ah, yes! Where else? Ze pool!"

Picking their way between rocky litter, bones and other artifacts, they stood once more looking up at the massive carving of the noble Agaja's face. Light glimmered blackly on the surface of the pool as Heather held the torch aloft, and Adam crouched down. He thrust his arm deep into the water, and she watched emotions—apprehension, doubt, realization, joy—race across his darkly handsome face in rapid succession as he drew out his hand and opened it, palm up, before her eyes.

A score or more of glassy lumps winked dully in his hands, and the shivery thrill of discovery swept through her, tingling down the back of her neck and dancing down her spine. Then she looked into Adam's radiant eyes, no less bright than the jewels.

"There must be thousands of them in here!" he breathed. "My God! We did it! We've found the treasure!"

She nodded, her smile reaching from ear to ear at the delighted expression on Adam's face.

The fabled Tears of Agaja were lost no more!

Tom, Ewasu and Ngudu were waiting at the surface when they exited the cave, blinking against the bright light. Tom hurried forward.

"Well?"

In answer, Adam held out his hand, and Tom lifted one of the knobbly lumps from it and held it up to the light. He let out a whoop of joy. "Congratulations,

462

Adam! You've done it! I couldn't be happier for you, old boy!"

"Correction, Tom. *We've* done it—you and I, and Heather, and Ngudu and Ewasu! None of us could have made it without the others' help. The treasure belongs to all of us," Adam declared solemnly. "Get the sacks from the bundles, and we'll fill them up. Ngudu, Ewasu, yes, you too. Come on!"

A grinning Ngudu eagerly did as ordered, but Ewasu hung back, shaking his head. "This place no good place, Bwana! Spirits bad. I feel it . . . here!" He gestured to his chest. "Ewasu stay here," he insisted firmly.

"As you will, Ewasu," Adam agreed easily. "Keep a watch on our gear, will you?"

An hour later, four small sacks had been brought to the surface, all of them bulging with diamonds. By now, the mellow afternoon light was rapidly fading into the violet and amethyst and gray of twilight; night was fast approaching. Ngudu built a fire, then announced that he and his brother would go in search of game for the evening meal. Taking up his rifle, Adam got to his feet to go with them.

"Where the devil do you think you're going, Markham?" Tom demanded.

"I don't know about you, Worth, but I'm starving!" Adam said. "I thought I'd go hunting."

Tom eyed him with disgust. "You don't realize when you're well off, do you, you bloody young fool? You came within a hair's-breadth of losing Heather, Markham, but you'd rather go off hunting than spend some time alone with her?" He shook his head. "You must not be thinking clearly yet, old chap! That crack on the head must have been worse than we thought!" He shook his head in disbelief. "I'd be damned if I'd prefer gallivanting through the jungle to Heather's company. You'd best keep a sharp eye out. I might be tempted to give you some competition!"

Anger flared briefly in Adam's face, but then he caught the sparkle in Tom's eyes and grinned. "Too bad for you, Worth, but my injury wasn't all that severe. I may be a little slower on the uptake than before, still I'm no fool! You've twisted my arm. You go. I'll stay here!"

With a laugh, Tom took Adam's rifle and clapped him across the back. "I should jolly well think so!" he declared as he left.

Alone, Heather and Adam sat before the campfire, gazing into the golden flames with starry eyes. "I never thought you could do it, but you've made your dreams come true, Adam," she murmured. "I'm so happy for you, my darling."

He shook his head. "No. My dreams came true a long time ago, my love—the day I came down the verandah steps back in Magadi and saw you there, heard you say you wanted to be with me always. The diamonds are just a pleasant bonus, as far as I'm concerned. They'll enable me to give you everything you deserve, everything I've wanted to give you."

"All I've ever wanted was you. As . . . as I want you now, Adam." She lowered her thick lashes and blushed.

"Here, you hussy?" he teased gently.

"Here. Now! 'Anytime, anyplace, is perfect for two people in love,' you said, remember?" Her lashes swept boldly up. Her violet eyes danced with challenge.

"You're a fast learner, Lady Heather," he breathed.

"I've an excellent teacher, Captain Markham!"

He brushed her heavy hair away from her rosy, fire-lit face and kissed the sweet mouth she gladly offered him. His eyes were alive in the flickering light, their gentian irises reflecting the golden flames as he pressed her down onto the blanket strewn before the fire. Caressing her lovely face, he leaned on one elbow and watched her, saw the love and tender yearning in her violet eyes as his touch worked its magic. Her breath was warm and rapid, gently fanning his cheek as he drew his lips from hers. Beneath his hand, her heart fluttered against her breast.

"Never change," he murmured, his voice husky. "Stay always as gentle and sweet and level as you are. I need you, Heather. I need you to steady me, to make me see things as they truly are. Before I met you, I thought the riches the Tears of Agaja could bring me were all a man needed. I was wrong! Without someone to share it with, their discovery would have been a hollow, empty thing."

"I'll always be there for you," she promised. "I'll steady you—and you can teach me how to dream."

He gathered her into his arms, his gently ardent embrace imparting a message of tenderness and love that was almost frightening in its intensity, his warm, demanding mouth reaffirming the promise of his arms.

Firelight danced over their bodies, catching the dark-fire glint of Heather's hair and the gleaming crimson of the silk *kanga* she wore, imbuing the ivory pallor of her rounded shoulders and slender limbs with a veil of pale gold as he drew the silk away. Her head pillowed upon the cascade of her perfumed hair, she gazed, through a fringe of dark lashes, into his handsome face, desire for him a flame in her half-closed eyes. Her lips were slightly parted, moist, her breathing quickened as she held out her arms to him and bade him come into them.

They made love without haste, without urgency, beside the fire, their sighs of delight loud in the jungle hush through which silent shadows stalked as night fell like a canopy about the little clearing, enveloping them in a velvety dark world of their own. With knowing lips, he tasted the loveliness of her, worshiping each alabaster inch of her flesh with a fierce devotion that elicited little gasping cries from her parted lips. She thrilled to feel his large, strong hands encompassing her breasts, molding their soft weight to fill the cup of his tanned fingers. Little shivers danced up and down her spine as the ball of his thumb drew whorls over the tingling areolas. Twining her fingers in his crisp black hair, she drew his head down to her bosom, gasping as he drew first one throbbing crest then the other deeply into his mouth, teasing the sensitive flesh with eager lips and teeth and tongue.

"I'd trade every last one of the diamonds for you, my red-haired minx," he breathed raggedly against her flesh as he lay back, lifting her astride his hips.

The moonlight caught the fire in her hair as she flung back her head; it glittered in the violet of her radiantly glowing eyes. Her breasts were the opalescent white of moonstones, half-curtained by her glorious, tumbling mane as she pressed down to take his hardness deep inside her. Lovingly, she watched his face as she began to move above him, saw his eyes grow darker and darker in the light of the fire as his passion soared. He reached up and captured her breasts, fondling them as he murmured incoherent love words, thrusting upward with his lean flanks to match her sensuous writhings.

Cicadas trilled. The roar of the falls seemed muted, distant. The moon rose to hang suspended in the small patch of indigo sky high above, a silvery gold ball enclosed in a dark frame. In the distance, a leopard growled as it prowled the forest. Still they loved. He rolled her now beneath him, his long, slim fingers caressing her as if she were an instrument and he sought to pluck the loveliest chords ever heard by man from her body. He played, and she sang—sang with every cell and nerve and muscle, her every vibrating pulse a rippling crescendo of delight coursing through her veins—every touch, every kiss, an overture to the rapture that she knew would follow, as surely, certainly as day followed night.

Strongly he thrust, losing himself ever more deeply within her, drowning in her glorious scent and taste and feel, filling her with his love and passion as surely as he filled her with his body.

Her arms tangled about his strong neck. Her fingers drifted through the crisp-silk texture of his hair as she surrendered body, heart, and soul to him. And when Rapture found them, reached out and lifted them in golden arms, they met her embrace eagerly, as one, their cries commingling, their glad hearts beating in unison, their limbs entwined.

Later, replete, Heather lay curled in Adam's arms, her head resting on the broadness of his chest as they shared an intimate silence in the afterglow of love-making, and from that silence drifted into sleep.

Dawn was painting the emerald blackness of night with gold and crimson borders when Heather stirred, yawned, stretched, and cuddled closer to Adam. The fire had burned down, she noted absently, and at some time during the night, Tom and the bearers must have returned, for meat was roasting and a billycan of water was boiling over the glowing embers. There was no sign of Tom and the others now, though, and she wondered absently where they had gone.

"How very touching!" A mocking voice rang out from the jungle trail, and she froze. "My adulteress wife and her lover! It's a pity I didn't come upon you sooner, my dear—in the act of your adultery!"

"Douglas!" Heather cried, her face paling in the dawn light. She sat up, gathering the silk *kanga*, loosely thrown across her bare body as she slept, closely about

467

her. She realized at that instant that Adam was awake at her side now, his body taut, his muscles tensed like those of a panther coiled to spring. He abruptly sat up.

"Ah, yes, Douglas!" her husband crowed. "Are you surprised? Did you honestly believe you could hope to escape me, my dear—with him?" He laughed harshly. "Never! There's only one way you'll ever cease being my wife, Heather. Just one."

Fear clutched at her as the import of his words struck home. It had happened as she had always feared it would. Douglas had found them. Oh, God! It was like coming face to face with a terrible nightmare!

Adam reached out and gripped her hand, reassuring her.

"And there's only one way you'll take her from me, Dennison," Adam said softly, his eyes a cold, dark blue that bored like steel into Dennison's mocking eyes. "Just one . . ."

Chapter Thirty-one

"We'll see about that, Markham!" Dennison sneered. "Personally, I'd say you're not in much of a position to threaten anyone, least of all me. I'm not alone."

They both saw then the others at Dennison's back: two swarthy, Portuguese-looking men with the muscular builds of laborers, and the pale-faced, fragile Philip Whiting.

"Who're your little friends, Dennison?" Adam drawled, uncoiling to rise and pulling Heather after him. "They don't seem your . . . type!"

Dennison paled, then his face filled with furious, mottled color. "Shut up, Markham, I'm warning you!" he barked. "You two, get him, and shut him up!"

He gestured to the two men.

They barreled forward and grabbed Adam by the shoulders, but he twisted free, sidestepped, and swung a punch at the taller of the two, clipping the man's jaw and sending him reeling. The shorter one then hurled himself at Adam, fastening his arms about his hips and sending him crashing backward under his weight. The fallen man, recovered now, came to the aid of his partner. Together, despite Adam's game attempt to

469

escape, they overpowered him and, breathing heavily from their exertion, quickly lashed him to one of the lichened idols, wrenching his arms back and up, then tying them behind him in such a way that any movement on his part would cause the bones to snap in two.

"Now for my lovely wife!" Dennison barked, and the excited glitter Heather had come to know only too well danced feverishly in his bloodshot eyes.

She darted forward in a vain attempt to evade the men's arms, but one of them quickly swept her off her feet and carried her, screaming and struggling wildly, to the second idol, which was but a few feet from where Adam stood. Despite her biting and clawing and her desperate lunges, the muscular pair overpowered her in short order and then tied her as they had tied Adam seconds before.

"How charming—and appropriate," Douglas jeered, strolling across to the pair. "Side by side in death, as you wanted so desperately to be in life. Within a matter of hours, it will be as if the two of you had never existed, nothing but your bones remaining . . . and the hyenas will take care of those, given time."

Heather closed her eyes, remembering the bearer, Sau, who had been killed by the leopard, his body reduced to mere bones overnight. Douglas was right, she realized, suddenly feeling ill. It would be as if they had never been!

"If you think you can get away with this, you're crazier than I thought," Adam growled. "Don't you think there'll be questions raised if we both disappear under suspicious circumstances? Heather has a family, as you well know—a family that loves her. Jamie Cameron won't let her death go unaccounted for, I'd be willing to bet!"

"Oh, but it *will* be accounted for," Dennison crowed.

"I shall, with tears in my eyes, of course, tell Cameron how my beloved, faithless wife left me for you, and how I came after you both, to implore her on my knees to return to me! But alas, I found that you'd both been killed—by savage natives, perhaps, or wild animals? There are any number of possible ways in which you might have met your end, are there not?"

"You've made your point, Dennison," Adam acknowledged, his jaw tight. "But with both of us dead, you'll be right back where you started, with no wife to present to the world. Let Heather go! She'll come back with you to Nairobi, and you can keep up the façade you wished to maintain. You'll have her, and the diamonds, Dennison!"

"Never!" Heather cried furiously, straining against her bonds. "Don't bargain with him, Adam, don't waste your breath! I'd sooner die here with you than live with him! He *used* me, as he uses everybody, for his own ends. As he used the little bugler, Paul, and Philip—yes, even you, Philip! Didn't I warn you of his true nature long ago?"

"And I told you then, Lady Heather, it isn't so!" Philip insisted hotly. "Douglas and I are—"

"You and I are *nothing,* dear boy," Dennison cut in silkily. "In fact, you've become quite a bore of late, with your possessiveness and your whining and your constant demands upon my time." He smiled. "I've been planning for some time to discreetly dismiss you from your position. Your damned father has been a little too insistent about you leaving my office of late! But I know you lack discretion and would create a nasty scene if I made that move, so I have postponed doing do." His face grew sly. "Perhaps you should join Lady Heather and her lover over there, eh, Phil? That way, I could kill three birds with one stone, so to speak?"

Philip's pale face revealed disillusionment, hurt, and then outrage. His green eyes blazed. "You wouldn't! You don't know what you're saying, Douglas!" he cried. "You don't—you can't—mean that? Why, I've given up everything for you! My father has disowned me. My mother—"

"Stop your sniveling, you spineless bloody weakling! Do you think I give a tinker's damn about you, or your cloddish father and mother? Ha! You've been nothing but a pretty, convenient toy! A *toy,* do you hear me, Philip, my dear?" His voice heavy with sarcasm, he laughed mockingly as the clerk, eyes blinded by tears, turned tail and scuttled away toward the pool, one hand pressed over his mouth to keep himself from sobbing aloud.

Douglas Dennison chuckled. "It's all worked out after all, hasn't it?" he said to no one in particular. "After all these years, I'll be even with you, Markham, and I'll have a fortune in diamonds into the bargain. My thanks, Captain! I could never have found them without you, and they more than make up for the loss of the brilliant military career I could have had, were it not for you and your meddling old fool of a father." He drew a hunting knife from his belt, and slashed open one of the makeshift sacks. Diamonds spilled out in a glittering shower. He picked them up by the handful, and let them run through his splayed fingers like sand. "Cut and polished, they'll be worth millions. They'll be known as Dennison's Diamonds henceforth. That has a nice ring to it, don't you think?"

Heather glanced across at Adam. His features were tighter and harder than she had ever seen them before. Fury blazed in his gentian eyes, and sweat stood out upon his brow in enormous, glistening beads as he strained at the ropes that bound him, cursing under his breath as they refused to yield. The cords at his

472

temples, neck, and shoulders became great knots beneath his tanned flesh with the effort.

"I love you, Adam," she whispered. "Whatever happens, remember that I always loved you!" She strained her fingers to reach out to him, to touch his hand one last time. But she could not. The idols were placed too far apart.

"You've got the diamonds." Adam's voice was surprisingly strong and even. "Kill me, if that's what you want, but let Heather go. She was just your pawn in this, and you know it. Her only fault lay in loving me. She can go back to England, live there quietly. I'll see that she never breathes a word of this to anyone. Be a man for once in your life, Dennison. Let her go!"

"Not a chance, Captain," he jeered. "Look at her! Even now, she loves you! It's there—in her eyes, in her face! Do you think she'd keep her pretty mouth shut if I were to kill you and let her go?"

"You'll let them both go!" barked a voice, and Heather almost cried out in relief, for Tom Worth stood at Douglas' back, the revolver in his hand leveled at Dennison's spine.

"You!" Douglas spat. "Get him, Silva!" Dennison's hired thug made a single move toward Tom and reached for the knife in his felt, but he instantly found himself staring down the barrel of Tom's revolver.

"Back off!" Tom ordered. "Hands above your heads! Trust me, Dennison, I won't hesitate to kill you! I stopped Adam from breaking your foul neck once, remember? I was wrong. I should have let him finish what he'd started, you bastard! Now, move!"

Not smiling now, Dennison raised his hands and backed away, his two men following his example.

"Be reasonable, Worth," Douglas said cajolingly. "The diamonds could be yours, don't you see, yours and mine! An even split, fifty-fifty. That plantation you've always dreamed about could be a reality. What do you say, eh, Worth? Put up your revolver and let's talk!"

"Don't make me laugh, Dennison," Tom said curtly. "You and I don't have a thing to talk about!"

Dennison's eyes were wild now. They flickered apprehensively to Tom and then Adam. He swallowed several times, and wetted his dry lips, watching nervously as Tom backed toward the idols and drew a knife from his belt. His weapon still trained on the three men, Worth began sawing at Adam's bonds.

Dennison inched stealthily forward, and his cohorts did likewise, ready to jump Thomas Worth should an opportunity present itself. There was no way he could take them all at once.

Suddenly, the larger of Dennison's men made a desperate lunge forward, knocking Tom's gun aside and grasping his throat, then squeezing it tighter and tighter until the revolver dropped from Worth's numbed fingers and his face turned bluish from lack of air.

Chuckling delightedly, Douglas straightened up, his confidence restored. "Ha! You almost managed it, didn't you, Worth? Almost. But then, at the last, you bungled it, just as you always bungled everything."

Unnoticed by anyone, Philip Whiting had returned. He held a hunting rifle in his hands as he silently walked across the grass, coming up behind Tom Worth. Dennison spotted Philip first, and a broad leer of triumph spread across his face. When Tom saw the youth behind him, his spirits sank. Inwardly, he groaned.

"That's my boy," Dennison chuckled, confidently starting toward the clerk, his handsome face wreathed in a cocky smile. "I knew I could count on you, Phil!"

But something in the youth's eyes halted him. He stopped in his tracks as Philip Whiting brought the rifle around, raising the long barrel until it was pointed at Douglas' forehead, not at Tom Worth's.

"You used me, Douglas!" the youth whispered, his lower lip quivering. "I loved you, and you used me!"

"No, Phil, you're wrong!" Dennison stammered, shaking his head in disbelief. "It wasn't that way at—!"

"Shut up!" Philip spat out, his green eyes ablaze. "Lady Heather was right! She told me once that you used people, that you were using me, but like a fool, I didn't believe her—until I heard it from your own lips today. She was right all along!" His voice broke, revealing his anguish. "I won't let you hurt them, Douglas. Let Mister Worth and Captain Markham go!" he ordered, his voice surprisingly strong." The man eyed the lad, and then the rifle, and with a curse he did as ordered. Tom staggered free. "Tie him up, Mister Worth," he added, nodding toward his former lover. "Then free Lady Heather and the captain. I'll cover the others."

In short order, Tom and Adam had a furious Douglas firmly trussed by the ropes which had held them captive not long before. Heather stood off to one side, rubbing her sore wrists. While Worth and Markham were tying up Dennison, his two henchmen took advantage of a momentary lapse on Philip's part and dived into the jungle. The youth wavered, looking at Adam, then back at them, the rifle shaking in his fists.

"Let 'em go," Adam instructed the frightened boy. "They'll keep on running back to whatever rats' nest they came from, without him to give the orders and see that they are paid!" He jerked his head toward Dennison. "We'll camp here for the remainder of the

475

day, then start back in the morning. It's over now."

Yes, oh, yes, Heather thought fervently, It is over!

"All set?" Adam asked, his black eyebrows raised as he looked across at Tom.

"All set, old chap," Tom agreed. "Ellen will be happy to see us. She was nicely on the mend when I left Kigali." He laughed. "Like I said, she's a tough old bird—but a real gem! She was giving the good Sisters of Mercy hell when I left. Ngudu! Ewasu! *Safari!*" The bearers grinned, taking up their bundles.

"Safari, Bwana Worth, ndio!" Ewasu agreed happily, glad to be going home.

"And what of our dear governor?" Tom asked, looking grimly across to where Dennison huddled under a tree, still firmly tied hand and foot. His formerly handsome face was ugly with impotent fury. Philip stood guard over him.

"We'll take him with us," Adam decided, "until we reach Kigali. Then we'll leave him with the authorities there."

Tom grinned. "With instructions not to unwrap this particularly unpleasant parcel until well after Christmas, right, old chap?"

"Right!" Adam grinned back. He drew the last stick of dynamite from one of the bundles, and stuffed it inside his shirt front, laughing at Tom's puzzled expression. "Just in case," he explained. "If Dennison gives us any trouble, I'll give him a 'cigar' I guarantee he'll never forget!"

Tom chuckled at his friend's bloodthirsty threat.

Adam looked down at Heather and smiled. "There's just one more thing Heather and I have to do, Tom, before we go back to Kigali for Ellen. Remember what we discussed last night?" Seeing Tom nod, he added,

"You go on ahead with our 'package,' and we'll catch up with you in a few minutes. Heather, will you come with me?"

Frowning in puzzlement, she nodded. To her surprise, he gestured to Ngudu, and the head bearer picked up two of the sacks of diamonds, while Adam picked up the remaining two. Without another word, he lit a torch and headed for the dark entrance to the cave, guarded by the ferocious idols.

The cave was as dank as she remembered it from the day before, the squeaking, rustling bats as horrid as ever. She gingerly followed Adam and Ngudu and the wavering beacon of torchlight deep into the earth, to where the long, sloping tunnel opened out into the vast cavern where they had found the treasure. The sound of running water still filled the silent darkness, coupled with the muffled roar of the falls.

The rush of fresh, sweet air from the hole in the tunnel ceiling revived the flagging torch, and the cavern was suddenly revealed, light puddling at Adam's feet and crawling halfway up one damp, craggy wall, so that the cobwebbed features of the enormous carved mask of Agaja the King seemed alive, mobile, instead of carved from wood. Small snakes, lizards and spiders and insects slithered away from the pool of light, and Heather shuddered.

"What are we doing here?" she asked.

Adam smiled. "I've had all night to think it over, and I've come to some decisions," he said at length, handing Ngudu the torch. He strode across to her and rested one heavy hand on each of her shoulders, looking down into her uptilted face. Her violet eyes were luminous amethysts in the torchlight.

"Old King Agaja was a wise man—a damned good king, to all accounts. The Oyos were punished for the theft of his treasure and for their greed by decades of ill fortune. Heather, if we take the diamonds from this cave, who's to say we won't be hounded by bad luck too? I don't consider myself a superstitious man, but damn it, I'm not willing to risk jeopardizing our future together! The real point is, they *belong* here, sweetheart. They belong to the people of this land. The diamonds are their heritage, not ours. Besides," he added, "we don't need them—at least I don't." He touched her cheek tenderly. "I have all the treasure I could ever ask for right here." He slipped his arms about her waist and pulled her close. "If you have no objections, we'll put the diamonds back in the pool, where we found them, where they were meant to remain."

"All of them?"

"Every last one."

"Couldn't we at least keep one, tiny little diamond, one just big enough to start a very small clinic for the native mothers and their children?"

"No," he said firmly. "It's all or nothing, my love. You'll have your clinic, but my way. It may take a little longer, take some hard work on my part, but you'll have it, I promise you—just as Tom will have his plantation."

"He will?" There was doubt in her tone. What madcap scheme does Adam have up his sleeve now? she wondered.

"One day, yes. You see, Tom and I have decided to go into partnership. Tea, perhaps, or coffee. Maybe sugar cane. It won't be easy, not to start with, but in a few years—"

"I don't care how long it takes!" Heather cut in. "It'll be marvelous, I know it will! You and Tom running the plantation—with Ngudu as your foreman, of course, if he's willing, and Ready running the house, while I—"

"While you see to the running of the clinic?" Adam grinned.

478

"Exactly!" she agreed, eyes shining. "But putting the diamonds back in the pool is such a terrible waste. Think of all the good they could do . . . for the African people. Our race has taken so much from them over the years, Adam, and so much from their continent—gold and diamonds and so on. Couldn't we, just this once, give something back? Ngudu would know what to do. He'd know where the diamonds could do the most good, wouldn't you, Ngudu?"

Ngudu stepped forward. *"Ndio,* Missie." His voice was strangely husky. "I know. There is much that needs to be done for my people."

Adam listened solemnly. "Then they're all yours, my friend," he said with a grin. He hefted the sacks into the bearer's arms.

Together, they helped Ngudu carry the sacks, bulging with diamonds, back up into the sunlight. Strangely, Heather felt not so much as a single twinge of regret as she did so. Well, perhaps just one, very *small* twinge . . .

They set off through the sloping tunnel to join Tom and the others, their mood light and eager. But their satisfaction turned to horror and dismay when they stood, gaping in disbelief, in the brilliant daylight. Douglas had gone! The ropes which had bound him lay coiled like snakes in the grass, and off to one side of the riverbank huddled the body of Philip Whiting, a neat black hole that oozed dark blood in his temple.

Adam hurried forward and rolled the body over, but it was obvious that the youth was beyond help. "Bloody, trusting young fool!" he gritted out, adding a curse under his breath. He stood and glanced around. "Dennison's free, and armed. I suggest we move out of here, and quickly!" he said grimly.

"What about Tom and Ewasu?" Heather cried.

"I'd say they went after Dennison. Come on! They'll need our help!"

They left the area of the cave at a run, plunging single file into the dense jungle.

Thanks to Ngudu's tracking expertise, they caught up with Tom and Ewasu downriver almost an hour later.

"Thank God you're safe!" Tom exclaimed when he saw them. "Dennison played on Philip's former feelings for him. That clever bastard talked Whiting into setting him loose; then he overpowered him, turned the gun on him, and ran off into the jungle before either of us could stop him!"

"We guessed as much when we saw Philip's body. Any idea where Dennison is now?" Adam asked curtly.

"Around here somewhere. Ewasu and I caught a glimpse of him between the trees."

Adam grunted noncommittally. "Our best bet is to cross the river and lose ourselves in the jungle. The current's pretty swift, but I think we can make it." A fleeting grin crossed his face, "At least we'll have paddles this time, right, love?" Heather smiled nervously and murmured agreement. Adam added, "Ewasu and Ngudu, you're handy with a canoe if we can find one, *ndio?*"

Ewasu and Ngudu nodded, and they and Tom went to search along the reedy riverbank for a Wanegi dugout, hoping against hope that they would find one.

Adam kept a lookout, Heather at his side. She was pale with fright, her violet eyes like two great dark holes in her face. At the squawk of a parrot high above them, she jumped nervously, and Adam took her slender hand in his and squeezed it reassuringly. Yet the contact did little to rid her of her fear.

"Even if we manage to get away this time, it won't end here," she said with awful certainty. "I know him,

Adam. I told you before, he won't give up until he sees us both dead. We'll always be on the run from him, no matter where we try to hide!"

"Then I'd best make damned sure I see him before he sees us," Adam said grimly, cocking Tom's rifle. His eyes were the color of dark flint; his jaw was set at a determined angle.

"No."

"No?"

"Don't you see, if you kill Douglas, then you're no better than he is! We'd have to live with the knowledge that we killed him, and that without his death, we could never have become man and wife." She shivered. "I know I couldn't live with that hanging over our heads, Adam!"

He was about to make light of her fears when her earnest expression stilled the words on his lips. She'd meant every word she'd said. "I understand," he began. "If that's—"

"Bwana!"

Ngudu's shout from the river spun Adam around. He saw that they'd indeed found a canoe, and that Tom and Ewasu were already inside it manning the paddles. He started toward the river as Ngudu leaped to the bank.

"Let's get the diamonds aboard and get out of here," he snapped.

Three sacks were already stowed in the bottom of the canoe and Ngudu was depositing the fourth in it when Tom gave a shout.

"Adam! Behind you! Look out, man!"

"Get going!" Adam yelled to those in the canoe. He swung about to see Dennison standing at one side of the clearing, revolver in hand. "Ngudu, run for it!"

He grabbed Heather by the wrist and together they raced back the way they had come. Vines and branches snagged at her flying hair. Roots snaked treacherously across the narrow path. They heard monkeys chattering in fright as their rasping breaths became louder and louder in the humid hush. Behind them charged Dennison, crashing through grass and creepers alike, hurling curses and threats in their wake. He squeezed off a shot, the explosion sending parrots into squawking confusion. They ducked and ran on, Heather's heart racing so wildly she could hear its thundering clamor in her ears.

"I should never have come after you to Magadi," she cried as they fled. "I should have gone back to England, I see that now. This way, I've put your life in jeopardy!"

He stopped abruptly and turned about, his gentian eyes crackling with anger. "Don't say that! Don't *ever* say—or think—that!" he growled, his strong fingers clamping her upper arms cruelly. "Do you think my life would be worth a tinker's damn without you to share it, you silly little fool?" He shook her roughly.

She forced a smile. "Nor would mine," she admitted breathlessly. "I'm sorry, Adam."

"There's my girl!" Adam rasped, "Come on! Just a bit farther, that's all! We're almost there!"

"Where?" she cried, gasping for breath.

"The cave," he flung over his shoulder as they sloughed through choking screens of vegetation toward their goal.

Behind them, unbeknownst to them both, Ngudu swiftly padded along, spear in hand, fierce loyalty in his heart. Bwana Dennison would not harm them! He, Ngudu, would see to it!

Minutes later, Heather and Adam stood in the wide treasure cavern beneath the earth, Dennison's crazed yells now reaching them only faintly as they proceeded down the long, sloping tunnel.

"I should have listened to you, darling," Adam said

regretfully. "You were right all along! He'll never give up, not as long as we live and breathe. You know what we have to do, don't you?"

She nodded, her lower lip quivering, her violet eyes suddenly shiny and brimming with tears in the gloomy light from the cave's mouth. "Yes—yes, I know. We have no choice, do we, Adam?"

"None," he murmured. "None at all."

"Then hold me. Kiss me," she implored him, and he saw that she was trembling violently.

He took her in his arms and lovingly stroked her back to calm her, tracing the delicate ridges of her spine. Then he twined loving fingers in her flowing dark-flame curls as he embraced her. His warm breath caressed her cheek when he placed his mouth over hers, and as their lips met in a kiss, a sad little sigh of longing broke from her. She clasped his dark head between her hands, and reveled in the cherished feeling of his crisp black hair beneath her fingertips.

"I love you so very much," she breathed when he broke the kiss, her voice tremulous with emotion. Their brows touching, they stood still, close to each other.

He drew her hand to his lips and kissed her fingertips tenderly. "As I love you! No regrets?"

"No," she confirmed softly. "No regrets. We were destined to be together from the first, the very first, moment we met. All that has happened since then was but a postponement of our destiny, I see that now. What we're about to do will seal that destiny forever!"

He nodded, drawing the last stick of dynamite from inside his shirt. His voice was husky when he spoke again. "Then, goodbye forever, Heather Cameron. Goodbye, Lady Dennison. Goodbye, my darling 'crimson angel'!"

Smiling through her tears, she gently touched his cheek, then glanced above them to where the blue, blue

483

African sky showed through the hole in the cave ceiling. A draft of fresh air from the opening riffled her hair as she turned back toward him. It bore the sweet promise of freedom on its cooling current.

"And 'farewell' to you, Captain Adam Markham!"

He drew a box of matches from his pocket and struck one against the craggy cave wall, holding it aloft to gaze once more upon Heather's lovely face in the tiny flare of its amber light before he touched it to the long, dangling fuse.

The massive explosion rocked the jungle. Parrots flew, screaming, from their treetop perches. Monkeys chattered and shrieked and leaped from tree to tree in terror. The ground shuddered violently as if torn asunder by an earthquake. Boulders were hurtled into the air. Fragmented by the force of the blast they bounced and rolled when they crashed back to earth. Dirt rose in great red clouds that drifted slowly on the humid air, as did the great gouts of smoke that had erupted from the center of the explosion.

When the choking dust cloud had settled, when the thick smoke had wafted away, when the ground was again still, the cave that had hidden the priceless Tears of Agaja for over two hundred years was no more. The lovers who had clung together and spoken their tender farewells, as King Agaja and his beloved woman warrior had once whispered their own tearful farewells, were gone. Only a mountain of smoking rubble remained to mark their final resting places.

Douglas Dennison, who had flung himself down onto his belly at the explosion, dragged himself upright and ran on, into the clearing.

He pulled up short and surveyed the ruin before him, his sky-blue eyes burning with fierce hatred. His torrent of curses was drowned out by the roar of the nearby falls. "No! It can't be! I'll find them!" he finally barked in the eerie hush that had resulted after the deafening boom. Scrabbling through the debris, he frantically repeated, "I'll find them!"

Ngudu had followed him, bent on protecting his beloved Bwana Markham and Missie Bwana, at the expense of his own life if need be. Now he came silently up behind the livid white man. In one hand he held a torn length of crimson silk that he had spied caught on a bush, where it had been flung by the explosion.

"You will never find them, Bwana," he said softly, great tears of relief rolling down his black cheeks as he offered the silk fragment to the white man. "Missie Bwana and Bwana Adam together now. Even you cannot follow where they have gone!"

"They're dead, you mean?" Dennison snorted and shook his head. "No, you sly black bastard, I won't believe that! Markham ruined my career—he stole my wife! And what of the diamonds? He *can't* be dead! He has to pay—they must both pay for what they've done!" He snatched the crimson silk from Ngudu's hand and held it fiercely in his own, which shook with impotent rage. His fair complexion had become mottled, had assumed a purplish hue. "They can't have cheated me again! They *can't* have, do you hear me!"

"Ah, but they *have* cheated you, Bwana," Ngudu murmured, smiling broadly now. "They have won! And there is nothing you can do about it. Look!" he urged, pointing to the smoking mountain of rubble. A silvery trickle of water was bubbling over the topmost ridge. A second joined it, then a third and a fourth as the raging Congo River reclaimed the land, its course altered and widened by the explosion. Soon, Ngudu knew, all that remained of the cave—and her secrets— would lie under water. And Bwana Dennison would suffer a thousand torments, for he would be forced to live with the constant doubts and questions that would plague him over the years. It was just and fitting that he should!

Ngudu put up his spear, turned on his heel, and melted into the steaming jungle, headed back down-river to where Bwana Worth and Ewasu waited with the canoe.

Dennison's hysterical curses and cries for him to return fell on deaf ears.

Chapter Thirty-two

"It says here that Captain Adam T. Markham, deceased, is to be officially recognized by the Royal Horticultural Society as the discoverer of a rare variety of red orchid, which will bear the name Markham's Crimson Angel as he had wished. Isn't that wonderful!" The newspaper, over eight months old, had arrived by riverboat that same morning, and the young woman was eagerly devouring the news and gossip from Europe, her black head with its elfin cap of short, glossy curls bent studiously over the printed sheets of the London *Times*.

"'Captain Adam Markham and his companion, Lady Heather Dennison,'" she continued, reading aloud, "'tragically met their deaths five years ago in an explosion in Africa, while exploring the Congo River. Markham was an avid orchidologist, and his close personal friend and confidante, Monsieur Marc Rivière, expressed his opinion in a letter sent to the Society at Kew Gardens that the deceased would have been most gratified to have his discovery named in his memory. Rivière, observing Markham's wish that specimens of the rare crimson orchid be taken back to his native country of England for study, entrusted this task to Mrs. Ellen Reading, companion to Lady Heather Dennison at the time of her death, who undertook the delicate transportation of the plant personally. Marc Rivière, a coffee planter of some reputation, lives quietly with his wife, Madame Angélique Rivière, in the area of the mission village of Linzola. Linzola was established in 1883 as the first mission to the interior of the Congo region and few Europeans . . .'"

Her husband smiled as she continued reading, comfortably leaning back in a wicker chair, his boots propped up on the verandah railing. As her voice rose and fell, he shifted his gaze to the terraced slopes below the sprawling bungalow, where low coffee bushes laden with beans spread down and across the valley as far as the eye could see. He could make out the roofs of the drying sheds in the distance, and beyond them the glinting ribbon of silver that was the river. There steamboats waited to carry his crops to the coast, and thence to the outside world. His blend of coffee beans had become enormously popular in the salons of Europe this past year, and discerning society hostesses prided themselves on serving only the dark, rich Rivière coffee to their guests.

The fond smile that played about his lips deepened to one of immense satisfaction. He and his partner had done it—proved that a plantation could be run profitably with paid labor. African laborers and pickers, yes, but there was no quota system on their plantations, and there were no harsh punishments. Workers who were lazy or unwilling to work were simply dismissed. If a worker seemed dissatisfied, he was given the option to leave. No recriminations followed, no threats to himself or his family. The men they employed stayed on because they wanted to, because they found Marc Rivière and his partner fair men to work for, and because the wages they were paid were sufficient to support their families. As a consequence the Rivière plantation had flourished, while those farther south—those run by the Belgians—were continually plagued with riots that frequently resulted in bloodshed and even death.

He looked up as a small boy ran across the shady verandah, yelling.

"Papa! Papa! I am going to the village with Maman today! Will you come too?"

Standing, he picked the child up, then tossed him high into the air, kissing the boy fondly upon the brow when he caught him in his arms. "Not today, Alexandre. Papa has work to do. But when you come home, we three shall play a game together, *oui?*"

"*Oui!*" Giggling, Alexandre flung his arms around his papa's neck and hugged him fiercely. His black curls, damp with perspiration, clung to his head, framing his flushed cherub's face with an enchanting, unruly mop. His dark eyes were shining as he released his father. "May I take Coco? May I, Papa, *please?*" he begged, eying his father hopefully. His father had little fondness for monkeys, he knew only too well.

"Go on then, take the little brute if you must. But watch him well! Father Breton was very angry when he found him in his mission last time, remember?"

"I remember," the child said soberly. "He was sitting upon the altar when I found him, Papa, and Father Breton threatened to have Coco made into monkey-meat steaks! When I asked him if monkeys were not also God's creatures, Father was very angry!" The child scowled in recollection.

His father laughed and tousled Alexandre's head. "Then it is up to you to see that Coco behaves, *n'est-ce pas?*" The little boy kissed his *maman,* urging her to hurry, and ran off. His father stood and retrieved his broad-brimmed woven hat from the wicker table. "I'll be off now, *chérie,*" he told his wife.

She looked up from the newspaper, and he saw suddenly that she was as pale as a ghost, her mouth working uncontrollably.

"What is it?" he demanded, going to her. "What's wrong?"

In answer, she handed him the *Times,* her hands shaking and causing it to rustle madly as she did so.

He scanned the black-bordered columns of the obituaries for several seconds, half-fearing what he would find; then the last entry on the page all but leaped out at him:

DENNISON, Douglas Ulysses, Tenth Earl of Kirkenmuir, 1856-1894

Lord Douglas Dennison, governor of the British Protectorate of Nairobi, Kenya, was brutally murdered January twelfth at his residence in Nairobi, East Africa. The authorities are holding Edward Whiting, Esq., a former friend and long-term associate of the Governor, for questioning in regard to the shooting death.

Tragedy had stalked the late earl in recent years. Three years ago Lord Dennison's beautiful young bride, Lady Heather Dennison (née Cameron) was herself killed in a mining accident while exploring the Belgian regions of the Congo River. The same explosion also claimed the lives of two others; Captain Adam T. Markham of Magadi, Kenya, who had served with the earl in India, and Master Philip Tyler Whiting, Lord Dennison's former clerk.

In his youth Lord Dennison served courageously with Her Majesty's Seventh Dragoons in India, rising to the rank of Major before resigning his commission. He left no issue. He is survived by his mother, Lady Winifred Dennison, who resides at Heathlands Hall, Kirkenmuir, Scotland. A memorial service is to be conducted in Glasgow at a date yet to be announced. R.I.P.

Shaken himself, he looked up. His wife still appeared stunned, but she was composed now.

"It's over," he said harshly, and she nodded.

"Yes. It's over!"

"Oh, Lord!" He took her in his arms and kissed her long and deeply. Her eyes were closed when he broke the kiss, and she opened them like one awakening from a dream, her long lashes aflutter. With an uncertain smile, he tousled the riot loose of black curls that capped her lovely head. "Three years, and I never once got used to this," he murmured, rubbing a glossy tendril between his fingers. He held her at arm's length and looked down at her thoughtfully. "I suppose I won't have to—not now."

"No," she agreed. "I don't suppose you will. I—I can't believe it. After all this time!"

"Have the past three years been so terrible, my love?" he asked quietly.

"You know better than to ask!" she chided gently. "I couldn't possibly have been any happier," she declared firmly. "It's just that now we can make everything right. For you and me. For Alexandre. And for the new little one." She pressed her fingertips to her belly.

He nodded and she slipped her arms about his back and rested her head upon his broad chest. For a few intimate moments, they simply stood there silently while memories crowded in, tenderly holding each other. Their faces were dappled by the dancing shadows cast by the blossoms of the jacaranda trees that shaded the verandah, the limbs tossing on a moist

491

and scented breeze.

"I'm all right now. It was just so—sudden. I really must be going," she whispered at length, reluctantly drawing away. "They're expecting me at the clinic. I promised yesterday."

He nodded. "I have to be going too. Tom's probably at the drying sheds already, waiting for me. Until tonight?"

"Tonight, *chérie*. And every night yet to come!" She smiled, then reached out and caressed his handsome, bearded face, warmth and tenderness sweeping through her. "But for now, my darling, Goodbye!"

"No, not goodbye," he corrected her gently. "We said our goodbyes a long, long time ago, remember? Never again! Henceforth, let's simply say adieu."

She nodded her agreement, a tender smile curving the lovely bow of her lips. As the warm breeze tousled her enchanting cap of midnight-black curls, her husband hesitated, then winked and rakishly doffed his hat to her. He strode from the verandah, knowing if he did not leave—and quickly—there would be no work done that day by either of them.

As he left, her heart sang with joy, for she had glimpsed the love and desire that glowed in his gentian eyes.

"Adieu, my darling Adam!" she murmured. "We're free, free of the past!"

She turned and hurried inside the bungalow, her steps light and eager as she cast off the last shadows of the past and went forward into sunlight to meet the future.

MORE ROMANTIC READING
by Cassie Edwards

SAVAGE INNOCENCE   **(1486, $3.75)**
Only moments before Gray Wolf had saved her life. Now, in the heat of his embrace, as he molded her to his body, she was consumed by wild forbidden ecstasy. She was his heart, his soul, and his woman from that rapturous moment!

ELUSIVE ECSTASY   **(1408, $3.50)**
Wild and free as the wide open Nevada territory that was her home, Kendra spent her nights dreaming of one man — a man she had seen for only an instant. But when at last they met again, she knew he hadn't forgotten her!

PASSION'S WEB   **(1358, $3.50)**
Natalie's flesh was a treasure chest of endless pleasure. Bryce took the gift of her innocence and made no promise of forever. But once he molded her body to his, he was lost in the depths of her and her soul. . . .

SILKEN RAPTURE   **(1172, $3.50)**
Young, sultry Glenda was innocent of love when she met handsome Read Baulieu. For two days they revelled in fiery desire only to part — and then learn they were hopelessly bound in a web of SILKEN RAPTURE.

122
134

THE BESTSELLING ECSTASY SERIES
by Janelle Taylor

SAVAGE ECSTASY (824, $3.50)
It was like lightning striking, the first time the Indian brave Gray
Eagle looked into the eyes of the beautiful young settler Alisha.
And from the moment he saw her, he knew that he must possess
her—and make her his slave!

DEFIANT ECSTASY (931, $3.50)
When Gray Eagle returned to Fort Pierre's gate with his hundred
warriors behind him, Alisha's heart skipped a beat: Would Gray
Eagle destroy her—or make his destiny her own?

FORBIDDEN ECSTASY (1014, $3.50)
Gray Eagle had promised Alisha his heart forever—nothing could
keep him from her. But when Alisha woke to find her red-skinned
lover gone, she felt abandoned and alone. Lost between two
worlds, desperate and fearful of betrayal, Alisha, hungered for
the return of her FORBIDDEN ECSTASY.

BRAZEN ECSTASY (1133, $3.50)
When Alisha is swept down a raging river and out of her savage
brave's life, Gray Eagle must rescue his love again. But Alisha has
no memory of him at all. And as she fights to recall a past love,
another white slave woman in their camp is fighting for Gray Eagle.

TENDER ECSTASY (1212, $3.75)
Bright Arrow is committed to kill every white he sees—until he
sets his eyes on ravishing Rebecca. And fate demands that he cap-
ture her, torment . . . and soar with her to the dizzying heights of
TENDER ECSTASY.

STOLEN ECSTASY (1621, $3.95)
In this long-awaited sixth volume of the SAVAGE ECSTASY series, lovely Rebecca Kenny defies all for her true love, Bright Arrow. She fights with all her passion to be his lover—never his
slave. Share in Rebecca and Bright Arrow's savage pleasure as
they entwine in moments of STOLEN ECSTASY.

*Available wherever paperbacks are sold, or order direct from the
Publisher. Send cover price plus 50¢ per copy for mailing and
handling to Zebra Books, Dept. 1783, 475 Park Avenue South,
New York, N.Y. 10016. DO NOT SEND CASH.*